THE FORGOTTEN PRINCE

TANYA ANNE CROSBY

Published by Oliver Heber Books

0 9 8 7 6 5 4 3 2 1

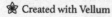 Created with Vellum

PRAISE FOR TANYA ANNE CROSBY

"I love historical legends woven into breath-taking new stories. The Goldenchild Prophecy is just one of those, yet an epic story all on its own. Tanya breathes life into this timeless tale of love and betrayal, blurring the lines of fantasy and history. "

— JEFF WHEELER, WALL STREET JOURNAL BESTSELLING AUTHOR

"Crosby's characters keep readers engaged..."

— PUBLISHERS WEEKLY

"Tanya Anne Crosby sets out to show us a good time and accomplishes that with humor, a fast-paced story and just the right amount of romance."

— THE OAKLAND PRESS

"Romance filled with charm, passion and intrigue..."

— AFFAIRE DE COEUR

"Ms. Crosby mixes just the right amount of humor... Fantastic, tantalizing!"

— RENDEZVOUS

"Tanya Anne Crosby pens a tale that touches your soul and lives forever in your heart."

— SHERRILYN KENYON #1 NYT
BESTSELLING AUTHOR

SERIES BIBLIOGRAPHY

THE GOLDEN PROPHECY

The Cornish Princess

The Queen's Huntsman

The Forgotten Prince

Arise the Queen

READER'S GUIDE

Main Characters

Adwen Bryn's uncle, Duke of Durotriges

Albanactus Brother of Locrinus; "founder" of Alba

Baugh Prydein thane, king in the north

Beryan Durotrigan alderman/warrior

Borlewen; Gwendolyn's cousin, daughter of Cunedda; died during the raid on Chysauster

Briallen Gwendolyn's cousin, daughter of Cunedda; died during the raid on Chysauster

Brutus Trojan by birth, "founder" of Britain

Bryn Durotriges Shadow Guard to Gwendolyn

Caradoc Chieftain of the Catuvellauni

Corineus, King *[cor-en-ee-us]* Gwendolyn's father

Cunedda, Duke; Gwendolyn's uncle; died during the raid on Chysauster

Eseld, Queen Queen consort and princess of Prydein

Elowyn (Ely) Durotriges *[El-oh-win]* Bryn's sister, and Gwendolyn's dearest friend

Emrys, Máistir Druid leader

Esme Faerie, with unknown allegiance

Estrildis Loc's mistress

Gwendolyn Daughter of King Corineus and Queen Eseld

Habren Locrinus' son by Estrildis

Innogen, Queen Locrinus' mother, wife of Brutus

Jenefer Gwendolyn's cousin; died during the raid on Chysauster

Kamber Brother of Locrinus; "founder" of Cumbria

Kelan Caradoc's son; Ely's husband

Lir, *Dearthair* Druid, brother of Emrys

Locrinus [*lock-ren-us*] Son of King Brutus of Troy

Lowenna; Gwendolyn's aunt, wife of Cunedda; died during the raid on Chysauster

Málik Danann [*mah-lick dah-nuhn*]

Ruan, Lady Talwyn's wife; Bryn and Elown's mother

Talwyn Trevena Mester at Arms

Taryn Beryan's daughter

Yestin Steward, Trevena

❧

Caledonia (n) Scotland/Scottish

Cymru "Land of friends"

Dryad/Drus Faerie oak spirit

Dumnonia Ancient Cornwall

Ériu [*eh-ru*] Ancient Ireland

Hyperborea Fabled land whence the Tuatha Dé Danann may have come

Loegria Essentially Wales. Old English, meaning "land of foreigners"

Plowonida Ancient London

Pretania Ancient Britain

Prydein Welsh term for the isle of Britain; for The Cornish Princess, specifically Caledonia/Scotland

Sons of Míl Hiberians who conquered the Tuatha Dé Danann and settled Ireland

Tuatha Dé Danann [*too-uh-huh dey dah-nuhn*] "Tribe of the

gods," ancient race in Irish mythology. Also, *Sidhe [shē]*,
Elf, *Fae*

Wheals Mines

Ysbryd y byd Spirit of the world.

The Four Talismans of the Tuatha Dé Danann

Claímh Solais [*Klau-Solas*] The sword of light

Lúin of Celtchar Lugh's spear

Dagda's Cauldron [*DAW-dYAW's Cauldron*]

Lia Fáil [*lee-ah-foyl*] The stone of destiny, upon which even
Britain's current kings are crowned.

Awenydds Philosophers, seeking inspiration through
bardic arts

Gwyddons/Gwiddons Priest-scientist, believe in divinity of
and for all: gwyddon, male; gwiddon, female

Druids Priests, teachers, judges

Llanrhos Order The most ancient order of Druids
occupying the area now known as Anglesey

Lifer Pol Order Druids occupying the area now known as
the Druids Crossroads

Dewinefolk Witches, faekind

The seven Prydein tribes

Caledonii Scotland during the Iron Age and Roman eras

Novantae Far northeast of Scotland, including the offshore
isles

Selgovae Kirkcudbright and Dumfriesshire, on the southern coast of Scotland

Votadini Southeast Scotland and northeast England

Venicones Fife (now in Scotland) and on both banks of the Tay

Vacomagi Region of Strathspey

Taexali Grampian, small undefended farms and hamlets

❧

Four Tribes of Ancient Wales

Deceangli Far northern Wales

Silures Southeast of Wales; "people of the rocks"

Ordovices Central Wales; area now known as Gwynedd and south Clwyd

Demetae Southeast coast of Wales

❧

Three Tribes of Ancient Cornwall

Dumnonii British Celtic tribe who inhabited Dumnonia, the area now known as Devon and Cornwall

Durotriges Devon and parts of Dorset and Somerset

Dobunni West of England

❧

Remaining Tribes of Ancient Britain

Atrebates Far south of England, along what is now the Hampshire and Sussex coastline.

Brigantes Northwest of England; Manchester, Lancashire and part of Yorkshire

Iceni East coast of England; Norfolk

Catuvellauni London, Hertfordshire, Bedfordshire, Buckinghamshire, Cambridgeshire, Oxfordshire, parts of Essex, Northamptonshire

Cantium Far southeast England, Kent and a small part of Sussex

Parisi North and east Yorkshire

Trinovantes Essex and part of Suffolk

FARGE MÔR
(GREAT OCEAN)

PRYDEIN
CONFEDERACY

7 TRIBES

MORIMARU
(DEAD SEA)

MUIR MENN
(CLEAR SEA)

BRIGANTES

PARISI

LLANRHOS
DRUIDS

DECEANGLI

CORIELTAUVII

CORNOVII

ORDOVICES

CATUVELLAUNI

ICENI

DEMETAE

TRINOVANTES

SILURES

DOBUNNI

CANTIUM

DUMNONII

DUROTRIGES

ATREBATES

MOR BRETANNEK
(BRITISH SEA)

LOEGRIAN TERRITORIES
CORNISH TERRITORIES

Surrounded by the spoilage of yet another day's battle—fourteen empty ewers, a stack of soiled platters, breadcrumbs, drained goblets, tapers burnt to the nubs—there was still no progress, no assent, and no additional confirmations for the *konsel*. Much to Gwendolyn's frustration, this task was proving to be more onerous than it should have been, considering the dearth of eligible candidates.

Of the twelve aldermen who'd once served under her father, only four returned to resume their duties. The rest were all presumed dead, murdered by the apostates who'd deposed King Corineus.

Naturally, Morgelyn, Petroc, Merryn and Crwys would continue to serve, and Caradoc, Kelan and Lir would join them. But those were the simple choices— Caradoc, because in Gwendolyn's absence, he would be called upon to lead; Kelan, because he came with experience after serving on his father's *konsel*; and Lir, because as a Druid, he was already a lawful arbiter of this land.

A few days ago, one minor victory: After *much* discourse, they had also agreed to accept Taryn, a woman, to the *konsel*, only because Gwendolyn had

insisted they must include a Durotrigan representa-
tive, and every Durotrigan elder was dead. Taryn, like
Kelan, Gwendolyn had argued, came with experience,
many thanks to her father. Beryan gave his life to save
Gwendolyn's, and it was her wish to honor him.

That was where all accord ended, and disputations
began.

Day after day, after day, after day...

All the shouting made Gwendolyn's head ache.

First Caradoc, then Crwys, back to Taryn, then to
Morgelyn, back to Petroc, now to Merryn—one after
another and another, no one prepared to concede,
each with an agenda, and everyone prepared to argue
against every candidate put forth.

Sadly, neither Málik's nor Bryn's silence was
helpful—Bryn because he held some ambivalence
where Gwendolyn was concerned, and Málik quite
simply because he was present. Gwendolyn was
careful to acknowledge him as little as possible. To
some, there would be only one thing worse than a
queen cuckolding her husband, and that would be for
her to cuckold him with an "Elf."

Unlike Lir, not everyone was so enamored by Fae.

Closing her eyes, Gwendolyn pinched the bridge
of her nose between a finger and thumb, listening to
the clash of voices—as violent in their conflict as
weapons of war.

Never once had she envied her father his seat on
this *konsel*, nor, until recently, had she aspired to rule
on her own. But never had she an inkling how bur-
densome it might be to manage a gripe of old men—
although, truth be told, some were not men, and some
not so old. Gwendolyn was tempted to allow them to
settle this dispute on their own—preferably after her
departure—but bearing in mind that there was no

guarantee she would return; it was crucial they fill these remaining seats. Indeed, the last time she'd found herself idle at this table, her silence had won her a mountain of grief. On that day so long ago, while these aldermen sat discussing her wedding to Loc, instead of speaking up like a grown woman should—as a leader should—she'd sat, dreaming all the while these graybeards argued like fishwives.

As they were doing right now.

But woe to them, unlike her mother, Gwendolyn had no artifice for negotiations. And finally, she'd had enough. "I choose Ely," she said, silencing the lot for the blink of an eye.

All eyes turned to her. But that's as long as the reprieve lasted. The declaration sent everyone into another shrieking match, wielding censure and protests like hammers and swords.

"This one aside," said Caradoc, flicking two fingers in Taryn's direction, rather rudely dismissing his Durotrigan counterpart. "No woman has *ever* held an alderman's seat. Must you now appoint two?"

Taryn was quick to defend herself. "If anyone should not serve here, Catuvellaunian, it should be you!"

To no one's surprise, Caradoc ignored her. But that, too, vexed Gwendolyn.

As a woman, Taryn's presence in this *konsel* might defy convention, but she was as capable as these men —perhaps more so. As a Durotrigan, her interests were more aligned with Gwendolyn's meanwhile Caradoc's were Catuvellaunian. But because the statutes of the Brothers' Pact governed this *konsel*—not the king, queen, or overlord—so long as all twelve seats were committed, there would remain a balance of power. However, with four seats remaining, and the military power favoring Caradoc, they still needed appointees and perhaps at least one dissenting voice who would carry sway with Caradoc's son. Ely's father was Durotrigan born, she Dumnoni raised, her husband Catuvellaunian—she was the perfect choice.

"Will you question *my* leadership?" Gwendolyn asked the Catuvellauni chieftain. "*I* too am a woman," she reminded him.

"Nay," he said, though his body language belied his denial. He sat forward, his arms extended across the table, where every so oft he would slam a fist and rattle the dishes. "I am only suggesting there is no need to burden the poor girl more than she is already —newlywed and grieving?" He shook his head. "Ely works too hard as it is! Last night my son ate cold gruel. Why should we include the poor girl when I have good men in the Cods Wold who would gladly answer my summons?"

"*Your* summons, *your* men?" Gwendolyn replied.

It wasn't an accusation. She simply wanted him to know she did not consider it to her advantage. A man would not mince words; neither would she.

As for Ely, it was true; she was working hard. Gwendolyn appreciated everything she was doing, but this would also give her a voice to accomplish more of what she wished to do, instead of begging this *konsel* for support, as her own mother was forced to do.

Caradoc's dark eyes glinted as sharply as his tongue. "Good men, regardless," he groused, and his gaze rounded the table, seeking support, settling upon his son.

Much to Gwendolyn's surprise, Kelan averted his gaze—perhaps because the appointee in question was his very own wife.

Gwendolyn smiled.

She would be lying if she said she wasn't counting on this.

Despite knowing this was the right thing to do, she couldn't leave a former enemy with the keys to her city without also leaving him with a *konsel* willing and able to oppose him. Ely would serve as a voice of reason. Even if Kelan wasn't persuaded to oppose his father, Gwendolyn had already determined he was devoted to his wife and he would respect her enough to allow her to vote her heart.

"We need *good* men in the Cods Wold, too," Gwendolyn allowed. "I insist Ely serves with her husband." She looked pointedly at Kelan to ask, "Have you an issue with this, Kelan?"

"Nay, Majesty," he responded at once. "My wife will serve this *konsel* with honor."

Gwendolyn offered the young man a smile, hopeful for the changing guard. Although there might be fewer men like her father and Beryan, whose knowledge came from age and experience, she was certain that, working together, this *konsel* would prevail, even with Caradoc at the helm.

"Very well," she concluded. "Ely will serve, and the matter is closed—on to the next."

"Majesty," interjected Lir, as he fiddled with one of his ear sheaths—silver leaflets emulating Fae ears to the point. "Do you think this prudent? It could be your dear friend will side with her husband, and what good would it do to have Ely serve this *konsel* if she'll not come with her own voice?"

Gwendolyn lifted a brow. "I assure you, *my dear friend* has no reluctance to speak her mind." She tilted Lir a questioning look. "What about you? You are neither Dumnoni, nor Catuvellauni, nor even Pretanian, for that matter. As a Druid, you might consider yourself above our ilk." She'd said it without condemnation, but his cheeks flushed red, and still Gwendolyn persisted. "Must I presume you will side with your Druid interests over those of my Cornish people?" Gwendolyn needed these men to understand whose interests were of utmost concern here. She meant to follow in her father's footsteps and unite Pretania's tribes, but Trevena's interests were still Trevena's, and in this city, she would not see Caradoc's will prevail.

"Nay, Majesty. I would not."

"And please tell; do you believe it entirely a man's prerogative to adjudicate fairly and objectively?"

For a moment, the Druid did not respond and Gwendolyn knew he resisted answering because *Druidkind* believed in the dominion of men. And despite this, she and Lir had been through enough together that she trusted he would do what was right for this realm, just as she trusted Ely to do the same. "Well?"

At long last, he shook his head, and Gwendolyn smiled. "You must trust this process," she told the men. "It is my opinion that regardless of a man's—or a woman's—personal views, once seated at this table, we must serve the good of the people."

Shifting her gaze from Lir to Caradoc, she added. "No matter how unjust this might sound to you, I will insist upon filling this seat with a native-born Trevenian. Your *good* men should remain in the Cods Wold where they've *chosen* to be."

"You do not trust us?" suggested Caradoc.

Opting for honesty, Gwendolyn replied, "Allied we might be, Caradoc, but you will agree your interests are not my interests. It is my intention to see *this* city returned to *my* people after we have removed the

Usurper from his stolen throne. You and I have a bargain, and I'll not fail to reward you for your loyalty."

Caradoc smiled ruefully. "My father once advised me that any man who'll not trust cannot himself be trusted. Have you not heard this?"

Gwendolyn returned his smile. "It is also said a wise *woman* will trust but give force to her interests. Wise words from my mother," she countered with a nod.

He sat back at last, exhaling, relenting, although not without a last jab. "Lamentably, I am reminded of yet another bit of advice my father gave me."

Gwendolyn lifted a hand, palm up. "Please share."

"*Never* argue with a woman," he said, after which the room erupted with laughter. And Bryn interjected, "Indeed, my brother, if you are fool enough to argue with a woman and you win, you still lose."

More laughter.

Gwendolyn tried not to take offense, though she thought it rude on both men's accounts. Still, she held her smile—until Bryn slid her a sheepish grin, and declared, "Especially with this one."

Her smile faded.

Leave it to Bryn to interject a word of caution in a manner that no man could take issue with. But, even laced with good-humor, there was an undercurrent of discourtesy to his warning. Her gaze sought her dear friend's, and he smiled, although the smile never reached his eyes. It tempered Gwendolyn's response. She felt a prick of regret for his sorrows, including the fact that he had once loved her, and she could not love him in return. Unfortunately, Bryn had changed, and she understood the fault was in part her own. Although, if she had it to do all over again, she would make all the same choices. She couldn't even regret their swim at Porth Pool because if she had not swum there with Bryn that day, and her mother had not discovered them together... and her father had not demoted Bryn, only to assign Málik as her Shadow... well... she would not have known Málik. Nevertheless, these past months had taken a toll on her friendship with Bryn—so much so that she sometimes questioned his loyalty. For the tiniest, most-terrible moment after discovering Talwyn in her father's chamber, when Bryn arrived behind her, she'd feared him a turncoat. It wasn't until he'd spoken that she'd rested easier. But it could certainly have gone another way, and now that she had his father's blood on her hands, she sometimes wondered if he would come to regret his choices. So far, neither brother nor sister seemed inclined to lay the fault for Talwyn's death on Gwendolyn's shoulders, regardless that it was her blade that took his life, but she could not tolerate insolence—not in this room. There was a fine line between Bryn's ease of comportment with her and the appearance of disrespect, and Gwendolyn could not afford for there to be any doubt about who was in command. She was.

"No more quibbling," she announced, and taking a lesson from her late mother, she added, with a nod toward Caradoc. "You've one last seat to fill and you've my blessing to fill it with whomever you wish."

It was Taryn who spoke now, clearly confused. "But Majesty... even with Ely, there are still three seats remaining, are there not?"

Gwendolyn looked first toward Taryn, then again to Caradoc. "One," she asserted. "To fill the other two, I've sent a request to the Temple of the Dead."

"Nay!" Caradoc exclaimed. "Not the Awenydds!"

"I did not misspeak," said Gwendolyn. "And please

do not tell me you fear the prospect of arguing against four women, even with a majority of fellows on your *konsel*? Certainly not a man like you?"

The Awenydds were female philosophers who sought inspiration through bardic arts. Her mother had favored them for a reason. While the Gwyddons had similar affinities, the Awenydds had a greater understanding of the past, and therefore, a stronger inkling of what they might need to return this city to its former glory.

Caradoc growled in response, the sound feral.

"Make no mistake, Dragon Queen, I remain your liege, but I will be heartily pleased to see the back of you! This city is too small for the two of us!" He tilted his head then, a flash of cunning in his black eyes. "Unless you care to seal our allegiance with a torc?"

Marriage.

Argh!

The thought turned Gwendolyn's belly, though this was hardly the first time Caradoc had suggested it. Regardless, she did not believe for a moment that he wished to marry her any more than she wished to marry him. "Are you asking me to defy the Druid's Law?" she said gently, referring to her existing marriage.

There was no way in Creation she would ever marry Caradoc, but she couldn't say so without embarrassing him for a second time today. Fortunately, her marriage to Locrinus had at least one beneficial use. She was already wed to that faithless charlatan, so she couldn't marry anyone else—not even the one she wished to wed. Without meaning to betray so much, Gwendolyn cast a curious glance toward Málik, only to find him unmoved by Caradoc's question. All this while, he had sat there in his chair, listening to the discourse, saying not one word.

Following her gaze, Caradoc added with a gleam in his eyes, "What *you* need, My Queen, is a man—a *real* man."

Málik did not stir.

Instead, he took a sudden interest in the condition of his fingernails—fingers that were too long to be human, and stronger than they appeared. The claws alone, short that they were, could gut a man as easily as a cat disemboweling a mouse.

For a moment, Gwendolyn allowed her gaze to linger on his too handsome face, daring to take comfort in his presence, despite his show of dispassion. In her heart, she held the faith that he didn't feel that way. Indeed, his actions too oft belied his words. He had never been more distant, yet he was also never more solicitous, anticipating her every need to the degree that she sometimes wondered if he knew her mind.

She understood Caradoc meant to needle him. Still, she said nothing, some part of her wanting him to raise Málik's ire—if only to provide some evidence that Málik still cared. It was perhaps ungracious of her considering all Málik had done for her, but Gwendolyn also knew Caradoc's words were not meant to anger. Rather, it was Caradoc's nature to test boundaries to glean what he wished to know. And it appeared to Gwendolyn that what he most wished to know right now was how close she had grown to Málik. Málik certainly knew this as well. She only wished she were as adept as Málik at hiding her feelings.

Gwendolyn could not afford to be led astray by her woman's heart. She still had much to prove. That they were still discussing a woman's role in her *konsel* when there was a woman on the throne was proof enough that her work was only beginning—especially if she intended to seize control of these lands.

And this she must do.

This she *would* do.

"We are through," Gwendolyn said, rising from her seat at the table, taking another cue from her dead mother. "Ely will serve the *konsel*. And you, Caradoc, you will choose another appointee—be it man or woman. I care not which, so long as all agree upon the appointment. No. Please stay, Bryn," she said, lifting a hand to stop him when he made to rise and follow. "In my absence, I intend for you to advise this decision."

And with that, Gwendolyn abandoned the war room, moving about the war table and into the hall without a backward glance.

For all his insouciance, Málik rose too, moving hurriedly to close the door, and Gwendolyn said nothing, not really knowing what to say.

Málik said nothing, too, because this was now his way.

E ager to put the unpleasantness of the *konsel* behind her, Gwendolyn hurried through the corridor, intending to seek a moment's respite in her mother's chamber. It cost her more than she'd like to confess to stand her ground, and no matter that she had somehow asserted a voice of authority, her limbs were quaking. It wasn't easy to rule over self-important men who would typically support another man, regardless of character, instead of a woman whose heart and intentions were true.

Of course, she was speaking of Loc more than Caradoc; but it galled her that Bryn—her own Shadow—would jest at her expense, and that Caradoc would tease at binding her with a torc.

And Málik, saying nothing, though perhaps by design and perhaps for the best. It wouldn't serve to be defended by someone perceived to be her lover—not that he was. He was not, though, not by her choice. If Gwendolyn could have her way, she would make herself a widow, but not before facing Loc with a babe in her belly and Borlewen's blade in her hand.

By now, Loc must have surely received the news that Trevena was lost to him and more, who had seized it. To make doubly certain he would learn of it, Gwendolyn released a scout they'd arrested to carry her message—pity for the poor soul. Loc would receive his news without mercy, and the scout's "reward" would depend upon Loc's mood. Doubtless, her husband was too cold and too brutal to consider the life of one man any great loss. It wouldn't matter how loyal he was; the man might, or might not, find himself without a head after delivering Gwendolyn's message. And despite this, not delivering it wouldn't be an option. At present, Loc and his brothers held the greater force in these lands. The messenger would never have one minute's doubt his commander would prevail. Because, of course, Loc wasn't a woman, and this was a man's world.

The afternoon's *konsel* meeting gave evidence to this, though at least Gwendolyn felt as though she had accomplished something. There was still much to be done before the morning's departure, but she would rest easier knowing Ely would have a seat on that *konsel*.

Now, if only for one moment, she could pretend everything was as it was before the Feast of Blades— that she was still the same wide-eyed little girl stealing into her mother's chamber only to catch a whiff of her sweet perfume. A heady mixture of lavender, rosemary, and pine, it lingered still on her furs, in her brush, and on her pillow.

Tears pricked at Gwendolyn's eyes at the thought of her mother.

Her heart wept over the news of her father's death, but her mother's somehow affected her more deeply —for all the time they'd lost and all the opportunities they would no longer have.

By now, she had exhausted every option in her

search for Queen Eseld and Demelza, her loyal maid. Gwendolyn had expended resources and soldiers Trevena could not spare, particularly when even bright-eyed Ely had lost hope. Their scouts looked high and low—east, west, north and south. They found no sign of Queen Eseld, Demelza, or even Ely's and Bryn's mother, Lady Ruan, and rather than glean any hopeful news, they'd heard more heartbreaking tales.

In one report, Queen Eseld was gathering her *dawnsio* students to usher them to safety, only to be stabbed in the back by Innogen herself—that one, told by the father of one of her mother's students, gave Gwendolyn a painful punch to the belly, and she longed to ride to Loegria, find Innogen and stab her through the heart.

Yet another story told of her mother casting her body over the king's, shielding him from harm. Right there on the dais, in the great hall, where they'd supped so many times, Innogen's second son, Kamber, ended Queen Eseld's life with a blade through the heart—once again, in the back, bloody wretch!

Unfortunately, the latter of these stories was easiest to credit. While the *dawnsio* students were Queen Eseld's greatest triumph, her love for the king was indisputable. Whatever affection she'd not provided for her wayward daughter, Gwendolyn never failed to spy in her mother's eyes when she'd gazed at her father. That Prydein maiden who'd once arrived as a price for peace came to adore her husband and king, and the passion they'd shared had once filled Gwendolyn's heart with hope for a love story of her own.

That was not to be.

A painful knot rose in Gwendolyn's throat.

She tried in vain to swallow past it, not daring to look behind her.

Málik's footfalls were silent as a ghost's. Still, she knew he was there, and even if her heart ached for more, she dared to take comfort in his presence.

Tonight would be her final moments spent amidst her mother's effects. Gwendolyn didn't know why that should bother her so much. Material things oughtn't matter. Neither gowns, nor cloaks, nor furs could make up for the loss of a loved one, but perhaps it was because, left intact, the queen's quarters were a refuge against the raging storm. Tomorrow, she would begin a perilous, new journey. But for now... everything in those apartments remained as her mother had left them... the same white shaggy sheepskin on her bed.

Her favorite claw-footed trunk at the foot.

The elegantly carved beeswax candles, purchased from a local artisan, half spent by her bedside...

If Gwendolyn sat long enough, closing her eyes, she could almost believe her mother might return... any moment, lifting those thick, dark brows as she swept into the room to press Gwendolyn over why she was lurking in her bedchamber like a tricksy little *knocker*. And considering that, a wry smile touched Gwendolyn's lips, because... well, she had pilfered a thing or two regardless that her mother had denied her little. Nothing except affection—a fact that Gwendolyn bemoaned whilst her mother still lived, and even now she could not lie to herself and say her grief was driven by true loss. It was something else—the rapine of something she never had, and now she never would. Despite that, her child's heart craved it—even as her woman's heart desired something else...

Daring to glance over her shoulder at Málik, she found his gaze intent upon her, and she lifted her shoulders and her chin, shrugging away the undeniable yearning.

Gods. She wasn't a child to allow herself to mourn over things she could not have, nor was she free to love where she would. She was a queen, wed to a tyrant, and it didn't matter whom she loved, or whether Málik returned her affection. Better to focus on practical pursuits—this moment, the question of her departure, and final preparations.

And speaking of her mother's apartments, instead of leaving them unoccupied, Gwendolyn intended to offer the accommodations to Taryn. It would be foolish to expect those rooms to lie unused so long. As yet, Caradoc had no wife, and those quarters so close to his own would be of no use to him. Meanwhile, Taryn made her bed wherever she could find one. And as a high-serving member of the Konsel of Twelve, they could not expect her to lay her head in a haystack.

By some odd stroke of good fortune, most of Queen Eseld's belongings had gone undisturbed during the coup that ended her father's reign. Gwendolyn discovered the room unoccupied, likely because Talwyn had been saving the quarters for his missing wife. There, along with the Queen's belongings were Lady Ruan's coffers—everything untouched since the Feast of Blades. Although Gwendolyn had since come to understand the depths of Talwyn's betrayal—his collusion with Loc—she hardly blamed Ely or Bryn for their father's betrayal. Earlier today, she had delivered nearly everything to Ely for safekeeping, but as far as Gwendolyn was concerned, Ely could keep it all. She could do with it whatever she wished. Gwendolyn had never been a collector of gowns. If she had a single good pair of boots and a pair of leathers, she was merry as a songbird. There were only a handful of things she meant to keep for herself, primarily the breastplate like the one her mother gave her to wear with the Prydein gown, this one fashioned of copper, with etchings of sunbirds. While it was not suitable for battle because the alloy was too soft, Gwendolyn was certain it had meant something to Queen Eseld, because even after all these years, it remained free of patina and shone.

Also, among her mother's effects, she'd discovered an arming sword like the one Loc stole from her to give to his mistress. But since Gwendolyn would not part with Kingslayer, she gave the arming sword to Ely as well—not because she felt guilty over her part in Talwyn's death, but because Ely and Bryn were the only family Gwendolyn had left. It made her feel good to give what she could. In the end, gold, gems—all of it was meaningless if there was no one to share it with. Besides, Ely would need a sword, and Lady Ruan was never the sort to own more than a delicate poniard. Despite that Ely was raised with gentler aspirations, she no longer had such luxury. Sweet Ely, with her golden beauty and soft skin, had been the object of Gwendolyn's envy for too many years—not because she was resentful of her lovely face, but because, for too long, Gwendolyn had believed her mother favored Ely above everyone. And perhaps she had, but for all Queen Eseld's fine gowns and jewels, Gwendolyn also found ample evidence that, regardless of her mother's aspirations to be more like the ladies of her father's court, Queen Eseld was still a Prydein maiden at heart. A warrior... in disguise.

They were more alike than Gwendolyn ever knew.

Once again, her emotions betrayed her.

Another sting pricked at her eye, and she moved

faster, rushing for the privacy of her chamber. If only her mother had lived...

There was so much Gwendolyn longed to say!

Why did you spurn me?

Because she saw herself in Gwendolyn and couldn't bear to remember that part of herself she'd lost?

Or because Gwendolyn was too stubborn and brash, and betimes too dirty and sweaty?

Or mayhap because she'd favored horses to jewels and gowns?

Because she couldn't dance, and spoke too freely?

Gwendolyn knew well that she was sometimes an embarrassment to her mother's aspirations. She was not the example Queen Eseld tried to mold her to be. So oft it appeared to Gwendolyn she was reviled for her face. But Gwendolyn had recently come to suspect her mother's feelings were more complicated.

"Majesty," came a shout at her back. "Wait! Please! Majesty!"

Swiping at the corner of one eye to mop a telltale tear, Gwendolyn turned to face Lir, but first slid Málik a glance. He averted his gaze—because he wished to save her the discomfort of noticing her flushed cheeks and moist eyes?

No matter; it gave her a moment to collect herself as Lir rushed down the hall.

"Majesty," he said again before he'd reached her. "I had hoped for an audience. Forgive me for abandoning your *konsel* at this hour, but I realize our time has grown short."

"Speak," Gwendolyn demanded.

Lir surprised her by kneeling—an act of obeisance Druids rarely offered, as they considered themselves the senior-most rás, second only to Fae.

"I beseech you," he exclaimed. "I know you wish for me to remain in Trevena, and I understand why, but I hoped you would allow me to join you." His soft-brown eyes were so full of hope. "Of course, I will do as you ask, but it has been my life's ambition to see the City of Light with my own two eyes."

Gwendolyn shook her head, not meaning to deny him, though she didn't believe allowing Lir to accompany her was the prudent thing to do. It wasn't simply that she wished for him to remain to serve the *konsel*—a task that for good reason he was well-equipped to perform—she was also mindful of the fact that, already, she and Bryn would be a burden to Esme and Málik. But at least they knew how to defend themselves if it came to that. Gwendolyn furrowed her brow. "I thought the position would honor you, Lir. It shows how much I value your good counsel—and I do," she said.

"My Queen," interrupted Málik, and Gwendolyn's heart tripped at the husky sound of his voice, her determination wavering with only his softly spoken words.

My Queen.

Even if only she could note it, the tenor of his voice betrayed affection, and gods knew, only hearing it, there was nothing he could ask of Gwendolyn that she would refuse—a truth that enslaved her even as it lifted her to unimaginable heights.

"He could be of use to us."

"How so?" Gwendolyn asked.

She would not relish the thought of having Lir's death on her conscience. Theirs was no pursuit for such a gentle soul—a man who'd never once wielded a sword in battle—and she couldn't imagine what use he could be.

Málik continued to explain. "As I have said... the Fae king will view your intrusion in the Fae realm as an attack on his sovereignty. Not only does he not believe you to be the rightful heir of *Claímh Solais*, he is quite certain you are not. The instant you descend upon his territories, he will send armies to end you. Howbeit, he has allies in the Druid village and Lir's presence may lend itself to diplomacy over commination."

The Fae king—not his father, nor Esme's.

Unless pressed, Málik would never confess their relation—most assuredly not in front of Lir, even if it seemed to Gwendolyn that Lir already knew.

She wanted to ask why Lir's presence would lend itself to diplomacy, but not hers. However, something in Málik's expression forbade the question. And it was Lir's eager expression that was Gwendolyn's undoing.

Gwendolyn sighed. It would be better for her if he did not go, but she would not make him stay. "Very well," she relented. "Go. Prepare for the morning's departure. But first, please return to the *konsel* to advise them to seek your replacement."

Caradoc would be all-too pleased to hear it, and the notion vexed Gwendolyn. No doubt he would install another of his own, but she hadn't any choice but to allow it. There was no one remaining she could trust to perform the duties of an alderman. It was a demanding job. And no matter that they no longer had the treasury to guard, it was so time consuming that poor Bryok and his wife had intended to flee Trevena in order to escape his duties. Gwendolyn was already feeling guilty for the strain it would place on Ely and Kelan's relationship. But though they might fall wearily into bed together at the close of day, at least they would serve together, and that must count for something. Gwendolyn inhaled an impatient breath as Lir turned to go but stopped him with a word of caution. "We depart at first light," she added. "If you are not ready, we will leave without you."

"Do not worry, Majesty!" he said excitedly. "I will be ready!"

The joyful glimmer in his warm eyes only served to further discompose her because that was the point: Gwendolyn *was* worried. She had grown quite fond of the youngling Druid, and she thought of him as a little brother, which was odd perhaps, considering their ages. But even with so many years spent in that Druid village, Lir was innocent as a babe. Once more, he turned to leave, and Gwendolyn stopped him again. "Lir," she said, her voice hard. "I will also insist you spend *every* spare moment crossing swords with Esme."

At the mention of his *Fae* adversary, Lir's joy seemed to dim a bit, but he answered without hesitation, giving her a nod. "I will, Majesty."

"Please call me Gwendolyn," she responded with a sigh. "I am still Gwendolyn." He gave her a look of utter confusion, and Gwendolyn waved him away. "Never you mind. Go!"

"Thank you! Thank you!" he said, and then, before Gwendolyn could think to stop him again or change her mind, he turned to rush back to the *konsel*, leaving her alone with Málik. Something like starlings took flight in Gwendolyn's belly as she cast him another glance, only to discover his magnificent lips twisted into a crooked smile—*amusement*? At her expense?

Gwendolyn glowered at him.

She didn't like how easily he could read her—nor that, when she tried to rule with her head and not her heart, she failed so miserably. How was she going to rule this kingdom if she couldn't even stand firm in her resolve?

Locrinus had no problem hardening his heart!

Málik said nothing, though he needn't speak a word. Betrayed by the twinkle in his steel-blue eyes, she knew what he was thinking.

Annoyed yet again, she spun about, continuing to her mother's bower, avoiding further conversation until they were alone, having learned to save all her aggrievements for private moments, when Málik was so much less reserved. However, the moment he pursued her into the antechamber, she turned to face him, confronting him at long last about his resignation as her Shadow. "I thought you gave up this position weeks ago? Why are you here?"

She didn't mind so much that Bryn had been reinstated—he was the Shadow she was most accustomed to—but she couldn't help but feel abandoned by Málik.

"I would think it obvious," he said easily. "Bryn cannot be in two places at once."

"Neither can you," she returned. "Doesn't Esme require your services?"

She knew she sounded like a resentful fishwife and loathed the sound of her own voice. But if it disturbed him, he didn't show it.

"I may have abdicated my role as your Shadow, but I am no less committed to serve you, My Queen."

"Gwendolyn!" she snapped, averting her gaze.

Of all her friends, Málik was the one with whom she most resented the use of formalities.

"Gwendolyn," he said silkily, and the sound of her name on his lips only made her heart trip once more —what a spiteful turn of fate! Either way, she was tormented, and nothing less would suit her now that she knew what it felt like to be held in his arms. As a matter of self-preservation, her gaze drifted to the cot Demelza had once occupied and fixed there as she regained her composure.

It was half the size of the berths normally afforded to a Shadow, but the beds belonging to her mother's guards had recently been relocated to the garrison to provide bedding for Caradoc's warriors. Caradoc had, of course, insisted, and Gwendolyn could find no reason to deny his request, when it made perfect sense to provide for the warriors who would defend this city. Her father's army was much diminished, but now, joined by Caradoc's warriors, the garrison was overflowing.

"Enough brooding!" she heard Demelza's faraway voice demand of her, and Gwendolyn hitched her chin, turning and moving from the antechamber into her mother's bower. Even in death, the maid would bedevil her! And it wasn't remotely sane to wonder whose side was on when Gwendolyn was only speaking to a memory.

Málik followed only so far as the door, and despite that Gwendolyn understood his given reasons for keeping himself apart, she didn't like it.

With as much as they had endured together, he, more than anyone, was the one she was most inclined to seek during these moments of uncertainty. Taking a moment to strike the disappointment from her face, she turned to meet his gaze.

Gods.

Standing in the doorway, he was no less beautiful than he was the first moment she spied him—his silvery hair spilling over his broad shoulders. Only now... she knew what it felt like to tangle her fingers into that hair...

Soft, like silk.

He remained in the doorway, watching as Gwendolyn unsheathed her sword, then laid it down atop the bed before she sat to remove her boots. However, nothing he ever did was by half-measure—not even the simple act of observation. His presence filled this room, so it was impossible for Gwendolyn's lungs to expand without encountering his essence—an earthy mixture of wood, smoke, sun... and something else unknown to her head, but not to her heart.

Distracting herself from wayward thoughts, she brushed a finger over the flat of Kingslayer's blade, where curious runes were inlaid.

This sword, along with the *mithril,* had been a gift from Esme during her kinder, gentler days. Even as her *mithril* was supposed to display extraordinary properties, so too should the sword. According to Esme, Kingslayer glowed blue in the presence of danger. But, like the *mithril,* which was purported to render the wearer unseeable by night, Gwendolyn had yet to witness any such marvel. She'd worn her *mithril* during the retaking of Trevena and though she had marched through these halls with nobody stopping her, that didn't mean no one saw her. And still, the *mithril* presented a stunning regalia, and not even the much-coveted Sword of Light Málik took from her father's treasury could surpass the beauty of Kingslayer.

But she needed *Claímh Solais.*

The Sword of Light was hers by right, and if she did not retrieve it, there would be no way to unite Pretania's tribes. She could not even count on her own grandsire to follow her without that sword, and, in the meantime, Locrinus would continue to grow his armies. Regardless that she had Caradoc's fealty, this would count for little in convincing the Iceni, Cantium, or Trinovantes. And, in fact, Caradoc's friendship would do the opposite. It was only with the Sword of Light that she had any chance of convincing Baugh to ally with her, and, if she could somehow convince him to raise his own sword to her cause, she might also win the Brigantes and Parisi. And finally, perhaps the Iceni, and with a little luck, Cantium and Trinovantes would follow.

With a sigh, she pushed the sword aside, returning her attention to her boot, plucking it off and dropping it on the floor.

Meanwhile, Málik kept his distance, his eyes following her every move, nothing escaping his notice. His gaze fell to the boot on the floor, then came back to her face, affixing there as Gwendolyn laid down her bare foot. And once again, like a bashful child, she was forced to avert her gaze, betrayed by her heart.

Her lips pursed because she loathed the way her heart raced in his proximity.

Only after she had gathered her composure did she dare look back, this time lifting her chin and holding his gaze, watching with wonder as his mercurial eyes softened to a wintry shade of blue. His mouth turned at one corner, scarcely concealing the fangs that to this day never failed to give Gwendolyn a shiver —not entirely with desire, truth be told. There was that about the Fae—an aura of danger and uncertainty that could never be dismissed, regardless of how much feeling lay between them. They were creatures born to inhabit the dark, evidenced by his luminous eyes and the keen, pointy ears, which could hear every sound in the darkness. Indeed, remembering the first time she'd traveled with him—the way his senses homed in on every movement in their path, like a beast of prey on the prowl—Gwendolyn wondered if they were always that way, or if their isolation deep in the bowels of the earth had somehow changed them.

She didn't ask, though, and Málik said nothing.

Meanwhile, Gwendolyn's annoyance was not assuaged. "You claim proximity will be our undoing," she argued. "How will you avoid this if we are meant to travel together? Or will you travel separately?"

The silver in his eyes glinted. "You mistook me, *Banríon*. It is not our proximity that endangers you— not precisely. It... is... complicated."

Again, with the queen, so formal. The sound of it tugged at one corner of her mouth, dragging her lips into a frown.

Gwendolyn dropped the boot and flopped back on the bed, lifting her gaze to the ceiling, trying not to think of all the complicated preparations that must still be imposed. Gods only knew she hadn't time to nurse a wounded heart—wounded without cause, because she knew he cared for her. And yet, here she lay, dwelling upon a kiss that should have been forgotten, brooding over—*what?*

Málik's decision to keep her at arm's length.

Even after weeks of preparation, Trevena was not settled, and time was not Gwendolyn's friend. Even now, Locrinus was marching across this isle, burning villages on his way to his precious Troia Nova. Once arrived, it would be an easy task to defend his plundered city with the number of troops he had gathered —ten thousand, so she had been told.

Ten bloody thousand!

And this didn't include soldiers sworn to his brothers—the ill-bred vipers!

On a good day, Gwendolyn might have... mayhap... four hundred, though not all were properly armed or trained for war. She hadn't even a makeshift army—one that could face a major force. Only Trevena's construction and placement on the Stone Isle made it possible to defend. And no matter how angry it made her, or how incensed—no matter how she boasted over the consequences of his actions—there would be no ousting Locrinus, nor defeating him, until she raised a bigger army.

That was why she must retrieve the Sword of Light, and then after, press north to conscript her grandfather's army.

Without Baugh's help, she wouldn't stand a chance.

But that gave her other worries—for one, his willingness to support her.

Would he look beyond her yellow hair and storm-gray eyes to see the turn of her mother's nose? Or the shape of her teeth when she smiled?

Or would he turn his back on her and withhold support?

"You are exhausted," Málik said quietly. "*Rest*."

"I can rest when I am deceased," Gwendolyn returned petulantly, not wishing to be told what to do. It had never worked too well for Demelza, and she didn't appreciate it now, coming from Málik, regardless of how she felt about him—but especially because of how she felt about him!

"A travesty which might occur sooner than you anticipate if you do not take care, Gwendolyn."

Gwendolyn...

Gwendolyn...

Gwendolyn...

The velvety sound of her name on his lips wove its way into her thoughts, obliging her to close her eyes... if only for a moment. And yet, eyes closed, she still found her voice. "I will try if you lay by my side," she said sleepily, patting the bed beside her and smiling, despite knowing the answer before he gave it.

He didn't stir from his place by the door, offering a dark, throaty chuckle instead, but then, just as Gwendolyn had expected, he didn't approach the bed.

Damn the sun and moon.

Damn the stars as well.

No matter. She didn't want him to come to her, Gwendolyn reassured herself, even if some silly part of her woman's heart couldn't resist testing him—why, she didn't know. It *always* made her feel worse.

Even now, the word "no" hung in the air as tenaciously as the scent of piss seemed to cling to her halls. He needn't even speak the word aloud for it to ring in her ears.

"The *konsel* will argue for hours to come," he suggested. "Once they are done, Bryn will rejoin you. Meanwhile, I intend to remain in the antechamber."

Damn herself as well, for caring too much—for desiring things she oughtn't to desire.

"*Rest*," he said once more, and even as he spoke the word, Gwendolyn's lids grew heavier and her breathing slowed.

Was he using powers of persuasion?

Nay. He wouldn't do that—not to her.

The truth was somewhat less unpleasant. Over the course of these past months, she had spent nearly every waking moment putting this city to rights. Now that it was done—at least for her part—the burden of her duties weighed her down.

"Rest," she heard him say again, and this time the sound seemed to come from faraway, as though in a dream, and Gwendolyn loosed all thought from her head... except one: The night Málik came to her on the ramparts. It was the most delightful moment of her life... the most tormenting as well. He had kissed her sweetly, offering his heart for the taking... and then... promptly snatched it back.

But nay, that wasn't true.

He'd been willing to run away with her.

It was she who'd refused.

For the second time.

Out of duty.

Even so... she loved him... with a desperation she daren't confess. More than anything, Gwendolyn needed him to join her on this bed, so she could wrap her arms about him, and then lie beside him, with her lips pressed against the warmth of his cheek... Alas, if, after all this time, there was one thing she found to envy about Ely, it was this: Ely had found her true love. And every night, they would curl up in each other's arms, and kiss...

Wistfully, Gwendolyn inhaled, filling her lungs with Málik's remembered scent, and somewhere in the distance, she heard a door close. Only then did she allow herself to drift into slumber... and... rest.

3

Morning?
       Truly?

The high-window revealed pearly light.

Gods. Gwendolyn loathed when *he* was right, and he was right too oft. She had been overtired and in need of rest. And judging by the heaviness of her limbs, she'd settled so profoundly into slumber that she'd slept throughout the night. Only now that she was awake, she found herself reluctant to rise.

Forsooth.

Lir wasn't the only one fascinated by the Fae.

All her life, Gwendolyn had heard wondrous tales of the Fae, and now that she was meant to see their world for herself, she was on tenterhooks.

The journey Below was not one meant to be made for leisure. She would descend with purpose, and if Esme's father refused to relinquish her sword, she would take it perforce. But neither would she face the Fae king with any great force. She would make her demands with only his foster son and his wayward daughter at her side. Only considering that Esme was supposedly also his favored daughter—no matter what her sworn affinity—when the moment of truth arrived, Gwendolyn couldn't be certain Esme would take Gwendolyn's side against her father and king.

All things considered, it didn't sound promising.

And neither did it help her mood at all to awaken and find herself alone—again.

Not that anyone would loiter whilst she slept. *That* would be unseemly, and Málik was too decorous for an Elf—yes, *Elf.* Knowing what she now knew, she no longer considered that word so profane. When speaking with Gwendolyn, Esme only ever referred to herself this way, and never as Fae.

To be entirely correct, they were Danann, although Gwendolyn now understood that to call oneself Danann came with certain political leanings, which was to say that any who called themselves by this name were loyal to the old king. Although it wasn't a crime against the laws of their kindred to call themselves by the name of their forebears, Esme's sire was the first half-blood king to rule the Fae realm. And purely because no one deposed him, he'd been their leader now for more than two thousand years. However, like Locrinus, he'd stolen his crown through subterfuge and treachery, and there was a rebellion rising against his reign.

Fae was the appellation the *"new"* Fae king preferred, and despite that there were still too many Danann to decry their ilk, he favored those who called themselves by his chosen name. Málik refused. The Fae appellation embodied everything he opposed— and, most notably, the Fae Usurper, who'd not only stolen his father's crown, but who banished the rightful Tuatha'an heir, to gods knew where. This was the only reason Málik had so oft corrected Gwendolyn when she'd used the Fae appellation instead of Danann. To his mind, he was Danann, not Fae. But though he favored Danann because he was Danann, he was an Elf by creed.

Elf—or white being—was the name once given to his ilk by mortal men who'd intended the epithet as a profanity. But these days, it held a deeper meaning for the Tuatha'an rebels who waged a secret war against the *Fae* king. So, Gwendolyn had learned, Elf was also the name given to the insurgents by the *Fae* king to denigrate their love for mortal men. But the rebels had embraced this epithet, imbuing the name with the strength of their convictions because, yes, they *were* lovers of men. The only reason Málik avoided using it was because he would see them victorious, and for him to champion their cause would be to end them.

Meanwhile, as her father's favored daughter, Esme was an officer in this revolution, operating without his suspicion. So then, was Málik right? Was she her father's spy, as he sometimes claimed?

It made one wonder. Why would Esme oppose the father who favored her... for Málik? Was she lying when she claimed she didn't love him? Or, like Locrinus, would she turn her coat and betray them all?

It wasn't enough that Gwendolyn had to worry about leaving Caradoc with the keys to her city—sooner than later now that the sun had risen—or ferreting out Loc's traitors; Esme's demeanor made her second-guess the Faerie's motives. And now she found herself worrying too oft that she would be walking with eyes wide open into Fae rebellion.

Already this morning, she felt something like angry bees buzzing about her middle over the prospect. As though it were a daily ration, worry settled in her belly, heavy like a brick of ore, and growing heavier when she heard the peal of bells.

Time to go.

It was Málik's suggestion to leave at the cock's first crow, instead of creeping away in the middle of the night. It was essential, so he'd said, that her people witness a strong, confident queen, passing her keys to her next in command. And perhaps this was sage advice. But right now, as too oft she did, Gwendolyn felt like an impostor in her father's shoes—a child merely playing at being a queen.

And sometimes... when her heart beat too fast for her breast, and her eyes stung with tears for all that was lost... in those disquieting moments she felt...

Vulnerable.

Uncertain.

Lost.

Alone.

But she wasn't alone, she reassured herself—even if Málik seemed so determined to avoid intimacy. He was still her huntsman, and with him by her side, she knew she could bear all the rest. Blowing a soft sigh across her lips, Gwendolyn slid a hand over the cold sheets... where, of course, no one slept. But, of course, he would not sleep here. Even if he hadn't another reason, Málik was too honorable to besmirch her reputation, no matter that she no longer cared what anyone thought.

Or rather, she did care, but as it was, she had sunk to ignoble depths in the eyes of so many. Many who didn't know her still believed she had plotted with Locrinus to supplant her father. And some who knew the truth—that she did *not* conspire with Loc, that he'd kept her like a prisoner in his palace, a pawn for his political machinations—considered her weak. *A woman discarded by the Usurper.*

Unworthy of sovereignty.

Unfit for the seat her father unwillingly vacated.

Unfortunately, reputation alone would not lift her —or her people—from this abyss. That would take work. With a weary groan, she hauled herself up from the bed. She had no need to call out to ask who occupied the antechamber this morning. She knew it would be Bryn. She rose, dressing mindfully, hoping to convey a certain image—one that Caradoc and his people, and her own, would respect. She chose her black *mithril*, along with her mother's soft black leathers. Her hair had grown a bit, and though she'd considered having Esme shave it, ultimately, she'd decided against it. It was easier to wear a crown when one had hair to keep it secure. Retrieving her boots from the end of the bed where she'd left them, she returned them to her feet and laced them. Next, she settled the gold-leaf crown Esme made upon her brow, and thereafter, tossed her father's blood-stained cloak about her shoulders, securing it with his dragon brooch.

There was no Demelza to launder the furs, nor servants to spare. She herself had applied a bit of limewater to the stains, but that only turned them purple. So, she left them... to serve as a reminder.

At long last, she retrieved Borlewen's blade and her Kingslayer before opening the door to face Bryn. She found him seated atop Demelza's old cot, dressed, with his boots on, his black hair neatly combed, and his black fur cloak resting at his side.

The Crone was slow to pass this year—not yet warm enough to go without a coat, but every day the wind blew warmer.

He grinned at her. "Any longer and I thought to go find Málik and send him in to wake you," he said with his usual insouciance.

Gwendolyn gave him a pointed look. "Since when do you fear waking me?"

He laughed, the sound like a scoff. "Fear?" he said. "Nay, Gwendolyn. But I have never known anyone to guard her sleep as you do."

"Did," she said. It had been a long time since she'd lingered abed. And still Bryn persisted.

"Someday, there will be bards who sing of a sleeping beauty who could not be roused, save by true love's kiss."

Gwendolyn gave up her pique, allowing herself to be amused. "Would not, or could not?"

"Does it matter?"

"Indeed, it does," Gwendolyn assured, with a half-smile. "If she'll not be roused, perhaps 'tis because she awaits her lover with intent." She winked. "If she cannot be roused, perhaps she is bespelled or poisoned, and the cure will be her lover's kiss."

He grinned. "Clearly, 'would not' applies here."

Still half smiling, Gwendolyn lifted a brow.

Little did he realize Málik was *not* her lover. Far be it from the truth. In all her life, Gwendolyn had been kissed only thrice—once by Bryn by mistake, and twice by Málik, though not since the night on the ramparts.

"He is not my lover," she said, though in her heart this was a lie. Perhaps not in deed, but he was in spirit. And, in her own mind, Gwendolyn had imagined herself wrapped in his arms. More than anything she envied Elowyn, who even now must be lying abed with her husband's fingers tangled through her lovely locks. But though the thought gave Gwendolyn a prick of envy, it assuredly was not because she begrudged Ely her joy.

She did not.

It was simply that, last Maytide, Gwendolyn had sorely hoped for this life to be her own—even if the man she'd promised to wed was not the man her heart desired. Regardless, she had intended to make Loc a good wife, and she had longed to know joy in his arms —giving birth to a love that would grow and grow, gifting them with children, and ultimately uniting their lands.

"As you say," Bryn offered, though he clearly didn't believe her—not by the dubious tilt of his head.

Or if he did, Gwendolyn detected a hint of bitterness in the glint of his eyes. No matter what he said, some part of his own heart must still be aching from her rejection, even as her own heart ached over Málik's. She recognized the shadow behind his eyes and vowed to never again be so blind to his pain. After all, he was still a fellow, with a heart too easily broken. Mending it would take time, she realized. But she wasn't about to tempt him again. Thus, if he must tell himself she and Málik were lovers, so be it.

Better to change the subject.

"Has the *konsel* settled upon the Twelve?" She adjusted the cloak and her brooch, hoping to present it correctly. She was nervous but daren't confess it, lest she fall into a heap on the floor and never rise again. "I hope Lir's announcement did not send them into another frenzy."

"Only for a while," Bryn allowed, rising from the cot. He dragged up his cloak to toss it over his shoulders. "But do not fret, My Queen. They settled the matter at last."

My Queen.

Those words, regardless of Bryn's feeling for her, never sounded quite the same as they did from Málik's lips. Nor was she accustomed to Bryn's recent sense of propriety—and, truly, like the jest he'd made at her expense in the war room, she now wondered if he sometimes referred to her this way as a matter of provocation. "Whom did they choose?"

"One of Caradoc's generals," Bryn said, laughing ruefully. "The bastard insisted, and, after much discourse, everyone agreed, if only to settle his ire over the 'host of women now serving on *his konsel*.'"

He said this last, mimicking Caradoc's voice—an accurate impression.

Gwendolyn lifted both brows. "*His konsel*?"

Bryn shrugged. "For the time being, you must allow it."

"Goddess, save us all," Gwendolyn said, agitated, though she knew Bryn was right. And regardless, the notion did not settle well in her already restless belly. She gave Bryn a frown, without intending to. "Speaking of Málik, where is he?" she pressed, trying to sound casual.

Bryn's vexing grin returned. "Oh, then... were we speaking of Málik?" Gwendolyn glowered at him, and he said, "If you must know, the last I saw of him, he was with Esme, preparing the horses."

Of course he was!

Another prick of envy assailed Gwendolyn. All the gods knew, so much as both had proclaimed their dislike for one another, Esme and Málik were *always* together, whispering like lovers.

"Art ready?" Bryn asked.

Gwendolyn nodded.

She was, and she wasn't.

However, she was as ready as she would ever be.

The last thing she intended to do now was reveal how nervous she was, not even to Bryn. She would do nothing more to disillusion him.

38 TANYA ANNE CROSBY

Oblivious to her thoughts, her Shadow made his way across the antechamber to retrieve his belt and sword, and Gwendolyn turned one last time to peer into her mother's bower, her heart pinching.

When they returned, this chamber would be different.

Not empty, just different.

The scent on the bed furs would belong to someone else.

The coffers would be Taryn's.

Although Gwendolyn would be pleased for Taryn to occupy these apartments, it still tugged at her heart. There was no help for it.

Her mother was gone.

Everyone was gone.

And, after today, she would be gone as well—perhaps forever.

"Let's go," she said, pulling the heavy door closed behind her. Marching past Bryn, she preceded him through the antechamber and out the door, determined not to look back. There wasn't room for doubt, *nor time for regrets.*

Come what may, as of this morning, Caradoc would hold the keys to her city, and if he kept his word, it would better serve them all.

If he did not... well, then... she would have one more battle to wage.

4

At long last, the palace had resumed its normal activities and Gwendolyn knew who to thank for the effort—Ely.

All the while they'd been arguing about whether to admit another woman to the *konsel*, Ely had been helping to set the palace to rights. Clearly, she had learned much through observing her uncle Yestin and, considering that, considering the old steward, Gwendolyn listened to Bryn's footfalls behind her, wondering if he, too, was as dismayed as she was by the state of this house. If she'd thought him reticent before the coup, he was more so now, keeping all his thoughts to himself. But if he was aggrieved by his uncle's incarceration, not once had he argued for his release.

Neither had Ely, for that matter.

Truth be told, even Gwendolyn was torn.

Yestin was the one who'd taught her to keep the household accounts. He was also the one who'd taken time to instruct her in her letters when the Mester Alderman grew frustrated with her mistakes. And yet, without Yestin, Talwyn could not have accomplished his coup, and if Yestin had simply remained loyal to his sworn king, everything would have transpired so differently.

Since reclaiming the city, Gwendolyn had spoken to him quite frequently and so it seemed, he'd had no inkling her father would be murdered—at most, deposed and perhaps incarcerated. But considering the king's health, Yestin had believed he was doing the right thing for Gwendolyn, so certain was he that she would return to rule by her husband's side. But more than anything, he had believed he was serving the welfare of Cornwall and Trevena. It was only after the Feast of Blades that he'd come to understand his folly. By then, there was nothing to be done, and so, for him, there was nothing to be done until Gwendolyn returned—*if* she returned.

More to the point, *if* Caradoc returned the keys to her city.

Whether he would or would not remained to be seen, but showing any manner of weakness would not bode well for her, or for the city. Unfortunately, releasing Yestin would make her appear weak, and weakness was not something she could afford. Yestin would have plenty of time to keep his own company and consider the enormity of his decisions. In the meantime, Ely would serve well enough as steward until they found a new one. But if recent changes were any indication of how she would negotiate the *konsel*, Bryn's younger sister would have every one of those quarrelsome old men lapping from her palm before Gwendolyn was gone a fortnight.

Gwendolyn need only look about to see how Ely dealt with everyone.

Bright and early, whistling as he went, the gong-farmer wheeled his smelly little cart up and down the halls. Gwendolyn couldn't fathom how anyone could whistle whilst pushing about that reeksome burden, but there he was.

Meanwhile, a runner carried buckets of steaming water to freshen each of the wash basins. On his back, he toted a sack of dried lavender. Gwendolyn caught the scent of the fragrant petals as he passed, a far cry from the stench of that gong cart.

She smiled at the runner but didn't recognize his face.

Unfortunately, the first thing she'd done after reclaiming the city was to dismiss every man and woman who'd remained to serve under Talwyn—very few, thankfully. Alas, there was simply no way Loc's coup could have succeeded without help from every sector of this household. It broke her heart to see the faces of those who had remained. But, judging by their lack of effort here, those who'd served under Talwyn had no true love for this palace, much less for the general they'd stayed to serve. Indeed, after Kamber and Albanactus departed, no one even bothered to keep up with their duties. Loc's brothers clearly had not deemed this bastion worthy of reinforcement. Or perhaps they had believed the claims that the city was impenetrable—and it might have been, but not to Gwendolyn, who knew its secrets. And regardless, even knowing what she knew, retaking this city could only have been possible because they were undermanned. Upon their departure, Kamber and Albanactus had taken most of the armed forces, leaving only a few guards, and the palace itself with a skeletal staff —none of whom had a care for the work necessary to keep the palace in order.

Not even Yestin could rally them to the cause.

Well, their loss was Trevena's gain.

Little by little, Ely was replacing the servants. And

no matter that Locrinus and his fool brothers might not have appreciated what her father built, this palace was nothing to fleer at. Influenced by some of the greatest cities across the sea, Trevena was the only port of its kind in all Pretania. As it was with the blueprints for their *piscina*, King Corineus had, throughout the years, incorporated many of the suggestions offered to him by visiting artists and architects, many of whom reassured him that Trevena, with its thriving seaport, robust trade, and wealth of ore, was in every way worthy of the glory. They'd regaled him with tales of hanging gardens in a city called Bāb-ilim, where flowers and fruit trees grew in the most unlikely of places—on rooftops, atop ledges, and on buildings constructed to emulate mountains.

After hearing those tales, her father dared to envision a city of equal splendor. Indeed, few things had compelled him more readily than the desire to raise Trevena's eminence amongst the world's greatest capitals. Her father had envisioned a flourishing metropolis that would bring more ships, more traders, more marvels. And, along with the peace he'd sought by uniting Pretania's tribes, he'd dreamt of a kingdom where no child would go hungry, nor any citizen fail to provide for his family.

This was the reason he'd welcomed King Brutus so readily, providing the exiled Trojan with lands of his own to keep. But, as far as Gwendolyn was concerned, he gave Brutus too much advantage. And, because of the terms of their alliance, too much of Trevena's wealth made its way into Loegrian coffers. Much to her people's dismay, Brutus arrived on their shores with promises of prosperity and discovered a king too willing to embrace him for the price of his flattery.

Soon enough, it became apparent that while her

father would prioritize the welfare of Trevena and its boroughs, King Brutus would not. His dream was something else—something that, if not shared by his odious sons, had certainly nurtured the seeds of their betrayal. And yet, considering his own death at the hands of his traitorous sons, Gwendolyn must believe that Brutus had allied with her father in good faith, content perhaps to unite their houses and rule this kingdom through his son and his grandsons. But all the while he'd been amassing armies, placing his wolfish sons in positions of command, his own city had languished.

Whereas Trevena's windows sparkled like Faerie dust beneath a midday sun, Loegria grew dim and dimmer throughout the years, with dirty streets, poorly constructed buildings that grew timeworn and in need of repair.

After having lived in his burgh, Gwendolyn surmised that every day of Loc's miserable existence he must have begrudged his father's austerity, and perhaps after seeing Trevena, his covetous heart turned sour. Alas, though Gwendolyn could easily understand why, she couldn't make allowances for his greed.

In comparison, Trevena was a wonder, boasting a stone palace the likes of which no one on these Tin Isles had ever beheld.

Not that Gwendolyn had ever spied the city from this vantage, but it was said that, to look upon Trevena from the heavens, it would appear to be a giant, dressed in a coat of many colors, with arms wide, and head bowed, and the crenelated ramparts serving as his crown.

From the main hall extended two corridors, each leading to apartments reserved for the royal household—one aptly named the King's Arm, and the other referred to as the Dancer's Hall, though Gwendolyn lived there as well.

Naturally, her apartments were considerably smaller, having to share the wing with the steward and his attendants. But all those rooms except hers were now empty, and without her mother's vision, Gwendolyn couldn't begin to consider accepting applicants for the *dawnsio*—nor would any of the tribes dare send daughters to a city under siege. As it was with the position of steward, the *dawnsio* would have to wait, and truth be told, without Queen Eseld, it might never return to its former glory.

Frowning as she wended her way through the familiar halls, Gwendolyn found herself incensed by the way her home had been treated during the occupation. There were still malodorous, yellow stains at every corner, where Loc's men had marked their territories like hounds staking their claims.

Here, along the interior halls, where windows were not practicable, the corridors were lit by torches, one every five alens—the length of five forearms. The result was a brightness that belied the windowless structure and betrayed its newly acquired filth. Swatting at a tapestry as she passed, Gwendolyn grimaced as black soot billowed in mockery of its former state. Fashioned of good wool and fine silk woven with golden threads, this was a depiction of her father's battle against the giant Gogmagog—a gift from a Cathayan merchant, who'd heard the tale.

Abused even so, it surprised Gwendolyn to find it intact, especially considering that it portrayed her father in such heroic light.

When Gwendolyn was ten, her father obtained a formula for a longer-burning resin made from a water-resistant solution of sulfur and lime called Hellas fire. Their chandler had become so well versed in the art of its creation that he'd kept the garner full of ready replacements. Loc's brothers had clearly depleted those stores and had used rushlights dipped in tallow to replace them.

Interesting to note, that was also what they'd used in Loegria, despite that the formula for Hellas fire had come from Queen Innogen's people—further proof, perhaps, that Loegria was never meant to be a permanent base.

Whatever the case, the reek of scorched pig fat vied terribly with the lingering scent of urine. But also, because the rushlights burned so hot, at every cresset, angry, black stains clawed at the white-washed stone. Sadly, though urine could be cleaned and aired—over time—these walls could not so easily be painted. The gypsum used for the whitewash was imported from Cantium, who were allies of the Iceni, and now her enemies after joining forces with Caradoc. The Catuvellauni and the Iceni were the bitterest of foes. But though this was something she intended to change, for now, she must be grateful that Ely had this palace so well in hand. It would bolster morale. But her people's true healing would not be possible until she eradicated the tumor growing in their midst—namely Locrinus.

As she neared the palace entrance, Gwendolyn heard the drone of chatter, growing steadily louder as they approached. Her belly fluttered as she spotted her traveling companions near the Mester's Pavilion: Esme, Lir and Málik.

Already, the horses were saddled—Aisling for Gwendolyn; Sheahan for Lir; Daithi for Málik; and Lorcan for Esme.

Only Bryn was not meant to ride one of Enbarr's

mares, but hopefully, his mount would be sturdy, and she would not come to regret allowing Lir to join.

Emerging from the palace, feigning a confidence she did not feel, Gwendolyn took the steps two at a time, alighting into the courtyard. But then her gaze swept the gathering to find Caradoc standing with his son and Ely, and her heart turned a somersault. Caradoc appeared formidable, as did his son—both with hair the color of obsidian. Beside him, even wearing her mother's copper breastplate and her gold-leaf crown, she would look small beneath her father's cloak—a child merely playing at this game of thrones. Dread made her turn and lift a hand to shade her eyes, pretending to admire the familiar slate stonework and the minarets surging against a cloudless sky—the brightness of it belying the crisp, cool day.

Enough, she told herself.

You are not a child!

This is not your sanctuary.

Not anymore.

It might again be, someday, but not if she did not fight for it.

With a lump in her throat, Gwendolyn tugged her father's cloak to cover her shoulders and then whirled to make her way toward the waiting horses, her heart tripping painfully as she turned to seek the one whose presence would help compose her... *Málik*.

5

He turned away.

No matter, Gwendolyn told herself.

She knew why he was behaving this way, and contrary to the way it was the first time she'd encountered him in this very courtyard, she understood it wasn't because he reviled her. She realized he didn't wish to inspire gossip, particularly today when there were so many eyes upon them. For weeks now he'd slept, gods knew where, and all because he'd wished to lift her in the people's eyes. Yet knowing this didn't make his repudiation any less excruciating. Nor were they fooling anyone with this contrivance. Anyone present could read Gwendolyn's heart in her eyes.

So be it.

This was for the best, she told herself.

She must be grateful he was so determined to push her away. Her love for him threatened to soften her heart, and Gwendolyn couldn't afford to be soft —not now.

Not on the eve of this quest with so much at stake.

"Caradoc," she said, presenting herself first to the man to whom she would submit her city's keys. Theirs was a tenuous friendship and the last thing Gwendolyn intended to do was to insult the man before their departure. As a fellow of convention, he was already struggling with the recent changes—foremost, a woman sovereign. To that point, his objection to having any woman on *his konsel* was in no small part a protest over having to bend the knee to a woman. But eventually, they would *all* succumb to a woman's rule, Caradoc included.

For now, she must take a few lessons from her mother, and she could afford to be open-handed, knowing that he needed her more than she needed him—at least until the moment she handed him the keys. Then she would be gone, and she must trust that Trevena was not his heart's true desire.

He responded with a polite bow of his head—a deferential gesture, to be sure, slight though it was. Even so, Gwendolyn was grateful for it. She knew that the head bow had cost him some pride.

His son made up for his father's meager tribute, giving her a full bow, and Ely's genuflection was unmistakable. Gwendolyn gave her dear friend a warm smile, gesturing for her to rise, before giving her new husband a grateful nod.

"Take good care of my dear friend," she charged him.

"I shall," he replied with a nod.

"Majesty," said Caradoc as he stepped forward to take Gwendolyn's hand, leaning forward to kiss it. But then, as Gwendolyn would have expected, his familiar, irreverent grin returned by the time he'd lifted his gaze. "I thought by now you would have reconsidered my proposal?"

Marriage?

Not whilst she had breath in her lungs!

"Lest you forget, my liege, I already have one husband to be rid of," she jested, then winked. "I shouldn't like to add another."

"Ah," he said. "Fret not, my beautiful queen. I enjoy a good tussle."

Gwendolyn blushed hotly, despite that she didn't wish to.

The man was incorrigible, with his incessant flirting—really, to the point that no one in their presence could fail to note it. And while it heartened her to hear his teasing, it came dressed with teeth. She knew he meant every word, and regardless, she wouldn't fool herself into believing his proposal was proffered with any genuine affection. They had grown as close as two contenders could be, but she knew him to be a practical man, and for his part, a betrothal would only secure his position. It would be far easier and less bloody than doing battling for Gwendolyn's crown despite that, as yet, she hadn't even an army of her own. No matter, she had the potential of aid from her powerful grandfather, and for now, that should be enough to temper Caradoc's avarice. But she would not delude herself into believing he cared for her or even feared her.

His answering tone was smooth as an eel, Gwendolyn thought. "If you but give me a nod, I would see it done," he suggested.

Murder Locrinus?

Gwendolyn almost laughed—almost.

He had yet to release her hand, despite that she tested his grip. He drew it back with subtle but unmistakable force, his grasp tightening on her fingers and Gwendolyn smiled, giving a glance about at so many eyes upon them, then relaxing her hand in his, capitulating with gritted teeth. Queen Eseld would have flirted back, so she gave it her best effort. She found

Caradoc responded better with a little teasing, trading quips until he had no more rejoinders. "Well," she said with a knowing smile. "Bring me his head! I may reconsider?"

He was quick to return her smile, but the fierce glint in his black eyes held a trace of annoyance, and he released his vise grip on her hand.

By now, she knew him well enough to know he would not be stupid enough to leave the safety of Trevena's walls, especially for some fool's errand. Caradoc's army and his people were still recovering from recent battles. He would not risk his kindred's welfare. Still, she winked once more, only to be certain he understood her challenge was made in jest.

One unwanted marriage was enough. She would not entertain another.

A young page arrived with supplies, saving her from further discourse.

"Travel well," suggested Caradoc, as Gwendolyn turned to watch the boy load their saddlebags.

Esme oversaw the effort, and Gwendolyn had every faith their needs would be met, so she didn't look closely at what was being packed. But she spied several lengths of salted meats, bread, canteens, flints and bolts making their way into each of the saddlebags, and finally, a small sack of gold coins into Esme's hands. Esme plucked up the sack by its velvet strings, then turned to hurl it into Bryn's hands. "For you," she said, "I've no use for trinkets."

Giving her a half-hearted smile, Bryn turned to tuck the sack of coins into his own saddlebag before returning to address his sister. He whispered into her ear, only to make her giggle and then made a show of embracing Kelan, bidding him, as Gwendolyn had, to take good care of Ely. He smacked the chieftain's only remaining son on the arm—hard—then stepped back to make room for Gwendolyn.

There was no use putting it off any longer.

With a last glance at the palace entrance—where she longed to flee, Gwendolyn embraced Elowyn, and then, lifting a finger to touch Ely's cheek, she said, "Take good care, my dearest friend. You are a sworn alderwoman now, and you must command your due respect. By law, they *must* heed your words. Accept misery from no one." She cast a glance at her new father-by-law. "Know your suffrage preserves the will of our people and our lands."

Ely nodded, her eyes brimming with unshed tears, and Gwendolyn reached up to swipe the glittering moisture away.

Gods. It was so difficult to leave her. They had once been like sisters. The minute she rode through those gates, she would leave yet another splintered piece of her heart. No doubt, she had battled a few demons where Ely was concerned, but not for one moment had she ever blamed Ely for any of it. Ely was like the sun to a blossom. "Weep not, sister of my heart. I have faith in you, and I promise to return your troublesome brother unharmed."

It was a promise she shouldn't make, but she vowed in that moment that whatever it took—even if it meant sacrificing her own life—she would do it.

Ely nodded, reaching up to wipe another tear.

"Enough!" Bellowed Caradoc. "You'll turn us all into weeping crones. Already, I find myself un-manned! Away! Begone!" he declared, waving a hand in a manner that could never be mistaken by the gathering crowd—shooing her like a dog.

Gwendolyn inhaled deeply and somehow re-frained from pointing out that he was not her sovereign. She would leave whenever it suited her, but as it so happened, it suited her to leave right now. *Canny old bastard.* But leave it to Esme to put his swagger to the test. No one could tell that surly Elf what to do, nor when to leave, and she was more protective of Gwendolyn than even Gwendolyn was inclined to be. Unsheathing her Elvin blade, she moved swiftly, turning the razor-sharp blade to Caradoc's throat. "*Banríon Dragan* will depart when it suits her, not before," she said, smiling, her lips pulling back tight over prominent fangs.

Startled, rearing back from the blade, Caradoc lifted both hands in submission, removing his throat from the vicinity of her sword. "Calm yourself!" he suggested. "No harm was intended." And then, only to be certain his position was clear, he fell to one knee before Gwendolyn, and said, "Go with the people's affection, Majesty. All will be as we said."

Gwendolyn swept a hand down, tapping his arm, bidding him to rise. She needn't see him so humbled, only a bit less... *despotic.* When he stood to face her again, she retrieved her father's judicatory brooch from the pouch at her waist—one similar to the ones worn by the *konsel* of Twelve. Only this one bore the royal seal and served as the city's symbolic key. So long as Caradoc held it, Trevena would be his to command. She handed it to him. "Wield it wisely," she charged him, withholding it only for a moment so the people could see she held it and gave it willingly. "Keep *our* people safe." Her choice of words was not by chance. His people were her people now, and she wanted him to feel the same responsibility for the ones she left behind. "We will return victorious," she promised. "And then, you and I will ride together as friends and allies to take back your rightful lands. I have given you my word and intend to keep it. Keep yours to me."

"I shall," he said, with a twinkle in his eye—the look far less reassuring than Gwendolyn had hoped for. Yet, she had no choice but to take him at his word.

It was past time to go—because if she did not leave now, she would lose her nerve, and run back into that palace to hide beneath her mother's covers and never again peek out. She released the broach into his hands, and then, swallowing her uncertainty, Gwendolyn spun about to find Esme mounted—so quickly she'd moved from Caradoc's throat to her horse, with her sword returned to its scabbard. Gwendolyn would never grow accustomed to that—the swiftness of the Fae's movements.

Lir, too, was mounted, eager to reassure Gwendolyn that he was ready to go.

Bryn's foot was in the bridle iron, and even as he swung his leg over the mare, Málik assumed his saddle as well.

Gwendolyn would be the last to mount.

No one advanced to aid her, but she didn't need help; she was an accomplished horsewoman. Even so, she experienced the tiniest flutter of nerves as she placed her boot in the bridle iron, thinking how cruel a twist of fate it would be if she should stumble now, leaving her people with a lasting impression of inadequacy—something she could not afford!

Too many years her people had floundered beneath an ailing king, and in the end, her father's weakness was Trevena's undoing.

The people's perception was a powerful force. This was why she needed them to view her departure as a willing sacrifice for Cornwall.

In fact, she'd once heard a tale about a king who

tumbled from his horse on the eve before a battle. His fall was presumed to be an ill-omen from the gods, and after the battle was lost, his people deposed him, allying themselves with his enemy. And truly, wasn't that what happened with her father? His most loyal subjects had judged and found him unworthy, opting for an outlander in his stead.

Mounted now, half-blinded by the morning sun glinting across her mother's breastplate, she lifted a hand to the crowd, waving. "We will soon return with *Claímh Solais* and all the fury of the North!" she declared, with a glance toward Caradoc, who stood, arms crossed, watching. It was Gwendolyn's not-so-subtle way of reminding him she had resources beyond his dwindled army.

He knew it and grinned as a chorus of huzzahs arose amidst the crowd.

Gwendolyn straightened in the saddle, unsheathing Borlewen's blade and holding it high so it winked against the morning sun. "Cornwall and her allies will prevail!"

Another concert of shouts, and Gwendolyn didn't wait to be led. Taking the reins, she wheeled Aisling about, pointing the mare's nose toward the Trade Streets. From there, the path curved northwest through the market, to the main gate.

It was a sovereign's duty to ride at the head of the army.

In his youth, her father would never have depended upon others to fight his battles, nor did he once depart these gates for war hidden behind his men. Rather, he'd ridden at the fore, always, unmistakable in his leadership. Gwendolyn wanted no one to mistake that she was in command. She shoved her cloak behind her with intent, wanting everyone present to see that she rode without a torc at her throat—unclaimed, unbowed, unwed!

She might have exchanged vows with that lying, conniving impostor, but she'd never once shared his bed—not even on the eve of their wedding, and so, in her heart, she was a free woman. And she would cut the heart from her own breast before she submitted to any man for the sake of duty.

Not Locrinus, not Caradoc—no man.

With thoughts of vengeance darkening her heart, she gave Caradoc one last glance and moved into the gathering. The rest of the party fell in line behind her, cantering toward the main gates. At the sight of her retinue, the people let loose another resounding cheer. "*My'ternes!*" They shouted. "*My'ternes!*"

Queen.

And still she would leave them, and there wasn't any guarantee they would shout her name upon her return.

It didn't matter.

Gwendolyn hadn't any choice.

They must do battle for the soul of this land.

In anticipation of the morning's departure, they had opened the gates during the wee hours of the morn. They would be lowered as soon her retinue crossed the threshold.

Don't look back, she told herself.

As she had done so many a time before, she waved to the guards as she veered onto the narrow bridge, even despite knowing these would be Caradoc's men. And then, even as the groan of chains began anew, she daren't look back. The boom that followed as heavy lumber and steel settled against unyielding stone sent a quiver down her spine. The terrifying finality of it lobbed another boulder into her belly.

"You should have allowed me to gut him," said Esme as she sidled up beside Gwendolyn.

Gwendolyn laughed, though she knew Esme wasn't jesting. And nevertheless, Gwendolyn answered in jest. "And then who would hold the city in my absence?"

The Elf's eyes glinted as sharply as her teeth.

"If that is your question, *Banríon Dragan,* perhaps you are still unprepared for the task you face."

It wasn't a question, and Gwendolyn knew Esme wasn't expecting an answer. But if it had been her intention to unsettle Gwendolyn, she had succeeded. Regardless of Caradoc's flirtations, Gwendolyn also knew he had spoken from his heart when he'd proclaimed this city was too small for the both of them. Now, remembering his words during yesterday's *konsel,* doubt reared its ugly, fanged head, and before she could stop herself, she wheeled Aisling about, turning one last time to peer at the city she was born in...

6

From this vantage, everything appeared quite ordinary—as it had a thousand mornings before. Except for the empty barbican, it was as though nothing had ever transpired in that city, and if only Gwendolyn returned to the palace with Bryn after the morning's adventure, she would discover her father seated upon his ancient throne, and her mother in the hall with her ladies in tow.

But this would not be the case.

No matter how Gwendolyn wished for it to be otherwise, her parents were gone, her life as it was... ended. No matter that she still considered Trevena her greatest love, she no longer recognized half the faces remaining. They were mostly Caradoc's people, and, with over six hundred to witness her bestowal, she had given her father's sworn enemy the keys to her city. Along with those keys, Caradoc would also assume command of the army and control of the harbor as well. And with the Dragon's Bay, he held the key to Trevena's advantage and the last of Cornwall's supplies—every last weapon, every brick of ore, every block of Loegrian steel...

Even as she watched, one thick plume of dark

smoke rose from the east end—the firing of the forges, she realized. As her final command, she had mandated the gathering of weapons, with the intent of repairing all the ones that were still serviceable and making new ones for those who had none.

War was coming.

There was nothing to be said or done to soften this truth, but the question remained: Must she now add one more battle to her list of battles to be waged?

Sensing her agitation, Enbarr's youngest mare stamped restlessly beneath her, eager to go... *one direction or another.* Gwendolyn's fingers tightened on the reins, second-guessing her plan. One small tug and she knew the mare would obey.

But it was too late; there would be no admittance to this city unless Caradoc ordained it and she had pressed her last advantage. The shaft housing the *piscina's* water screw was now permanently sealed. By her own command, the outer barbican had been vacant for months, the gates secured, with no one admitted for any reason at all, not even to seek sanctuary.

Now with the Dragon's Flame restored—the light in the cave which guided ships safely into the Dragon's Bay—trade could resume. All supplies they would need could be procured or received through the newly re-opened port. It was perhaps not the greatest solution for local farmers or merchants, but for them, there would be access to the beach via a path down the cliff side, and from there, entry to the docks. If anyone should require admittance to the city proper, it could be granted from below and all wares could be lifted from the docks to the ramparts—a painstaking effort, and more precarious than traversing Stone

Bridge, but so long as there were ample precautions, it was a viable solution.

Meanwhile, the main gates could easily be defended by a handful of archers... even if Caradoc's bowmen weren't as skilled as her father's.

And still, every muscle in her body ached to fly back.

She *could* try... if only to see whether Caradoc would reopen the gates, but what good would that do? If he refused her, it would force her to deal with his defiance here and now, and she couldn't afford to waste more time.

Even worse, rushing back to shake her banners at the towers, demanding reentrance... this would only serve to pin an epithet of "mad queen" to her already abused reputation, and no one could afford that.

Don't do it, she begged herself.

Don't.

Don't.

Don't.

"If you tarry long enough, you may hear him celebrating," said Esme, chortling, and Gwendolyn cast the Elf a backward glance, but she refrained from responding, loathing how true she spoke. Caradoc would indeed be compelled to celebrate her departure, but Gwendolyn also trusted he would keep her people safe, and that's what mattered most.

Far more than her ambivalence toward Caradoc, it was Esme's demeanor that bothered Gwendolyn most. Changeable as the wind, her sense of humor—if it could be called that—had turned dark and biting and there was an edge to the Elf's temper that was sharper than Borlewen's blade. And considering the countless hours Gwendolyn had spent honing her cousin's blade in anticipation of exacting her revenge, it was razor-edged.

Gwendolyn didn't know what happened in the Cods Wold, but something must have. This was *not* the Esme she'd first encountered in the Druid village. She was moody and contentious of late—as a sister would be, one moment doting and sweet, the next bitter and grudging, given to rivalry.

Pivoting in her saddle, she watched Esme approach Málik, her heart squeezing when she saw them resume their heated whispers.

"Something is amiss with those two Elves," said Bryn, as Lir rode by—slow as freshly sapped honey, even despite riding one of Enbarr's mares.

Gwendolyn looked at her oldest, dearest friend, arching a brow. More than anything, she longed to point out that the same could be said for him, though she was more concerned with the tone of his voice. It wasn't so long ago he had been Málik's most ardent champion, but she couldn't fail to note the bitterness that lingered in the glint of his brilliant blue eyes. She wondered over the cause of it, but suspected she knew. "You shouldn't call them Elves," she rebuked.

"Why not? *She* refers to herself that way."

She was Esme. And, indeed, *she* did.

Gwendolyn refrained from pointing out that Málik and Esme could call themselves whatsoever they pleased. There was nevertheless something about Bryn's use of the word that unsettled her. He didn't know what she knew. To him, the Faerie nomen was interchangeable with the age-old insult, and his use of the word only depended upon his mood. And perhaps that's what Gwendolyn didn't like. He only ever called them Elves when he was annoyed by them.

"I can never quite decide if they are enemies or..."

"They are *not* lovers," Gwendolyn asserted.

"Perhaps," Bryn allowed. "But if you have a doubt, Gwendolyn—any at all—now would be the time to confess it. Once we leave, we'll be at their mercy."

Not till they descended into the Fae realm, but Gwendolyn understood what he was saying. They shared a look—one she feared revealed too much, and then averted her gaze too late.

"Do you trust him?"

Gwendolyn answered without hesitation. "Of course, I do."

"And Esme?"

This time, her nod came hesitantly, regardless that she trusted Esme—so much as she could trust anyone, including Bryn.

Bryn was her oldest, dearest friend.

She *needed* to trust him.

She should trust him.

Even after she'd failed him so grievously, he'd stood by her, regardless of her ill-considered choices —defying his own parents, and even his king. In the end, Bryn made the ultimate sacrifice for Trevena... by helping Gwendolyn defeat his turncoat father. Still, there was something about his reticence these past weeks that gave her pause... did he regret having helped her?

Was he still bitter over Málik?

Even now, she had the distinct impression he wanted to say more; still he refrained. As children, they had been so quick to understand what the other was thinking without any need for explanation. A single word conveyed so much. But, of late, Gwendolyn didn't feel attuned to him, and she wondered if they would ever overcome their misfortunes. "If I did not trust her, I'd not keep her close."

His tone darkened. "My father oft warned me to keep friends near, and enemies nearer," he offered.

"As did mine," Gwendolyn allowed. "Regardless, I've been close enough to the worst of them to know *all* vipers should be kept at arm's length."

"Perhaps," said Bryn, nodding, but then added, "I am told they cannot lie, but... those two are certainly keeping their own counsel and I will caution you to remember that a lie of omission is still a lie."

"True," said Gwendolyn, but she suspected Málik's silence was because of something else. Sometimes she had the sense there were words that might fly from his lips if only he could speak them, and the struggle was clear in the storm of his eyes. Whatever the case, she had more to worry about than Bryn's reticence or Málik's silence—foremost, how to convince Esme's father that she was the rightful heir to *Claímh Solais*. And getting to the Druid village in one piece was hardly the least of it while Loc's men plagued the area, raiding and burning villages.

One last time, her gaze sought the comfort of Trevena's spires. But there was nothing more to be done, she told herself.

"It's not too late," Bryn suggested.

"It is too late," Gwendolyn responded. "The way back is before us," she said, with certainty, and putting the decision behind her once and for all, she wheeled Aisling about, and said, "Let's go. I've one last thing to investigate before we're away."

7

Giving her mare a heel before anyone could stop her, Gwendolyn flew toward Porth Pool.

"Wait!" Bryn shouted. "Gwendolyn!"

Nay. She would not wait. It had been too long since she'd had the chance to inspect Porth Pool—not since hers and Bryn's ill-fated swim a few weeks before her wedding to Locrinus. Before leaving, she needed to see how it fared. Every time she had previously suggested they should inspect it, excuses were made about why she should not—particularly by Bryn, who'd insisted she not expose herself to Loc's assassins. And perhaps there was merit to that argument, but here they were now, and the pool wasn't far.

Besides, Málik and Esme were too preoccupied with their discourse to miss her for as long as she would be gone.

At any rate, she trusted Bryn would follow. And even if he didn't, she knew these woods better than anyone. In their current state, there was no cover to be found; so far as she could tell, there were no scouts in the area—not anymore. But if she was wrong, she would welcome the swordplay. She could use an opponent other than Málik or Bryn. Málik's thoughts were clearly elsewhere, and Gwendolyn's skills had long surpassed Bryn's. Even Caradoc, with his brawn, had been too slow for her.

Leaping over a large puddle, Aisling missed dry land by a shred, sending up a slosh of muck. But Gwendolyn didn't care. She had weeks to go on the road without a change of clothes. She was bound to get dirtier still, as the condition of these woods were atrocious and growing more so by the day.

Behind her, she heard another splash and Bryn's pursuant curse.

He'd missed his mark, landing in the puddle.

Gwendolyn didn't stop.

The sound of Bryn's pursuit recommenced, and in scant moments he could rejoin her and scold her all he wished—gods, it felt good to ride!

It had been too long.

Her heart sang, her veins stirring with anticipation.

She loved Porth Pool so much.

Ever since she was a girl, she had cherished every moment spent at that pool, only waiting to return to its pleasant, restorative waters.

The first time her mother sent her there—ostensibly to restore her complexion—Gwendolyn bemoaned the need for it, but once she'd waded into that pool, and discovered those *piskies*... she was... beguiled.

To her knowledge, there was no place like it in all Pretania—where divine creatures still thrived. Demelza once told her that their presence here was a measure of the gods' favor, and if the *piskies ever* abandoned the pool, all hope would be lost.

Hidden within a coppice, it was easy to miss. Betimes, travelers came seeking its warm, curative waters, and perished before they ever found them, especially during the long winters, rife with ague. Gwendolyn knew that only because after the snows melted in the spring, their bones were uncovered amidst the bracken—so near to their destination, without reward. Today, in the sixth moon since *Samhuinn*, these woods were alarmingly bare, and the lands were boggy. Just when the dark half of the year should end, and *Calan Mai* grew near, when her people were normally frolicsome, and preparing for the Fire Festival, the forest appeared as though it was still bracing for winter.

Slow to grow and slow green, what few leaves had appeared on the trees looked sickly—as though they too would perish seeking a cure. Despite that, Gwendolyn took heart because this was not the first time their lands had been so mired.

She was scarcely old enough to recall the Great Southern Storm, and this reminded her of that— browning leaves on once-verdant trees, despite the endless precipitation; wetlands that appeared from nowhere, made to swallow horse and rider.

After the storm, her father opened the city gates to men and women traveling from more devastated southern regions, and soon after, the rains stopped, the bogs dried, the land healed. But before that, entire provinces and forests were lost. And still the land recovered. Everyone celebrated, praising her father for his generosity of spirit.

Until one day, his flesh turned sallow, and his limbs began to quake.

And thereafter, as Gwendolyn feared, the beginning of his wasting illness foreshadowed the return of the Rot.

"Whoa, girl! Whoa!"

Aisling whinnied, tossing her head, and Gwendolyn tugged at the reins as the mare skidded to a halt before the path's end. She quickly regained control of the horse, but her jaw fell and her eyes widened at the sight that greeted her.

Blood and bloody bones!

There was a pit between two large ash trees, where the pool had eroded the land allowing the pool to drain. It poured from its reservoir.

Trickled more like.

The water remaining in the pool could scarcely be seen from this vantage, despite bared-limbed trees. But it was the condition of it that rent Gwendolyn's heart and robbed her of breath and hope...

The surface of the pool appeared black and oily beneath the sun's watery rays. And, even as she considered this catastrophe, a glance up revealed more storm clouds gathering overhead.

So stunned was she, so dumbfounded, that she was only vaguely aware that Bryn came trotting up behind her, reining in his mount. "I am sorry," he said at once. "We meant to tell you."

Gwendolyn slid her gaze to his. "We?"

"Málik," he confessed, with a bloom in his cheeks. "He told me not to tell you."

Gwendolyn frowned. *Why?* To spare her? Did they believe she would never find out? "Málik has seen this?"

Bryn nodded, his gaze moving past her to the devastated pool. "Aye," he said, looking chagrined, though at least Gwendolyn didn't have to drag the explanation from his lips. "The day we captured Loc's spy. He fell into this pit." He gestured toward the crevice below, where a gnarled tangle of roots had prevented a full collapse of the forest floor. "That's how he broke his leg," he said, before turning again to meet Gwendolyn's gaze. "The horse fared worse. We put it down before dragging the idiot to his cell."

Gods. That was weeks ago! Gwendolyn realized. So long ago that the spy Bryn was speaking of was the same man she released to carry her message to Loc. He'd had ample time to heal in his cell. *He'd kept this news so long?*

No, not *he... they.*

Her jaw clenched.

And Esme? Did she know, too?

Admittedly, Gwendolyn had been mired with preparations for their departure, but this was something she would have wanted to know.

"Why didn't you tell me, Bryn?"

He shrugged. "I am sorry," he said again. "You had so much on your mind," he added. "I did not wish to add to your burden."

"Blood and bones!" Gwendolyn exclaimed, her gaze returning to the decimated pool, fury burning hot through her veins.

This... pool... it was nothing as it was when the two of them had swum here together only last spring. Despite that the Rot was evident even then, there had been a glimmer of hope in its condition.

Their journey was only beginning, and Gwendolyn knew she must temper her words, but she barely restrained fury. "Never again will you lie to me," she said.

"It was not a lie—"

"It is a lie, "Gwendolyn argued. "Was it not you who only moments past reminded me that a lie of omission is still a lie?"

"Yes, but—"

"Never again!" Gwendolyn declared. "You will not

spare me any truth. It is my duty to protect these lands, and how can I do this if you will not apprise me?"

"I am sorry," he said, but Gwendolyn didn't trust herself to say more. Disheartened, she turned Aisling away from the pool.

And yet, she must take part of the blame here. She had known for so long that something terrible was happening here, and she had been too afraid of angering her father or turning the people against him. She had worried incessantly, when what she should have done was to summon every bloody Druid from every corner of this isle—every Gwyddon, every Awenydd. She should have attended all her father's *konsels* and persisted with her concerns, instead of allowing a few doddering old fools to dismiss her concerns. Instead, like the day they'd discussed her betrothal, she had behaved like a sullen child.

Quickly on the heels of her fury came fear—bone rattling fear.

Gods.

The condition of this land did not favor her, and if Porth Pool was lost... she must retrieve that sword with all due haste and return.

Only what if she failed?

What if the sword would not burn for her?

What if she wasn't worthy?

What if she couldn't heal this land?

What if she wasn't able to unite the tribes?

What if they turned away from her, even with the sword in hand?

Gwendolyn's journey was only beginning, and already she had a knot in her belly the size of the yew tree. But she took heart in this: If she'd had some part in this land's demise, she was unwilling to accept that she had no part in its recovery. Somehow, she would heal this land of Rot.

There was no time to wallow in self-pity.

She must keep her mind on the task she was given. As it was, the journey to Lifer Pol would prove treacherous and long—no less than a fortnight wading through boglands while Loc's armies continued to scour the area. *To find and kill her*—wasn't that what he'd commanded his men?

I mean to put an end to that Cornish vermin once and for all.

All this time later, his voice still rang in her ears, the vitriol consuming every word uttered. How pleased would he be if he learned how thoroughly the gods had abandoned her?

Soured by the morning's discovery, the buzzing in Gwendolyn's belly quickened to a full-on ache.

Bryn said nothing more as they made their way back, and when she caught up with the party, Lir blinked at her like a buck facing a bow. He twisted away, peering up—anywhere but at Gwendolyn—pretending to study a storm cloud. But Gwendolyn could tell by his expression that he, too, had known.

Had everyone known?

Málik gave her the briefest of glances before resuming his conversation with Esme, and Gwendolyn couldn't help herself. A prickle sidled down her spine. Something dreadful was driving their discourse—something Málik was unwilling to discuss with her, or even with Esme, judging by the rigidity of his shoulders.

Conversely, Esme seemed quite adamant he listen, and whatever she was saying commanded all his attention—so much so that he hadn't even bothered to give chase when Gwendolyn made off for the pool, leaving Bryn to see to her safety.

Another prickle ran down her spine, a feeling Demelza cautioned her not to ignore—a pip of intuition borne in the gut and perceived by the heart. *What was it trying to say?* More than ever, she missed Demelza's counsel and candor. Her mother's maid had been one of her most trusted advisors, always telling her precisely what she needed to hear, not merely what she wished to know. But suddenly... with the hiss of wind through the trees, she heard the ghost of Demelza's voice whisper in her ear...

Slay the child, arise a queen.

Gwendolyn lifted her shoulders and chin.

She had an impossible task now before her, with impossible odds, and despite this, she had no choice but to embrace the quest.

There was no turning back. No matter how much she wanted to.

As she'd apprised Bryn, the way back was before them and their only hope lay in the Fae realm.

Once more, her gaze returned to Málik.

To accomplish her goal, she needed both Málik and Esme, yet she could afford to trust no one. Twice, Málik had claimed to love her, and she trusted that in this, at least, he'd spoken true. However loving her wouldn't prevent him from doing whatever he believed he should. In the end, if loving her meant he must leave her, Gwendolyn knew he would do it. *Hadn't he proven that already?*

Indeed, he'd promised not to go, and still he did, but that wasn't the worst of it. At her father's behest, he'd stolen her sword—the one she must now reclaim —never once giving her the opportunity to prove it should remain in her keeping.

If he had, they mightn't now be forced to go beg for it...

Or steal it.

Worse yet, kill for it.

She loved Málik, but since that night on the ramparts when he'd bared his heart to her, telling her so much, and still too little, he had grown more and more distant. Meanwhile, he and Esme seemed to have grown closer—close enough to argue like mates. *Look away*, Gwendolyn told herself. *Look away and guard your heart.*

Slay the child, arise a queen.

8

Gwendolyn's mood foundered as they wended their way north through wet and withering woodlands, her thoughts pervaded by dark thoughts.

Furious as she was at Bryn and Málik, she was also deeply concerned for her people. All she could think as they rode through this endless slough, was that if this Rot persisted, there would be no grain for the fall.

Already, the planting of spring crops had been delayed by a full month, and no matter that they had reopened the port, the garners were nearly depleted.

For too long, they denied merchants entry to the port; it only stood to reason there would be fewer ships. It would take time to ramp up trade again, but her people needed food now, and it didn't take a *grandmester* to deduce that without an immediate increase to their supplies, filling those garners—much less maintaining them, for winter—would prove a difficult task.

Especially with the threat of Loc's soldiers in the area.

If they used up all their remaining stores whilst waiting to plant, it would set them behind by months and months.

While much of their food could still be sourced from the Cods Wold, which were a bit less mired, that settlement was too young to spare much.

The Atrebates and the Dobunni were neutral tribes, but perhaps because her father had aided the Atrebates during the Great Southern Storm, they might return the favor. And even though her uncle and Lowenna were gone, she might still find allies amidst Lowenna's tribe. Lowenna's brother, Mawgan, was a chieftain of the Dobunni. Why hadn't she sent emissaries to inquire?

Because she was afraid of revealing Trevena's weaknesses?

She had perhaps been too concerned about the forging of weapons, and not worried enough about providing food for her people's bellies.

As though to emphasize the point, her belly grumbled, and she peered up at the blustery skies, wondering if this was a message from the gods.

And simply because she felt guilty over it, she didn't reach back into her saddlebag to see what victuals she could find. If her people must ration, so too must she...

Bryn sidled up beside her, riding companionably by her side, as he used to before the trouble began.

"Art still angry with me?"

"Yes," Gwendolyn said evenly.

"Will you forgive me?"

At least he was asking forgiveness. Meanwhile, Esme and Málik had little to say to her, and if anything was vexing her at the moment, it was that more than anything. She dared to take comfort in Bryn's presence, though she daren't reveal her innermost thoughts, not wanting to burden him, nor confess her inadequacies. But she didn't have to say anything.

He knew...

And perhaps that's one reason Gwendolyn had grown distant from him. Whilst Málik saw her potential and encouraged her to greatness, Bryn still thought of her as that mischief-making little girl.

"I do forgive you," she said, at last. "But you will not disrespect me again. I am not a child, Bryn, nor are you. If you are tasked with my safety and wellbeing, I am tasked with yours no less than I am the rest of my kingdom—and make no mistake, this kingdom is mine, and I am your queen. When you speak my title, you will speak it without disdain, nor will you mock me for it."

"I meant noth—"

"It doesn't matter what you mean or did not. As my Shadow, you must realize that your respect for me will set the tone for how others treat me as well. In private, I insist you call me by my given name—as I have all my friends—but in public, you will not jest at my expense, nor will you make jests to belittle my womanhood."

"Apologies," he said. "Truly. I meant no harm, Gwendolyn." And then he sighed. "I suppose it made me feel... more a man... to square my shoulders and speak like Caradoc, but, truth be told, not even Kelan behaves this way, and I can only say for myself that Loc's treatment of me in Loegria unmanned me. And then, my father—"

"You need not apologize for Talwyn," Gwendolyn said. "Your father's mistakes are not yours, and I would never blame you or Ely for his quisling position."

He nodded, and they fell into silence. So much of what she'd said had been walled up inside her, only waiting to escape. His dishonesty over Porth Pool was the final insult. It didn't matter how well they knew each other, she couldn't allow him to dishonor her again, and this made her feel even more alone.

It wasn't easy to rule, and no one ever taught her how. Everything she'd ever learned was meant to assist the husband at her side.

Neither did her father ever take her in hand to explain the requirements of his office. Gwendolyn had learned by observing him. And yet, to be fair, neither could she fault King Corineus for her ignorance. No one ever advised her to be like her mother and Lady Ruan, certainly not him—nor did prim and proper Demelza. Rather, Gwendolyn had too easily accepted her station, never once questioning her role, nor expressing any genuine interest in attending her father's *konsels*—so of course he would assume she didn't care. And it was true: Gwendolyn didn't like *politiks*, but not liking something did not mean it should be neglected or dismissed—just the same as liking, or not liking one's husband was not a prerequisite to the exchange of torcs. Perhaps she could do worse than to accept Caradoc's proposal for marriage? They didn't have to like each other to work together for the sake of this kingdom. Nor did she have to share his bed.

Her cheeks heated over that notion, remembering Caradoc's bawdy jest—*good tussle, indeed!*

Not if her life depended upon it!

Neither could Gwendolyn imagine kissing anyone but Málik.

And still, she took comfort in knowing that Caradoc would know what to do about their garners. Unlike Gwendolyn, he was an experienced leader, and, in part, that was why Gwendolyn had chosen him. As bad as the Rot might be here, his eastern fenlands oft fared worse, and she had every faith he would find a way to feed her people. Against all odds, hadn't he sustained over three hundred souls in those bogs?

Indeed, Gwendolyn found some perverse pleasure knowing that Locrinus would find himself ill-prepared to deal with the problems arising from the Catuvellauni wetlands. *He* was spoiled more than she —indulged by his mother when he should have been taught to value others. He was too quick to discard anyone who did not serve his purpose, and from what Gwendolyn could tell of him, he cared so little for anything or anyone—not even Estrildis, truth be told.

No matter what Loc believed, Lundinium would not welcome him with a lover's open arms, nor would he find his victory there rewarding or immutable. He would discover a province in ruins, and his lack of experience—more so than Gwendolyn's—would leave him unready to deal with the fens.

The very worst of Loegria's tidal basins lay south of his capital—south of Caerdyf and north of Cantre'r Gwaelod, where Duke Osian had failed to defend his coastline against the Endless Sea. Sixteen villages were destroyed on Osian's watch. And that, among other reasons, was what led her father to seize his territories and offer them to a foreigner from Troy— more's the pity. But those floods came long before Loc's time. He would have no inkling how to buttress Lundinium, and in the end, this should work in Gwendolyn's favor. Her revenge would be sweet, and she would savor it when it came, but, in the meantime, she still had Trevena's welfare to consider, and, bearing in mind the season, she made a few calculations in her head... Even if the fight never came near Trevena, and the journey Below went well beyond their expectations, even if she were granted the sword without question, they would still not return in time to oust Locrinus and his armies from their lands in time to plant and grow crops. She wouldn't see Trevena again for a year or longer because, thereafter, they would still journey north to Baugh—another four or five weeks for that alone if luck was on their side. And then, gods knew how long it would take her to unite the rest of the tribes before she could even think to face Loc.

"I was thinking about the Atrebates," she told Bryn, thinking to put him out of his misery. The poor soul had ridden beside her for all this time, long-faced after Gwendolyn's reproach. "I know they will not join us in war, but their lands have long since recovered from the Great Southern Storm. When we arrive at the Druids' Crossroads, please help me remember to send a messenger to Caradoc so he can approach their *konsels*—Mawgan as well. I will have him inquire if they can spare some grain."

"That's brilliant," he said, smiling. "Your father would be proud, Gwendolyn."

Gwendolyn's mood lifted at once, though even as she lifted her shoulders, her fleet-footed mare stumbled, sinking to the cannon bone in the soft, stinking muck and she whispered an oath beneath her breath.

"It gets worse and worse," said Bryn, plodding through the mire.

"The land weeps," said Málik, trudging by, and the revelation struck Gwendolyn like a bolt of thunder. It never once occurred to her that the land could weep as people wept. But of course, it could.

What had Esme told her?

We are all the same in this world, living and dead. The Aether absorbs our emotions; this is the ysbryd y byd. The spirit of the age. It weeps like men weep, over time, seeping into everything it touches. Gwendolyn had always

known the king—or queen, as it were—was connected to this land, but perhaps she had not considered it well enough. She had certainly connected her
father's illness to the land's decline, but rather than it
be a measure of *his* health, it was a measure of the
people's spirits, and, really, no Druid, or Gwyddon, or
Awenydd could heal the land without lifting the people's spirits. No prayers, nor balms, nor alms could
atone for the lack.

Only faith and peace could restore this land.

Despite that Gwendolyn had given her people
hope, there was still much to be done before their
spirits were healed, so rather than focus on curing the
land, she must focus on healing her people. Unfortunately, considering the current condition of these
woods, she feared they would encounter worse when
they entered Loc's demesne, and now she worried
anew about Bryn riding an inferior horse. Enbarr's
mares could traverse this land without trouble, but already, he was falling behind, and over the course of
the day, Gwendolyn began to realize that she was
slowing her pace only to keep him company instead of
the other way around.

9

The following afternoon, the skies opened up, battering an already abused landscape. When Bryn fell woefully behind amidst a worsening quagmire, Gwendolyn finally resolved to send Lir home.

Now would be the time to do so, before advancing further into enemy territory.

As far as she was concerned, it made more sense to continue the journey with Bryn riding Sheahan. Quite deliberately, she had chosen her companions to make the best use of Enbarr's mares. The fact that three could ride more swiftly and pass easier without detection was in part the reason she'd settled on such a small retinue. And nevertheless, here they were, slugging along, impeded not merely by the fog that settled so densely about them, but by the boggy terrain as well.

Settling Aisling by the stream to drink her fill, she sought Málik and found him rifling through his saddlebags. "Tell me again why Lir must accompany us?"

Her tone was perhaps a little too reminiscent of their former, contentious relationship. But she had good cause to be annoyed with him, not the least for which, she didn't enjoy being ignored, and less so by the one being she needed and trusted most. But, more, she was still vexed about Porth Pool and that was a matter she intended to broach as well.

"I told you," he said, peering back at her over his shoulder. "Though if that's not reason enough, he's also a healer. Remember? This is why he was appointed to join us in the first place. You didn't believe we could do battle against the *Fae* king and march away unscathed?"

Gwendolyn frowned, resting her hands upon her hips. "So certain are you it will come to that?"

Málik shrugged, but he continued to fiddle with the contents of his satchel, appearing to readjust everything, finally removing a bundle of cloth, unwrapping it, then proffering the contents to Gwendolyn—ordinary wafers, not Hob cake. She shook her head, refusing it, far more interested in his explanation than she was over the prospect of filling her belly. But neither was she hungry—not after chewing so long on questions that left her belly unsettled.

"It's not wise for him to join us," she persisted. "We will travel faster without him."

"And you would deny him the chance to return to his village only to serve on your *konsel*?

"I do not require that of him. I only asked because I wished to honor him, but if he does not wish to do so, I would not force him."

"We are nearly there."

"We are not nearly there!" she argued. "We must still travel through Silures, Ordivices and Deceangli territory. I fear for his life!"

Málik shrugged, placing one wafer between his teeth, before settling the rest atop Daithi's saddle.

Once the cloth was free of its contents, he then removed a flint from his saddlebag and wrapped it within the cloth.

"I can summon fire," he said, as though she couldn't remember that he had done so in the *fogous*. Taking the wafer from his mouth, he handed it to Gwendolyn. "But that would be unwise." He finished wrapping the flint in the cloth, then lifted it to show Gwendolyn. "This won't do us any good if it's wet. Doubtless, your page has no experience with packing for travel, else he'd have known to make certain to keep it dry. Damp food may be unpleasant, but we can still consume it. But it'll be a chilly night without a fire." He then returned the bundle to his saddlebag, and though she tried to hand him the wafer back, he wouldn't take it.

It didn't matter; she didn't intend to eat it any more than she intended to allow him to change the subject. "What good is a healer if he dies before we cross the Veil? The chances are good we'll encounter Loc's men on his own lands. Lir cannot wield a sword. I would wager he might not even know how to carry one, much less wield one."

Málik gave her a forbearing smile. "I would argue a keen mind can be far deadlier than a sword," he said, but his response only vexed Gwendolyn because she didn't believe he was taking her concerns seriously. "He could *die*," she said, emphasizing the last.

"Indeed, he could," agreed Málik. "So, too, could you."

That was true. Gwendolyn had no argument for that, but she could far more easily bear the possibility of her own death than she could Bryn's, or Lir's or Málik's—she wasn't worried about Esme. Esme was too mean to die. However, not only would Lir slow them down, having one hapless soul to defend could be their undoing, and Gwendolyn was unapologetically concerned about that. Frowning, she peered over her shoulder at the Druid where he knelt by the stream, tending to his thirst, even as the horse refrained. Not once had he shown himself prepared to do battle, even with his words. Gwendolyn appreciated his calm demeanor, especially considering the company she was keeping, but he was Esme's victim to such a degree that it would force Gwendolyn to keep watch over him more than she could afford to do so. In Esme's present mood, she would chew him to bits before they ever arrived at their destination—never mind Loc, or his men. "I've no proof his mind is lethal or else wise," Gwendolyn contended. "To be sure, Málik, he scarcely speaks, even to defend himself."

Málik thrust a hand into his silver mane, sweeping it away from his face. "A wise man knows to spend words like gold."

Gwendolyn huffed, growing frustrated, because, as usual, this conversation was going nowhere—at least not where she expected it to go. But more, although she had prepared a lengthy explanation for all the reasons Lir should return to Trevena, she was no longer so certain he should go. Admittedly, she hadn't considered the fact that he was also a healer, and this was the reason he'd joined them to begin with. If he'd not come along, Bryn would have died after the battle defending Durotriges. So now, she was second-guessing herself and loathed to confess it to Málik, especially considering the knowing smirk that curled his lips.

"Blood and bones. I don't know what to do," she conceded, and the admission didn't come easily.

Clearly, she needed help, and Málik was the one she trusted to ask for it, but after the way he had been behaving, it was difficult to admit such a thing to his face.

He lowered his gaze, answering with silence, perhaps weighing his words, and that vexed Gwendolyn, too, because Bryn was right: A lie of omission was still a lie.

What was he keeping from her?

She knew Esme's father wished to see them wed.

Did Esme want that, too?

Did he?

Once returned to the Fae realm, would those two be forced to submit to their king's demands? Was this why they were quarreling?

Blood and bloody bones!

Distressed over all the possible answers, Gwendolyn shoved the wafer into her gob, chewing with vigor, perfectly aware that he'd compelled her to eat it or waste it. But he wasn't as clever as he believed himself to be, and Gwendolyn wasn't as dense as he might wish. Gods knew, if his feelings toward her had changed—if his silence was because he still had feelings for Esme—Gwendolyn could not allow this quest to be undermined. Not even for love. She'd spoken true that night on the ramparts: It was her duty to seek her birthright. Whatever came of her relationship with Málik, it must come second to her duty to Pretania. And regardless, she would like to know the truth. "Málik?" she prompted, slapping the crumbs from her hands.

"I am sorry," he said, and Gwendolyn felt an immediate sense of dread over his tone.

"For what?"

For forcing her to eat the wafer?
For ignoring her?
For lying?
For loving Esme?

Gwendolyn reasoned with him. "Speak to me! How am I supposed to prepare myself for this quest if you will not counsel me—nor even speak to me about what we may encounter?"

A muscle ticked at his jaw. "I... *am*... trying."

Gwendolyn lifted both brows. "*Trying?*"

"To prepare you."

"With your silence?"

And then she couldn't help herself; she missed him furiously. "Mayhap through your endless quarrels with Esme? The two of you have more than enough to say to each other," she complained, loathing the way she sounded. "I, for one, enjoy it enormously when you whisper like lovers, and hush at my approach!"

He arched a brow. "You think us lovers?"

Gwendolyn's cheeks heated.

"Art jealous?"

"Siblings," she amended. "Why must you always be so evasive?"

"You know why," he said, eyeing her pointedly, and when Gwendolyn deepened the furrow in her brow, he added, "Do you not recall the day you tried to tell your father about our time in the *fogous?*"

She did. The words had rested so eagerly on the tip of her tongue, and yet every time she'd attempted to speak them aloud, her voice had faltered. She'd learned so much about Málik in those *fogous*, and still she could share none of what she'd discovered. He nodded, seeing that she understood.

"Some things I *cannot* say. I—" He hushed

abruptly, then groaned and sighed. "For one, even spoken in jest, words are indissoluble. If I am heedful —particularly around her." He gave Esme a dark look —one that both eased and troubled Gwendolyn at once. "It is because some words carry too much weight. Do you take my meaning?"

Glancing over her shoulder, Gwendolyn found Esme once again hounding Lir. Even from this distance, she couldn't miss the spiteful tone.

"Youngling Druid. Will you don those lovely ear sheaths for our *Fae* king?"

Lir said nothing, and Esme grinned, showing a mouthful of porbeagle teeth.

"I do hope so, because then you may see what 'flattery' buys you." She chortled nastily, and Gwendolyn gave Málik a sideways glance.

"See what I mean?"

Lir was too docile, never standing up for himself. And if that was the way it was to be, healer or no healer, Gwendolyn would soon regret having brought him along, especially since it left Bryn with the disadvantaged horse.

When she turned again, it was to find their conversation dismissed. Málik had returned the untouched wafers to his saddlebag, leaving them on top, within arm's reach. "Málik," she begged. "Please! Tell me something!"

"Very well," he said, turning to face her. "I will tell you... *something*... Do you remember what I said to your uncle about the purpose of those quoits?"

Gwendolyn nodded impatiently. "You claimed they were portals?"

"I did," he said. "At one point, there were many across these lands, all accessible to *Faekind* and mor-

tals alike. But. now, only one passage remains. This is
the way through the Lifer Pol village." It was, he explained, why nothing in the Druid village seemed ab-
solute. In that location, the *Féth* was still discernible to
mortal eyes. "When the time comes, you must not
enter lest I tell you. Its boundaries push and pull
against the mortal realm, forming traps. If you enter in
the wrong location, you will be lost, never to return,
never to be found. No one will find your bones."

"Why would I enter without you?"

His tone revealed his impatience. "Simply promise
me, Gwendolyn."

"I said I would not! Why would I not do as you
say?"

He gave her a pointed look. "Quite oft, you do not
listen," he said, and though Gwendolyn took issue
with his complaint, she couldn't argue it wasn't true.
Unfortunately, Bryn could attest to it with much ag-
gravation, though she had mostly learned her lessons
after Bryn's demotion.

"That was the old Gwendolyn," she reassured, a
tentative smile returning to her lips. "I have changed."

"Have you?"

"I have," Gwendolyn insisted.

"What about the other morn?"

She knew she sounded far more innocent than she
was. "What morn?"

"The pool," he said, and Gwendolyn's smile faltered because that was altogether a different matter.
Indeed, she had a lot to say to about that as well, only
now was not the time.

She lifted her chin. "I needed to see that pool," she
explained. "And since you have refused me at every
turn, I took the opportunity whilst you were busy
quarreling with Esme."

There appeared a knowing glint in his eyes. "I should apprise you nothing is more capable of subverting reason than jealousy," he said. "No good ever came of it."

It wasn't jealousy. Gwendolyn was queen now—and not that she should do what she pleased because of it. But sheltering her from the truth was not something that should be done. "I *needed* to see the pool," she persisted.

"Needed or wanted?" he asked, and when Gwendolyn didn't answer at once, he added, "Did it ease your mind? Or did it reveal aught more than you already knew?"

"No," Gwendolyn said petulantly, feeling chastened, though it wasn't fair. Emotions ruled her at the moment, so she tempered her response, knowing he wasn't truly her subject. He was with her only because he believed in her cause.

Málik reached out as though to touch her, then dropped his hand by his side, the look in his eyes full of torment. His voice was sober when he spoke again. "Gwendolyn," he begged. "I need you to understand the gravity of this situation. I need you to listen to me and I need you to trust me—above all, trust me."

Gwendolyn exhaled a breath she'd not realized she'd held, her gaze dipping to the hand resting at his side. She hadn't realized how much she'd missed his touch until he'd teased her with the possibility of it. "I *do* trust you," she said as sincerely as she could because it was true. "But I also need to understand what we face. You cannot keep me in the dark—I beg you, Málik! If I am to be queen, I must rule, and in order to rule, I must know what it is I must rule."

He smiled, but the smile was sad.

He reached up now, giving her face the sweetest,

gentlest caress, before withdrawing the hand, and Gwendolyn felt the separation acutely. She had to resist the urge to lift her hand to the spot where his fingers brushed her face.

"As you no doubt may have surmised, the Lifer Pol Druids are guardians of the portal," he continued to explain. "Scholars, as well as healers, though they have agreed to guard that portal according to our covenant."

That was why the secrecy over the location of their village—the portal? Not simply because they had stumbled upon an abandoned Fae village?

"They've not kept their place so long by taking their duty lightly. The covenant is inviolable. If aught but peace is brought to either realm through any culpability of theirs, my father's retribution will be swift and fierce. With that in mind, Emrys may not allow us to pass."

Gwendolyn blinked. She had a hundred thousand questions, but she asked the first that came to mind. "So, you believe he will refuse us?"

Málik shrugged.

Gwendolyn blinked. For the second time in the space of a single day, she found herself gobsmacked. If they could not cross the Veil, and there was no other passage in this realm, how could they retrieve her sword? "Can he prevent us?"

"Not *us. You*."

"But..." Gwendolyn said, shaking her head, confused. "I don't understand... I thought he supported me?"

"I am certain he does," Málik allowed, and the furrow in Gwendolyn's brow deepened. She didn't understand. If Emrys supported her bid for the throne, and he understood she *must* traverse the Veil to retrieve *her* sword, why then would he not allow her to do so, regardless of the consequences for his village? The repercussions for Pretania were far worse than to lose the right to occupy a village—extraordinary though it may be. Loc's reign would be the death of this land.

She opened her mouth to ask why Emrys should refuse her, but before any words could leave her tongue, Málik continued. "He is only one man. Our timing could not be worse. Even were our mission entirely peaceable, he could not guarantee—because you cannot guarantee—that we'll not raise arms against the Fae king if he refuses your behest." He gave Gwendolyn a pointed look. "Can we?"

She shook her head, because, in truth, she could not.

If the Fae king did not return her sword, Gwendolyn was duty-bound to seize it, one way or another—at any cost. She could not abandon her duty to Pretania, nor could she abandon her sword—justly hers—in the hands of a king to whom it did not belong. Only now she wondered why Málik had not brought this up sooner, when everything depended upon her retrieval of that sword.

Where were they going, if not to the portal and the Druid village?

"So, you are saying he *must* deny *me* passage? What then? Do we battle with friends?"

Málik sighed. "As I have said, allowing you to pass will risk the village."

"Has Emrys ever crossed the Veil?"

"Nay," said Málik.

Gwendolyn's frown deepened as she peered over at Lir. "How then can *he* help if no one has ever crossed the Veil?"

"You mistake me. I did not say no one ever crossed. I said Emrys has not crossed." He cast the young Druid a glance. "I suggested Lir join because perhaps if Emrys knows Lir will accompany us, he may yet agree."

"Why Lir? Why not Emrys himself?"

"Because... Lir has spent the entirety of his life studying our covenant," Málik explained. "He is a student of Tuatha'an law as well as the laws of men. He will understand every nuance of every word my father utters, and simply because of this, he will make certain everyone adheres to that covenant—my father included. You included."

"Why can't you or Esme help with this?"

He said her name, like a prayer. "Gwendolyn."

Gwendolyn knew that tone. This would be his ultimate word on the matter. He would say no more, regardless of how she pressed him. That night on the ramparts, by his own admission, he'd left so much unsaid, and to this day, no matter how many times Gwendolyn pressed him over it, he'd yet to reveal more.

"Blood and bones!" she exclaimed, turning and walking away, realizing that an argument with either of these two Elves would be pointless. Neither would speak a word until it suited them, and Málik had decided answers were beyond her privilege. *Gods. He... he was... maddening.*

Frustrated, she made her way to her mare and stood a moment, thinking as she rubbed Aisling's shoulder. "Sweet girl," she crooned.

And then she opened her saddlebag to remove the golden tiara Esme had fashioned for her, only to see how it fared...

This crown, without her sword, would serve no

purpose. Loc stole the real crown—the bronze circlet of flowering myrtle. No one would even recognize this as a sovereign's coronal, but the circumstances of its creation were as extraordinary as the crown itself, with its delicate beauty and indestructible composition. It had spent these past days stashed in her saddlebag, amidst items that could easily have ruined or bent it, and still it remained perfect, shining as brightly as it did the day it was formed. Whatever the reason for Esme's temper, and Málik's forbidding demeanor, she must look to this crown as proof of their loyalty—and she must not be thwarted.

She sighed. And determined to make the best of it, she put the crown away and took the mare's reins, drawing Aisling away from the stream.

"Let's go," she said, passing Bryn, though she didn't look back to make certain he followed, nor to see whether Málik and Esme came after, because the moment she'd abandoned Málik's side, Esme returned to him, and now, again, they were discussing some private matter. She didn't know what to do, but for now, doing nothing seemed most appropriate.

To her surprise, it was Lir who caught up to her, and he said, as though he'd somehow read her mind, "I wished to thank you again, *Banríon*. I vow to serve you well and to give you no cause to regret my attendance."

So much for sending him home.

Even if Málik's defense of him had failed to convince her—which it did not—she found she could not disappoint Lir. He was such a kindly soul, and she wanted him to see the City of Light—wearing those silly ear sheaths if he must.

Drawing Aisling onto the dirt path, she hauled herself into the saddle and said, "See you do not." But even as she said it, she regretted it, feeling like a shrew, hating herself for her tone of voice.

Truth be told, Gwendolyn already regretted Lir's presence for all the reasons she'd conveyed to Málik, and a few more she did not.

More than aught, she was worried for him. She worried about what they would face, and neither of her *Elven* companions seem the least bit inclined to enlighten her. She didn't relish the thought of having Lir's death on her conscience, nor could she bear it if his inability to defend himself put others she cared for at risk—Bryn, for one, and not simply because he was astride the weakest, slowest mount, but because, despite a lifetime of sword practice, Gwendolyn feared he was as unprepared for this battle as she was. More and more, she feared death would result of this quest, and nothing Málik had shared with her had renewed her faith.

Unlike Lir, Gwendolyn knew Bryn would not hold his tongue. Nor would he hesitate to wield his sword in her defense, and that could well be the death of him, and that Gwendolyn could not bear. *Gods.* If she should live, and Bryn did not, she would have to face Ely with tears and apologies. And this time, unlike with Talwyn, her brother's death would destroy her. Gwendolyn had promised to return him, but it was a promise made in vain because Gwendolyn couldn't even control her testy companions.

Resigned to the journey as it was, she dared to cast a backward glance, and found that, while Bryn had caught up with Lir, riding companionably beside the young Druid, Esme and Málik had yet to remount. Once again, with their heads together, they stood by the stream, and a shadow fell across Gwendolyn's heart.

Let them stay. She would not wait.

She knew the way to the Druid village, and they would know where to find her. If she would lead, she must lead. And, unless those two confessed their quarrels, she could not consider them first. She must follow her heart.

10

G reen!
    Loc's lands were green!

It should have filled Gwendolyn with hope, but as the rich canopy grew thicker and more verdant the farther they ventured into Loc's territory, a most unwelcome thought began to brew in her head...

If this Rot reflected the king and his people, there must be more to the story than what she'd been told. If Trevena's parklands were already so wasted, she would have expected to find Loc's worse. But it wasn't, and it now appeared to Gwendolyn as though the disease began near Trevena, and her precious city was the root, if not the cause.

But that made no sense. The condition of this land was not something she had expected to encounter and neither could she fathom why Loc's lands should be flourishing. Meanwhile, hers lay rotting.

It confused her beyond measure.

Doubtless, the return of her sword was paramount to the prosperity of this kingdom, but what good would it do to rule over wasted lands, or people who were dead or dying? Would her people prefer a kingslayer to a sovereign queen? Truly?

Unfortunately, the answer to that question might easily be deduced by the weeks and weeks of discord she'd had with her *konsel*. Truth was a bitter pilule; it was past time to swallow it. She could not force the will of her people, and if their hearts would not embrace a woman as queen... *what then?*

A man would have had an easier time of it.

So few had rallied to Gwendolyn's cause, despite that, by now, news of the coup must have reached every distant shore.

Even so far north, her grandsire must have heard, and months and months had passed since the Feast of Blades; despite that, she had yet to receive a messenger from his tribe—nor from any of the Prydein confederacy. Even Talwyn had considered himself the better choice to lead in her stead.

Unfortunately, to their minds, Gwendolyn must appear the weaker contender for her father's throne... Of course, she was a woman, and, amidst these male-governed tribes, that was proof enough against her. But being the daughter of a deposed king, and the bride of a man who'd discarded her with impunity... that would seem to be death knells for their support. Perhaps, to their view, she had been a willing participant in Loc's treachery, only to end with nothing because she was too feeble to stand up to her husband. But Gwendolyn would rather swallow a viper than to sit idly beside Loc as his queen—let him have his simpering mistress.

Like metal to a lodestone, her gaze sought Málik... as it happened the night of her Promise Ceremony, only to discover him and Esme with their heads together—yet again. Gwendolyn couldn't help herself. Envy burned through her veins.

Watching the two of them together, she endeavored to harden her heart, vowing to shed no more tears for the silly girl she had been.

If, for the good of her people, she must purge Málik from her heart, so be it.

Like her father, she was a servant to the people. It was her gods-given duty to see the land restored, come whatever may.

Nor did it matter what doubts Esme had placed in her head over leaving Caradoc to rule in her stead. That was the only decision she could have made. If she was not the one meant to govern these lands, she would accept this fate...

But first, she would carve the heart from Loc's breast.

Not for the first time, her hand sought Borlewen's blade, her calloused thumb caressing the dragon hilt, the black pearl eyes... remembering the look in Loc's eyes as he'd butchered her hair.

The night of her Promise Ceremony she'd felt such a fool, and more the fool now that she understood what Loc must have been doing all those hours whilst his father made excuses for his tardy son. Even then, he must have been planning his coup—unbeknownst to his father, and certainly to hers. Meanwhile, like a love-starved girl, Gwendolyn had sat there, waiting, and waiting, until, at long last, he'd deigned to appear. And then she had been so blinded by his shining splendor and silken robes that she'd never once questioned what dirty work he might have been doing.

Would she have carried on so if his countenance had displeased her? Or would she have done instead what so many had done to her? Dismiss him for his face?

There was no way to know, but it forced Gwendolyn to confess that she had so much preferred Loc to Urien, his older, sickly brother. She had counted herself fortunate to have been dealt another fate—a younger son, whose face and mind were allegedly forged by the gods. However, beauty was no virtue itself, and it would seem that she, more than anyone, should have minded this lesson. Her Prophecy should have taught her that above all else. Neither was a sharp mind necessarily a good mind. Loc was evil, but she had realized this too late—only after her mother and father were both slain, along with poor, sweet Demelza.

Gwendolyn had once believed herself astute enough to judge the character of others by the way she was treated, but Loc had sat there beside her at the high table, whispering sweet nothings into her ear, telling her how lovely she was, how well matched they were, and she had believed every beautiful lie that sprang from his lips. And now, she feared she had herself more to blame than anyone else because she had suspected Loc's character, and despite that, she had ignored her intuition.

A lesson well learned.

She would not do so again.

For all that time imprisoned in his palace, she'd discovered her heart as ravaged as this land, but she was more than a princess, waiting for a crown.

More than a bride, waiting for a husband.

More than a woman, waiting for a purpose.

For now, she was a queen without a throne, but she had rediscovered her purpose in the most unexpected of places... locked in that prison chamber. For too long after the fall of Trevena, she'd been forced to endure the evils of her husband's court. Come what may, she would be the one to end him and if anyone dared to stand in her way, she would end them as well. Once more, her gaze traveled to Esme and Málik, frowning. More than anything, she wanted to give Aisling a heel and insinuate herself into their conversation.

"What do you make of it?" Bryn asked, sidling up beside her.

During the past few days, he had been much more companionable, his demeanor not unlike the Bryn she knew and loved. She waved a hand to indicate the bewildering spectacle of green. "You mean, this?"

"Indeed," he said. "This land is far from wasted."

Gwendolyn's gaze bore into Málik's back, reluctant to meet Bryn's knowing eyes, lest he glean what was lurking in her heart. Málik was right. She was jealous, and jealousy was a bitter, grudging creature. Even a queen wasn't immune to her siren's song. "I don't know."

As soon as she had a moment alone with Esme, she would ask about it. Cantankerous or not, Esme was never so reticent as Málik. Indeed, she had plenty to say to everyone, and far too many words for Málik. Gwendolyn wished to believe Málik when he'd scoffed at the possibility that they were lovers, but those two were up to something, and whatever it was, their confidence didn't include Gwendolyn.

"A copper for your thoughts?" Bryn suggested, and Gwendolyn wondered if he already knew what she was thinking, judging by the coyness of his tone.

She loathed he knew her so well.

"I was thinking about something Esme said," Gwendolyn lied, turning to assess his reaction. Although, in truth, it wasn't entirely a lie. Gwendolyn had been contemplating the Rot, and Esme, as well, and she remembered how Esme once told her there were lands where the *ysbryd y byd* would not be affected by Pretania's trials. She simply never disclosed that those lands could be Loc's!

"Something you wish to share?"

"When I've made more sense of it," Gwendolyn promised. "Though I wonder about your thoughts on the Rot?"

"Mine?" said Bryn, blinking, his hand lifting to his leather-vested chest, patting himself. "Since when do you wish to know what I think?"

"Always!"

He lifted both brows.

"I speak to you oft—"

"About *your* thoughts, *your* fears, *your* concerns," Bryn said, interrupting her. "I do not recall a single time when asked for mine."

"Truly?" Gwendolyn asked, appalled. "Did I never?"

Certainly, she'd worried enough about both her dear friends. Had she never once confessed as much? Indeed, so oft, she had championed both, and Ely in particular, especially when she'd longed to quit the *dawnsio*. Gwendolyn only ever wanted the best for both. "You must know I value you?"

Bryn shrugged. "You mistake me, Gwen. I do not complain," he said. "You are... like your father—so certain of your way. I knew it from the moment you and I returned from our adventures at the Giant's House, when your father took me aside to apprise me I would become your Shadow... you were the one who mattered most."

Gwendolyn twisted her fingers about Aisling's reins, listening.

"Indeed, I took it so much to heart that I gave you,

not only my fealty, but my heart as well... regardless that you did not ask for it."

"Oh, Bryn," she said with heartfelt sorrow.

"Don't," he said, lifting a hand. "This is my lot, and I do not bare my soul for pity's sake," he said. "You have never been aught but kind to me, Gwendolyn. Your friendship I've held true. I love you, truly, but I was born to love you, and I cannot find regret for that love."

Gwendolyn met his sad blue eyes, feeling horrid that she could not return his affection—not the way he'd wanted her to. Still, she loved him... simply not the way he deserved to be loved.

His gaze found Málik as he added, "Not even after you gave your heart to *him* did I begrudge this, and even now, as you pine for him, and I cannot find any joy seeing your pain."

"I do not pine for him!" Gwendolyn argued. Though even as she said it, her gaze returned to Málik, her heart squeezing as Esme leaned close.

Bryn's gaze returned to her, daring her to deny it to his face. "Do you not?"

"*Gods' blood.* Am I so easily read?"

"To me, you are. I know you better than I know myself. You've not smiled since we left, and 'tis no mystery why—not to anyone. My only concern is that *he* has yet to notice—and not that I believe he has feeling for Esme. But..."

"But what?"

He frowned. "I've a feeling in my bones, Gwendolyn."

"What feeling?"

He shrugged, but then had no further explanation. No matter, he needn't define what he was feeling. Gwendolyn felt it, as well—stronger now after encountering Loc's lands. And still she could not name her fear, nor point a finger to any specific reason for the affliction—aside from the obvious. Ever since leaving Trevena, a shadow had pursued them like a brume, not so much a temper of the sky, so much as a temper of the soul.

Doubtless, she was enraged over Loc, but until a few weeks before their departure, she had still felt hope. But right about the same time they'd begun to argue over those who should serve the *konsel* this persistent shadow had cast itself over her heart.

"You must have noted... I rode awhile with Esme this morn, trying to determine what she and Málik are discussing."

"I did," Gwendolyn said. "I thought you were protecting Lir?"

"That too," Bryn confessed. "But truly, though she pretends to revile that poor lad, she does not. In fact, if I did not know better—know what a ruthless fiend she can be—" He said this last with a bit of a grin. "I would say she is only trying to protect him the only way Esme knows how."

It was Gwendolyn's turn to lift both brows. "How? By hounding him so mercilessly that he remains in his Druid village?"

He lifted a shoulder and said, "Something like that." And despite that, he maintained the crook of his lips, and Gwendolyn thought about that a moment...

She had once harbored a suspicion that Esme was sweet on Lir—in much the same way a rude little boy might tug the pigtails of a little girl he was smitten with. However, her teasing of late had taken a darker turn, and Gwendolyn had discarded the notion. Ever since the Cods Wold, Esme was not the same, but Gwendolyn didn't believe she was working at cross purposes. After all, it was she who'd pressed Málik into taking the blade to snip Gwendolyn's hair, and it was that effort that had revealed Málik's true heart. Without realizing it, Gwendolyn's hand lifted to her growing tresses—still too short and shaggy. It was also Esme who'd fashioned her crown, and then placed it atop Gwendolyn's head, and then, bending her knee, she was the first to shout, "The king must die. Long live the queen!"

Why, then, was she behaving so oddly?

"As for this land," Bryn said, thrusting a hand into his shining black mane. "I loathe to disparage the things you believe, though perhaps 'tis as Morgelyn says—merely a natural occurrence, and there is nothing you or I, or even Locrinus, can do to cause or prevent it."

Gwendolyn blinked, shocked to hear him say so.

In her grandfather's day, even voicing such a fanatical view could find one's head on a pike. But during her father's reign, a few of his aldermen had dared propose this blasphemous notion. While her father did not sanction their views, neither had he discouraged them. And nevertheless... to suggest that the natural world could operate free from the will of the gods, that the king was not their appointed... this was a heresy, and even the Gwyddons, whose beliefs were all based upon natural observations, would never deny the gods their due.

"Do you believe that?"

Bryn shrugged. "I sometimes do not know." He pointed to the woodland. "Betimes, up seems down and down seems up. Only think about it, Gwen. If it is as you believe—that the king is so connected to the land—these lands should not be so vibrant. Whatever issue I might ever have taken with... our friendship, I have always, always held you in the highest regard. Your heart is good and kind."

It warmed Gwendolyn to hear him say so. "Perhaps," she allowed. "And yet in my heart of hearts, I feel I must have failed in some way, and I mean to ask Esme about it." She gave the Elves another glance. "If they ever cease with the bickering."

Bryn laughed. "Good luck with that!"

A devious smile turned Gwendolyn's lips. "Perhaps you should toss a frog on her head."

Bryn grinned so wide that Gwendolyn wondered if it hurt his face. "She would skewer me," he declared, with little fear of it.

"Or turn your frog into a prince and kiss it?"

There was a certain look in his eyes that Gwendolyn couldn't quite decipher, but he said, laughing, "Or eat it! She has the gob for that."

At that, both laughed, although Gwendolyn could see Esme doing the last of these things. Hadn't she once claimed to eat babies? And, surely, in her present mood, anyone could easily believe it.

"Gods forbid," said Bryn, and he shuddered. "No thank you! I would die for you, My Queen, but I'd not wish to tempt *that one!*"

Gwendolyn laughed again, warmed by their rediscovered fellowship, but suddenly she shuddered, remembering how Málik once advised her to note there were few occasions when the goddess' creatures were made without regard to their needs. *If you spy claws, or fangs,* he'd said, "*Run.*"

For all her other-worldly beauty, Esme had both.

11

These were all once Cornish territories. And yet, before Gwendolyn's marriage to Locrinus, she'd never once ventured north of the *Aber Hafren* and its estuaries. Despite this, she knew the lay of the land, as she knew the Druids' Crossroads—from the detailed map in her father's war room.

As a girl, she had studied every beautiful detail, sweeping her finger from north to south, west to east, memorizing every dip and swell in the painted clay. She had marveled over the wheals—the tin and copper mines that provided Cornwall's wealth and were so numerous that the Phoenicians had appointed their island *Cassiterides*, meaning 'tin island' in their native tongue.

She had studied the coastal plains where Duke Osian's villages surrendered to the sea, and scrutinized every slight variation as lowlands gave way to hill and dale, and then to the *mynydds—mountains*.

But there was one feature not on her father's map.

After arriving in Silures, they discovered the new border wall—an immense earthen embankment the height of two hulking men and fronted by a quarry as wide as four cubits across on the east side.

To Gwendolyn's dismay, it was obvious what guide the builders had used for the demarcation. On the west lay verdant fields interspersed with rich farmlands. To the east stood withering trees and stinking rivers.

Somehow, she had missed this development in her flight from Loegria. But now that she had found the wall, and could follow its length, it raised myriad questions. Ostensibly, King Brutus had begun to partition their lands before the Feast of Blades. *Why?* Did he do so to prevent the Rot from spreading west? Or was he simply separating what was his?

Gwendolyn had never considered greed or excess among Brutus' sins. On the few occasions she'd met him, she'd had no sense of his avarice, or vainglory. He was modestly dressed, and even unclean—so much as to arrive at Gwendolyn's Promise Ceremony unwashed and smelling of horse and sweat. But this was a matter Gwendolyn could hardly fault him for when she might have done the same if she could. How many times had her mother chided her for the smell of her horse?

Nay, if Brutus was greedy for aught, it was for power. But power came with the acquisition of lands, and partitioning these territories did not strike Gwendolyn as a wise thing to do, especially when he was in accord to merge his house with hers.

And regardless, someone had intended for this wall to be a border betwixt their lands, and Gwendolyn knew it wasn't her father. King Corineus had well-known aspirations to the contrary—open borders across the entire island.

Yet neither did she believe this was Loc's work. As well as she knew him, she knew he would no more be content to remain in *Westwalas*, enclosed by this immense wall, than he would have been with Gwendolyn by his side. Therefore, she must conclude this was Brutus's work; only why was a question.

Beginning north of *Aber Hafren*, the wall persisted north, and the demarcation remained the same as far as the eye could perceive. Only for some odd reason, construction seemed to have halted, and Gwendolyn wondered if it might be because, after setting his sights on the river-fed territories in the east, Loc no longer intended to base any of his armies in Loegria. After all, why should he bother when his people's safety was not his concern? Even so, it was difficult to believe that anyone could discard such rich lands, or the possibility of a thriving western port. But she had an inkling it could be the same reason Locrinus could not envision himself settling in Trevena—a city founded by someone else, revered for its culture and renown by so many across the Endless Sea. It was not his work, and Locrinus was egotistical enough to require the glory to be all his.

Though maybe it wasn't Brutus, either?

At intervals, they encountered abandoned towers that could have been intended for a watch. Scarcely a league apart, some were complete, some only partially so, but very clearly, no one had ever bothered to occupy them. Only a steady stream of bird droppings gave any indication any living creatures frequented them.

"Should we return to the road?" asked Bryn.

"No," Gwendolyn said, surveying the wall as they rode.

With Málik in the lead, and Esme riding ten rods to the east, Lir another five behind, they should be careful to remain close to the dyke, away from the Brigantes' lands.

Gwendolyn wasn't ready yet to deal with that quick-tempered chieftain, nor did she wish to drag anyone into the conflict until she could fight if she must—later, she decided. Later when she had more sway. In the meantime, she was counting on the fact that Loc's army had already traveled east.

So she had been told: Not long after her escape from Loegria, he'd marched off to Lundinium, taking his mistress along with him, and leaving his bastard son in the care of his mother. But that could be his worst mistake ever, Gwendolyn mused, because Innogen would sacrifice even her own sons if it granted her the right to rule through her grandson. After all, wasn't it her idea to pit her sons against her husband? Next, she could pit them against each other. Gwendolyn knew better than to trust her, and she had long suspected that Innogen—vindictive and sharp as a thorn—had coordinated every aspect of the planning for the Feast of Blades. Her sons were only pawns in a game of Queen's Chess.

Indeed, Brutus' consort was no fool—too shrewd to allow Loc to take all their troops east and leave her with none. She would insist upon keeping a proper garrison, and with her grandson in her care, her son would have had no choice but to agree. He might like to believe himself a leader of men, but Gwendolyn knew too much about his relationship with his mother to doubt who was in control.

But, like her son, the people of Westwalas were not Innogen's concern. She cared only for her own welfare and that of her grandson. So bloody far from Loegria's capitol, this half-formed wall should hold no interest for her—unless... unless... she intended to use it to prevent her son's return?

What could be her endgame?

Could she have so much influence without her husband and son?

Enough to convince the neighboring tribes to build this wall?

Although it appeared deserted, perhaps Innogen was only starting?

Looking for clues, Gwendolyn insisted upon following the wall north, a seedling of a plan beginning to germinate... there might eventually be some way she could use this to her advantage.

❧

THE SUN and moon came and went, rising and lowering for three days without their party encountering a soul. On the ensuing day, they came across a traveler on horseback—an Ordovician soldier. At Málik's behest, they hid until the soldier passed, and then continued north, following Innogen's wall until they were well into Ordovician territory. Thereafter, they retreated east again, though not too far east. Unless they wished to add days, perhaps even weeks, to their travels, it would be necessary to stay close to the wall until they reached the River Dee. From there, they could follow the tributary on the east side, till the Mersey and Dee emptied into Lifer Pol Bay. That's where they would encounter their destination...

The Druids' Crossroads.

Without knowing what Gwendolyn knew, those blood-painted stones would frighten even the worst of trolls, but though it was no longer a destination to be feared, she dreaded the meeting to come, yet not because of the Druids.

The Lifer Pol order was not what they once led her to believe. Those men might not welcome tribunals, nor visitors, but it wasn't because they were murderous fiends. Along with their guardianship, the order was renowned for *shamanic* ceremonies, most oft performed in the grotto beneath their tree-bound village—a ceremony *Máistir* Emrys most often officiated, evidenced by his much-aged form. He and Lir were brothers, separated by less than three years, but the *Máistir* appeared more than three times Lir's age. And now, for the first time, Gwendolyn considered what might happen if *Máistir* Emrys continued to descend from his village to perform his pookie ceremonies. Would he age enough to die?

Casting a glance behind her at Lir, riding with shoulders back, wearing his dignity like a royal cloak, she wondered if he had ever considered his brother's mortality. To Gwendolyn, it seemed Lir had lived too sheltered a life to remember his own, much less his brother's, and this gave her pause.

So far, luck was on their side, but they had a long journey ahead, and even once they arrived near the Crossroads, they would not be safe until they ascended into the village itself. Lir was too innocent and too peaceable to perceive how to defend himself. And, truly, despite their reputation, none of the Druids she'd ever met seemed remotely capable. How they had survived in their tree-house village so long was a mystery nearly as great as that of the portal.

For one, the stories circulating about the Druid Orders, frightening though they might be, were not the only reason people avoided that area. Warring tribes occupied those lands—most allies of Loc's. Brigantes to the northeast, Deceangli and Ordovicians to the north and south, and Loc's own territories to the southwest. And yet, despite their allegiance to Loegria, two of those three did not even get along amongst themselves. The third, the Brigantes, were loyal to none. As long as Gwendolyn could recall, their fidelity swayed like reeds against the gentlest of winds. Though she found comfort in this: Loc would keep loyalties only so long as he maintained the upper hand. None of these tribes had any stomach for weakness, nor was Loc of their blood, and blood must count for something. For the time being, Locrinus held the advantage—no matter whether gained through subterfuge and treachery—but the instant he lost it, the tribes would turn against him.

To Gwendolyn, if she had anything to do with it.

She didn't have to like or respect them—or even trust them—to make use of their armies. And neither could she afford to allow pride to turn them away. Before long, she vowed, they would all bend the knee to her—as Caradoc had done.

As Loc would do.

Only for Loc, there would be no mercy.

He would meet the same unsparing fate he'd dealt her cousin.

As Danu was her witness, Gwendolyn would not rest until Locrinus tasted the sting of her blade. And even as she considered this, her hand sought the dragon hilt of Borlewen's blade, seeking solace from the weapon Loc once used both to strip her of her dignity and to end her cousin's life. But the feel of the cold steel in her hand never failed to bring a sting of tears to her eyes.

One day, she would put this dagger to his throat and make him beg for his life, but if the gods were merciful, he would breathe his last in those fens—and perhaps take his simpering mistress along with him. It would save Gwendolyn the trouble of killing them both. But come what may, Loc's son would not inherit his father's crown.

In the end, Gwendolyn vowed to make Locrinus suffer for every offense he'd delivered, not only to Gwendolyn, but to her people as well.

It was one thing to betray his own sire and hers as well. But that he'd brought so many innocents to bear for the issues he took with the old kings... and with her... This was... *unforgivable*.

"We should make camp," suggested Bryn, peering up at the heavens, turning his hand up as though to catch a drop. "I feel rain," he said.

"That is *not* rain you feel," said Esme, the tone of her voice lifting the hairs on Gwendolyn's nape. She, too, peered up at the heavens, and Gwendolyn did as well, noting the strange light permeating the skies.

"They know we are coming," Esme added darkly, and Gwendolyn might have asked who, but she didn't have to...

She knew.

12

"T hey" were *Fae*.

It wasn't Locrinus Esme was speaking of, of that Gwendolyn was certain. Else, by now, Loc's men would have had them surrounded, and if that be the case, nothing could save them. They were only five against too many.

Would the Fae king assail them here in the mortal realm?

Did they know what Gwendolyn was after?

Did he mean to deny her?

Was the Fae realm, even now, preparing for war?

Gwendolyn didn't know the answers to these questions, nor was she certain of Esme's warning, but Esme's present mood did not invite questions, and neither did anyone seem overeager to place themselves at her mercy.

At one point, while Gwendolyn reminisced about Demelza with Bryn, Esme rolled her eyes and said, "Your tales of this simple maid have grown tiresome. You speak as though she were your blood."

Surprised by the vehemence in her voice, Gwendolyn tried to explain that, when everyone else had feared reprisal from her mother, Demelza was her greatest ally, defending Gwendolyn even when many had suspected her a changeling. In fact, even when her father dared not intervene, it was Demelza who'd dared to defend her.

Esme's response was devoid of compassion or good humor. "Mayhap you *are* a changeling," she'd said shrewishly, and Gwendolyn resolved to avoid her thereafter.

She was *not* a changeling, though her mother had too long accused her, and the memory of her treatment never failed to bring an ache to Gwendolyn's belly. How many countless years had Queen Eseld marched those contentious physicians into her bedchamber to inspect every freckle, every mole, every finger, every toe? It went on so long that, at long last, it forced her father to call a halt to the endless investigations, and no one ever found reason to suggest Gwendolyn was aught but a girl.

"What does this prove?" Esme argued. "That Demelza herself believed it an abomination they should denigrate you by calling you a changeling? I do not find this behavior admirable," she said. "Please spare me the endless extolling of this maid's extraordinary virtue."

Gwendolyn bristled over the condemnation, but tempered her response, realizing that something more was bothering Esme than having to bear witness to Gwendolyn's tales.

No one said anything, and Esme left off, swallowing her words as she swallowed a wafer, and then rose, slapping her hands on her leathers and, giving Gwendolyn an indignant backward glance, left.

Gwendolyn let her go without reproach—who could reproach Esme, anyway? Hoping to make nice, she refrained from pointing out how vulgar it was to disparage a grieving person's dead loved ones.

But that was not the end of it.

Later the same day, when Gwendolyn and Málik were discussing the Rot, Esme insinuated the worst. "Perhaps it follows you?" she'd said with a tilt of her head—as though Gwendolyn herself could be the cause.

After so many days on the road, Gwendolyn hadn't the tenacity to fight with her, and even Málik seemed to grow weary of Esme's temper, judging by the rigid set of his shoulders and the way he turned his head every time Esme approached.

One thing was certain: For all Gwendolyn's initial concerns about Lir, he was the only one whose presence wasn't dispiriting. For all the abuse the poor lad endured over the past days at Esme's goading, he more than anyone remained uncomplaining, brushing off Esme's barbs with a natural forbearance, which was far more than even Gwendolyn was inclined to do. Indeed, observing Lir filled Gwendolyn with a burgeoning sense of respect, and she understood why Bryn had risen to the young Druid's defense. Gwendolyn, too, felt defensive of him, and without advising him what she was doing, she drew him close by her side, despite that this was specifically what she did not wish to do. But they were too far down the road to turn back now, or to send him away. This was the company she had, and Lir was an integral part of it. Come what may, she would protect him and keep him safe— as much from Esme as any of Loc's men.

As the days wore on, Esme's temper remained disputatious. She was abominable in every way she could manage, arguing with Málik, bullying Lir, and avoiding Gwendolyn. Only Bryn seemed to take her mood in stride.

"Something is troubling her," Gwendolyn said to Málik on the one occasion he was drawn to her side. When he didn't reply beyond the lift of his brow, Gwendolyn tried changing the subject. It had been too long since they'd had much discourse, and she was desperate for conversation with him. "You were right about Lir... I was too quick to judge." This earned her an even higher lift of his brow, but still he said nothing, and Gwendolyn tried once more to find a worthy topic of conversation—something they could latch onto and seek respite from this bothersome silence. Sadly, being queen did not save her from awkward conversations. "You know, I wondered... when you said our journey was ill-timed, were you referring to the state of our *konsel*?"

She'd used the word *"our" quite* deliberately because she'd never once viewed this role as hers alone. If they were going to return the spirit of this land to its former glory, she couldn't do it alone. She needed every member of her team.

Málik peered at her, and she added, rambling, "Caradoc will honor my wishes, I believe."

"Art trying to convince yourself?"

Gwendolyn's tone betrayed uncertainty. "You think he would defy me?"

"It is not what I think that matters, Gwendolyn. I do not confess to knowing the turn of *your* minds."

Your minds?

Yours

Plural.

Gwendolyn blinked at his choice of words. Did he now lump her with all her mortal brethren? Was there nothing sacred between them?

She tried not to take offense, still she did.

Day by day, she felt their closeness dissipating.

In part, it could be because Esme was chipping away at their bond with every wrathful word she uttered, yet Gwendolyn had done nothing to deserve the distance Málik was raising between them.

She lifted her chin. "I think Caradoc mightn't like it that I placed Ely on his *konsel*, but she's wed to his son. I do trust Ely to do what is right, and I am quite certain—as Caradoc should be—that she will consider his concerns with great care."

Still, Málik said nothing, and Gwendolyn continued. "She is young, mayhap, and inexperienced, but I know her heart—more than I can say about some," she said with growing impatience.

Without meaning to, she had perhaps revealed her own worst fears—that she would place her own trust in the wrong hands. But rather than bother to reassure her, Málik said, "Good."

"Good?"

Good?

Gwendolyn blinked with confusion.

Gods.

She was trying desperately to lift the mood. But nothing she said or did seemed to make any difference. Bryn, Málik, Esme—all three of the individuals she most trusted—grew more preoccupied and quarrelsome as the days wore on. Even Bryn took every available occasion to slip into the woods for peace of mind—not that Gwendolyn blamed him. She was growing weary of attempting to placate her ill-tempered companions. Her own mood mightn't be exemplary, with all she had on her mind, but she was trying. And, on top of everything, this incessant drizzle left her cold to the bone. But above everything —more than any other concern she was realizing how connected she was to Málik. If only he would give her a smile or glance, she could deal with anything, and she didn't like the revelation.

He turned his too familiar gaze on her, and said, "It *is* good, is it not?" He awaited her response, and Gwendolyn pursed her lips, seizing hold of her reins.

"Indeed," she replied, and that was the end of their painful discourse.

For the love of the goddess, she wished she had asked Caradoc to join them! At least then he would have had her smiling over his silly male swagger! In Gwendolyn's mind, she had envisioned this journey so differently.

And more, if she must confess, despite that she and Málik were not alone on this road—with no aldermen present to tug at her sleeves, nor governmental issues to resolve—she had looked forward to spending a moment alone with him.

Apparently, that was not to be.

Of course, he had explained why he was keeping his distance, and she understood his reasons, but that didn't appease the ache she felt over the growing rift between them—a chasm already and growing more by day.

She didn't enjoy feeling so petty, nor having to confess that she lived for Málik's smiles... even if she did. Whatever they might be to each other, he had become her touchstone and Gwendolyn needed him as fiercely as she needed air to breathe.

This, too, was a revelation she didn't relish.

After Gwendolyn's escape from Loegria, during

those long weeks when Bryn had so little to say to her, it was Málik she had turned to. He'd remained her closest confidante. And then, during the first days after returning to Trevena, he had remained steadfast by her side, counseling her, keeping her safe.

Thereafter, it wasn't long before he'd begun to distance himself. Firstly, he'd returned Bryn to his "rightful" place as her Shadow, and when Gwendolyn asked him about it, he'd claimed it to be for her own good, giving her the most vexing of explanations—vexing because she didn't understand it. He'd claimed his father would scent their bond the same way her people viewed a torc about the neck. But it wasn't as though they were rolling about together. Gwendolyn had hoped the journey would give them a few moments alone to discuss the matter further. Instead, she felt the rift growing and growing and it pained her as it would if someone were to thrust a lance through her belly. *No matter,* she told herself.

She didn't need distractions.

It must be enough to focus on making it safely to the Druid village, preferably with *all* her ill-natured companions in tow—including prickly Esme.

Certes, Málik's aloofness made it easier for Gwendolyn to forget how it felt to be in his arms. And gods knew, there was too much at stake to pander to her woman's heart—if only he would reassure her now and again that the reason for his troublesome formality was on account of his father, not that he'd grown weary of her, and no longer cared. He slid her another glance, and, to Gwendolyn's dismay, she could read too little in his expression—nothing more than boredom—and it soured her belly. Disheartened, she fell back, allowing him to lead unfettered by her presence, certain that, at the least, with his keen eyes and sense of smell, he was the one best suited to the task.

Unbidden, the memory of their first travels together assailed her...

He was the same then—focused and taciturn, his blue eyes ticking back and forth across the woodlands, like a wolf seeking its prey. Every sound, every hare, every bird in the trees caught his notice.

At least she could say with certainty that no matter what his mood, she felt safe in his presence—at least, until he lost his temper with Esme.

It happened quickly.

Esme said something that angered Málik and his response was startling. For the first time in the history of their acquaintance, Gwendolyn witnessed Málik in all his terrible splendor—a creature not of this world. Snarling, he bared his teeth at his Fae counterpart, and Esme brandished hers in return. The two hissed at each another. Málik's hackles rose, and in profile, his was a fearsome visage, his jaw lengthening to what appeared to be a snout, fangs bared, long and cambered. Small horns presented themselves atop his forehead—as they had the night on the ramparts. The confrontation ended abruptly with a furious Esme tugging at her reins. She disappeared into the woods, only to return hours later, with a glint in her eyes like daggers, casting glares at Málik, and a few more for Gwendolyn.

If nothing else, that vicious exchange was a keen reminder to Gwendolyn, that no matter what she felt for Málik, he and Esme came from a world apart.

Gwendolyn was no longer a child, and she believed herself strong enough to do what must be done to win against mortal men, but despite waking each day to Esme and Málik's foreign faces, she often over-

looked the truth of what they were. What if some day
they were to turn the full force of their anger against
her? What power did she have over them, save love
and friendship? And both these things seemed tenuous and growing more and more questionable.

Moreover, this display was perhaps only a preview
of what awaited her in the Fae kingdom—an army of
like creatures.

How could she prevail against them?

13

The journey went from bad to worse.

No one ever said it should be pleasant. But it was far less so with Gwendolyn's band of not-so-merry minions. To make matters worse, it was the rainy season, with abrupt downpours that soaked everyone to the flesh.

At the moment, even the insides of Gwendolyn's good leather boots were sopping wet and the tiny hairs of her *piloi* were squishy. She was pretty sure that when she removed them, her toes would look like prunes. The one blessing about wearing her mother's breastplate was that copper didn't rust. Lamentably, it was quick to warm to the heat of one's body, and when the temperature plummeted, it drew it away, leaving her cold and shivering.

Over time, they made their way west, then east, and west again, weaving in and out of Brigantes and Ordovician territory, traveling as much as possible by night. Considering the dearth of people they encountered on the road, Gwendolyn grew certain Loc had conscripted every able-bodied man in Westwalas, and if that was the case, perhaps the women and children had gravitated toward the shelter of the capital. Deer, they found plenty, as well as coney, badgers and foxes. A few owls kept watch over the night, and once, a bat swept close to Gwendolyn's head, making her squeal. They slept wherever and whenever they could, and once, when the drizzle escalated to a downpour, they dared to shelter in one of Loc's half-built towers. On another occasion, they hunkered within the dyke itself. Most often, they took shelter in the thickets, careful to avoid open spaces. Fasting by day, they hunted at twilight, then supped by night. And, when they slept, and were compelled to build a fire for warmth, they dug pits to conceal the flames.

Unfortunately, as it must eventually, their luck ended halfway through Ordovician lands, when, ironically, the construction of Loc's wall ceased altogether. There, in the dying light of a watery sun, they encountered a horse and rider, both wearing Loegrian livery. On one of her scouting missions, Esme spotted the soldier and doubled back to rush them all into a nearby thicket. Moving quickly to settle the horses, Gwendolyn waited with bated breath for the soldier to pass, her eyes narrowing on the tattered attire...

Loc's serpent reared its head on the man's worn leather jerkin, and Gwendolyn's jaw clenched at the sight of it, considering for the first-time what Loc intended with the melding of their standards. With that simple design, he had too easily replaced her father's sigil with one still recognizable to her people, giving the impression he belonged on the Cornish throne— that his blood was the blood of the Conservators. The sigil was both brilliant and abhorrent at once, making it clear to Gwendolyn that this plan of his had been in the works since long before their betrothal.

Estrildis had spoken true. Gwendolyn knew it then, as she knew Loc was a monster. The toad murdered his brother! Either he did, or his mother did, but regardless of who performed the deed, those two were one and the same.

Gods.

Was the sigil Innogen's vision?

As it was to murder Brutus' first-born child and Brutus as well? Along with her father, her mother and everyone Gwendolyn held dear?

The notion sickened Gwendolyn.

So many had perished on account of their greed, and evidently, it wasn't enough that, through their marriage, Loc would someday come to possess the Cornish throne—he wanted it now!

Gwendolyn had suspected much of this, but it was difficult to argue with evidence. That this lowly warriors' dirty, ragged uniform was emblazoned with the standard gave clarity to the grandiosity of their scheme—like that wall that should take ages to complete. Indeed, the time and effort it must have taken to design the sigil, and then apply them—even to scouts, who, for the most part were never meant to be recognizable apart from the army—bespoke such arrogance. Those men were meant to travel undetected, solely to report the state of the realm. Not only was dressing this fellow such a stunning form of hubris, it was also quite revealing because this was not a feat that could have been accomplished overnight.

Gwendolyn's eyes misted.

Wet, dirty and cold, her emotions roiled.

On the eve of their nuptials, only Locrinus had arrived wearing that sigil, and yet... this man's uniform was not new. Clearly, he'd needed her to believe his gesture was a measure of his affection for her—a merger of their houses, a symbol of their unity.

It. Was. Not.

With his greedy little mistress awaiting him at home, he'd simply needed Gwendolyn's compliance—until the night he'd snipped her hair, and found, to his disgust, it was simply hair, not gold.

And then he'd decided her Prophecy was a lie.

He'd rebuffed her. Discarded her. Left her to rot in the room where his brother died, perhaps hoping his black-hearted mistress would do the same to Gwendolyn.

The soldier trotted past, oblivious to his audience, but Gwendolyn's fury ignited with remembrance—that moment of her violation.

The look of disgust on Loc's face as he'd pulled and hacked her locks.

The fury with which he had hurled Borlewen's blade into the bedding.

The glee with which he'd conveyed the truth of her cousin's death.

The injury it left in her heart!

Gods. She'd sat so dumbly on that bed, so expectantly, only waiting for a husband's love... and what she'd received instead was revilement, rage, and shame.

Acting on impulse, Gwendolyn drew her dagger to cut the offending serpent from the man's breast, incensed that he would wear it. But before she could hurl herself into his path, Málik produced a fairy flame and dispatched it. With her dagger still in hand, Gwendolyn watched as the fool hastened after it, none the wiser over their presence in the bush—or how close he'd come to tasting the tang of her blade.

Borlewen's dagger screamed for vengeance.

Gwendolyn's legs trembled with fury.

Her gut burned with rage.

So much she could taste her own bile.

Bryn's hand closed about her upper arm, drawing her gently back as she watched both horse and rider chase the fool's fire.

"Gwendolyn," he said. "He is gone."

Not yet, he was not. Gwendolyn could still see him, her eyes following him as he jumped over fallen logs and ducked beneath low-hanging limbs.

If she but mounted Aisling, Enbarr's mare would overtake him. And yet, it wasn't that man's fault—not really. And now his fate was sealed.

From a distance, in the dark, those Faerie flames could easily be mistaken for lanterns, but the light was not golden-hued. The fool had likely recognized it for what her people knew as *piskie* lights or Foolish Fire, aptly named because that flame would lead him astray, and to his doom. They had nothing to do with *piskies*, though her people still believed in the old tales —that if one could capture a will-o'-the-wisp, it would bind itself to you, and lead you to untold riches.

Pity for that horse and rider, Gwendolyn knew better.

That flame served one master and she needn't ask who when it returned a few hours later to shadow Málik... *alone*. No one spoke as they returned to the road, silent and brooding, and this time, it was Gwendolyn's mood more than anyone's that darkened the brume. Meanwhile, like an annoying little biting midge, Málik's flame buzzed about his head, eventually coming to rest upon his shoulder, but not before buzzing back to glare at Gwendolyn. Indeed, she could swear it did so—even without a face. And then, finding her dull perhaps, it returned to its master, staying close to him until early the following morn, when it vanished at the break of day.

Gwendolyn was relieved to see it gone. This one

was nothing like the one she'd named *Sterenglas*—*blue star*. At Málik's behest, that one had remained dutifully by her side, keeping her company, making her wish she could have one too.

This one had been... hostile.

She'd been apprised that every flame had a will of its own, and once given life, they burned till no longer required, seeming to comprehend when they'd outgrown their usefulness, extinguishing without ceremony. They were indisputable reminders of their eventual destination—a place unknown to Gwendolyn.

How was she supposed to win back her sword if she knew so little about the Fae realms?

Her gaze slid to Lir, and she realized that if she wished to know more, there *was* one person she could ask who wouldn't evade her questions.

There was more than one way to skin a rabbit, she decided, and silently thanked Málik for the unintended suggestion.

14

From her mother, Gwendolyn learned there was a place and time for political machinations; careful planning served one best. Therefore, she waited until Bryn and Esme were preoccupied with conversation, and Málik content with his solitude, before sidling up beside Lir. She gave him a tilt of her head and, smiling, gave their Fae leader a quick nod. "So, I am told, *you* are the expert—not merely with Pretanian histories, but Málik claims you are also quite proficient with the Fae's as well—particularly brilliant with the peculiarities of their language."

Lir cast a glance at Málik, and even as Gwendolyn watched, his spine straightened. "He said that?"

"Indeed, he did." Gwendolyn made a pretense of reaching out to pat Aisling's withers, not quite able to meet Lir's gaze—not because she was lying. Because she was not. Málik had said those things, more or less, but she didn't wish to make it seem too important. She'd rather Lir believe she was only making conversation—not that Málik had refused to elaborate, and it reduced her to ferreting out the rest of the information from others.

"Well..." Lir said, eyes brightening. "I must confess, I do not know so much as I'd like to know. As I have previously expressed, for all my life I've longed to cross the Veil to see the City of Light. I cannot help but think that to see it would be even more illuminating— did you hear what I did?" he said, pleased with himself over the reference to light regarding the City of Light.

Gwendolyn smiled, amused. Of course, she remembered him saying so, but she feigned ignorance, asking conversationally, "City of Light?"

"Tír na nÓg so it is called in their tongue—the land of the ever young. To hear the stories told, the city shines eternally, even without the light of the sun."

Gwendolyn's brow furrowed.

That really shouldn't be possible.

She had always envisioned the Underworld as a dark and grim place, with tunnels like fogous and creatures like rats burrowing through inky passages— a place where *spriggans* dwelt, despite that Málik said they did not exist. Indeed, more like her uncle's *fogous*, occupied by bats, beetles and rats. Now, she was genuinely curious. "What do you suppose provides this light?"

The Druid shrugged. "I cannot say, and they will not."

He hitched his chin twice, once toward Esme, then Málik. "What we know, we have gleaned from our past encounters with the Fae. Their ambassadors oft used to visit, and, in fact, it was from them we first learned about *pookies*. I am told they were planted in our mortal realm by Faekind and, like their creators, they are far more remarkable than anyone could suppose. Did you know that *pookie* are connected to the trees through tiny threads, like roots? They form a vast web across this isle, and perhaps even the entirety of this world."

"Fascinating," Gwendolyn allowed. And truly, it was. But hadn't Málik claimed everything was similarly bound?

That day when Málik saved her from Loc by doing whatever he'd done with that tree, later, in order to explain this phenomenon, he'd patted the tree at his back, and said, "What one knows, all will know." And he'd spoken of the roots running deep.

"It is the opinion of some in my order that *pookies* contain the mystery of life. Therefore, we consume them frequently—seeking wisdom. Hidden in the fiber of those *mushrooms* is the very book of life!"

Gwendolyn laughed softly over his unrestrained exuberance.

He continued, describing his dream of building a temple full of tomes, and then told her about a magnificent library in the city of Rhakotis in the harbor of one Pharos on a river called Nile, where it was said that more than forty thousand scrolls were secured, some unraveling to the length of two full-grown men, with every space filled with scribblings of note. "I would build one in the Druid village if there were room, but our poets are nowhere near so prolific as they."

And despite this, they had already amassed a proper library. The difference being the manner of their storage. The Druids had developed a method of binding, wherein the parchment must be folded, and then sewn together with strong cords or ligaments that were attached to wooden boards, then covered with leather. So, he claimed, every time they partook, they rendered this experience to a written word—sometimes by the one experiencing what he called a journey and sometimes by another. Occasionally, what came of the sessions were nuggets of wisdom or accounts of the past or future—as it must have been the case with Gwendolyn's pookie dream.

"Even now, we are still remembering all we forgot," said Lir. "None of my Druid brethren ever imagined the Fae ambassadors would forsake us."

"There were ambassadors?" Gwendolyn asked.

"Indeed," said Lir, and then he sighed. "It was they who stole our memories. Were it not for our precious tomes, we'd know little of those days. Lamentably, it was far too long while before we began compiling our histories, and we lost so much during the interim."

Gwendolyn's face contorted with confusion. "But, Lir, you are still the same people," she suggested. "It is not as though your stories have been passed down through the ages—you yourself lived them!"

"True," said Lir. "True. But, alas, time is the bane of our human minds. I might not look my age, but this body has been well used, even so, and the mind cannot keep all we expose it to, more's the pity."

Gwendolyn wondered if they might allow her to peruse those volumes, but evidently Málik spoke true: The value of Lir's experience was immeasurable. "Why do you suppose they stole your memories?" Gwendolyn pressed.

Lir shrugged. "I don't know. Mayhap because they believe our ignorance will keep them safe?" He shrugged again. "That is my brother's opinion... alas, they took our memories and now bind all Fae who visit—like her," he said.

"Bind?"

"Compel," he said. "Constrained. Think of it like a gag put into one's mouth, only without the foul-smelling rag. Fae magic," he said.

"Bespelled?"

"Yes, and willingly, so I am told—as a matter of return for any passage into the mortal realms. I know not how it works, but it is a trick of the mind, I believe."

Gwendolyn frowned, wondering if Málik had bound her too. She remembered his explanation of her inability to recount everything she had discovered in the fogous, but he had very conveniently refrained from saying who had kept her from it. "By whom, I wonder?"

"His father, his king, I would suppose." And then he said, "It is unlawful for any Faekind to speak of the Fae realms, or any account thereof. So I am told, much of their knowledge was used to their detriment by the sons of Míl."

Gwendolyn knew they were exiled through some trickery by the Sons of Míl; this made sense to her. Her gaze slid to Esme, where he'd pointed. "Did you know her before I came to your village?"

"Indeed!" he said. "*She* was one of our original ambassadors, and so I am told she's the only one her father trusts to come and go as she pleases—in part, to keep an eye on *that one*." This time, he indicated Málik. And he put his hand to his mouth as though to whisper behind it. "I am told *he* was exiled, but as he has never corroborated this, and Esme will not speak of it. I do not know if it is true. And nevertheless, there is a persistent rumor—do not take it as truth, mind you—that he was banished for love of a woman, compelled to seek her endlessly, only to lose her again and again every time he finds her."

You have been my weakness for a hundred thousand years...

Gwendolyn blinked with sudden foreboding.

She had considered his profession only an embell-ishment—a expression of his affection. Poetic words to win her heart. But if what Lir was saying was true, if the woman he was speaking of was Gwendolyn, could it be that she was the love he had lost... and would lose yet again?

Málik had also claimed Gwendolyn was part Fo-morian. But Gwendolyn hadn't any understanding of what that meant, only that, according to Málik, her mother's people were descended of this rás of demigods—so was the Fae king.

Unbidden, Gwendolyn remembered a conversa-tion a few days past, wondering at Esme's vehemence when she'd spoken of Gwendolyn in terms of being a changeling. The very notion that Gwendolyn or Demelza might find it abhorrent had offended her.

During the time she had been speaking to Lir, Esme had abandoned Bryn and now sat discussing some private matter with Málik, only this time they were no longer arguing. Gwendolyn frowned. "Málik said you knew their language well. Do you know what Tuatha means?" she asked, merely curious.

"Kindred," he said.

"So... Tuatha de Danann means... kindred of Danann?"

Lir gave her a shrug, then a nod, and Gwendolyn continued, wondering aloud. "Where is Danann?"

"Or who," he said, with a half-smile. "No mortal can say, and no Fae will. But I do know this realm they now occupy is not the land of their birth. Their moth-erland was a land of great riches, where death and dis-ease did not exist. I believe they called it Hyperborea."

"Hyperborea?" Gwendolyn's head snapped up, having heard that name before—from, of all people, Loc. But what should he know of that? And why had he brought them up in conversation? But then something occurred to her. "If they do not speak of this place, how do you know its name?"

"Pookies," he explained.

"So, you've never discussed this with them." She hitched her chin in Málik's direction.

"Of course not!"

"I ask because Locrinus once told me he traveled there."

His gaze shot to hers. "I do not believe this!" he declared. "More likely, he heard the name during his sojourn to Ériu."

It would not surprise Gwendolyn to learn Loc had lied. But why would he bother to do so when she herself did not know of this place?

Every learned person knew of the four cities from which the Tuatha hailed—the sunken city of Murias, the city of Gorias, and the cities of Finias and Falias. But this was all her people ever knew.

"Interesting," Gwendolyn said, trying to recall what else Loc had claimed during that pompous conversation—too much, she'd thought, and most of it blather. Mostly, he'd yammered about things he must have gleaned would impress her, and certainly, he had, much to Gwendolyn's disgust. But that conversation was when she had begun to suspect Loc's character—speaking ill of the Temple of the Dead, and the consortium of tribes that governed it. He'd referred to it as the Æmete Temple, referring to the people as ants, and telling Gwendolyn they were inconsequential.

After that, she never recovered her opinion of him, but neither did she go tell her father, which was what she should have done.

Gwendolyn had so many regrets.

Lir gave a flourish of his hand, speaking as though reciting some passage by rote. "When they came, they arrived on a mighty cloud! Sailing without ships! And the truth was ne'er known beneath our sky of stars, whether these gods flew from Albios, Bitu, or Dubnos!" Aside, he explained behind his hand, "Albios, Bitu and Dubnos are the names attributed to the White World in the heavens, our own mortal realm, and the Black Realm below."

The man was a walking tome!

He knew things none of her tutors ever shared.

Nor were any of these stories taught by the *dawnsio*.

Even as wise as he had been, the old Mester had never even believed in Gwendolyn's prophecy. Still, it came to pass, evidenced by the crown she now had stashed in her saddlebag—made of her own cut locks, and fashioned by Esme's deft hand. No matter what naysayers might say all who were present knew the truth: Her hair turned gold by true-love's hand. And simply by virtue of this truth, her marriage to Loc—despite so many having concluded he should be The One—was not the union she should have made...

Her gaze sought and found Málik, finding him too beautiful for words. A lump formed in her throat and she felt anew the pain of their estrangement.

Clearly, aldermen were *not* infallible.

Now, after everything Gwendolyn had witnessed, she no longer had any doubt in the existence of Faeries or magic. Certainly, as fanciful as Demelza's tales may have been, there was proof of Fae magic even in Trevena, in the Dragon's Lair.

That sacred place in the cliff-side was there when her people first settled on the Stone Isle, and throughout their tenure in the city, no one could ever account for the source of that flame, regardless that her father invited the most scientifically minded to investigate. Over the course of the years, the alcove was laid bare to all, yet no one ever explained why the Dragon's Flame existed, nor why it burned so brightly by night. And despite its name, no one ever found a dragon in that cavern, though if anyone would have, it would have been Gwendolyn. So many times she and Bryn had snuck up to the cavern, hoping to catch a peep at some mysterious beast. Never once did they do so. Despite that, the flame burned bright and true. Each night, the altar lit of its own accord, revealing twin flames within the "dragon's maw." Somehow, even after the deluge that took the original Fae villages many generations ago, that flame never extinguished, except during that short time after her father's death—not because the tarp was drawn. But, rather, the flame, like her sword, refused to burn, as though it *knew* of Loc's treachery and declined to light.

And this was perhaps the reason Trevena depleted its stores during her absence, because for months and months, no ships dared enter that harbor. It was likely also the reason Loc's brothers left Trevena so poorly defended. As remarkable as the city and palace might be, without a means to procure sustenance, a walled city such as theirs would effectively serve as a tomb— a mere monument to the stupidity of men.

Or even the Fae, truth be told. After all, Trevena was not the first village to grace the Stone Isle. Long before the battle between the Sons of Míl and the Tuatha, there was yet another village there whose history they lost as surely as the Fae realm was shrouded by the Féth. If any soul remained who could remember those days, the details had grown smoggy, like the Druids' memories. And yet stories persisted, passed down through the ages by wizened old nurse-maids, like Demelza.

"Málik was right. You are a wizened man," Gwendolyn allowed. "I shall make you a bargain, Lir."

He lifted a finger to his pointy ear sheaths, cocking his head. "Bargain, Majesty?"

"Indeed," said Gwendolyn with a wink. "I will teach you to wield that poor, neglected sword in your scabbard, and since I cannot seem to pry a word from our Fae companions about what to expect once arrived in the Fae lands, I would have you teach me everything you know of their world."

"Everything?"

Gwendolyn nodded. "Everything."

"Our volumes are quite lengthy," Lir said loftily.

Gwendolyn was undaunted. "No matter," she said. "We have time, and it will serve us all better if you can wield your sword aptly, and I know what we face."

Lir agreed. "Indeed. Very well. We've a bargain."

Gwendolyn smirked, casting Málik another glance. Leave them to hiss at each other like cats. Gwendolyn would learn what she could from Lir, and in the meantime, she would teach the poor man how to wield his sword, and together, they would lift the odds no one would die.

15

By the eleventh day of their travels, Gwendolyn knew much more than she feared her brain could hold. Much to the contrary, Lir was only marginally better at wielding his sword. In his defense, it was certainly easier to converse while on horseback than it was to spar, and there had only been a few occasions where it was safe to practice swordplay. Undoubtedly, the arrangement benefited Gwendolyn most. For one, she had never realized how tricksy the Fae could be even despite that Demelza had warned her. Not that Gwendolyn hadn't believed her, it was more perhaps that the stories her maid told seemed contrived—so much so that the Mester Alderman had admonished Gwendolyn not to believe them. Still, so much of what she'd learned from Lir seemed apropos to Esme, even though Lir advised her to be wary of *all* Fae, including Málik—particularly, the words that came out of their mouths. And this would appear to be the reason Málik himself had counseled Gwendolyn to allow the Druid to accompany them. There was a wealth of information to be gleaned from every aspect of their communication, including their tone, and even the construct of their words. Neither did their bent for deception need be done with any malicious intent. They simply could declare one thing and mean another, and the trick of the matter was to listen to every word uttered and look for hidden clues.

For example, if one said, "Yes, I would give you the sword" this didn't reveal when, or how, or, under what conditions. It might be given in one's hand, or thrust into one's breast, or even offered to the bearer whilst he stood in chains, locked away in some *gaol*, where the sword might never be wielded to its purpose.

Or, if one said, "I should give you the sword." *Should* did not convey any true intent, any more than *would*. Instead, it could express duty, wistfulness, or even obligation without action.

Every word had some nuance, like an artist with his palette.

But neither was cornering an Elf for answers so easily done. They invented language and had many ages to learn to wield words as deftly as weapons.

Gwendolyn tried to determine whether she'd ever felt Málik to be evasive, and certainly she had. To be sure, even now—especially now—conversations with him were more frustrating than they were with Esme.

Although what had Lir said? Esme was the only one her father still trusted to come and go as she pleased, most probably to spy on Málik.

Was this what Esme was doing all this time? Did Gwendolyn's cause mean nothing to her? Was this also why Málik mistrusted Esme?

Gwendolyn noted that, even now, Málik didn't return Esme's conversation with any great relish. He responded with the same economy of words that always vexed Gwendolyn so much.

Gwendolyn didn't wish to believe he was capable of deception—at least not with her. But he had warned her she could not rely on him nor Esme to manage negotiations with his father. This should give her pause.

Riding alone, for once, without Esme by his side, Málik's back was straight and proud, his attention on the road ahead, his silver mane shining beneath the morning sun like silver spun... But even as Gwendolyn watched him, she knew...

He knew more than he would say.

And not only about the Rot.

Indeed, Gwendolyn suspected her plight was no mystery to either of these Elves, and she grew certain Málik wasn't the only one keeping things from her.

Curious how Esme might answer in her present mood, Gwendolyn waited for the Elf to tire of her one-sided conversation with Málik, and then sidled up beside her.

"You once advised me that the *Aether* absorbs our spirit. This is the *ysbryd y byd*. But I do not understand why the Rot is worse near Trevena, when my father tried so hard to rule as the First Men ordained."

"Did he?" Esme asked.

"I believe he did." Gwendolyn furrowed her brow, taking issue with the flippancy of Esme's tone, and when Esme responded with silence, Gwendolyn continued. "Clearly, he *made* mistakes, else we'd not be where we are today. But he considered the Brothers' Pact with the utmost respect. All he did, he did to honor our Conservatorship."

Esme slid Gwendolyn another glance, her gaze slippery as an eel. "Aye, well... I will argue that a pact between warmongering mortals intent upon dividing lands not their own should never be commended. Instead, perhaps your tributes should be offered to the land?"

"Are you suggesting my father forsook his duties?"

The Elf gave an exaggerated sigh, once more turning to Gwendolyn, her eyes shining curiously. "Gwendolyn," said Esme, with scant patience. "You know the answer to this question already. May I ask what your father hoped to gain with the Loegrian alliance?"

Gwendolyn responded without hesitation. "Peace, of course."

She knew this beyond a shadow of doubt. Everything her father ever did, he did for the sake of peace —the taking of a Prydein wife, the treaty with Leogria, the money invested in the *dawnsio*, the honoring of ancient wisdom through his patronage of the Gwyddons and Awenydds—not to mention his affiliation with the Druids.

"And you're certain of this?" Esme asked. "Because I assure you, the Spirit of the World does not wither and die of its own accord."

Gwendolyn's frown deepened. "Perhaps I should ask instead, why does this land thrive in the heart of a Usurper's demesne? Why would hopelessness and despair not manifest itself like a cancer upon this land, as it has in Cornwall?"

Esme tilted her head, as though she found it difficult to explain. And then, settling upon an answer, she lifted a finger. "When there are no expectations, there can be no disappointment. There is a certain... fervor —if fleeting—in the freedom granted an unbound soul."

Gwendolyn considered that explanation, but before she could consider it too carefully, and ask questions, Esme added, "Anger bears its own force, as does fear."

Gwendolyn thought about that as well.

"So, you are saying there is power in the spirit of anger?"

"Life is passion and passion is life," Esme explained. "Loathing is not the opposite of love, *Banríon*. Dispassion is. Hatred might sustain life... for a while —did you never hear it said a man was too mean to die?"

Indeed, Gwendolyn had. She had said just such a thing about Esme. She lifted a hand to her lips, as though to keep herself from expressing that fact.

"There is truth in this," Esme said. "But the energy of it is short-lived, even by mortal years. Eventually, all things perish without hope, and hatred's roots, no matter how deep, will not sustain. Only a true sanguineness of spirit may do this."

"So... you are saying... Loegria thrives through Loc's wrath, and meanwhile Cornwall's spirit withered before my father did?"

Esme gave her a nod, then shrugged. "Something like that. Though I do not scry, so I cannot tell you at which point your people's hope died, only that you should seek your testimony in the land itself."

As much as Gwendolyn loathed confessing to it, it all made sense.

Ruefully, though she herself had been quite sensitive to the state of the land, watching for the smallest of changes, she had, undoubtedly only done so after the onset of her father's illness—and then, only so she could find hope for the king's recovery. To Gwendolyn's mind, she had believed her people flourishing. After all, how could they not be? Their city was the greatest in all the land and the most prominent of merchants passed through their port and gates. Trevena was a melting pot of cultures, a bastion for the arts and intellectual achievement, its architecture unparalleled. Even so, Gwendolyn had begun to note a certain restlessness that only worsened as her father's illness progressed.

As Esme suggested, had it begun with the Loegrian alliance?

Did the people worry when her father offered their lands to outlanders?

Did they believe him when he said he'd formed the alliance for the good of the kingdom?

Did they fear the soldiers Brutus sent?

As part of the alliance, her father had agreed to accept a contract of defense in the form of trained soldiers, whom he further compensated with room and board.

In the end, it was he who allowed Brutus' influence into their garrison, placing the enemy under Talwyn's nose. And yet, Gwendolyn knew her father believed this was the right thing to do, trusting that Brutus would honor their pact.

For a time, the alliance with Loegria had proven to be mutually beneficial, providing their armies with the finest of weapons and armor made of Brutus' new alloy. But it wasn't simply the new alloy to be considered: Together, Cornwall and Loegria had made a formidable pair, strengthening their positions against the rest of the tribes. Allied with King Brutus, Cornwall would be difficult to defeat.

Did the people believe her father greedy for power?

Did they find his motives less than pure?

Was there yet another reason her father had to ally with Brutus? Something Gwendolyn did not know of?

A thousand questions assailed her—none of them pleasant to contemplate.

Esme gave her a simpering look, and Gwendolyn wondered if she had somehow gleaned her thoughts.

But then, one quick glance over at Málik, and she discovered his gaze boring into her for the first time in days. However looking back on the last one she...

Or rather... he had been watching her, but surreptitiously pretending to keep his interest elsewhere. But she knew he was watching her every move.

He didn't appear to like it she and Esme were conversing. But this was not to be helped. If he didn't wish her to press Esme and Lir for answers, perhaps he should be more forthcoming. And yet, regardless of whether he approved of Gwendolyn's inquiries, she didn't care. Right now, the Rot was a grave concern. Gwendolyn had considered her father to be a man of the people, but perhaps this was how she saw him only because she'd loved him and because she'd wished to believe him noble—as she did all she valued, Bryn and Málik, included.

Given bitterly, or nay, Esme had at least given her much to think about.

Was there no inkling of greed for her father's motivation?

No trace hubris in the construction of their palatial city?

What was it about her father's policies that killed the spirit of her people?

Indeed, Porth Pool had been deteriorating since Gwendolyn could remember... undetectably at first. But then, after a time, the winters grew colder; the trees lost their foliage sooner, and the sun shone with less brilliance... It was only after her father grew ill enough that his limbs grew unsteady and his hands shook that Gwendolyn took a keener interest in the changes. And then, one day, his illness grew worrisome. His aldermen became more vocal about their displeasure, perhaps less secure with his decisions.

Their arguments grew fiercer, and this was the reason
Gwendolyn so oft dreaded going into his *konsel* meet-
ings. However, looking back on the last one she'd attended whilst her father yet lived, there was a wealth
of information to be gleaned. Mentally, she sifted
through conversations, recognizing so much discord—
most notably, complaints over her broken betrothal to
Urien, her betrothal and marriage to Locrinus, her
mother's Prydein kinsmen, the allegiance with Loegria, the output of their wheals, so many household
quarrels...

In that meeting in particular, her mother had
smashed her palm upon the table and walked out
after an altercation with several of the aldermen
who'd dared to question her position as the king's
lawful consort. Most of the palace staff had feared her
mother, but the aldermen did not. They didn't even
fear her father—why should they? The king could not
remove a sworn alderman. Only if one broke faith, or
died, they could replace one; this was why Gwendolyn
had been so adamant that she must put her own
trusted men and women in that position.

They could be most unreasonable to deal with—
as they were too oft with Gwendolyn, dismissing her
concerns, thinking her too young to have a valuable
opinion. Every time she had brought them her concerns about Porth Pool, they'd sent her away, begging
her not to speak of the Rot or the pool, lest the people
turn against the king. Only recently had they acknowl-
edged there was a problem. And despite this, Gwendolyn had consulted with them before leaving
Trevena, with no true consensus over the cause of the
Rot, nor about how to prevent it, much less to stop it.
Old as they were, most of those graybeards considered
themselves wizened old souls, and, like the old

Mester, they argued it was a natural occurrence, denying that Trevena could have any part in the Rot's conception or its spread.

However, after everything Gwendolyn had witnessed, and all she had endured, she knew enough to know that not everything was born of this world. Science was not to be dismissed, but neither could they disregard the king's role in the land's decline. *"The land is the king, the king is the land"* was a maxim so integral to her people's faith that they had carved it into stone at the base of her father's throne. Howbeit, Gwendolyn no longer believed it was simply a matter of angering the gods. Rather, it must be the culmination of a thousand injuries, perhaps beginning with the granting of Cornish lands to a foreigner. And nevertheless, if her father ran afoul of his duties, Gwendolyn felt in her deepest of hearts it must have been unwittingly. As ill as he'd been, she knew he would have abdicated his throne if it were the will of the people. He had been a reasonable man, who'd cared little for amassing riches—evidenced by his untold generosity with Brutus, even against the bitter opposition of his *konsel*. In her father's mind and heart, Gwendolyn was certain he had bartered for a powerful ally, not merely to defend his crown, but to further his dream of a united Pretania. But what if that was not the way it was meant to be? What if these lands should not be one land? They might all share a bond, but they were nothing alike.

16

The rain returned, forcing Gwendolyn and her company into a small copse, where they settled within a thicket in time to watch the passing of a stranger—an elder man, journeying afoot. Now and again, with a backward glance, the stranger pulled his sopping cowl over his face, and kept on marching, too preoccupied with what came behind to worry about who might be watching.

It wasn't long before they discovered why.

Soon behind the old bod came a motley crew of soldiers, seven drunkards—three on horseback, four marching—passing a flask betwixt them. Gwendolyn counted it her good fortune Caradoc was not here to hear them crowing over his misfortunes. He would have met their rude song with a hammer.

"Down she came, down she came by the sea pen," they sang of the Catuvellauni fortress. "Off they went, off they went, marching to the fens!"

They laughed then, chortling nastily over the ignoble fate dealt to Caradoc's proud tribe, and Gwendolyn longed to defend her friend's honor by silencing these mouthy, drunken fools. If she'd wondered how she felt about Caradoc, she need wonder no more. He might be a vainglorious big-head jester, but he was *her* vainglorious big-head jester! *Imbeciles!*

The Catuvellauni were now Gwendolyn's allies, and she admired their fortitude. Unfortunately, between the battles they'd fought against the Iceni, forced starvation, swamp sickness and whatever else they'd endured before she'd discovered them, they were not the force they once were. But if Gwendolyn had aught to do about it, they would return stronger than ever.

The men carried on, turning the conversation to Gwendolyn and she grit her teeth as they made jokes about her face. "I got she was born with the face of a horse," said one. "Bloody hag!"

"No wonder her husband kicked her out of bed!" laughed another, and then he made horse noises, whinnying and snorting in turn.

"Shut up and listen to my song!" scolded another man.

"Elf lover!" said another man with lime-washed hair. "If you ask me, the bitch got what she deserved," he groused.

"No one asked you! Shut yer filthy gob!"

And then the man next to him crooned...

E' came t' slay the Rot King!
For the prize of a gold bride!
Snipped her dirty yellow mop, n' cried.
To see the changeling he was poking!

All together, they laughed, and Gwendolyn's heart rent to hear the inglorious song and the reference to her countenance—a rudeness she'd not suffered since her days with Loc. But as unflattering as the ballad was, it was the first and last lines that infuriated her most—an ugly reference to her father as the Rot King and the lie about her wedding night.

Her hand flew to Kingslayer's hilt as she made to rise, intending to shove *her* poker down the fool's filthy gob.

Faster than she could blink, Málik was behind her, squeezing her shoulder firmly, pushing her down. "No," he said. "They aren't worth it."

Gwendolyn disagreed.

More than anything, she longed to silence their song for all time—cut out their tongues and feed them to the wolves.

Who were these stupid fools who would crow over the fall of Lundinium and, in the next breath, the death of their king?

The only thing that kept her still was the reminder that, while her Elven companions would give Loc's soldiers a fight to remember, she knew immortality did not make them invincible. The one Lir had pointed out only yesterday had little to do with the other. If Esme or Málik should take a mortal blow, and succumbed without intervention, they would die as surely as Gwendolyn would die.

Gods help her. That was the one thing she feared most of all—more so than the possibility of returning to Loc's prison or facing him blade to blade. To her view, those would be acceptable risks for this quest... losing Málik was not.

Nor could she live with herself if she risked Bryn or Lir.

They were seven against five. And, though, in her fury, she would take them all, she was unwilling to ac-

cept the slightest disadvantage for her companions—
not unnecessarily. As it was, she would endanger them
soon enough. But there was too much at risk to throw
it all away for the sake of pride.

Grating her teeth, Gwendolyn settled back down,
sinking to her knees in the muck, taking comfort in
the hand that rested atop her shoulder.

Málik's.

She heard his sigh of relief as the men disappeared
around the bend, and it was only then, as Esme, Lir
and Bryn moved away as well, that she felt the warmth
of his breath at her ear... and a whisper so low that
only Gwendolyn could hear it.

"You are a rare flower," he said, pressing his cheek
against hers, as he swore, "I will make certain they
choke on their words." And then he planted a chaste
kiss upon the curve of her neck, and said, "Art beautiful, Gwendolyn."

For a moment, Gwendolyn's heart ceased to beat.

When it resumed, it tripped most painfully, its ca-
dence now as erratic as her thoughts. She swallowed
convulsively.

This was the first time in so long that Málik had
placed his fiery lips against her wanting flesh, and it
was all she could do not to turn and face him, rise up,
wrap her greedy arms about his neck, draw him close
and kiss him.

More than anything, she longed to know him, as
Ely did Kelan.

But, alas, despite that, Gwendolyn could remain
here for the rest of eternity, basking in his warmth... if
she kissed him now, she would forget herself forever.

He rose then, stealing her chance, and with a sigh,
his hand slid off her shoulder.

For the longest moment, Gwendolyn couldn't move.

She didn't turn. She knelt there in the muck too long, staring beyond the thicket where Loc's men had gone.

17

This was as good a spot as any to camp whilst they waited for the weather to turn. The maples and oaks served as a natural cover, and the entire perimeter was ringed by brushwood and brambles.

During their time there, several travelers ventured by, and Gwendolyn deliberated why, after so many long hours on the road, there were so many soldiers now roaming the area. All throughout Silures they'd encountered nary a soul, and here, as they grew closer to Lifer Pol, there were sundry troops in the area.

It could be they were brigands—and perhaps that man whose song had cut her to the bone was only an opportunist, hoping to join with the Usurper now that Loc was in control. Unfortunately, there would be many who would do so, Gwendolyn realized. There were some who might consider him the better choice only because the tide had turned in his favor. Loc was charming when he wished to be, and even Gwendolyn had longed so desperately to believe in him...

Until that day in the grotto, when he'd put his hands upon her, and sent her flying from the cavern.

Even now, the look of fury on Málik's face filled her with shame—not because Gwendolyn feared he had judged her—she knew he did not. Because she had put herself in such an untenable position. If not for Málik's intervention, that day could have gone so dreadfully wrong, and she would have lost her virginity to the one man she now most despised.

It was only Málik's defiance that saved her.

Remembering that day, she considered... what if those hands had been Málik's? What if he had been the one to put her back against the wall then laid his palm against her hip? What if it were Málik who'd leaned close... pressing the heat of his chest against her own... with the rush of the ocean drowning out the beat of her heart? Would she have let him lay her down?

Would she have lifted her face for his kiss?

Would she have drawn him closer?

Even as she'd wished to this afternoon?

And thereafter, would she have given him her heart?

Gods. Even then, she had loved him—with his unapologetically crooked smile and his storm-filled eyes.

One thing was certain, she would never have wed that monster.

Shrugging away impracticable thoughts, Gwendolyn busied herself preparing a pallet. Each of them had only one blanket, but she had her father's cloak, and that had been enough to keep her warm, although she longed for the heat of Málik's body to warm her through the night—indescribably delicious, especially on a freezing night. But though she somehow settled herself without giving away her yearning thoughts, she had trouble extricating the memory of his lips from her skin and his whisper from her ear. It harassed her, like a stubborn midge fly, buzzing at her ear. Long into the wee hours, she could still hear his silky voice. It made her smile, but along with those sweet words, he had shattered her heart into a thousand bits. Lying alone beneath the stars and moon, she was having a difficult time reminding herself why she must fight.

Already, the battle seemed lost.

For one, she had abandoned her city to a man who could too easily take it, and if she lost Trevena, she had an army of only five to retake it—including Lir, who'd yet to prove he had the wherewithal to fight.

And Esme, whose mercurial mood left Gwendolyn wondering.

Even as she thought this, she watched as Esme stole away into the woods, and Gwendolyn turned upon her pallet, huffing a sigh of irritation over their current state of affairs.

Why did she think she could do this?

Who was she to believe that any man would follow her?

It was enough to make her weep, but tears would gain her nothing and lose her much—the confidence placed in her, for one. But here in the darkest hour of the night, she must confess, if only to herself, her mettle was mostly a ruse. And though she liked to believe herself hard-wearing and her heart made of stone, neither of those things were true—not if one tender word from Málik could penetrate her well-shored armor.

Very well, not one kind word, two.

"You are a rare flower," he'd said, and then, "Art beautiful."

Two compliments given with the bestowal of a kiss.

The memory of it made her lips tingle and her skin burn.

Groaning inwardly, Gwendolyn turned again, putting her entire body into the effort, impatient over the way she felt—the ludicrous thoughts now rampaging through her brain. From the day she could walk and talk—nay, from the instant she could understand the conveyance of a look—she'd known her mother found her wanting. And no matter that her father had cared for her, and always treated her with sincere affection, he was never the sort to speak of love.

As for Demelza, her mother's maid had had so many compliments to give throughout the years, but none ever spoken with such love and conviction as Málik.

Certainly, Bryn had made her feel lovely, and she knew he'd harbored some affection for her. Despite that, no one ever made her feel as Málik did.

The way he'd looked at her, the way he'd spoken to her, the way he'd touched her—so rife with feeling... More than anything, she longed to crawl over and curl up beside him, then wrap her arms around him, and hold him until her dying breath.

With all her foolish heart, she wished she were only an ordinary girl, loving an ordinary boy, but Málik was no typical boy, and Gwendolyn was not a simple girl. Still, she loved him with an intensity that frightened her, and some part of her wished she could change her mind... leave Trevena to Caradoc, and Pretania to Loc... go tell Málik, yes! She would leave with him.

But she could not.

Her responsibility to Trevena and to Cornwall was as much a part of her being as the nose on her face. Come what may, she could not leave her people to suffer under Loc's rule.

Of course, he slept, oblivious to her thoughts, with Bryn and Lir between them.

Gwendolyn did not know where Esme had gone.

More oft than not, she stole away whilst they were preparing pallets, and for all Gwendolyn knew, she was spying for her father. But since Gwendolyn still couldn't prove it—not yet—it would be a grievous accusation to make. So she said nothing when Esme returned in the small hours.

Her thoughts still in turmoil, she turned again, facing Málik in the darkness, counting every thundering beat of her heart until sleep finally found her.

18

Morning broke with the light of an anemic sun. Gwendolyn woke, daring to hope the day would brighten and warm, but as the morning carried on, the skies turned ashen, like flesh turned gray and cold in death.

It continued to drizzle as well—a willful, freezing mist that persevered, gradually penetrating even through her leathers.

To make matters worse, for the past two bells, she'd had a feeling of foreboding—a tightness in her chest she couldn't escape. Something hung about this forest—a shadow that unsettled her so that gooseflesh erupted on her flesh. For a good league now, they had encountered no travelers—neither man nor beast.

No deer.
No foxes.
No coney.
No chirping birds.
Not. One. Creature.

When Gwendolyn's nose detected a trace of smoke, she turned to Málik, and mouthed the word, "Fire?"

He nodded once, drawing his sword, and Gwendolyn understood that to mean he didn't believe the fire was an accident.

Presently, they discovered the reason for the unnatural silence.

In the aftermath of whatever had transpired in this Ordovician village, the adjacent woods were bereft of life.

"*Gods*," Gwendolyn said, swallowing convulsively over the sight that greeted them as they entered the once-verdant glade, now decimated by flames. "Who could have done such a thing?"

No home was spared.

No soul reprieved—not one man, woman, child or beast.

Aisling whinnied in protest as she by-stepped over the still smoldering remnants of a luckless soul, his body prone and burnt to the bone. What flesh remained was being picked at by carrion, whose gluttony for carnage could not wait for the smoke to clear. Gwendolyn swung her blade and the large crow shuffled out of the way, squawking in protest. Peering back over her shoulder at the body, she saw no sign of weapons anywhere near his person... although, in truth, it could have been a woman. Simply to look at the corpse, it would be difficult to say. The hair, like the clothes, was burnt to crisps.

"Raiders," suggested Bryn, though he couldn't possibly know. The single word was more a question.

"Loc's men," announced Esme, with ill-concealed revulsion. "If I had known when they passed, this is what they were about, I'd have cut their throats myself."

Lir nodded, perhaps in agreement, perhaps only a nervous gesture. "I've never known the Deceangli to raid like this," he said, speaking of his nearest neighbors.

Gwendolyn agreed. This was not Deceangli, nor Silures.

Silures' lands had never grown beyond their original borders. For as long as she had lived, that tribe seemed content enough to live and let be. That they had allied with Loc had more to do with their proximity to him than any intent to rally to his cause. Moreover, the Silures' chieftain may have given his fealty to Brutus, but he'd more often appealed to her father for judicial intervention. Until Locrinus' betrayal, their kingdoms had shared constabulary duties. And neither was it unheard of for King Corineus to settle debts for disadvantaged farmers, even for those not of their province. As for the Deceangli, Lir would know their disposition, having lived around them for more years than any living soul could remember. He and his Druid brethren had occupied these woodlands for more than seven hundred years.

"I cannot believe men would perpetrate such a thing," offered Gwendolyn.

Indeed, she had known none to be so...

Violent.

Brutal.

Heartless.

Savage.

Studying the carnage, Málik said nothing. His wintry gray eyes perused the village, his gaze moving haltingly from hut to hut—or what remained of them —and perhaps beyond. Gwendolyn followed his gaze, hoping to find what he was searching for.

A tribal flag flew fitfully, like the final, desperate thrashings of a dying beast. The fire that had swept through this close-built village was guttered now, reduced to plumes of life-choking smoke. A young cock lay with wings spread, as though it ran, collapsing as it fled. Its torso lay crushed, trampled by hooves.

It startled Gwendolyn to find that they had slaughtered even the village goats, then burnt them—not one living creature spared.

Children. Dogs. Goats. Women. Men. Horses.

The stink of charred flesh was unbearable.

Mingled with the smell of the Rot—ever so slight here, but present—the combination was insufferable. And yet, the underlying dampness of this sodden ground had contained the flames, so it didn't reach the woodland perimeter. Whatever transpired here was less than one day past, not more than that. The dead were fresh and still without the telltale scent of decomposing flesh.

Not yet.

Clarity assailed her—sharp and immediate.

This was why she must fight.

This.

This was a brutal reminder of Loc's cruelty and judging by the way these people fell—as though running for their lives, some covering their faces as they stumbled to their deaths, it appeared as though Loc's men had ambushed them. Perchance by night as they'd slept? A judgment against this village. For what? These were Loc's own people—had he perhaps received some intelligence that they had softened toward Gwendolyn's cause? Or had Loc's soldiers acted alone, greedy for pillage? Had they ravaged this village for supplies—weapons or food?

It sickened Gwendolyn to note there were too many empty hands amidst the slain, although one woman died making a fist, as though the handle of some weapon had been pried from her fingers.

Gwendolyn felt a potent surge of nausea.

Whatever the case, she could not pass through this village without seeing to the care of these wretched souls. Against Esme's bitter complaints, she commanded everyone to dismount to see to a funeral. Except for Málik, whom she sent to investigate the surrounding woodlands, everyone expected to dirty their hands, including herself. By the end of the day, Gwendolyn herself had dragged more than twenty bodies into a pile at the center of the village, whispering apologies to deaf ears. There wasn't time to bury them, but though Esme also objected to a pyre, Gwendolyn couldn't bear to leave them as they were.

"This is a mistake," complained Esme. "The fire will lure them back," she warned, flinging one corpse after another, as though they were only piles of dirty laundry. By the eyes of Lugh, Esme's strength never ceased to amaze Gwendolyn.

Neither did her cold demeanor.

"There are children here," Gwendolyn said. "I'll not leave innocents to have their sweet faces plucked by vultures!"

The first thing she came across thereafter was the most heart-rending discovery of all—a young woman with a babe still cradled in her arms. Intending to carry her to the pyre, Gwendolyn flipped her over to discover that they had fallen together, and in her tumble, the babe lay crushed and smothered. Her throat constricted at once—and not because of the lingering smoke. Some heartless miscreant ran them both through with a blade—both mother and babe. The child's little body, covered by his mother, had been shielded from the flame, but not the sword. Between them, fresh blood pooled from a wound at his belly, and his dirty little face lay planted in the stinking muck.

Gods.

Gwendolyn couldn't bear it.

The poor child looked as though he might be sleeping. She gave a little keening cry, and for a moment, worried it could be the child. Lifting him into her arms, Gwendolyn left the mother where she lay, and carried him ever so gently to the pyre. Swallowing the salt of her tears, she laid him down in a place where he could rest, surrounded by his kin, and then made a place for his dear mother.

This, again, was why she must fight—for this child —for every poor soul who had no chance without her support.

Gwendolyn wept, and she didn't care who saw.

"Get over it," scolded Esme, as she laid down another body. "They are dead now. Whatever honor they should have been granted should have been offered whilst there was breath to be had. Now they are fodder for worms!"

Horrified by the truth in her words, as cold as they were, Gwendolyn spun to face Esme, her brows colliding, and for a moment, the two locked gazes.

"Fodder they might be," Gwendolyn allowed, once she found her voice. "But we will not leave this place until we've given every one of these people their due respect. If I have to carry each one to the pyre myself, I will do it!"

Esme sneered at her. "We've not traveled so far only for you to find yourself with a blade at your throat, *Banríon na bhfear.*"

Queen of men.

But this time, unlike the first time she'd said it, it was not spoken with respect or affection. Rather, this was Esme's way of reminding Gwendolyn of the obligation she faced... and no matter. She couldn't leave them.

What manner of queen would she be if she disrespected her people?

It didn't matter who they were.

"Leave if you must!" Gwendolyn said, furious. "I will not!"

Esme shook her head as she returned to the search for bodies.

Bryn said nothing, but Gwendolyn knew him well enough to know he would agree with her. His sense of decency ran too deep, and Gwendolyn had never known him to shy away from duty, no matter what disadvantage it gave them. Come what may, they would do as they must, and if Loc' soldiers—or whomever it was who had perpetrated this atrocity—returned whilst they were burying the dead, what better time for sword practice? Even now, Gwendolyn's blade thirsted for blood over this offense against her people —her people, not Loc's, because these were still her kin by blood. Give or take, all children of the Sons of Míl.

Unfortunately, if the raiders returned, she knew Lir would find himself tested, but he had insisted upon joining them and Gwendolyn could not consider his needs above the honor of these children.

Eventually, Málik returned, and it wasn't long before they had rounded up all the dead to prepare for the pyre. Gwendolyn couldn't help herself. She took their bloodied, burnt and mangled arms, folding them atop their breasts in order to see them into the After Life with some small vestige of dignity. Meanwhile, Bryn gathered wood and once they were ready, Lir spoke words and Málik lit a flame—a flame unlike the cool wisps Gwendolyn had witnessed before. He stood at one end of the pyre, and the firestorm came roaring from his mouth, golden-hued and consuming everything in its path. This was no wee flame like that one he'd nestled in the palm of his hand in her uncle's *fogous*. This was a raging torrent.

Blinking, Gwendolyn turned to give Esme a questioning glance, to which Esme replied with a knowing smile, "Dragon fire."

Stunned, Gwendolyn turned again to gaze into the pyre.

Every time she thought she knew Málik, he surprised her again. But... she didn't know how to feel about this discovery—only that, once again, she must face a terrible truth: If this was the power of the creature she loved, and he could not defeat the Fae king... how could she do so?

His dragon fire made quick work of the remnants, turning everything to dust. Not one cloth survived the blaze, and she thought back to the day he'd lectured her about the wet flint, wondering why he'd bothered if he could produce a flame like this... And yet... she must confess, there was nothing elegant about this flame. It was hotter than Hellas fire. Even from where Gwendolyn stood, twenty paces away, she could feel the intensity of the blaze.

"Let's go," Málik said once he was done. "The smoke will be visible for leagues."

Peering up, Gwendolyn watched as thick, black plumes eddied into a watery sky.

19

Gwendolyn's arms ached, and her heart hurt—
which one worse, was impossible to say. They
didn't go far before stopping for the evening. But
having gone as far as they physically could, Gwendolyn was certain no distance could take her far
enough from the savaged village. And judging by the
sullen expressions she faced when she dismounted,
she wasn't the only one unable to forget the day's
carnage.

They found a secluded spot near a small *bourne*,
and no one spoke a word as everyone, except Bryn,
went straight for the stream to wash.

Bryn stayed to dig a pit for their campfire.

One year ago, if someone had told Gwendolyn she
would spend the better part of an afternoon gathering
bodies for a pyre—thanks to the husband she'd
wedded but never bedded—she'd have judged
them mad.

Then again, one year ago, she was still a silly little
girl, incensed by everything her parents did and said,
looking for any cause to defy them, too naïve to realize
how difficult life could be.

Perhaps even to the day she and Bryn were swimming in Porth Pool. Wincing, she pulled at her shoulder to ease the ache. What she wouldn't give for a soak in those warm, healing waters!

The stench of death permeated even her clothes.

But far, far worse than any filth or physical discomfort, the memory of that poor child haunted her still—that dear, sweet babe and his mother.

"Monsters," she whispered.

Some might call Málik and Esme monsters, but despite Esme's foul temper, Gwendolyn knew she hid a mountain of sorrow for those villagers. She might never confess it, but Gwendolyn could see it in her eyes. Even now, as Esme stood, splashing water into her face, she did so with a ferocity of temper that betrayed her grief. And then suddenly, Esme froze, sensing Gwendolyn's regard. She turned and sent Gwendolyn a look of fierce imputation that forced her to look away.

It was not that Gwendolyn felt guilty for having forced her company to deal with the dead—she did not. But she suspected Esme was struggling with something, and Gwendolyn wanted to give her as much privacy to deal with it as was possible.

In the meantime, she had her own aching body and mind to tend to.

Ash blackened her hands and charred flesh wedged beneath her nails. She would gladly strip bare, but for the lowering temperature. And neither had she a proper change of attire. As disgusted as she was with her state of disrepair, worrying about it was pointless. That little brown mud-stain she'd acquired near Porth Pool was the least of her defilement. Sadly, she would have to wait until they arrived at the Druid village for a simple change of clothing. Neither could she afford to sleep in wet attire, so she washed as best she could, and resigned herself to live with the rest.

Tired and ready for bed, she returned to camp in time to watch Málik retrieve the flint from his saddle-bag. Without a word, he kindled a fire in the pit Bryn dug, before departing to hunt for supper. That was perhaps a moot effort, Gwendolyn thought. Who could eat after the atrocities they'd witnessed?

As though to illustrate the truth of that, Bryn sank to his arse beside the firepit without bothering to wash, and then sat, staring into the rising flames, his expression haunted.

"I'll go tend the horses," offered Esme, returning from the *bourne*.

Lir rushed to help her and Gwendolyn hoped the gesture would prove a balm for Esme's mood, but that was not to be.

"I don't need help!" she snapped when he tried to hobble her mare. "Enbarr's mares do not wander," she apprised, and then hitched her chin at Bryn's distressed mare. "Hobble that one if you feel the need to pretend you're of use," she said, then casting Gwendolyn a withering glance, she added, "Better yet, take the horse and go home!"

Not that he was ever compelled to do so, but Lir didn't argue. The sweet Druid abandoned the Faerie mounts, moving at once to the only horse in their company born of mortal stock. *Poor Lir,* Gwendolyn thought. There was nothing about Esme's treatment of him that felt the least bit tender. If, as Bryn seemed to believe, she held some measure of affection for him, it wasn't clear by her demeanor. More than aught, Esme seemed affronted by his very presence.

Too tired to intervene, Gwendolyn sighed, and she,

too, sank to her bottom by the campfire next to Bryn, placing a hand atop his shoulder.

As it once used to be, they did not need words between them. Gwendolyn gave him a nod of appreciation, grateful beyond measure to have him by her side.

ALTOGETHER, they gathered about the campfire, partaking of Málik's contribution in silence—forest grouse. And regardless that Gwendolyn hadn't believed she could find her appetite, she did.

After a solid week with only foraged berries, wafers, and nuts, she welcomed a warm meal. As well stocked as they had been for the journey, they had depleted their stores, except for a few wafers and lengths of salted meat.

Simply for the matter of expediency, they'd not lingered long enough at any given camp to hunt, much less cook. Tonight, this grouse was like manna from the gods and Gwendolyn hadn't realized how famished she was until she tore the first bite. Thereafter, she swallowed her meal so rapaciously that she later found herself embarrassed by her lack of decorum. Gods knew the sight of her would have horrified her well-mannered mother. But Gwendolyn was a long way from home, and a long, long way from the conventions of her father's court.

Most significantly, her mother was dead. Queen Eseld need never again worry about Gwendolyn's prospects.

"You missed some," apprised Bryn, reaching over and plucking something from Gwendolyn's dirty mop of hair.

Gwendolyn laughed, horrified, to find that he held up a bit of greasy meat. And yet, much to her dismay, she was also quite relieved to discover it was grouse and not refuse from the village. He offered it to her with a weary smile.

"No, thank you," Gwendolyn said. "I am quite satisfied. Do enjoy."

It was Bryn's turn to laugh. "You never were one for proper graces," he said warmly, and Gwendolyn had no argument for that. It was true, perhaps, though neither had she ever been so befouled. What she should do right now is lift her bottom and go back to the stream, drag Bryn along with her. He smelled, too. But, as weary as she was, she was looking forward to a good night's rest, and she didn't care how unkempt she was. She hadn't any idea how many people she'd carried to the pyre. She'd stopped counting at thirteen— and more than a few had had houses atop them, so removing the debris had been an effort all on its own. For once, when she closed her eyes tonight, there should be no rumination to keep her awake. Even now, her eyes were threatening to close, and her arms and legs felt as quivery as meat pudding. She was so tired, in fact, that she hadn't even bothered to deposit Kingslayer into her saddle sheath, and it lay by her side.

Málik and Esme might feel comfortable wearing their swords in the most awkward positions, even whilst riding, but Gwendolyn had yet to accustom herself to sitting with the point of a sharp blade nestled in the cleave of her bottom.

Fortunately, one glance up through the treetops revealed a night sky peppered with twinkling stars. The skies were clear; the rain was gone, and the woods were quiet as a broom handle. Once she closed her eyes, she was fairly certain that not even a deluge would wake her again.

"Do you think those were Loc's men?" Gwendolyn asked no one in particular. She hadn't any need to say of whom or what she spoke.

She was certain the culprits were those men whose song had so affronted her; they were the only soldiers they'd encountered in these woods who seemed capable of such a crime. And they were coming from this direction. In retrospect, Gwendolyn remembered them being as filthy as she was tonight. And she wondered if those mongrels had pilfered their mead from the hardworking men of that village.

Seemingly so.

"Difficult to say," said Bryn. "The cruelty is reminiscent of Loc."

He should know. He'd spent enough time in Loc's barracks to know what type of soldiers the man was raising.

Gwendolyn considered the cruel way they'd fought at Loc's behest. And, in her mind's eye, she could still see them from the crack in her window, and no doubt Loc had declined to fix the window because he knew Gwendolyn would be watching. Bare chested, they'd practiced with fine-steel, without armor, painting the dirt red with their blood. Once or twice, the injuries had been fatal. And more than twice, Gwendolyn had feared Bryn would be among the casualties.

But, of course, Gwendolyn knew Loc was cruel.

Hadn't he been cruel to her as well?

So was Estrildis, with her lover's blessing. Those two deserved one another. But right now, Gwendolyn was too weary even for the thought of vengeance.

Already, so much blood had been shed.

So much death...

Slow to finish his meal, Lir tore a bite from his own

portion of meat. "Unless Loc has the power to turn a heart black, I do not believe any of our neighbors would treat one another with such disdain—and believe me, I have seen my share of war."

"Have you now?" taunted Esme, with a contorted grin. "Amidst all your seven hundred and two years?"

Lir sat, unfazed. "Three now—my birthday came and went a fortnight past."

"Oh, nay!" Gwendolyn exclaimed. "Why did you not speak of it?"

Lir shrugged. "We were preparing to leave; it did not seem of import."

"Of course it was, brother!" Bryn argued. He winked. "Perhaps for you, having weathered so many, it might not seem so remarkable an accomplishment, but every year survived is a triumph to be celebrated!" He reached out to clap a hand on Lir's back. "I'll tell you what; first chance we get, you and I must share a pint. Then we shall see if your seven hundred and three years have taught you how to endure your mead better than me."

Gwendolyn laughed, enjoying their light-hearted banter—such a boon after a harrowing day. "Do you remember that time you and I got into Yestin's store of mead, prepared for the Carthagian emissary?"

Bryn grinned, ripping off another bite of meat and talking through the chew. "Do I ever? That was your first time pissed, and we tried to hide it from Demelza —remember? —by securing you into your bedchamber and telling her you were ill. But she knew."

Gwendolyn laughed, the sound as drained as she was. "Of course, you fool, she smelled it on you. But, regardless, no one could never pull the wool over that one's eyes."

"Ah, yes! The maid, Demelza, because she was so

utterly brilliant," suggested Esme, and finally, Gwendolyn turned to look at her, tilting her head in question. "What ails you, Esme? Why are you so full of enmity? Have I done aught to anger you?"

"Nay, of course not!" Esme said. "Art perfect, Gwendolyn!"

Gwendolyn stood. "I am not, but neither are you, no matter that you seem to believe it." They were behaving like sisters, though Gwendolyn didn't like it one bit. Why couldn't it be a sisterly affection? She was on the verge of asking where the nice Elf had gone, because she missed her fiercely, but Esme stood suddenly, shoving Gwendolyn back onto her bum with such force that it brought a cry of pain and a sting of tears to her eyes.

"Hey!" Gwendolyn exclaimed, but before she could rise again, an arrow came flying through camp, embedding itself into the tree behind where Gwendolyn had stood. Another whizzed toward her as Gwendolyn leapt to her feet. Málik caught it midair before it found Gwendolyn's eye.

"We have company," he said, as a chorus of steel rang against the night.

20

Chysauster again!

Armed men exploded into their camp.

Rushing from the woods, a few on horseback, some afoot, Gwendolyn recognized the one with the lime-washed hair, and the other whose song had enraged her. But all thought of vengeance flew from her head as another warrior advanced upon Bryn. Panic seized her heart.

Moving to defend Lir, Esme beheaded one assailant, sending his head rolling toward Gwendolyn. Without missing a beat, Gwendolyn booted it away, sweeping up Kingslayer, and then flew to Bryn's defense, placing herself betwixt Bryn and his attacker—Loc's soldiers, each wearing Loc's golden serpent!

A scant moment ago, Gwendolyn couldn't lift her arm for the day's efforts, but she refused to be defeated by her own exhaustion.

Raising the pommel, she swung, missing—knowing she would. Her intent was only to stop this miscreant's advance. If she must die today—here and now—she would die fighting. But whatever it cost her, Bryn would not be the first to fall.

But too many had set upon them, even if already

Málik and Esme had felled four between them. Dancing about Gwendolyn like a blur of glinting steel, both *Elves* struck and withdrew, struck and withdrew, struck and withdrew, each time leaving broken, twisted forms in their wake. They would have been a marvel to watch if only Gwendolyn had the leisure to do it. She did not.

She danced about her quarry, giving Bryn a chance to find his sword.

They were unprepared for this—so stupid! So stupid! They had been too arrogant, too unaware—nursing their wounds like old men!

Merely because those idiot soldiers did not spy them hidden in the thicket did not mean they would not find evidence of their presence. Esme had warned them of the smoke, and knowing in her heart she could do nothing differently, Gwendolyn had ignored the warning. Only now, in the heat of battle, with so much at stake—the direst possibilities flashed behind her eyes, none good—she must confess it may have been a mistake. If her mission should end here—if she died, should Bryn fall, or if Málik or Esme should perish, even Lir...

Gwendolyn's feet worked by rote as she advanced upon one soldier, moving with purpose, remembering her lessons, gaining her bearings so that, when she swung again, she swung with confidence, missing only by a fraction.

Ducking to miss the swing of an axe leveled at her head, she sprang to her feet yet again, leaning into her strike, putting her might into the blow, ripping the blade across the golden serpent on the man's breast.

The man howled in pain, his face twisting with surprise and anger.

"Dragon queen!" he spat. "I knew I smelt Cornish offal!"

Gwendolyn refused to trade insults with this fool. There was no satisfaction to be had by it. She would rejoice once he was dead.

"You will die today!" he said, and his smile was cruel as he advanced upon her once more. But nay, she would not! She had not practiced daily over these past six months, sweating every loss, only to fall prey to this mangy dog.

Nor was she the weakling girl she used to be; her arms were strong, and her will itself made of Loegrian steel. Thanks to Málik, she understood every aspect of swordplay, knew intuitively how to fight her enemies, big and small. Day after day, Gwendolyn had proven that, besting every opponent she faced, except Málik, and even Málik when she did everything right.

Ignoring the man's taunts, she forced all thought from her head. Málik had taught her the first to anger would be the first to fall.

She did not intend to fall.

She parried each time the man swung, pushing him back, back, back—away from Bryn. Nimbler than he was, carrying less weight, Gwendolyn danced about his sword, her lips turning with grim satisfaction as his arms tired and his smile faded. And still she did not taunt him; he wasn't worth the loss.

Another of Loc's soldiers—the one with the lime-washed hair—advanced upon her now as well. Gwendolyn's eyes moved behind him to Lir, who had only just now recovered his sword. Once again, her heart tripped as she watched another of Loc's soldiers go after him, preparing to stab him in the back. She couldn't make it in time. She had two warriors to dispense with first.

Glancing at Bryn, she commanded him with her eyes to shield Lir. Bryn's intervention came just in time. Even as the soldier made to plunge his blade into Lir's back, Bryn struck his blow, sending the warrior to his knees.

Meanwhile, Gwendolyn circled the campfire with both her warriors, striking blows at her, one after another—both advancing from the same direction, too stupid to press her between them.

Miss. Duck. Miss again. Duck. Again.

Saving her strikes for when she knew it would matter, Gwendolyn kicked at the fire with her boot, sending glowing embers at one man's loosely clad shins. The burning coals sizzled through his breeches, scalding his flesh. Still, he smiled.

"You will swallow my blade!" he said, skirting the fire to her left.

The idiot took one hand off his sword long enough to cup his bollocks, and Gwendolyn used this moment to her advantage, pouncing at him and thrusting her weapon straight through his eye. Dropping his sword, the fool stumbled to his knees, but even as Gwendolyn booted him away, retrieving her sword, the second warrior came stabbing at her, laughing maniacally. Skirting his blade, moving aside, and placing the pit between them, Gwendolyn readied her blade, raising her pommel.

"Bitch!" he shouted.

Swing. Miss. Parry. Swing again.

Circling the pit, Gwendolyn waited, watching for the right opportunity, understanding the limitations of her sword.

She could reach him across the flames, but to wield a sword of this length, she must be able to step into her blow. Kingslayer weighed less than Málik's bastard sword, a bit more than her arming sword, but it needed the support of her entire body, or the sword would miss its mark.

In the space of a breath, Málik was by her side.

"Aim high," he commanded, though Gwendolyn never saw his mouth move. The words flowed through her like a whisper in the wind.

Meanwhile, Loc's man continued to advance upon her.

Gwendolyn lifted the pommel higher, preparing to strike, knowing its weight would drag the sword tip down the instant she extended to strike.

"Elf lover!" said the man, but though Gwendolyn was not Málik's lover, she wished she were. His taunt was no insult. If she were, she would be the first to say so.

"You're better than him," Málik assured, his words nourishing her like sustenance. *Take him down. You can do it.*

Indeed, she could.

Gwendolyn knew Málik spoke true. Still, his reassurance gave her daring. Intending to disarm the man, she did what they expected no gentle woman to do. *She stepped into the burning coals.* Resisting her fear, she leaned her body into the blow and the look that entered the man's widening eyes as her sword found him was one of bewilderment. He could not move quickly enough to escape his fate. Gwendolyn sliced her blade across his throat, beheading him as expeditiously as Esme had her prey. Then, she pulled his body over the firepit, dropping him belly first into the coals, withdrawing her sword.

Málik grinned, eyes glinting with pride.

And then he was off again, arms and blades swinging, legs dancing so nimbly that even Gwendolyn's practiced eyes could not follow his movements, even after months of sparring with him.

One by one, their attackers fell.

Joining the fray, Lir thrust his blade through one man's back, then hid behind a tree, punching his blade through the back of another man's neck as Esme did battle. The warrior gagged, surging forth with the agony of Lir's knife, impaling himself on the end of Esme's sword. "I told you, stupid Druid! I don't need your help!" insisted Esme ungratefully. "Go hide beneath a rock!"

Lir turned and ran as yet another soldier advanced upon him, and Esme moved between them to dispatch the fool. "Thank you," said Lir, as Bryn felled another. And Málik yet another.

"Don't thank me, you pretentious fool," said Esme, as she moved away.

Working together, they proved to be an effective team, although Gwendolyn hadn't time to be impressed. She swung, and parried till her arms felt as though they would fall off, and soon enough, they had dispensed all but one... and that man Esme dragged into their camp by his hair, shoving him down onto the ground before the firepit, kicking his mate's body from the coals, then putting her sword tip into the much-revived flames. Freshly fed by the fallen man's attire, the fire licked higher, burning brighter, greedy for more kindling.

Bloodied and battered, the soldier's eyes grew wide as Esme leered at him, revealing the full effect of her porbeagle teeth. And even as her sword began to glow, Gwendolyn spied piddle flowing from beneath the man's rear.

"Who sent you?" Esme demanded.

Wiping her blade on her leathers, Gwendolyn approached, and then one after another, so did the rest of her companions, moving into a circle to hear the man's confession. Afraid though he must have been, he spat on Esme's boots.

Esme did not instantly respond. She kept her gaze trained upon him, her sword in the flames as it flared. "How did you know we would travel here?" Esme demanded. The man said nothing, and she turned her blade, never taking her eyes from his face. "Were you searching for us?" she persisted.

Still, the man did not respond.

"How many returned to Loc?"

Gwendolyn furrowed her brow, wondering how Esme could know.

"Vermin!" the man spat. "I do not answer to Elvin fiends!"

"Nay?" said Esme, her lips curving cruelly as she took a step forward. "I would send you away whole with a message for your gutless master, if you but answer one question." She tilted her head at the man. "Wouldn't that be better than dying?"

The man spat again, this time at Gwendolyn, and Esme drew her sword from the flames and moved upon him so swiftly there wasn't time to blink.

"Wait!" Gwendolyn demanded. "You cannot—"

"Slaughter innocents?" Esme asked, stopping, turning to face Gwendolyn, with a note of challenge in her voice and a gleam in her eyes.

Gwendolyn reasoned with her. "I would not suggest he is innocent, but you cannot murder this man. He hasn't a weapon!"

"Not anymore," Esme argued, tilting her head to peer over her shoulder. "I shoved it in *that one's* arse."

Behind her lay a man with an axe in his buttocks. The sight of it made Gwendolyn grimace, but such was the savagery of war. And regardless, it gave her no satisfaction beyond the fact that they had survived this attack.

"Is it not against your laws to slay an unarmed man?"

"Who told you that?" Esme asked, casting an amused glance at Málik, and then added, "You should know *his* laws do not apply to me." And then she raised her glowing sword above the man's head, and before anyone could stop her, she thrust it down, skewering him through the pate of the head. The light left his eyes at once, and Esme put her boot against his face, pushing him away to retrieve her sword.

"Why would you do such a thing?" Gwendolyn asked, appalled. "He could have told us more."

"He would not have," Esme countered. "I am well enough versed with the hubris of men to recognize truth when I hear it." And then she turned, swiping the blood from her sword with her bare hands, leaving Gwendolyn to stare after her.

21

T hey arrived at the Druid village at the break of day on the twenty-fifth day of the sixth moon of the year.

There was no need to pull the bell in the grotto. As though expected, a welcome party descended to escort Gwendolyn and her party into the village. Bright-eyed, with some nameless emotion in the ferocity of her gaze, Esme cast Gwendolyn a parting glance, then rushed ahead, ascending into the village without invitation.

No one stopped her. But then, who would dare?

Gwendolyn hadn't spoken to the quarrelsome Elf for days. She didn't understand what changed, or when, but by now Gwendolyn had had enough of her ready ire. Every time she thought about the cold-hearted manner of her dispatching of Loc's man, it soured her belly. Gwendolyn liked to believe herself a hardened warrior, but after witnessing such a brutal execution, she knew it mustn't be true, and she was glad of it. While it might be true that she wasn't the same girl she once was, neither did she wish to become such a heartless monster for whom a man's life could so easily be dispensed. To be sure, Gwendolyn had oft imagined herself cutting Loc's throat—and given the chance, she would do it without hesitation —but *that* was different. Loc stole her life. He'd murdered her family, stole her dignity, and then cast her away as though she were nothing more than offal. But that man wearing Loc's livery was her enemy in name only. Perhaps given the opportunity to end her life, he might try, but like so many others, he had been misled, and if Gwendolyn slaughtered every man, woman or child who followed Loc, she would massacre thousands—too many—for no other reason than because they dared to raise a golden serpent as their standard.

"I know you do not wish to hear this," Málik had said, when Gwendolyn pulled him aside to discuss the matter privately. "There wasn't more to be done. We couldn't have brought him with us. What else could Esme have done?"

"You're defending her?"

It vexed her even if he spoke true. "We could have released him," Gwendolyn persisted. "They could not have located this Druid village without us, and there is no way that fool would have dared pursue us without his companions. I must presume he would have returned to Loc."

"And that would have been good?" Málik asked.

Gwendolyn frowned. "At least he would know—"

"What, Gwendolyn? The direction we were traveling? To what end? The Druid village is not impossible to locate, merely difficult. The last thing we—or they —need is for Loc to send his armies north to search for you. Better one man should die than to risk your mission."

Gwendolyn huffed with frustration. "Perhaps," she relented, though none of it suited her. Nor could she bear it that Málik would argue in Esme's favor, nor how he could watch that execution so impassively.

No one ever told that man where they were going. He'd had no cause to follow them without his cronies to support him. It would have been a suicide mission and Gwendolyn didn't believe he would dare. She might be young yet, but she was no longer naïve. She might lack experience, but she'd watched her father rule long enough to understand that there was more to governing a kingdom than to rule by might. If her father had failed at his conservatorship, it wasn't because he didn't care about his people, nor was he a stranger to mercy.

Gwendolyn longed to be better than Loc—better than her father, as well.

Executing unarmed men, regardless of what they said, was not the way to do it. If that man was guilty of murder, they should have taken pains to prove it. All they had proof of was the attack on Gwendolyn and her party, not the village itself.

The fate of this kingdom lay in Gwendolyn's hands, and she would not fail her people, nor would she shed blood without justice. Fear had a purpose, but she would not become the thing she opposed, nor would she settle for being queen only because her people feared her. Her people mattered most of all, and she was determined to earn their trust, or step aside and allow them to choose a new leader as the First Men once chose her forebear. If they gave her the chance to prove herself a worthy champion, those men might have changed their minds. But they could not win dead men to anybody's cause.

This quest was not over, and they had many moons to go before she returned from the Fae realm. In the meantime, how many men would Loc win to his side? Should everyone now die because they'd dared to raise the wrong flag?

No. The answer was no.

As they ascended into the village, with Esme so far in the lead, they could no longer spy her, Gwendolyn dared to broach the subject with Málik once more. "You must know what is bothering her."

He lifted a brow. "Must I?"

Gwendolyn frowned. "I know you do, Málik. Why will you not answer me without riddles or questions?"

He cast her a sharp-eyed glance, his irises the soft gray of a summer cloud, with the barest hint of blue sky. He sighed. "All I have leave to say is that they have tasked her with something she does not wish to do."

"They? Who?" Gwendolyn pressed. "What task?"

He shook his head. "This I cannot say."

Of course, he could not!

Why should this answer be any different from the hundreds of responses to the hundreds of questions asked before?

"If she does not wish to do it, why do it?"

"She hasn't a choice," he said gently, perhaps to deflect Gwendolyn's ire, but, once again, this was the end of their discourse.

He turned away as they entered the Druid village and found Esme huddled with one of the Druid brothers, speaking in whispers. And, seeing Lir, the man extricated himself from their conversation and approached Lir. "I have dreadful news," he said. "It is Máistir Emrys."

"My brother?"

The Druid nodded. "He has... he... is... unwell," the man finished, casting Gwendolyn a wary glance, even as Esme's burning gaze met Gwendolyn's.

Before Gwendolyn could say a word, Esme spun

on her heel and marched away, disappearing into the mist. His Druid brother nodded toward the place she passed, and Lir followed at once.

A frisson of fear rushed down Gwendolyn's spine and she grasped the Druid's arm before he could leave. "What is it? What's happened?"

"Go," said the Druid heavily. "See for yourself."

Gwendolyn bolted after Esme and Lir.

22

Máistir Emrys lay insensate.

He had been this way for days. No one
could say whether it might be because of his advancing age, or whether it could be something...
more... *deliberate*.

A few days ago, he had descended into the grotto
for a counsel with some nameless emissary from a
nameless tribe. He'd arranged it; no one was aware of
any request made by any presiding chieftain. He'd told
them what he was doing and descended alone. At sun-
down, when he did not return, his Druid brothers
went searching and found him resting on the floor beside the pool in the grotto. There was no sign of any
disturbance. No emissary to be found. No evidence
anyone came or went. The *Máistir* lay upon his back,
his shoes off and arms crossed over his chest, as
though simply napping. But every attempt to wake
him had proven futile, and he had yet to open his eyes.
Then, yesterday morning, someone discovered a
small, but unusual wound at the back of his left ear,
where a bruise about the injury had spread.

"Poison," declared one of his brothers, and regardless that no one else agreed, there was no one who

could refute it. But if this were poison, it was unlike any poison Gwendolyn had ever encountered. She was quite well versed in every manner of toxin, considering the fact that, for years, she had ingested a special *theriac* to raise her tolerance against the most heinous.

After hearing the tale of an entire household who fell prey to poison-laced mead served from ewers that were made from the bark of yew trees, her father thereafter insisted that the entire royal household should guard against such treason. Even the servants partook, although everyone's formula was different. For Demelza, the potion was weaker, and this was because she had to sample *theriacs* for both Gwendolyn and her mother, and the physicians feared too much would hasten her demise. For Gwendolyn, it was stronger, comprising many of the most common poisons employed for assassination—insect, plant and reptile venoms, as well as arsenic, and more. Containing forty in all, the formula was painstakingly prepared, the process meticulously regulated by their royal physician. Meanwhile, the king's *theriac* included sixty known toxins, and because of the number of toxins contained therein, the potency of his *theriac* was greater. However, he had insisted upon this, even against the physician's recommendation, and Gwendolyn had sometimes worried that this had contributed to the decline of his health.

Until a few weeks before the journey to Chysauster, she had carried a small vial filled with a powerful antidote. Unfortunately, that antidote was only good for a short while, and after Alderman Bryok's death, when it was determined there was a breach in their security, no more *theriacs* or antidotes were made thereafter. And regardless, Gwendolyn's life had been so full of madness since her return from Chysauster that refilling her vial was the last thing on her mind, despite that she could produce the *theriac* herself if she were so inclined. Not only had she been present for much of the brewing, she was also required to study the properties of most of the toxins she and her family consumed. Ultimately, this was how she had known poison was the culprit when Owen fell from his horse after eating Aelwin's prune. She had recognized the symptoms and knew how to read the body.

When she examined *Máistir* Emrys, she found nothing to prove there had been an attempt upon his life. The slight wound behind the *Máistir's* ear could easily be attributed to other causes, including the filigrees from his ear sheaths, which, it also happened, he was still wearing when Gwendolyn examined him. Removing both, she took care not to damage either as she scrutinized them. Fashioned ever-so delicately, she had never seen such spectacular artistry. It was as though they were woven like silk thread, but there was no method known to her people that would allow for such an intricate weave of something so rigid as metal —and these were, doubtless, some type of alloy. The entire appliance was made of a single piece, with two points at each end of the manipulated metal. The point at his left ear was exposed, so that it could have caused the *Máistir's* wound when he fell... particularly if he fell in such a way that it smashed the sheath against his head. The bruising could thusly be explained and since, at the moment, the *Máistir* was breathing easily, Gwendolyn couldn't agree with his Druid brother's verdict of poison. Still, she considered it.

There were, in fact, a multitude of poisons that

could cause this type of torpor—henbane or yew, were two. However, were henbane or yew poison responsible for his condition, the *Máistir* would be dead by now. If, for example, yew poison had entered his system, he would have hours, not days. And, in fact, the yew poison was so toxic that her father's armies had often infused the toxin into their missiles. And, obviously, yew wood was so deadly that those ewers her father spoke of would have had to be burned outdoors, with the fire-tenders wearing cloth masks to protect them from the fumes. Therefore, she must conclude this was not henbane or yew.

She lifted his hand, finding it stiff—the fingers unyielding.

Much to her chagrin, that wasn't the only thing that was stiff. Averting her eyes from the bed, Gwendolyn made it a point to ask if anyone had discovered any evidence of spew anywhere near the vicinity of the pool, where he was located. So many of the poisons she was familiar with would cause some manner of regurgitation or foaming at the mouth, even when injected.

According to their palace physician, whenever the heart and lungs could not function because of certain types of poisons, it caused fluids to gather in the lungs and manifest like foam in the mouth.

Also, while many common poisons worked rapidly, affecting the muscles and the lungs and heart, and could well lead to such torpor, they often caused excitation and delirium—which was to say that even if the body appeared to be restive, the heart was a teller of tales. The *Máistir's* heartbeat remained slow and steady, with no worrisome symptoms.

Laying the ear sheath down on the bedside table in plain view, Gwendolyn considered other poisons as she examined the *Máistir's* arms, his nail-beds, and hands. Even thorn apple, which was a milder poison, and had the added benefit of giving the recipient amnesia should he survive, would manifest itself with some manner of flushing about the skin.

Of all the poisons Gwendolyn knew of, there were two that caused extreme sedation rather than excitation and delirium—a rare poison called Hul Gil that was imported from Mesopotamia, and... mandrake.

The Hul Gil, so she'd been told, could slow the heart to such a degree that one might mistake the living for the dead.

But neither of these poisons would explain the bruised flesh about the Máistir's neck. That was a mystery to Gwendolyn, as much as was a lack of a motive. As far as she knew, *Máistir* Emrys had been the order's beloved leader for more than seven hundred years, and that was a long time to lead for there to suddenly be an issue with his authority. But, even if there were some undisclosed issue, Gwendolyn must presume there was another way to remove a *Máistir* from his role without resorting to murder. Indeed, even now, two of the elder Druids stood outside the *Máistir's* chamber, discussing the necessity of electing a new *Máistir*, regardless of whether Emrys recovered. But this discussion had nothing to do with any discord they had with the *Máistir* himself. Rather, they feared for his life, arguing that his age had become a complication. They believed his only chance to live long and prosper was to keep him from leaving this village. Naturally, they valued his knowledge and posited that he, alone, knew the intricacies of each of the neighboring tribes. Now, when war was so close at hand, it was imperative to keep his counsel. Meanwhile, they argued it was past time for him to retire before it was too late. Next time, his visit to the grotto could prove his last. While here in this place, no illness or age existed, beyond its borders no man could save anyone from his destiny—be they king or queen. To live was to die, and to die was a human condition.

Lir had nothing to add to their deliberations, perhaps knowing how much it meant to his brother to lead this order. After so long, who would Emrys be if not the *Máistir*? But Gwendolyn also knew he didn't wish to lose his brother. Looking more troubled than she had ever seen him, he sat beside h*is brother's* cot, suppressing tears, begging Emrys to wake and promising not to leave again if only he would open his eyes.

Gwendolyn's heart swelled with pity for him. The normally sober, stoic, even-tempered Druid maintained his frown, and every now and again, reached out to test the back of one hand against Emrys' forehead. "Still, no fever," he would say.

"That is a very good sign," Gwendolyn reassured, because it was true.

Fever would be a definite sign that there was a battle being waged by the *Máistir's* body. But he was neither too hot, nor too cold—another reason Gwendolyn didn't believe this was poison.

"Has anyone kept a record of his time beyond this village?" she asked. "How many years has he accumulated below?"

Lir shrugged as he considered the question. "Who can say? There is no reliable means to measure the passing of time." He shook his head then, refuting himself. "None beyond the shadow clock we keep in the grotto. But those are useless here. The sun does not shine as it does there. And regardless, my brother will not have kept track of his time below. Nothing like this has ever happened before."

Gwendolyn wondered how they could ignore the fact that every Druid who ever left this village showed signs of aging. Although she had no way of knowing how old these men were when they arrived here, it was easy to ascertain who descended regularly and who never did. Lir was one of the latter, scarcely aged a day over these past centuries, his skin smoother than hers.

"We have used candle clocks to some success," she suggested. "Though I have only seen a few in all my years. They are expensive and quite rare." The science was not so simple as marking a burning candle. The wax must be of a specific variety that burned strictly over a measure of time, and the formula for those clocks were never shared. Rather, sometimes merchants brought a few to sell—but again, rare. So strange that only a few days ago she had wondered over this very dilemma—the quandary of aging in this Druid village.

She passed a glance to Málik. "He might not like to hear it, but it might be a good time for the *Máistir* to retire," she suggested.

"If he recovers," interjected Lir.

"If he recovers," Gwendolyn allowed. "Let someone else lead for a change. His knowledge and experience will make his guidance invaluable. Yet he need not be the one to expose himself to the ravages of time."

She averted her gaze from the bed to the door, wishing her royal physician had lived through their coup. He would have known more than she. But sadly, even he was lost. For now, she had only her studies to guide her.

Outside, night was lowering, but as Lir had pointed out only moments ago, she could neither see moon nor stars, much less the sky. Even having visited this village before, the make of it still awed her, though it was as illogical to try to tell night from day in this place as it was to perceive the construction of the walls confining this room. Made of the strangest of substances, and shimmering in shades of green, they were not transparent, but neither were they solid— like some strange, tightly woven tarp made of silk spun from a spider's spinnerets. Remembering the story Esme told of the ill-fated weaver Arachne, she wondered if she'd had a part in its creation. There was a certain property about the walls that reminded Gwendolyn of her black *mithril*...

Noticing that the Druid elders were gone now, she crooked a finger at Málik, drawing him aside to ask, "Do you believe this could be poison?"

Málik crossed his arms and shook his head. "Impossible to say. But, Gwendolyn, I am unfamiliar with the poisons of your realm. Those in mine could easily affect a man aversely, and favored though he might be, he is still a man—mortal, as you. For too many years, he has descended into that grotto. There's no telling whether he descended once too oft. Your human form is not meant to endure."

"And yours?" Gwendolyn dared ask. "Lir claims you, too, can die?"

He nodded in a manner that led Gwendolyn to believe the prospect did not concern him. "I could," he agreed. "But do not worry, *Banríon*." He offered her a winsome smile, one without teeth. "To manage such a feat, I would have to be stupid, or—"

A sudden shadow fell across the door, but by the

time Gwendolyn turned to see who it might be, the figure was gone.

Málik left her to peer outside, frowning as he turned to meet Gwendolyn's gaze. "Stupid," he said once more. "Or... betrayed..." And there was a certain something in his tone that gave Gwendolyn pause.

Esme... was the first thought that entered her head.

23

I n Emrys' stead, one of the elder Druids had taken
up the *Máistir's* staff, and now sat in Emrys' chair
at the head of the *Máistir's* table in the Hall of Feasts.
Having requested an audience, Gwendolyn was told it
would be most propitious to conduct their meeting at
the dinner hour. So, at present, the knives were in the
meat, and the drinks in the horns. Gwendolyn had
never witnessed a Druid table so replete.

All the while the *Máistir's* fate remained uncertain,
these men were feasting, and if she didn't know better,
it would appear to be a celebration. And yet, despite
this, Gwendolyn could not imagine any Druid taking
glee in the *Máistir's* death, nor planning for it besides
—not even this sober-faced prelate seated across
from her.

He took his time, pulling a slice of bloody meat
from his poniard, and waited to speak until he had
thoroughly masticated the bite, then, using his greasy
hands, he tucked his long black hair behind his ears.

"Nay," he said at last, and with such finality that a
less determined soul mightn't dare ask again. "I'm
afraid granting you passage is *not* possible."

Gwendolyn couldn't accept that answer. His village

did not fall within her dominion, but there was too much at stake to let his decision stand. If she could but convince the Fae king to give back her sword, the rest would come easier.

But it all began with *Claímh Solais*.

Her sword.

The one Málik took from her.

The one her father denied her.

Gwendolyn made a fist beneath the table, squeezing.

If only Málik had not taken it away—she glanced at him now with some measure of annoyance—she mightn't be forced to press the issue with these Druids. For once, there was regret in the turn of his gaze. But that wasn't enough to appease Gwendolyn at the moment.

Truth be told, she didn't wish to be angry with Málik, but this *was* in great part his fault. After everything they had endured together in Chysauster, even if her father hadn't believed in her, Málik should have.

Or, if he'd had any doubts over Gwendolyn's ability to keep the sword safe, he should have taken it and hidden it somewhere of his choosing—some place they could retrieve without defying the Lifer Pol Order. Instead, that day in her father's vault, he'd left without a word, taking her sword without allowing her the chance to try it. And he, more than anyone, should have known it would come to this... the possibility of war betwixt two realms that could otherwise have stood together against the scourge that was Loc.

Then again, she vacillated. If that sword hadn't been scuttled away, perhaps it, too, might now be in Loc's hands, and she understood that regardless of whether the sword would burn for Loc, it would remain a powerful symbol of sovereignty. Simply having it in his possession would create allies of foes—but why, oh, why, did Málik present it to the one creature whose distrust of *mankind* could cost Pretania its future?

But the most pressing question right now was: Who was this greasy fool who held the *Máistir's* staff?

Gwendolyn found she didn't like him. He was stubborn and self-important, and perhaps he believed he was considering the Druids' best interest, but he was working at cross purposes.

Considering her words, Gwendolyn unclenched her palm and flattened it atop the table, calling upon all her patience and strength.

The child in her longed to rise up and command he acquiesce, though she was no longer that spoiled, youngling princess, and neither was she fool enough to make demands of these men. *Now was no time for tempers.* Somehow, they *must* find a way to work together for the sake of this realm.

Her father had considered the good of his kingdom in every decision he'd made, but she also knew his temper was many times off-putting, and there was something of that arrogance in the lift of this man's chin—an inflexibility that demanded silence from her. Gwendolyn vowed she would never be so unswerving.

She said calmly, "I am certain that if *Máistir* Emrys were here with us, he would agree with *me*."

"Well, then, perhaps 'tis a good thing he is not," suggested the Druid, his tone rife with disapproval. "My brothers cannot afford to disregard our covenant with the Fae. I know too well what the consequences may be."

Gwendolyn cast Málik another glance, begging him to speak on her behalf. For the past bell, he had been naught but a spectator in this debate, as he was in her *konsel*, and she had run out of reasonable arguments. When he persisted with silence, she continued. "Mayhap," she allowed. "But the consequences will be worse for Pretania if you do not allow me to cross the Veil. Surely, you must realize this? An exception *must* be allowed, or life as we know it may cease."

"Life as *you* know it, *Banríon*. But I can assure you, change is not always a loathsome thing..." He'd used the Fae word for queen with no reverence, the look in his eyes making it clear he did not bow to her now, nor would he ever. He had been quite definite that this village did not fall within Cornwall's jurisdiction. Nor Loc's either, he was quick to point out. The conflicts of this mortal world were not his to prevent nor to encourage.

She turned his argument against him. "I beg to differ. We have appointed you and your brethren arbiters of this land. You make judgments of this nature upon request quite frequently. Why else would a tribunal be called?"

"I would not say we offer tribunals frequently," he argued, tearing another bite from his meat and talking with his mouth full. "In fact, we profoundly discourage it. Why else do you think we have placed those blood painted stones—for their ornamental value?"

Gwendolyn frowned.

The Druid turned to address one of his brothers. "I would say it's time for another gruesome rumor to illustrate what happens when men come knocking upon our door unnecessarily. Put your heads together over that one. Clearly, the possibility of having one's entrails spilled for the sake of judgment is not enough of a deterrent."

"We have been considering one already," answered a Druid brother. "How does this sound? Along with human sacrifice, we have a taste for human blood?"

"That could work," said another, and Gwendolyn rolled her eyes over the inane conversation. To think she had once feared these men. Despite their age, they were like a pack of shavelings with the sense of humor of little boys.

And regardless, she continued to reason with the leader. "Perhaps, as you say, change is not always such a loathsome thing; but perhaps it is time for a change for Druidkind as well? Give me passage, and I will provide you the means to work and live as you will."

"Nay," said the elder Druid, picking rudely at his teeth. "I cannot allow you passage, lady queen."

Was it truly necessary to call out her gender? Gwendolyn bristled, but she was near to begging. "It would be a dreadful thing if Locrinus were made king."

"Fie! He is king already," argued the Druid, wiping the lingering grease from his hand across the front of his robe. "To that end, my spies report his lands are far less ravaged than yours, *Banríon*. This would indicate to me that the evil we fear is not the change you oppose." He eyed Gwendolyn with meaning, and she felt the prick of his accusation like a dagger to her heart. Heat crept up into her neck, then ignited upon her cheeks. This was not the first time that insinuation was broached—in fact, the first time by Gwendolyn herself. Still, she could not conceive why her father's reign would be worse than that of a murdering, usurping madman. And no matter, she did not intend to rule as her father did. Woman or not, she would not make the same mistakes—even if she didn't yet know what those mistakes were. She would continue seeking answers, and she would not rest until her lands were healed and her people contented. However, she couldn't address these matters until she had the sword in hand.

Despite the hysteria welling within her, Gwendolyn kept her voice calm. "Esme will be the first to apprise you—as she once did me—the future for Pretania will be bleak if we do not prevail."

The elder Druid waved a hand about the table. "And yet... our esteemed Fae princess is not here," he said. "Why do you presume that may be, *Banríon Dragan*?"

Gwendolyn had no answer for this, and seeing she did not, the Druid continued. "I must suppose she knew you would seek an audience with us for this purpose, and yet she has declined to appear by your side?"

"I don't know where Esme is," Gwendolyn confessed, sliding Málik yet another pleading glance. Trying not to panic, she peered down at the hand she'd laid flat on the table, her finger itching to find Borlewen's blade. But that would not be the noble way to solve this problem, and neither were the Druids her enemy.

Neither was the Fae king, for that matter, but she would make him one for the sake of this quest. She *needed* that sword.

"*Deartháir...*"

"Harri," the Druid said. "I am *Deartháir* Harri."

"Well, *Deartháir* Harri," Gwendolyn repeated. "I really do not mean to place your village at peril, but you must realize it is my duty to retrieve *my* sword. I was rather hoping..." Again, she peered at Málik, begging with her eyes. "I was hoping Lir might accompany us. His counsel would be invaluable to me, and I am certain that with Lir by my side we would strive to safeguard the interests of your village, even as we do mine."

"*Dearthair* Lir has agreed to this?" interjected another Druid.

"Well... yes... he did... before." Gwendolyn averted her gaze.

The elder Druid narrowed his eyes. "You mean... before he arrived to find his brother afflicted?"

Gwendolyn nodded. "But it was his suggestion. And Málik concurred that his counsel would prove fortuitous."

Every Druid turned to look at Málik now, but again, Málik declined to speak, allowing their silent questions to go unanswered.

"No Druid has ever dared venture beyond the Veil," said *Dearthair* Harri. "Not since—well, that is neither here nor there. But we cannot condone this, and particularly now with—"

Gwendolyn interrupted. "But if the *Máistir* recovers, you will approve?"

"*I* would not!" Harri said decisively. "Nor can I say what others might do. But kings and queens will come and go. This village has stood longer than the seven hundred years we Druids have occupied it—so I am told, since the First Dawn. We've been apprised that anyone fortunate enough to live here will remain so long as our covenant remains unbroken. Therefore, no Druid I know of will presume to allow what you propose. Even as it is our duty to enforce the laws of men, it is also our duty to defend the Veil against those who are not welcome to cross."

The man was impossible to argue with.

Even more so than Málik.

"It may not come to war!" Gwendolyn argued. "It

could be the Fae king will happily agree to return *my* sword—and in such case, there would be no dissent between our realms. All you will have done is to allow a mortal to cross the Veil."

Deartháir Harri directed his gaze at Málik, and, finally, Málik spoke to agree with Gwendolyn. "It is not expressly forbidden for a mortal to cross," he said, and *Deartháir* Harri persisted.

"Can you swear to me on your Fae honor that no blood—neither mortal nor Faerie—will be shed for this cause?"

He was silent for a moment, and it was impossible to say whether that was because *Deartháir* Harri had referred to him as Fae. Gwendolyn knew he did not like it, but she also sensed that he knew it would not be in his best interest to deny his affiliation here and now. Or was he trying to answer without lying?

Málik shook his head, and Gwendolyn's hopes fell.

"There we have it!" the elder Druid declared. "Therefore, we cannot allow it! I will bear the *Máistir's* staff only a short time, but I'd not have it said I was the one who ended our habitation in this village—or worse!"

But that was precisely what Gwendolyn was afraid of! Deep in her heart of hearts, she knew that whatever came of Locrinus' reign would be far worse for Pretania than whatever might be visited upon this fellowship of old men who'd been fortunate enough to live on borrowed time in this abandoned Fae village. But what could she say to convince this man? *Give up your purpose and your lives so I can fulfill my destiny?*

Indeed, Gwendolyn would sacrifice her own life to make things right, but how could she force others to sacrifice what they would not?

Neither could she swear to this man that her quest would not end with crossed swords.

Sick to her belly, she peered down at the medallion of venison that graced her plate—too bloody for her tastes. Neither was it something she had expected to find at a Druid table. After the sparse meal she'd shared with them during her previous stay, she'd presumed their tastes leaned toward... well, *pookies*. In light of the moment, the blood that lay congealed beneath her cut of meat seemed to be an ill omen.

She tried to find something to say, but any decent argument eluded her. So, she said, "Wise men must be brave men. We must accept some manner of risk to ensure the longevity of Pretania, not solely *your* Druid village! You hold it has existed since time immemorial, but if the gods intended for it to survive in perpetuity, they would have kept the village for themselves instead of abandoning it to a pack of greedy old fools!"

The Druid elder was unmoved. He cocked his head back, staring at Gwendolyn with slightly lifted brows that conveyed only boredom.

"Please," Gwendolyn begged.

The elder shook his head, and Gwendolyn straightened her spine, rising to her full height in her seat. "I am charged with the well-being of this land and its people! I'll not accept your answer, *Dearthái* Harri. I will pray and hope *Máistir* Emrys wakes soon, and that he sees the truth in my words before all hope is lost!"

"Even if he wakes," argued Harri. "He should not and cannot decide this matter alone." He lifted his staff and slammed it down on the wood floor. "We hereby deny your request to cross the Veil!"

24

The first thing Gwendolyn noted upon entering her assigned bower—the same bower she'd occupied during her first visit to this village—was the garment that lay folded atop the bed. She recognized it at once as her mother's Prydein gown, unmistakable for the symbols. The last time she saw it, it looked worse for the wear, and she had abandoned it here, opting for the *mithril* Esme gave her. As promised, the gown appeared to have been washed and mended, and the sight of it now turned the corners of her lips, even as it brought a sting to her eyes.

That gown was all she had remaining of her mother, and seeing it, she felt a failure. More, she despaired ever to wear it again. Not only was she certain it would not fit in her current state, she didn't intend to wear it until she rode north to face Baugh—a quest she could not embark upon until she had the Sword of Light in her hands.

Stubborn, short-sighted fool!

Didn't he understand? If she failed to unite these tribes, his purpose in this village would come to naught. These Druids were arbiters of the laws of men, but they were so well respected only because of their relationship with the tribes. If there were no tribes to arbitrate, what then? What motive could the Fae have to give mere mortals dominion over their precious portal? The answer eluded Gwendolyn, and no doubt, escaped the Druids, as well.

She had used every argument to convince *Dearthái* Harri, but that man was an irascible buffoon, who believed himself *chosen* for a task he had merely been fortunate enough to hold—with his pretend Fae ears, and his haughty demeanor, one would think he considered himself a king.

Poor Emrys was never so despotic!

Unfortunately, Gwendolyn had counted on the Lifer Pol Order.

Without them, the situation seemed hopeless.

For one, she didn't have the Sword of Light, and without that sword, no certainty anyone but Caradoc would follow her—and even with Caradoc Gwendolyn had concerns. Meanwhile, Locrinus had many thousands of warriors more than she did, and her lands continued to be ravaged, and Loc's were not.

Already, Porth Pool was lost! What might be deduced from that?

On top of everything else, her city's fate lay in the hands of a man who was once her rival. And for the ultimate injury, *Máistir* Emrys was deathly ill, and no one seemed any wiser about how to help him—certainly not Gwendolyn. And she felt like the very worst of villains for worrying more about trying to find a way across the Veil than she was over the *Máistir's* health.

She inhaled a breath, exhaling with patience.

And then again.

And again.

And then, curiously, she wasn't worried about anything at all. Her outrage dispelled with the swirling mist—a mist whose very purpose appeared to be to inspire forgetfulness. It held the same odd, dreamlike quality she'd experienced when Málik turned her into a tree—a fluidity that made it impossible to distinguish contours, edges, or extremities. Gwendolyn didn't remember this mysterious effect from her first time in this village, and yet, truth be told, neither did she recall anything at all beyond the *pookie* stew and those odd prophetic dreams. She'd left here with only the vaguest sense of the village itself, and now she wondered if her meal had once again comprised more *pookies*.

No matter; if it did, for once she was grateful.

She'd not had much rest during their journey north, and she would like to sleep tonight—without worrying about being set upon by Brigantes or Loegrians.

In the meantime, her thoughts were both the clearest they had ever been, but also the fuzziest—like the feel of these marvelous walls…

With unvarnished wonder, she smoothed her fingertips across the fuzzy surface. Made of a substance she'd never encountered beyond this village, the entire edifice reminded her of an enormous leaf, although if she was standing beneath a leaf, it was the largest leaf Gwendolyn had ever encountered, and she, beneath it, must be the size of a flea!

The interior was no less… peculiar.

At first glance, it was hardly remarkable—perhaps even austere. Precisely what she might expect for an order of reclusive prelates.

Along with a small tub—which, by the by, appeared to be filled with warm water if the steam was any indication—there was also a bed, a small table,

and a stool. Else wise, the chamber was unfettered by
frippery—no tapestries on the walls, no baubles, nor
even a simple candle gracing the bedside table. Instead, the room's only true source of illumination
came from the muted light filtering in with the breeze,
and a small golden orb resting atop the table, its gen-
tling pulsing light casting a soft yellow glow against
the swirling mist.

Did she come here to sleep? Or bathe? Gwendolyn
suddenly couldn't recall.

Whatever the case, no one had come or gone since
she'd arrived, and despite this, steam curled up invit-
ingly from the interior of the tub, sending tendrils of
wispy fingers to beckon her into the bath.

At the far end of the room, the bed lay atop what
appeared to be a thatch-woven dais, and save for the
furs that lay atop it, the berth reminded Gwendolyn of
a bird's nest, complete with a feather-stuffed pallet.
She almost expected to find it occupied by cheeping
birds, but nay, she was alone. In her stead, Málik had
gone to inquire about the *Máistir's* condition, insisting
Gwendolyn retire for the evening. There was little
more to do, he'd said, and unfortunately, this was true.
Whatever ailed *Máistir* Emrys, it was nothing she had
any knowledge of, and in the meantime, she was bone
weary and filthy and they had another long, arduous
journey ahead.

She refused to be thwarted.

Brooding, her gaze returned to the small tub
gracing the center of the room. It wasn't so elaborate
or grand as the one she'd enjoyed in the bathhouse,
where she'd first met Esme, but the water was still
warm. And, recognizing that even in this odd place, it
was bound to cool, she undressed, and waded into the
tub, sinking down into the temperate water—again,

deeper than such a tiny tub should allow. But Gwendolyn was beyond questioning the peculiarities of this village. As Bryn once said, up seemed down, and down seemed up, and she had far more pressing matters to consider—for one, how to cross the Veil if *Dearthair* Harri continued to refuse to allow it. Intent upon cleaning herself in the meantime, she found the cloth that lay draped over the rim of the tub, along with a small wedge of delightful smelling soap, and washed—vigorously scrubbing the scum from beneath her nail-beds, her face, ears, breasts. No one should come to the bargaining table so defiled! It was perhaps no wonder *Dearthair* Harri had peered down his nose at her.

Before long, Gwendolyn forgot to scrub so ruthlessly, and sighing over the enchanting scents accosting her—oddly reminiscent of her mother's perfume—she laid her head back and closed her eyes, reveling in the bath.

Quite thoughtful, despite the mulish, half-witted arguments...

At home, a bath like this required the service of an army of servants—a number to heat the water in the kitchen cauldrons and too many to rush the buckets to her chamber. Gwendolyn had preferred bathing in Porth Pool. Unlike her mother, she could never justify the use of her people for such an effort—not that she didn't appreciate being clean, mind you. She did, and particularly now, after having mired herself with the soot and grime of that wretched village Loc's men destroyed.

She tried not to think about the woman and her sweet, dead child...

Tried not to think about the brave men felled there, defending their families...

Nor, again, the execution of Loc's man...

Gwendolyn didn't wish to upset Lir's village, nor his order, but she knew in her heart that, no matter how Loc's land fared right now, there was no joy or hope to be borne by a tyrant who cared nothing for anyone except himself.

What had Esme said? Eventually, all things perish without hope, and hatred's roots, no matter how deep, do not sustain.

The people feared Loc, but this was not the same as whatever her father inspired. Like his sire, the only thing Loc cared about was power and gold, and even with all the wealth her father had sent his way, he'd coveted more. He'd never wanted her. He'd only coveted the gold promised by her prophecy. And then, after discovering her hair was simply hair, he'd chosen bloodshed and betrayal over any true alliance. With his choices, he'd stolen her life—her hopes, her dreams, and her trust.

With a pang, Gwendolyn recalled the look on his face as he'd snicked her hair, and even now, it made her long to cut out his heart.

She would not play the fool for anyone ever again.

After everything Loc had done, she refused to believe any good could come of his reign, and, even if she was not the one who should rule in his stead, Gwendolyn was destined to liberate Pretania—sooner than later, else there would be more of what they'd encountered en route to this Druid village.

Burnt villages. Murdered innocents. Such cruelty.

This land would become a lawless land without hope, and, without hope, it would wither, even as the lands surrounding her own beloved Trevena now withered.

She slid lower into the tub, turning her thoughts to

more pleasant ones... specifically, the moment when Málik placed his hand upon her shoulder... his lips against the curve of her throat.

That was the first genuine show of affection he'd given her since the night he'd kissed her on the ramparts, and she sighed over the memory.

What if she should perish in pursuit of this sword? She would die with such bitter regret for never having known a lover's touch...

For never having known *his* touch.

Sinking lower into the tub, she dared to imagine how it might have been if they had been alone in those woods... and then, quite rudely, a bell startled her from her reverie, sobering her at once. She sat straight, but before she could call out to say she was indisposed, the curtain parted to reveal Esme—once again intruding upon her bath, only this time, she was not welcome.

25

G wendolyn closed her fist about the shard of soap as Esme came strutting into the room, clapping her hands, her mood unquestionably lighter than Gwendolyn had witnessed from her in many moons. "Lovely," she said in a sing-song tone, her gaze sliding to the bed, alighting on the Prydein gown. "I see you've found it!"

"What do you want?" Gwendolyn pressed.

Esme was not who she wished to see right now. In fact, she was the last person she wished to bandy words with.

"I came to be certain you found your mother's gown," she said conversationally. "As promised, I had it mended for you, and cleaned—and yes, it was me who ordered the bath as well." She grinned a little wider, displaying a mouthful of porbeagle teeth. "After all we have endured, Gwendolyn, I thought you would covet a nice, hot bath."

"Thank you," said Gwendolyn, though she could summon little gratitude. The journey had been too long and arduous, and she had encountered too many disappointments. Nor did she have the energy to share polite conversation with a murderous fiend. Ignoring her, Gwendolyn ducked beneath the water, soaping her hair, washing it vigorously, holding her breath for as long as she dared, hoping against hope that Esme would leave before she re-emerged.

She did not.

Much to Gwendolyn's dismay, Esme remained, greeting Gwendolyn with a ready smile when she resurfaced. And then, without asking permission, she turned about, pouncing upon Gwendolyn's bed, and settling herself atop it.

Naturally.

It wasn't Esme's way to beg for anything, nor was she ever sweet for no cause. She wanted something, Gwendolyn knew. The question was, *what*? Any other day, she might have more patience to ferret the answer, but more than anything, at the moment, Gwendolyn longed to curl up in that bed by herself.

Well, not really by herself, but that was neither here nor there.

"Why are you here, Esme?"

"Please, *Banríon Dragan.* Do not be cross with me," she cooed. And then, leaning back on the bed, she lifted one leg over a raised knee and bounced her bare foot as she continued to stare. Gwendolyn glared at Esme's toes—never having really noticed them before. They were like her own, except for the nails, which were more like claws... perhaps a cat's... and if only one dared to rub her belly, she would rip out their entrails. Gwendolyn blinked, shaking away the thought, blaming the mist for her jumbled thoughts.

Clearly, Esme had bathed already. Gone was any evidence of her blood lust, and she sat before Gwendolyn in the most diaphanous of gowns, one that revealed too much. And yet, like the mist in this Druid village, too little as well. Once again, Gwendolyn found herself curious over the differences between their bodies—not much, from what she could tell. Despite that, driven by curiosity—it was difficult not to look when Esme lay reclining on her bed with her legs in the air—Gwendolyn peeked at the shadow betwixt her thighs. For so long she had wondered over the differences in their anatomy—not so much regarding Esme's. But rather, she wondered because she'd never once dared to peek, nor had Málik revealed himself.

If they wished to couple... was that possible?

Esme caught her glance and smiled coyly. Mortified to be caught peeping, Gwendolyn averted her gaze, rising from the bath. Eager to be dressed, she stepped out, and Esme produced a towel from beneath the Prydein gown, tossing it to Gwendolyn. "Here," she said, and this time, it was Esme's turn to gape. And despite Gwendolyn's discomfiture, there was little she could say when, only moments ago, she had done the same. But honestly, she couldn't count the number of times she'd stood naked in front of Ely, and Ely in front of her, but, somehow, that was different. Ely was like her sister. Esme was... *not*.

"You have... changed," Esme said.

"Have I?" Gwendolyn's laugh was quick and short. "*You* are the changeling, Esme!"

"Me?" Esme laughed now, too, but instead of sounding annoyed as Gwendolyn was, she sounded amused. Patting herself on the chest, Esme said, "I must wonder... do you even know what a changeling is, Gwendolyn?"

Gwendolyn's frown deepened, incensed by the question. Of course she knew! For so much of her youth, they had examined her to exhaustion—with every inspection focused on her flaws—of which there appeared to be many! *Her arms were too short. Fingers too long. Her hair like straw. Canines a bit too pointy. Skin too pale.* The list went on, and on, and on...

"A changeling is simply an *Elf*, that is all. A Faerie." Esme explained. "And therefore, you have simply called me what I am. Should this truly anger me?"

Gwendolyn blinked, her outrage silenced. She had never thought of it quite that way. It would be easy to see why some mortals considered the Fae countenance to be monstrous, but Gwendolyn never had. Considering her own trials, she had always felt there was beauty to be found in *all* creatures. And while so many times it had unsettled her to be treated so poorly by those who saw her as a "changeling," the first time she'd set eyes upon Málik, she only ever saw the beauty in him. And no matter, she didn't wish to defend herself, nor reassure Esme, nor confess that she had envisioned a changeling much opposed to the creature who now sat before her on that bed. Rather, she had thought them like... ghouls—hideously deformed, not with such delicate, ethereal features, even if her teeth were frightening to behold.

"Please go," Gwendolyn begged. She wrapped the towel about her torso and stood, arms crossed.

"If you think about it," Esme continued. "That is a stupid name... *changeling*. Don't you believe so? And, truly, I must take issue with it because I—" She pressed a claw to her breast. "Have not changed one bit in my life. I am as I was conceived, no more, no less."

Gwendolyn cast the Elf a dubious glance. "So, you were born fully formed?"

"Don't be silly," Esme said insouciantly, laughing, waving Gwendolyn away, with fingers like claws. "All creatures arrive in this world as innocent babes."

Gwendolyn rolled her eyes, unable to envision

Esme as innocent, even as a babe. Indeed, as a babe, she would have crawled about on all fours, gnashing her porbeagle teeth and feeding on other children.

But, really, if she were in the mood to argue, she might point out that the last time she'd spent any time alone with Esme in a bath chamber, Esme had seemed an entirely disparate creature. Gwendolyn no longer trusted her.

"Will you please get off my bed."

It wasn't a question.

Gwendolyn knew full well Esme would rise when it pleased her to do so and not a scant moment before —not even at the point of a sword. Even now, she proved that theory true by ignoring Gwendolyn and changing the subject.

"I only wonder if you will heed some advice?" Esme asked, though she didn't wait for Gwendolyn to agree or disagree before continuing. "Find your true self, Gwendolyn. But do not seek her in a glass. You will not find her there. And regardless, if you manage to do so, you might yet earn that reward you seek without bringing war to both our realms."

"Esme," Gwendolyn said impatiently, begging now. "I haven't the presence of mind to decipher your riddles. If there is aught you came to say, please speak, then go. I am weary to my bones!"

"I only came to help."

"Isn't that what you claim to have been doing all along?" Gwendolyn countered. "Or will you confess, as Málik appears to believe, that you have been working at cross-purposes with me all along?"

As nothing else seemed to, that revelation appeared to wound her. Esme's smile faded. "Málik said that?"

"Not precisely," Gwendolyn allowed. "Though I can tell he does not trust you."

She sounded affronted. "I have *never* worked at cross-purposes with you, *Banríon*." And then, having declared as much, she glanced away. When she turned again to meet Gwendolyn's gaze, there was a suspicious gleam in her eyes that gave Gwendolyn pause. "At any rate, I have come to beg a favor."

"You, beg?" Gwendolyn responded. "Alas, no favor you ask will come without a price."

"You wound me," said Esme.

Gwendolyn sighed. "I do not wish to wound you, Esme. Truly, I do not. But I am exhausted. I have tried so desperately to befriend you. You have called yourself my friend, and I once believed you. But I do not understand why you have become so bitterly disagreeable."

Esme shrugged, then sat upright, dropping her legs off the side of the bed, all trace of her belligerence gone. "I have good reason."

"Explain."

"I cannot," she said. "But you well know I have had much discord with my father."

Perhaps some answers at last? Gwendolyn secured her towel as she approached the bed, interested.

"As I have said—as Málik has told you—my father took his crown without right, and his rule has been... well, difficult. You must know I *have* worked at cross-purposes with him, but—"

"Yet you do not lie? How is it possible to work at cross-purposes with your own father and not lie?"

Esme shrugged. "Clearly, he has never challenged me. I've never given him any cause to doubt me and he believes I come to spy... when I come... to protect you."

"Me?"

Esme nodded somewhat petulantly. "You."

"From?"

She was silent a while, clearly reluctant to answer, and then she did. "Málik."

Something about her confession summoned a memory... of Gwendolyn with Málik in the *fogous*...

How came you to be in my father's employ?

I was sent.

By whom?

My father.

Gwendolyn's heart twisted.

She sank beside Esme on the bed beside, the truth apparent to her in that moment of clarity. "He came to assassinate me, didn't he?"

Gwendolyn knew the answer to this question before she asked it.

In the beginning, she had sensed Málik's ill will toward her... and now she understood why. Her impression of the Fae had changed after he'd arrived, and despite her awe of him when she first laid eyes upon him riding through their gates... she promptly changed her mind. She had sensed a darkness in him... and soon decided he was a demon incarnate. She grew to loathe him despite... everything—despite that she never wished to.

I was sent.

By whom?

My father.

Esme was still watching her, and there was no joy in her expression. If indeed she considered Gwendolyn a rival, this was not the emotion she spied in the Elf's eyes.

It was more like... *sorrow?*

Pity?

Regret?

"Yes," she said. "That was my father's plan."

"Why?"

Esme shrugged. "It is foretold; your reign will bring war to our realms and will end my father's reign. But Málik did not agree to this task of his own accord. Gwendolyn..." She reached out, settling a hand atop Gwendolyn's. It was then that Gwendolyn realized she was trembling. "Our true names compel us; thus we do not share them. He was compelled."

"If this is true, why am I not dead already?" Gwendolyn freed her hand from beneath Esme's, clutching at her towel.

Esme shrugged, and Gwendolyn peered down at her bare feet, staring again, unwilling to believe it, despite that she sensed the truth in Esme's words— Faeries did not lie, but there was no need for lies when their mastery of words enabled them to twist them into traps. "So then, you would have me believe you —*you*, who has not spared me one kind word of late— came to defend me? And Málik—"

Came to kill her?

Blood and bloody bones.

For some reason, though Gwendolyn thought about it, she couldn't complete the thought aloud.

Esme blew a sigh. "I perceive what you leave unsaid. But simply because you do not speak a thing aloud does not make it untrue. I will not lie to you," she said. "Yet nothing is as it seems. Believe me, I have little doubt of Málik's affection for you, Gwendolyn, and regardless of whether he has completed this task my father has assigned him, someday, he will be compelled to finish what he started."

She gave Gwendolyn a moment to process that information, and then continued. "Meanwhile, although I was sent to spy, and I have done so, it is not my true

purpose, nor have I been entirely candid with anyone... not even Málik... until now. I bare my heart to
you in order to save his life... and yours."

Málik's life, as well?

She meant to save Gwendolyn?

It was too much to conceive.

Gwendolyn's heart twisted over Esme's brutal reve-
lations, and still... she could not believe Málik intended to harm her. He loved her. Hadn't he said so?
Faeries did not lie.

Esme must have sensed her ambivalence because
her tone took on a sharper edge. "You may have conveniently forgotten that no matter whether there is love
between us, Málik is still *my* betrothed. He is our
Dragon Prince, Gwendolyn—forgotten though he
might be. How can you expect he should give up so
much for you? My people need him, but if he is
dead—"

Gwendolyn blinked, swallowing past the knot in
her throat. "I have not asked him to give up anything,"
she argued.

Esme's delicate brows collided, her eyes narrowing
to slits. "To this, I respectfully disagree. By your own
enchantment, you compel him to give up *everything*,
including his life, Gwendolyn. You must listen to me;
what do you believe my father will do once you face
him with your demands, and Málik stands by your
side, demanding the sword?"

"*My* sword," Gwendolyn reminded her.

"No matter," said Esme, and once more, a telltale
gleam appeared in her eyes. "My father will call him a
traitor, and he will deny you and destroy you."

She whispered brokenly, and her expression soft-
ened. "You will be the end of him. And no matter what

Málik may feel for me, I love him and I have loved him longer than he has loved you."

Gwendolyn's shoulders fell. She felt numb. "What are you asking of me, precisely?"

"Demand he wait for you in this Druid village. Do not allow him to journey with you below."

"Demand?" Gwendolyn snorted. "How can I demand aught of Málik? You know he will do as he pleases."

"Not if I provide you his true name," Esme said. "And I will. For the price of your agreement, I will give you he means to stop him."

Tears pricked at Gwendolyn's eyes. She didn't wish to compel Málik. She daren't even have his true name. More than anything, she wanted him to love her of his own free will, and if Esme gave it to her...

"His name is—"

Gwendolyn lifted her hand to cover Esme's mouth, shaking her head. "Do not speak it! Do not! But if I agree to do as you ask, how will I cross the Veil and find this City of Light without help?"

"I will go with you," Esme declared. "I will stand by your side when you face my father. We will cross the Veil together, and you will leave Bryn and Lir with Málik. I alone will stand by your side."

"What if your father calls *you* a traitor?"

Esme twisted her lips ruefully. "If he does, it would be true."

Gwendolyn's mind raced with all the arguments for and against. She did not wish to imperil anyone—especially not Bryn, nor Lir. Lir had enough to contend with in dealing with his brother.

And Málik...

Esme anticipated her thoughts. "None of us will fare well in the Fae realm—especially Málik. Forsooth, Gwendolyn, I cannot guarantee you will return —nor I. To stand by your side, I will risk my father's wrath. He will suspect the very thing I have somehow kept from him all these years."

"Your rebellion?"

Esme shook her head, averting her gaze, looking down. "Something else—something I dare not speak aloud. Though if you will but trust me, Gwendolyn..." She closed her eyes, and then reopened them, meeting Gwendolyn's gaze, and in that glance, Gwendolyn saw the Elf she'd first met in the depths of Esme's bright, green gaze—green, just as her eyes had appeared on that morning she'd gifted Gwendolyn the *mithril*. "You *must* trust me," she insisted. "You *must*!"

With both hands now, Gwendolyn clutched the towel to her breast, too many thoughts rushing through her head. But there was something else Esme would not say. This moment she had the same desperate look in her eyes that Málik once had on the ramparts...

"Lir cannot help you," Esme insisted. "Bryn cannot help you. Neither Málik nor I can truly help you. Only you can sway my father before he strikes you down. But if you dare to utter the wrong word, or if you do not answer every question to his satisfaction, blood will spill, and it will not be his. He is too strong, Gwendolyn. Why do you suppose he has reigned so long? Why do you presume no one challenges him? If you cross the Veil with your army of five, he will view this as a declaration of war, and I promise you there is no more you will accomplish if you face him with five than you will if you face him alone."

"So, then... you and me?" Gwendolyn pointed first at Esme, then herself, recognizing sincerity in her tone. Despite that, she knew better than to agree too eagerly, keeping in mind Lir's warning. "I will consider it," she said. "I swear it."

"Indeed, you will." Esme hardened her gaze, "And you will agree, because if all I say is not enough to convince you, I come bearing news you will wish to hear; only to hear it, you must first swear to my terms."

"What news?" Gwendolyn demanded.

Esme lifted her chin, her green eyes turning a shade of green closer to steel. "Promise you will do as I say."

"I could promise, but what guarantee have you I won't lie?"

Esme smirked. "Have you ever lied?" she asked, her tone again with that sing-song quality.

Come to think of it, Gwendolyn never had. She was not the lying sort. Even when it might have saved her from her mother's wrath. Resigned, Gwendolyn nodded, but hesitantly. "Very well. I promise," she said. "Tell me your news."

Esme's smile returned, revealing the tips of her porbeagle teeth. "Tell no one, and if you do, you will regret it, Gwendolyn."

"For the sake of Danu, Speak!"

"Your mother lives," Esme said, and Gwendolyn's fingers released the towel; thankfully, it remained secure.

"*My* mother?"

Esme nodded, and Gwendolyn's heart squeezed painfully. "Where is she?"

"*After* we have returned, I will tell you everything."

"What if we do not?"

Esme shrugged then, her demeanor returned to the manner she'd displayed over these past weeks—cold and firm. "If you do not, what good will it do to know where she is? Retrieve your sword from my father without finding one through your little mortal heart, and I will happily take you to her myself. In the meantime, take this as a token of my goodwill."

She seized Gwendolyn by the hand, turned it upside, then dropped a small trinket into her palm. Gwendolyn stared, blinking away the sudden prick of tears.

In her hand, Esme had placed her mother's ring—a simple copper ring with two small flowers on either side, each bearing seven petals representing the seven Prydein tribes. It was a ring Queen Eseld was never without.

"Wear it in good health," said Esme. "Until you can return it yourself."

26

H er mother was alive!

How?

How could this be?

Despite all her searches and inquiries, Gwendolyn had never uncovered a single clue that would suggest this was true. All throughout the long months in Loegria, Queen Innogen and Loc had behaved as though both her parents' deaths were a given, taking too much glee in Gwendolyn's grief.

And later, during the mayhem of those weeks after returning to Trevena, there was never one clue to suggest anyone had escaped the Maytide coup.

Then again, neither was there any evidence of Queen Eseld's demise—no body, no witnesses to her execution. Nothing except a handful of contrasting stories.

It could be true, and, for the first time in so long, Gwendolyn dared to hope.

"What about Demelza and Lady Ruan?" Gwendolyn pressed. "Did they escape with my mother? Why does no one know this but you?"

"Did you not wonder where I was off to so many

times? I have my ways." And then, crossing her arms, she offered a stubborn tilt of her head and gave Gwendolyn a coy smile that said with certainty she would say no more.

It didn't matter. *By the eyes of Lugh!* Gwendolyn didn't need proof. No matter how mean Esme had been, she felt in her heart that, knowing how much this meant to Gwendolyn, Esme would not toy with her heart.

And regardless, if someone told her now that she must go present herself to Locrinus in order to save her mother, she would do it. Consequences be damned. Right or wrong, Gwendolyn was driven to make amends with the woman who gave her life. Too long they'd been at odds, and Gwendolyn never even once considered how desperately she would regret every argument they ever had.

Only now...

She was alive, and Gwendolyn would do *anything* to see her again.

Anything!

The satisfied grin on Esme's face as she departed left a smoldering pit in Gwendolyn's belly. "Remember, Gwendolyn, tell no one." She lifted a finger to her lips. "Especially not Málik." And no, she had insisted, not Bryn—not even to provide him a shred of faith that his mother, too, might have survived the Feast of Blades. Esme was concerned Bryn would tell Málik and that Málik would attempt to stop them. And this was her way of trying to save Málik from her father. And this alone was reason enough for Gwendolyn as well. But if she could help her mother, and Málik as well, and still keep Bryn from losing his head, and somehow manage to accomplish this task, it would be the best of all worlds.

Gathering herself, she went in search of Bryn and meanwhile continued poring over the exchange with Esme, if only to be certain there was nothing she had missed—something Gwendolyn had inadvertently promised or failed to exact, a turn of the phrase that promised more than it gave or took more than Gwendolyn could afford. But there was nothing. Their exchange had been short and Esme's bargain straightforward. The only problem Gwendolyn could foresee was that she didn't know how to keep this secret from Bryn. She wasn't a good liar, and Bryn knew her better than anyone, no matter that they had grown apart over these past months.

Quite literally, Bryn had known her since she was a babe. Along with his mother and his father, he was the first to "meet" the new princess in her crib. And no matter that he was barely a year old at the time and couldn't recall the occasion, his mother had oft told the tale of how her eldest son cooed with delight as he'd peered into Gwendolyn's crib—a love story for the ages, she'd many times proclaimed, and perhaps Bryn took it too much to heart.

Gwendolyn loved Bryn like a brother, and as her beloved brother, she would prefer not to see him flayed for his support of her. Unfortunately, he could read her too well. Avoiding him would only make him suspicious, and so she devised the perfect plan to keep him preoccupied—if only she could find him!

Losing herself amidst the twisty paths, the long ramps and endless cross points, Gwendolyn grew agitated. Walking in circles, she passed the feast hall where she'd argued with *Deartháir* Harri and supped on *pookies*.

She passed the audience hall where she'd first met

Emrys, and then the bathhouse, where she'd bonded with Esme—three times each!

Somehow, through all her rounds, she never once encountered Esme again, nor Bryn nor Málik, and she wondered if Esme had put a hex on her to keep her from seeing anyone and betraying her secret. In fact, as tired as she was, she nearly gave up, until she stumbled on the *Máistir's* chamber at last.

Poking her head inside, she found Lir where she'd left him, at his brother's side. Apparently, he'd not left Emrys since they'd arrived. Gwendolyn stayed long enough to re-examine the *Máistir's* breathing and his strange wound and spreading bruise. Regretfully, there was nothing she knew to do—nothing better than to assign Bryn the task of searching for his assailant, if there was one.

Leaving Lir with words of encouragement, she resumed her search for Bryn, wondering how he was faring in this place. Except for the sojourn to Loegria after Gwendolyn's wedding, and then a single visit before that dreadful day, she knew he'd never traveled beyond their territories. Chysauster didn't count. Nor did the wheals. Together, she and Bryn had traveled oft to check on her father's mines, but this place was far from home and from anything Bryn might be accustomed to. She suspected it might overcome him as she was, and here, again, she was not by his side, leaving him to investigate this sprawling village and its odd denizens alone.

Nothing was as it seemed, Esme had said. Certainly, that was true of this place. Until this afternoon, Gwendolyn hadn't even realized how many Fae still lived in the village—all male, in keeping with the Druid tradition. During her last visit, none were anywhere to be found, but this time, they walked about conducting business as though it were the most ordinary thing to do. And yes, they were Fae. Gwendolyn recognized them by their ears, despite that the Druids also wore the ear sheaths—and now it made sense to Gwendolyn that these Druids should wish to blend among the Fae. However, unlike the Druids, the Fae's "ears" were neither shiny nor was their flesh all the same, though always with the slightest iridescence. As though the essence of magic must be woven through the fabric of their being. And regardless, it was only when one smiled as he passed, showing his porbeagle teeth, that the revelation suddenly occurred to Gwendolyn...

The Druids did not live here alone.

No wonder they guarded this village jealously.

No wonder they were so careful to adhere to the covenant.

No wonder *Dearthair* Harri was so reluctant to give her passage.

At last, she dared to stop and ask one of the Fae as she passed. "Have you seen my Shadow?"

He peered down at the ground, blinking. "Shadow?"

Gwendolyn looked as well, and nearly said—no, not that one—but then she found she had no shadow at all. Perhaps because this place existed in the twilight? "No," she endeavored to explain. "Not *my* shadow, shadow. My... guard." She made a sign as though to unsheathe her sword, which she did not have on her person.

"Dark of hair?" the creature asked and, for a moment, Gwendolyn couldn't help but stare at him. He, too, like Málik and Esme, was uncommonly beautiful—his smile and bright green eyes more like Esme's, though his hair was the same silvery shade as Málik's. The Elf smiled again, a smile that beguiled her.

"That way," he said, pointing, and Gwendolyn said, bemused. "Thank you."

The Elf frowned at her, and turned abruptly, marching away without another word and Gwendolyn hadn't the first inkling why, but she had the oddest feeling it was because she'd thanked him. She made a mental note to ask Esme about that, and whether she had offered some slight. So far as she could recall, neither Málik nor Esme had ever behaved so rudely over words of gratitude. Scratching her head, she returned to her search, and soon found she had worried for naught. She found Bryn, at last, in the one place she should have looked first, although how he'd found his way to the cookhouse bedeviled her. Not even Gwendolyn had visited this dwelling before, and regardless, she should have known that if anyone could sniff out morning cakes, it would be Bryn.

"There you are!" she exclaimed.

He wasn't alone.

Here with a Druid escort, he sat on a stool, one leg up with an elbow resting atop his knee, and a something like cake in his mouth. He could barely talk for the mouthful. "Delightful! You must try it!" he said, holding a bit aloft. And then, somehow, managing about another mouthful, he exclaimed, "Hob cake!"

Yegods.

Gwendolyn knew enough about Hob cake to know that the amount he was consuming boded ill for him. Without waiting for her to accept his offer, he shoved the last heaping handful into his mouth and cheerfully munched away, already with a loopy smile.

Gwendolyn shared a glance with the Druid cook.

The man shrugged.

As Gwendolyn entered the kitchen, the most unimaginable scents barraged her senses—too many to distinguish, and yet, some so achingly familiar it brought a sting of tears to her eyes. *Lamb stew. Nettle pudding. Roasted boar. Carp pie. Dormouse. Fried cheese curds. Shardbread. Fresh oysters. Smoked fish. Hevva Cake. Pottage stew. Mushroom pasties. Crispels basted in honey.*

All these scents accosted her at once—and more!

Regardless, when she looked about the cookhouse, she saw nothing to account for the scents. Only a circular hearth, about which everything in the room was arranged, with a heaping, smoking cauldron in its middle. On the farthest counter on the opposite side of Bryn sat several Hob cakes, fresh from the griddle.

"No thank you. I've had the pleasure," Gwendolyn said, smiling wanly.

"I cannot believe it!" Bryn declared. "One bite tastes like eggs with honey, and another like good Cornish beef!"

Much to Gwendolyn's dismay, she found herself craving a bite, though she knew how addictive that cake was, and she daren't indulge—not now. Tomorrow, Bryn would heartily regret eating so much of it. But that could well work in Gwendolyn's favor. "Take one to go," she said. "I've something I wish to discuss."

"Gladly," Bryn allowed. And then, to the cook, he asked, "Do you mind?"

"Certainly not," answered the Druid. "Take two."

Gwendolyn noted the answering grin that split Bryn's face, and he responded, "Three? May I?"

"Please," said the cook. "We've plenty."

Looking like a wee boy on his Name Day, Bryn hopped down from the stool enthusiastically, and went to retrieve his bestowals. He tried first to carry them in his hands, but they wouldn't fit, so he stretched out his tunic and set three in the cradle it formed. Then, peering back at the Druid chef, he plucked one more Hob cake for good measure. And once he had his tunic filled, he gave Gwendolyn a wink, and then, together, they filed out of the kitchen. They hadn't gone two steps before he offered a portion to Gwendolyn.

Gwendolyn couldn't resist. "Just one bite," she said, pinching off a bit from one corner, not daring to take more. As they walked, she popped the morsel into her mouth, and her eyes rolled backward into her head at the remembered taste of salted pilchards —those flavorsome little fishlings her uncle used to scoop out of the Bay of Dunes and serve with *hevva* cake and mead. Simply by the taste of it, she could almost see herself seated across from her cousins and her sweet uncle, with Málik by her side, and Lowenna plucking the last of the pilchards from a pan.

"Gods," she said, but refrained from begging another bite, knowing through experience how much she would regret it later.

"The cook also made stone soup," Bryn declared. "A bit like Hob cake, though somehow the taste, elusive anyway, was too fleeting. No sooner did I heap a spoonful into my mouth when the taste of it was forgotten. I remember only loving it but can't tell you what it tastes like."

"Made with *pookies*?" Gwendolyn asked, dreading the answer.

"Nay," he said. "When I asked for the recipe, he said it was stones—one stone. He said that stone was a gift from the Fae when they first arrived in this village. Like the Dagda's Cauldron, its bounty never ends. He has cooked every pot of soup with that same stone for seven hundred years!"

"Seven hundred and *three*," Gwendolyn corrected and Bryn furrowed his brow. "That's how long they've been here," she explained.

"Fascinating. I love this place!" he said. "Everyone is so agreeable. I am certain he would have allowed me to take another three." And then he gave her a sheepish grin. "I wouldn't have taken another if not," he asserted. "That would be stealing."

Gwendolyn snorted. "No doubt," she said, smiling, though she felt compelled to caution him as he lifted another bite into his mouth. "Go easy with that Hob cake, Bryn. It's quite potent as well as flavorful."

"Dagda's balls!" he declared suddenly. "Do you remember those bloody oysters we fished from Dragon's Bay? That summer when the currents were so strong, and the waters warmer than usual?" He grinned, waving the bite in his hand. "That time when Ely spewed from the ramparts and found the head of one alderman? Well now, this bite! This bite!" he declared. "It tastes like those oysters."

Gwendolyn couldn't help herself; she giggled, her mood lifted as much as she could manage, considering the circumstances. Bryn's expression was one of wonder—one that must mirror the look on her own face when she'd first tasted Hob cake. In fact, Gwendolyn was envious that she could no longer experience that wonder for the first time. Despite Málik cautioning her against eating too much, she, too, had stolen little bites all day long—in part with disbelief over the fact that every bite could taste so extraordinarily different, so delectable besides. The confection was incredible—as though it somehow replicated one's most beautiful memories regarding food. Every dish she had ever loved, that's what Hob cake tasted like.

"Hmm" she said, wondering about that stone soup.

Truth to tell, she would like to try that, as well, but dared not—not today. She would have to wait until she returned, and perhaps if *Máistir* Emrys was well enough, she would beg him for some, and they would celebrate together with stone soup and Hob cake and if she slept for a week thereafter, and woke with an aching head, she would endure it most gleefully.

At any rate, she believed it was the *pookies* she'd eaten after her arrival in the village that affected her so horribly. And somehow, the combination of the two had also given her those prophetic dreams. In the end, it was those dreams that had given her visions that helped her to win Caradoc to her side, and also save Ely—although, admittedly, Ely hadn't needed saving. Thus, she allowed Bryn his newfound delight over the discovery of Hob cake and took a bit of joy in his bliss. No doubt, they'd all had too little joy since the Feast of Blades.

As to that matter, it was the most difficult thing Gwendolyn ever had to do not to blurt out the news of her mother's escape—not merely to share her own burgeoning joy and sense of relief, but to give Bryn some hope that his mother might have survived as well. Gwendolyn sighed. "I remember that day all too well," she said fondly, though Ely mightn't recall the occasion so fondly, since she was ill for two days after.

"This one!" Bryn exclaimed, once again waving the Hob cake, Ely's encounter with summer oysters forgotten. "Oh, gods! 'Tis better than Cornish oysters!"

"Be warned," Gwendolyn said, feeling guilty for not fessing up sooner. "You might discover yourself asleep for days. Málik warned me, too, but I did not listen."

"Cheese!" Bryn exclaimed, ignoring her warning. "Freshly made!"

And then, perhaps only recalling that Gwendolyn had come searching for him for a reason, he asked, "What did you wish to speak to me about?"

27

B ryn's delight over the Hob cake dimmed after Gwendolyn finished sharing her suspicions— well, not *her*s precisely. She was *not* the one who'd voiced them, nor did she believe them. However, she was not above using the Druid's proclamation to her advantage. As far as Gwendolyn was concerned, there was no evidence of poisoning. And despite that, if she did not investigate this case, and someone in this village was behaving nefariously, they would perhaps try again. Gwendolyn didn't wish the good *Máistir* to expire, simply because no one had treated this concern earnestly. It was enough that *someone here* thought there was an attempted poisoning, and by engaging Bryn to investigate the matter, she could slay two hares with a single arrow. Indeed, not only did she trust Bryn to leave no stone unturned, this task would keep him from scrutinizing her own actions too closely. While it was his job to do so, she didn't intend to have him following her about, asking questions. As it was, it was killing her not to tell him what Esme had revealed about her mother—and mayhap his as well. But there was yet another reason to task Bryn with this. As one of only two women in this Druid village—and being the one who'd so vehemently insisted upon accessing their portal, she was quite sure she would have eyes upon her. No one would miss her poking about, and meanwhile Bryn, being of the male persuasion, would have more freedom to uncover the portal. If he found it, Gwendolyn might have yet another option should Esme decide to betray her, and Gwendolyn could still not convince *Dearthair* Harri to allow them passage into the Fae realm. Naturally, Gwendolyn didn't tell Bryn her true feelings about the first reason, nor did she reveal the second, but she suggested the third.

He slid her a frown like so many he'd given her throughout the years—a frown that said he didn't approve. "Have you not had enough playing the sleuth-hound, Gwen? Do you remember what happened the last time you set about investigating?"

Gwendolyn returned his frown. "Don't make this about that, Bryn. As I've said, we need to locate the portal. Without it, we can proceed no further." She averted her gaze, unwilling to allow him to study her eyes. Somehow, he had *always* gleaned when she was hiding something, and although the past year had hardened Gwendolyn, she wasn't so complicated or unknowable to Bryn's discerning eyes.

She slid him a careful glance. "I assure you, this is not that," she asserted. "But, no matter, even if this were solely about the *Máistir*, I cannot ignore this matter. I know and care for the old bod. Before we go, I would like to be sure no one will make another attempt on his life."

"Do *you* believe someone tried to poison him?"

There was doubt in his voice, and Gwendolyn feared he'd read it in her voice. *No.* She didn't believe the *Máistir* was poisoned, but neither she didn't wish to admit that to Bryn.

Nor, in truth, was she willing to be judged for her investigation into Bryok's death. That occasion was gone and done, and perhaps if she hadn't bothered to do so, her uncle and his family would still be alive, but so much as she wished things were different, they were not. Much to her eternal regret, she went to Chysauster, everyone died, she returned none the wiser, and nothing changed for Trevena. But at least Alderman Aelwin spent some time in *gaol*. And now Gwendolyn had the chance to locate her mother and make some things right—for Bryn and for her.

Anyway, having Queen Eseld by her side might also help convince Baugh to fight with her against Locrinus. So, this wasn't only about mending her broken heart. Strategically, Gwendolyn *needed* her mother as well.

This was the right thing to do.

She felt it in her bones.

At least she thought so.

Gwendolyn slid Bryn another mindful glance, intending to lie to him now, but what came out of her mouth was another version of the truth. "I don't know what I believe, but his Druid brother believes it, and *Máistir* Emrys is our ally—one of too few. I'd not abandon him when he needs us most."

"What about the Fae?"

"What about them?"

"Do you suspect them?"

Gwendolyn's brows collided. "Are you suggesting Málik or Esme would do the *Máistir* harm? They were with us, Bryn."

He inspected the Hob cake in his hand. "I suggested no such thing," he argued. "But they are not the only Fae to be considered here. What I'd like to know

is what motive there is for murdering our good
Máistir?"

"Precisely!" Gwendolyn allowed, and then she suggested, "Perhaps to keep us from crossing the Veil?
Deartháir Harri was quick to refuse me. He opposes
the notion and swears it will make no difference who I
ask, and that Emrys will uphold his decision, but I do
not believe him."

"*Deartháir* Harri?"

Gwendolyn shrugged, remembering belatedly that
Bryn had yet to meet him. "He is the acting *Máistir*
now that Emrys is so ill. Perhaps *he* has a motive?"

"What motive, precisely?"

"They will lose this village if we spill blood in the
Fae realm, so I presume he cannot face his own mortality." Even as Gwendolyn spoke the possibility aloud,
the argument grew stronger. "He would rather stay
here than allow me to cross the Veil to retrieve my
sword. He would put himself and his youth before the
good of Pretania!"

Bryn lifted a dark brow as he popped another bite
of Hob cake into his mouth, then used the free hand to
brush a lock of shining black hair from his face.
"What do you propose we should do? Will you have
me spy upon our hosts? Peep through windows and
skulk about the kitchen, making inquiries?"

Gwendolyn offered him a crooked smile. "Isn't that
what you were already doing?"

"Well, I wasn't skulking," Bryn argued. "I was there
for the precise purpose of filling my empty belly," he
said. "Not to gather intelligence so I can accuse the
chef of poisoning our good *Máistir*."

Gwendolyn's gaze snapped to his. "You suspect the
chef?"

Bryn frowned. "Well, more than any, he would

have the knowledge, wouldn't he? After all, it was our kitchen service we employed to produce the *theriacs* we took. They must also have some knowledge of plants in order to cook without unintentionally murdering everyone. But nay, if indeed *Máistir* Emrys was poisoned, I must believe they perpetrated it another way. For what it's worth, I do not believe that kind chef would hurt a flea."

"Why?" Gwendolyn grinned. "Because he was kind enough to gift you Hob cake?" She sobered again. "Perhaps that, too, was by design," she suggested. "Again, I would take care with that Hob cake," she advised.

Still, Bryn ignored the warning, taking another hefty bite, and Gwendolyn noticed his hands were no longer quite so full. "There are no windows, anyway. Have you noticed?"

Of course, she had. This Druid village was nothing like any place Gwendolyn had ever encountered. "I am not suggesting you should peep into windows, Bryn. I don't know how you should go about your investigation. I only feel in my heart this is the right thing to do."

"My investigation?"

"Yours, yes," she agreed, avoiding his gaze.

There was so much Gwendolyn couldn't say, and the worst of it was withholding the possibility of his mother's escape. She longed to reveal that news most of all but dared not. Not only had she promised Esme, but she could not yet verify it as truth, and she would not raise Bryn's hopes only to dash them again. As it was, she was well aware of how much grief she had already caused him, and she refused to do aught more that would undermine him or their friendship. Slowly, but surely, they were rediscovering their amity, but this would end swiftly enough if Gwendolyn wounded him again.

Or... if he perceived she had lied to him.

A feeling of dread formed in the pit of her gut.

Gwendolyn trusted Esme only so far as to know the Elf could not wittingly lie. But to that end, Esme never actually said anyone besides Queen Eseld had lived.

Or had she said even that much?

A dark thought occurred to her—one she'd not considered before now, regardless of the differences between hers and her mother's countenances...

Was Queen Eseld her mother?

Could it be that her true mother still lived, but Queen Eseld was dead?

Blood and bloody bones.

Gwendolyn was too aware now of the possibility of crosstalk in every Fae agreement, and her heart sank over the deliberation.

But nay, she had her mother's ring for proof.

Still, Esme could have somehow discovered it, and used it to deceive her. That would be clever—to offer it as proof, without ever speaking her mother's name.

She tried to recall if Esme even once spoke it aloud and could not remember.

Ambling along, she was silent a long while, considering the possibilities, listening to Bryn swallow and chew bite after bite of Hob cake—devouring it as though he had gone for months without sustenance. He seemed fine at the moment, but he might yet come to regret his belly full—and so might she.

He would not be alone in his inebriation.

Long ramps made of ropes connected the village, intersecting at intervals by cross points where Druid prelates sat meditating and smoking their reeds.

These men were all so preoccupied with their *pookies* and their pipes, and their Hob cake and mead, it was little wonder how they accomplished anything at all.

Were they all this way?

Even the Llanrhos Druids had seemed immensely preoccupied with inducing their "visions," and Gwendolyn now wondered if they'd only ever visited Trevena in order to swelter beneath their ancient yew, filling their lungs with vapor.

The thought made her glower.

At long last, Bryn finished the last of the Hob cake. "Parsnip puffs!" he blurted, and Gwendolyn lifted both brows at the mention of the dish, made with salted, boiled parsnips and heaped with cream, butter, nutmeg and eggs. It had been so long since their cook had made it, but the first time she recalled eating parsnip puffs, Bryn had pushed an entire salver into her face, and then laughed and dashed away. They were twelve and eleven that summer—the year before she'd met Urien for the first time. Poor man, she thought. He had seemed hale enough in those days, and Gwendolyn's only thought had been one of horror over the possibility of wedding a man nearly her father's age. She wondered when his stepmother had begun to poison him, and felt terrible for his fate, despite that they did not perpetrate the crime on her behalf.

Bryn gave her a familiar grin, telling her he remembered that day as well, and Gwendolyn laughed and said, feigning irritation, "Parsnip puffs, humph!"

Of course, he would remember that occasion and dish—he had relished every moment of Gwendolyn's shock when he'd pushed the salver into her face. His laughter, as he'd run away, reverberated for weeks throughout Trevena's halls. Alas, if it was his intention to divert her, she would not be—not even by such pleasant memories. "Whatever you do, do not stir suspicion," she persisted.

"Discretion is my true name."

"Is it?" Gwendolyn knitted her brow. "Since when?"

For the first time in months, her childhood friend's cheeks mottled red. "Since my father discovered me in the stables with Caja."

"Caja!" Gwendolyn blinked. "The kitchen maid?"

Bryn nodded, his cheeks coloring deeper.

Gods. How was it she'd never known this? "You never said."

"Why would I?"

The question sobered Gwendolyn at once.

Why would he, indeed? Gwendolyn had always been aware of his feelings for her. But she'd also learned that his father never refrained from using the lash on his only begotten son. Bryn was too proud to tell her and Gwendolyn wanted to kill his father all over again, solely for the possibility of his having taken the lash to his sweet little boy—a just and honorable soul, who'd deserved more than what he got.

Including from her.

Gwendolyn owed Bryn so much.

Someday, she would honor him rightly.

Someday, she hoped he would find his own true love, as Ely had—hopefully, not like Gwendolyn, always wanting, wanting but never having.

Already, he'd known too much of that.

Indeed, the thought further sobered Gwendolyn, filling her with guilt. It was no wonder Bryn's mood grew ever more somber. Even now, though she could see the sadness in his eyes over the mention of his father, it also glinted with an underlying fury—perhaps because Talwyn always held him to such high standards, and meanwhile, would stoop so low as to commit treason—rotten, misbegotten cur.

As yet, she and Bryn had not had a suitable occasion to explore the events of that day—specifically, the death of his father by her hand. She sensed he didn't blame her, but there was still too much left unsaid.

"Everyone has secrets," he said, as though he'd read her mind. "Including me."

Now it was Gwendolyn's turn to flush because it was true, and clearly, she was keeping a few of her own.

He fixed her with a pointed glance, before relenting. "Very well. I will do as you suggest—as though there ever was a doubt. I am far too soft where you are concerned, Gwendolyn. Don't worry, I shall be discreet," he promised. "But I will only investigate under one condition..."

Gwendolyn slid both hands behind her back, linking her fingers, trying for a lighter tone. "And that would be?"

"You must allow me to deal with this my way, with no intervention from you. And furthermore, you must abide by my conclusions. In the meantime, you will worry only about getting us through the portal. No matter how charming this village, or how good the Hob cake, I'd not like to see us waylaid. For that matter, I heard some gossip in the kitchen, and it does not bode well."

"What gossip?"

He exhaled wearily. "There have been emissaries coming and going for the past two moons. Many from the Brigantes tribes, and a few from the Deceangli and even the Votadini. Locrinus has been busy wooing them, with a bit of help from Mona."

"Mona!"

Mona was the home of the Llanrhos Order.

The red in Bryn's cheeks spread to his neck. "Yes. Locrinus has sued for the return of his bride."

Sued? Gwendolyn felt a prick of fury over that news.

Over her dead body would she return to that ill-bred viper! "How dare he!" she said. "All the while, he travels with his mistress by his side!"

"From what I have been told, the Llanrhos Order has denied him, but they came to speak to the *Máistir* to glean his thoughts on the matter."

Gwendolyn felt her shoulders tighten.

Could that be who Emrys had met with in the grotto? If someone had poisoned him, she would loathe to think it could be anyone from the Llanrhos Order.

What had begun as a means to keep Bryn preoccupied now looked to be a matter of prudence. The more Gwendolyn heard, the more she was afraid there was foul play.

"Have we a bargain?"

"Yes," Gwendolyn said. "Of course."

Bryn tilted her a wary glance. "That was too easy."

Gwendolyn shrugged. "Mayhap I have learned my lessons, and therefore I have asked you to investigate in my stead. I know you will see everything more clearly than I will." That was and wasn't true. Bryn might be more broody than she, but he had the most annoying habit of seeing only the best in those he loved—that included Gwendolyn.

"Leave it with me, then." He grinned at her. "To begin, shall we pay our favorite brothers a visit and see how the *Máistir* fares?"

Gwendolyn stopped abruptly, peering about, dropping her hands by her sides, realizing they were lost. "Bryn? Where are we? Do you know how to find the *Máistir's* chamber?"

"I do," he said, turning to face her and skipping backwards, pointing to the bark of a tree. "Note where the moss grows. Always, on the north," he then said, pointing again, only this time to the courtyard itself. "Also, note the corners," he suggested. "They marked every corner with symbols, showing what lies ahead."

"That's brilliant," Gwendolyn allowed, wondering why she'd never noticed those before. But that would make sense, when otherwise, there was nothing in this village that gave one any sense of direction. One could not glimpse the sky, nor the ground in this village, nor was it possible to distinguish day from night, except in the vaguest sense—which was to say that, if the sky was dark, even by day, then the light was minimal, regardless of the hour. And despite this, the hour was never too dark to see one's hand in front of one's face. From outside, every dwelling looked the same, except for the length of the chambers. That was the only reason she had known which was the *Máistir's* Hall and which was the Hall of Feasts. Or the bathhouse— she'd recognized the last by the outpouring of steam. But even that wasn't foolproof. The curling mist was ever-present, light but impenetrable, so that even as one passed through it, knowing full well what was left behind, every sense of what was gone was forgotten, and a glance ahead revealed nothing more than billowing mist—like a waking dream, even without the aid of *pookies,* everything illusory. Only this time, that quality left Gwendolyn unsettled. This was a village lost in place and time, and perhaps someone intended for it to remain that way...

At the cost of Máistir Emrys' life.

28

As heartening as their conversation had been—giving Gwendolyn a much-welcome return to normalcy regarding Bryn—she sent him on his way, reassuring him most vehemently that she could locate the *Máistir's* chamber on her own. She alone would check on Emrys and Lir. And, instead, Bryn should begin his investigation. The longer she remained in his presence, the greater the chance he would suspect her ruse. But Gwendolyn didn't have to lie: Their time was growing short. She told him so, and he gave her a dubious tilt of his head. "Art certain, Gwendolyn? I haven't seen Lir since we arrived. Shouldn't I lend support?"

"Later," Gwendolyn pressed. "We haven't time, Bryn. Go discover what you may. In the meantime, I will see to Emrys, and I promise to tell Lir you will visit soon."

He scratched his head. "Very well," he relented, and walked away, and though Gwendolyn had the feeling he suspected something, he didn't look back.

Once he was gone, she made her way at once to Emrys' quarters, using the symbols Bryn had pointed out. It wasn't quite so simple as Bryn had suggested, but the marks made it easier to find. Unfortunately, when she arrived, it was to discover the *Máistir's* condition unchanged. He wasn't improved, but neither was he in immediate danger, and Gwendolyn took comfort in that, at least.

He rested easily, with no fever. No bluing of his skin. No flushing. Only this odd bruising, which seemed to have traveled from its point of origin—that, and his hands were now stiff as a boar's bristle. As though he were already dead, rigid, despite most certainly being alive. It was the most perplexing array of symptoms, and the only thing that gave her any pause. Because, if, in truth, the cause of his illness was his advanced age, there shouldn't be any symptoms at all.

Frowning, Gwendolyn smoothed a hand over his forehead, then patted his cheek with affection, hoping he would recover, although she must consider that these Druids had put off for seven hundred years what most mortal men experienced after fifty or less—only if they were fortunate. Many men expired younger, and though her father had lived more than most, despite his illness, he did not come close to *Máistir* Emrys' age. Alas, no one could cure old age, nor prevent one's natural death. Sliding her hand from Emrys' cool forehead, she considered the color of his skin—neither pale nor flushed. For all that he had endured, he appeared as though he were sleeping. "Has he stirred at all?" she asked Lir.

Solemnly, the young Druid shook his head. "Not once."

BY THE FOLLOWING MORNING, when Gwendolyn had yet to receive Esme, she rose and set out to find her.

Normally, the Elf appeared whenever it suited her

to do so. Half the time during their travels, Esme hadn't even slept when they slept, abandoning camp at twilight, and returning in the wee hours, only to continue the journey in the morning as indefatigable as Enbarr's mares. And yet, considering the urgency of this mission, Gwendolyn would have expected to leave by now, and nevertheless, Esme was nowhere to be found.

Oddly, neither did she encounter Bryn, and Gwendolyn wondered if he was making progress—or even if there was progress to be made.

By early afternoon, she grew frustrated. She had looked everywhere. In the bathhouse. In the *Máistir's* chamber. She'd checked the dining hall, the kitchen, and once, entirely by accident, she poked her head into a strange Druid's quarters, searching for Bryn, and found the man on his knees, nude, and crawling about on all fours. Stifling a yelp of surprise, she backed away without disturbing him, befuddled over what he might be doing, and thereafter resolved to at least clear her throat before entering any quarters.

Having spent too little time in this village the first time she'd visited, she had had no genuine sense of how curious this place was. The entire village was a spidery maze, and the mist, she suspected, muddled the mind.

For all Gwendolyn knew, she'd only dreamt the conversation with Esme, and only wished her mother was still alive.

Gods. Had she?

Gwendolyn hoped not.

Not only did she long so desperately to see her mother again, but the more she considered Esme's plan, the more she felt it was the right thing to do. She couldn't live with herself if she endangered others. Not if there was *another* way.

And there was.

Bryn, for one, couldn't think clearly where Gwendolyn was concerned. If he believed for one moment that it was for the best to defend her, she could not be certain he would stand down, even if she commanded him to do so. It didn't matter that she had survived Loc's wretched court, nor that she had rallied a once-sworn enemy, nor that she had stood up to Caradoc, besting him at swords, nor that she herself had devised the plan to save Trevena, nor that she had been the one to climb the *piscina* shaft to see her plan to fruition. Gwendolyn could defend herself but judging by the way Bryn had spoken to her yesterday afternoon, he would always see her as the youngling princess he was sworn to defend, and she might never outgrow his solicitousness, nor his dubiety. When they faced Esme's father, Gwendolyn must be certain she was the one in command, and that no one would undermine her efforts to retrieve her sword. A peaceful negotiation was preferred, but if blood must be shed, it should be hers—not Bryn's, and not Lir's.

Nor Málik's, though she felt like eviscerating him herself.

Indeed, she had to restrain herself from accosting him when, late in the afternoon, he found her wandering, and insisted she join him to sup.

Angry though Gwendolyn was, she had no choice but to accept his offer if she didn't wish him to suspect. But this was the first time since learning the truth that she'd had to look him in the eyes and knowing that he had been sent to assassinate her, not confronting him over it was the most difficult thing she'd ever had to do —more so, even, then keeping the truth from Bryn.

No, she wanted to say.

Bloody liar, she wanted to shout.

It didn't matter whether Fae couldn't speak untruths. Bryn was right: A lie of omission was still a lie. And Málik's lie was not a small one.

He came to kill her? Truly?

How dare he claim he loved her when all along he was carrying such a dark secret, with even darker intent?

Seated in the hall now, with Málik by her side, Gwendolyn turned the ring Esme gave her under the table, flicking her thumbnail against the little flowers —proof that she and Esme had spoken... proof that her mother lived.

So long as Gwendolyn had a memory of it, her mother had never once removed this ring from her finger. Even when she'd dressed for the finer occasions, she had worn this relic of her Prydein youth. She must believe Esme spoke true.

Turning the ring around and around and around her finger, Gwendolyn sat on pushpins, eager to be done with the evening's discourse and entertainment... eager to speak with Esme again, intending to press her about her mother. If she could not answer with conviction, or if she digressed, Gwendolyn would know to suspect.

But then what?

Did she go back to her original plan and concede to the danger it would pose to Bryn and Málik? Never mind Lir; she couldn't bring him now, not with Emrys so ill. But then, after all, Esme had been so adamant that Málik and Lir should be left behind. Had she changed her mind? And if she did, what about Gwendolyn's mother? What about the portal?

Gwendolyn would have thought for sure Esme would have found her by now.

Her thoughts spun like the ring on her finger as her gaze sought the door beyond the creature seated atop a stool on the dais, praying Esme, or even Bryn would come save her from this pretentious discussion.

And meanwhile, now and again, her gaze fell upon the odd little creature in the center of the room, whose fur alternated between black and white.

Introduced as a Púca, Gwendolyn soon discovered it had the same peculiar quality as Hob cake. Only instead of becoming what others wished to see, it transformed as it pleased—one moment, a tiny blue man with pointy ears, singing at the top of his lungs, another moment a three-headed beast, still singing, but each head crooning a different verse. The cacophony gave Gwendolyn a pang in her ear.

Meanwhile, Málik sat beside her, watching her with unbridled interest, and Gwendolyn daren't speak a word lest she give herself away. Foremost in her mind was Esme's disclosure, and though she longed to ask him, why—not so much why he would agree to his father's command, but why, after everything they had endured together, he had not revealed the truth.

"Tricky little beasts," Málik said, hitching his chin at the stage and rubbing the stem of his wooden goblet between two long fingers.

The silver glint in his eyes gave Gwendolyn the strangest feeling that, for the first time, she was witnessing his inebriation. She frowned, peering at the goblet in his hand. Like you, she thought, quietly seething. She had the distinct impression he wasn't talking about the Púca right now, and she longed to challenge him and turn the table. But no matter how sore her heart, she couldn't divulge any of the things

Esme had told her. If her mother still lived, and she had any opportunity to reunite with her, she would not spoil the chance by tipping her hand.

For now, she must keep her thoughts to herself and her mother's ring beneath the table. But this marked the first time since Chysauster that she'd held back from Málik, and she sensed his chariness... multiplying by the moment.

Picking anxiously at a biscuit with her free hand, Gwendolyn averted her gaze when he tried to peer into her eyes. Only when he returned his attention to the Púca did she relax. Meanwhile, the Púca stopped singing, and the dining hall chatter, without the accompaniment of music, had a more soothing effect on Gwendolyn, reminding her of the dinner hour in Trevena's hall. It wasn't so long ago that her worst problem was how she was going to get away from her mother long enough to ride, swim, or hunt. At the moment, she would give anything to be away from this hall in search of the one person she had spent so much effort to avoid.

On the stool in the center of the room, the three headed beast shifted form into the shape of a horse's tail, flicking with annoyance—only the horse's tail, mind you, no torso, no head, no neck, or limbs. Somehow, that tail clung to the stool, all the while swishing back and forth, as though it could read Gwendolyn's mood and she watched it, wondering why a horsetail. She would have asked Málik but didn't wish to make polite conversation with him—not now when her emotions were in such tumult. And despite this, she was aware of his every move made, every gesture... the way he held his goblet... and the way he fingered the odd wedge of yellow fruit that reminded Gwendolyn of a lime. And she was so focused on Málik she had

somehow missed the salver behind the yellow fruit...
until now.

Hob cake, and no matter, she daren't take a single
bite—not an easy feat, when every morsel she had
ever consumed was like reliving a lovely memory.

Following her gaze, Málik said, "I am surprised
you've refrained." He flicked a finger at the Hob cake.

Meanwhile, on the dais, the horse's tail whipped.

"That's the thing," Gwendolyn said, with meaning.
"I perhaps like it *too* well. I should endeavor to resist."

Swish went the horse's tail.

"I mustn't forget how it affects me—to my undoing. It seems so innocuous, though I have learned it is
not, and I—" She corrected herself, smiling ruefully.
"*We* cannot afford for me to lie abed for days now, can
we? Nor am I willing to court any more *pookie*
dreams."

"A bite shouldn't hurt."

*What about you? Will you do me harm, Málik? Would
you oppose me? After everything you have said—after all
we have suffered?*

The questions caught in Gwendolyn's throat,
making it burn.

But that was the thing. Already, she was hurt, and
if he took his blade and slit her throat, her heart
would not bleed any more or less.

"Last time, the *pookies* compounded the effects. I
requested they not be served you this eve." He gave
her a playful wink, and Gwendolyn said, "Thank you."
But what else had he warned the Druids not to say
or do?

Was he the reason they would not allow her to
cross the Veil?

Was he pretending to be her ally, all the while
working at cross-purposes? For all this time, Gwen-

dolyn had suspected Esme of doing just so, but never once did she suspect it of Málik. Gwendolyn had trusted him implicitly. How dare he look at her now and make her feel like the worst of villains for lying to him, when she knew he was lying to her still?

How came you to be in my father's employ?

I was sent.

By whom?

My father.

Swish, swish went the horse's tail.

Gwendolyn offered a half-hearted attempt at a smile. "Apparently, Bryn is taken with the Hob cake," she allowed.

Swish, swish.

"For all we know, that is why he's not in attendance tonight. He's like to be flat on his face in bed, and we can't have two drunk on Hob cake, can we?"

Swish, swish.

Málik laughed, the tenor rich and low—an achingly familiar sound Gwendolyn hadn't heard in far too long. *But how could he laugh when her heart was breaking?*

Swish, swish.

"Really," she said, animated now. "I found him loitering in the cookhouse, of all places. Who knows how many cakes that greedy pig has consumed?"

"He'll be fine," Málik reassured. "A nap will do him good. It was a grueling journey north. He should rest, and so should you."

Swish, swish.

"You needn't worry about me," Gwendolyn said, noticing only belatedly that *Deartháir* Harri was also missing from this hall, and she wondered where he might be. "How well do you know *Deartháir* Harri?"

she asked, changing the subject to something less indicting.

"Well enough."

She pretended an interest in a slight scratch on the wooden table as she asked, "I wonder... how many times have you visited this village?"

"Over the past seven hundred years?" His tone suggested it would be impossible to count. "A few times, I suppose."

"And Esme?"

"More than me."

As usual, no answer he ever gave offered more than the meagerest of information.

Swish, swish.

"Well," she said, once again turning her mother's little ring beneath the table, perhaps as a reminder. "There is something about him I do not trust."

The Púca suddenly returned to its three-headed form and shrieked at the top of its lungs with every voice—a terrifying sound that felt as though it would shatter Gwendolyn's eardrums. But it sounded the way she felt—ready to shatter. When the creature's "song" subsided again, she offered, "That is quite an annoying creature."

"Can be."

"What language does it speak?"

"Gaelg."

Gwendolyn tipped him an inquisitive look.

"The First Tongue."

"And what does he sing about?"

"A song prohibited in the Fae realm."

"Why?"

He shrugged. "On the one hand, it reveals too much, on the other, too little."

How appropriate, Gwendolyn thought, though she

nodded without remark, returning her gaze to the salver of Hob cake. Unaccustomed to this dance of words, especially with Málik, she was trying in vain to make polite conversation. Forsooth. Even when their discourse had been inimical, they were never at a lack. And now she had reason to guard every word that came out of her mouth. "I visited with Emrys this morn," she said, offhand.

"And?"

"He's the same. His symptoms unusual. Nothing like I have ever encountered."

Málik lifted his goblet, tilting it one way, then the other, considering. "As I told you, there are substances in the Fae realm that could affect a mortal aversely."

"What sort?"

He gave her a pointed look, once again deflecting the question. "Which reminds me, Gwendolyn... if they ever invite you to sup, you must consume nothing, unless I tell you it is safe." Gwendolyn frowned— for the most obvious reason: because he wouldn't be with her. But also, because how could she *ever* trust him again?

And regardless, she agreed without argument. "I will not." And then she tilted her head, smiling coyly. "Any further counsel, now that we are down to it?"

"Oh,, then? Has *Deartháir* Harri changed his mind about the portal?"

"Nay," Gwendolyn said, feeling thwarted. "He has not."

And then, despite his obvious aversion to truth, she opted for honesty on her part. "It doesn't matter; I *will* cross the Veil."

He smiled, then raised his glass, winking. "I place my wagers on the Cornish princess," he said amiably, but Gwendolyn had the unmistakable impression his thoughts were swirling with speculation and suspicion.

She couldn't afford for him to wonder, so she tried for an easier tone, one that bespoke their previous fellowship. "Have you any new opinion on the *Máistir's* condition?"

"Nay. I've no additional information to provide. And yet," he said, continuing, watching Gwendolyn with unbridled interest. "If one of our medicaments, or even some harmless victual has been provided to these Druids, it could well render him just so. That is why it is forbidden to trade with mortals."

Gwendolyn cast a glance at the salver. "What about Hob cake?"

"That is different," Málik said. "It is the only Fae substance approved for this realm. Essentially, there is only the slightest deviation from your *pookies*—a component that accounts for the illusory taste. Howbeit, the rest of the ingredients are already available and growing in the mortal realm—*pookies*, as I said, but also Hul Gil, which I believe you sometimes use medicinally?"

"Only when it can be procured," Gwendolyn allowed. "It turns up most oft on Sumerian vessels, though some years ago my father requested the drogue not be traded in our markets, because... well..." She gave him a rueful smile, one without mirth. "A certain someone thought he could fly and broke his arm and three ribs after jumping from the ramparts."

Málik lifted a brow. "Anyone I know?"

"Perhaps," Gwendolyn said, though she didn't intend to say. It was Alderman Crwys, and he'd nearly paid for that reckless stunt with the loss of his position, but as it was, there was plenty Málik was keeping from her and it might be silly, considering the circumstances, but Gwendolyn didn't wish to share. "It wasn't me," she said.

Málik smiled thinly, and Gwendolyn endeavored to change the subject, her hand returning to the ring beneath the table, and, unintentionally, her thoughts were revealed. "Do you remember your mother?"

"I do not," Málik said. "I only know she was Fèinne."

"Fèinne?"

"A freeborn guard to the High King."

His ready answer piqued Gwendolyn's curiosity. She had never known him to be so forthcoming about his private affairs. "Do you know her name?"

Málik's pale blue eyes glinted like Loegrian steel. "Has no one ever told you there is power in a Fae's true name?"

Gwendolyn's heart beat faster.

He smiled. "Her name is not mine to share."

Gwendolyn hitched her chin. "Because you do not trust me?"

"*Should* I trust you, Gwendolyn?"

Gwendolyn's face burned hot. "I might ask this of *you*," she countered, if only to divert the question, and he laughed darkly.

"Well played, *Banríon*. You will do well in conversation with my father. But that only proves my point."

Gwendolyn's heartbeat tripped. "What point?"

"We dance about the question, but we both know the answer." His gaze skewered Gwendolyn as surely as his sword might have done. Beneath his scrutiny, Gwendolyn felt wholly exposed, all her secrets laid bare. *But, thankfully, not all her secrets.* As far as she knew—by his own assurances—he could not read minds. Yet now it begged the question. "Must I presume Málik is not *your* true name?"

He lifted both brows. "Must you?"

"Málik, I beg, for once, you would answer my question without deflection."

"And give you the power to compel me?"

Gwendolyn's heart twisted. "You would have no qualms if you trusted me," she returned, and so quickly, her ire had returned.

"As you trust me?" he replied. Once more he lifted his goblet and made a show of taking a sip. He then tipped it slightly so Gwendolyn could glimpse within the cup. *The liquid was blue.* "It is not simply our elements that can affect a mortal aversely. The same holds true for those found int he mortal realm. For example, there is a flower called the butterfly pea, which grows in your realm. It is known to be a truth serum. For that reason, whilst they do not proscribe it from our realm, they prohibit it from being served to any Fae without the accompaniment of this yellow fruit they call a lemon." He lifted the small wedge and turned it to show it to her, pinched between two fingers, then he lifted it over his cup to squeeze a drop into his drink, setting the lemon down after. "It reveals the elixir for what it is. A single drop deposited into the drink will turn the serum red." He tilted his glass again to show her. *The liquid was red.* "For us, the butterfly pea is quite compelling, and the smallest of sips may render us unable to prevaricate."

Gwendolyn felt the burn of tears return to her eyes. "You mean lie?"

"Well, you may call it that, and perhaps it is true, as you once pointed out, that a lie of omission is still a lie, but I am certain you've also been told there is no cunning, like Fae cunning?"

"Indeed," Gwendolyn said, her neck and throat burning with ire. "So I have been warned—by you, no less. Isn't that why you suggested Lir should accompany us?"

"So, if you must know," he continued, ignoring the subtle accusation in Gwendolyn's tone. "All these things I have told you about my mother and my father, these are forbidden for me to speak of, and still I have been able to share them tonight, aided by this tea." His winterbourne eyes shone. "Mind you, I do not know how it works, only that it does, and despite that the effects are more compelling to my ilk, it seems to work on *mortals* as well." He placed the glass down and pushed it toward Gwendolyn, then said, "Won't you try some?"

Gwendolyn stared at the goblet, blinking.

There was a shadow growing in Málik's eyes that warned her against drinking even a sip. He knew something. That glint in his eyes gave her every assurance he would press for answers. Discomposed, she pulled the glass closer—close enough to peer within. The bright red liquid seemed to have grown brighter. When she peered up again, he smiled, giving her a glimpse of his fangs. Gwendolyn shoved the glass away, dropping her hand to her belly.

"I am not thirsty," she proclaimed, and then rose from the table as the Púca once more began to wail. "I am knackered," she said. "I must bid you good eve."

His eyes glittered as she rose. "Sleep well. Don't let the bedbugs bite," he said, and he didn't bother to rise to see her out. "I mean to stay. I've been watching for Esme. If you see her, please tell her I would like to speak with her."

"I will," Gwendolyn said, and hastened away.

29

H*e knew.*

That was the first thought Gwendolyn had upon waking, and she squeezed her eyes tight against the brightening light.

Last night had been the single most harrowing night between them, and she loathed their dance of deception. Nor did she know what more to do. She'd spent half the night waiting for Esme, and Esme never arrived.

Fatigued and troubled, she opened her eyes to a curious display of dust motes dancing along a nimbus of morning light—nay... *not* dust motes. They were wriggling.

Bedbugs? She thought, remembering Málik's send-off, but nay. Although they were certainly small enough to be bedbugs, bedbugs couldn't fly.

Could they?

Momentarily disoriented, she peered about to find herself alone in the chamber, and then, blinking, she tilted her head up to study the swarm...

Piskies?

Indeed.

They were *piskies.* The tiniest of creatures flocked

above her head, like gnats... or, truly, more like minuscule winking stars floating along in the soft morning light.

Blinking again, she stared in wonder.

Never was she afforded such an opportunity to watch so many up close, nor had she encountered them anywhere besides Porth Pool.

As they did there beneath the surface of the water, they sailed over her head, swimming through the air, effortless in flight. And yet, if they had wings, they fluttered them so quickly it was impossible to see them, and it was only once she'd lifted a hand and one landed atop the butt of her palm that she could actually see the filigreed wings—tiny, but perfectly formed. And no wonder they twinkled! What might have been hair sprang from its wee head, reflecting golden light.

For the space of an instant, Gwendolyn daren't blink as the bright speck bounded over to land atop the tip of her nose, where she could further make out its pointy little ears—like Fae. She peered at it through crossed eyes, afraid to breathe lest it startle like a nervous fly. "Hello," she said as the *piskie* crouched, lowering its face... to sniff?

Or.... *Did it intend to bite her?*

Poke a finger into her eye?

Demelza used to claim whenever Gwendolyn awoke with sore, red eyes that she must have angered a *piskie*. She'd claimed they liked to sprinkle dust like glass into the eyes of those they did not like.

Even now, as Gwendolyn watched, she half expected to feel the prick of teeth. But when the bite didn't materialize, she smiled and cooed. "Look at you!"

How adorably fierce it appeared, gazing at her

with such unbridled interest, simply watching to see what Gwendolyn might do. For the sake of the moment, Gwendolyn did nothing, not wishing to frighten it away. They could be wicked, perhaps, but they also had a desire to champion good. Demelza also told her a tale about a fellow arrived in their city, who'd set about wooing a young maid. One evening, he'd lured the lovesick girl to Porth Pool, and there, took her virginity, after which, the girl told him her father would welcome a match between them. The young man laughed in her face and then sent her away sobbing. He never returned to the city, and they discovered him the following morning, covered in blights, lying amidst the bracken with a look of terror on his face. *Piskies*, they'd claimed.

From that day forward, only the purest of hearts ever dared swim at Porth Pool—and perhaps Gwendolyn subconsciously considered that on that day she'd contemplated taking Locrinus to the Pool. Somehow, even knowing so little about him—only that he was a pompous, vainglorious man—she hadn't believed he would fare well in her special place. So, she took him instead to see her stone maidens. What a disappointment that was, too. He'd trod all over her maidens with his rude horse, showing such disrespect that Gwendolyn had longed to smack him, even then. Conversely, Málik had stood back to honor the fallen, kneeling beside her stone maidens to pray—why, she still didn't know. But it was during that moment Gwendolyn had seen him differently—not as the belligerent creature she had tried so hard to make him to be.

A tear stung one eye, and she pushed the memory away. She had been such an innocent, with no notion of how much pain she would come to endure.

Today, she must talk to Málik, she decided. They mustn't go on this way. She didn't know what to say. She only knew that if he had wanted her dead, he would have slain her long ago. He'd certainly had many opportunities, and instead, had shielded her, not once, but so many times—including the other day in the woods, when she'd nearly leapt out at Loc's men. It didn't matter how her swordplay had improved; she had been one against too many. Altogether, they would have cut her down before she could plunge her blade into a one, and she would have endangered Bryn and Lir.

She swallowed with some difficulty, remembering Málik's expression as she'd walked away last night... so much suspicion and disappointment.

Gwendolyn couldn't bear it.

And yet... she still could not reveal Esme's plan—she daren't.

It wasn't simply because her heart yearned for the woman who gave her birth... she needed Queen Eseld as well. With her mother at her side, there was a far better chance Baugh would fight by her side, and she needed Baugh. More than ever, Gwendolyn was convinced he was the key to her success. Even if she faced him wielding *Claímh Solais*, there was no guarantee he would see it as a divine sign. What had Málik said? *He might be your grandsire, but he'll never be swayed to your cause solely because his blood flows through your veins.* During all those years, her mother had lived in Trevena, never once had he traveled to see her.

For all this time, the *piskie* remained on Gwendolyn's nose, watching, and then it bounced away with the spryness of a flea to rejoin its swarm. Suddenly, they put their voices together, forming a single, coherent word—a swelling sound formed of a thousand voices.

Danger!

Gwendolyn blinked, staring at the swarm.

Danger! They bellowed again.

"What danger?" she asked, and then, without warning, the swarm dove toward her face, giving her cheeks an odd sting. Startled, Gwendolyn sat, swatting them away, and the little buzzing creatures flew away, toward the door, and out, the swiftness of their flight leaving Gwendolyn with a sense of unease, but for what, she couldn't say. And then... she heard voices outside.

Familiar voices.

Málik and Esme?

Whispering.

Quickly but quietly, Gwendolyn cast away the furs, thrusting both legs off the side of the bed. She landed on her toes and made her way to the door.

"Once again, you've appointed yourself her Shadow?"

"What business have you with her?"

"*My* business with *your* queen is for her ears, not yours."

Gwendolyn sidled closer to the door—well, not a door, more like a curtain, and despite that she knew by experience that these walls were sturdy enough to hold her, she couldn't be certain they wouldn't betray her presence if she leaned against them, so she tipped forward, careful not to touch the wall, only listening.

"After weeks of disregard, you come crawling now?"

"Mayhap you've forgotten, *dear betrothed*. You are not the only one with business here."

As though buffeted by her words, Gwendolyn rocked back on her heels.

Dear betrothed.

With so much enmity between them, it had been too easy to forget their relationship, but he was Esme's before Gwendolyn ever knew him. And no matter, she was so startled by the endearment that she missed what else they were saying, and now she focused again only to catch the last of it...

"...Please, Málik! You will risk all *we* have worked for."

We? Perhaps she meant the rebellion? Although, as far as Gwendolyn knew, Málik had taken great pains to keep himself apart from that effort...

"No matter what you do, or what you say, he'll never concede the sword, and you well know it!"

"If I must, *I* will take it for her," Málik said darkly.

"By the eyes of Lugh! Have you forgotten who you are?" Esme whispered fiercely. "A prince of the realm! Why would you give up so much for her?"

Confusion swam in Gwendolyn's head. *Gods.* Esme sounded so bitter—like a spurned lover. Did she, or didn't she, intend to help Gwendolyn?

There was a note of menace in Málik's response. "It suits me better to be a lowly huntsman than to wear a black-horned crown!"

"My father will flay you!" Esme warned.

Gwendolyn didn't know what to think.

Who was helping whom?

Who was the villain and who was the champion?

Whom should she trust?

The more she heard, the more muddled her mind, and this morn, she couldn't blame it on the mist.

"So be it," Málik said.

"Málik," Esme said, begging now. "Please, allow me to tell her."

"No."

"Even if you cannot, I am not bound."

"No," he said once more, and Gwendolyn recognized the finality of his tone. She had been the recipient of it a few times.

It didn't matter; she'd heard enough.

"Tell me what?" she asked, pushing her way through the curtain and presenting herself.

For the first time in their acquaintance, Esme appeared to blush—a burst of pink appearing on her otherwise pale cheeks. "I came to speak to you, but this sour-faced lout will not let me pass!" She waved a hand with an angry flourish at Málik, whose arms remained crossed.

His narrowed gaze remained fixed upon Esme. "I asked what business you had. You refused to say."

"A prince of Tír na nÓg, and you will lower yourself to be a huntsman!"

Málik's arms did not unlock, and Gwendolyn noted the tick at his jaw.

For a long, awkward moment, Esme stood firm, fury clear in her own unwavering stance. Her green eyes flashed with unmistakable ire, and yet behind the fury, Gwendolyn also recognized desperation. "You need not guard me from Esme," she said. "If she has aught she wishes to say to me, I will hear it."

"If she has aught to say to you, she may speak it in my presence."

"What if I prefer to speak to her *alone*?" Gwendolyn was beginning to feel like a rag doll being tugged between two rival children.

"Have you secrets to keep?" Málik challenged.

"No," Gwendolyn said, feeling guilty for the lie, because she *did*—and not a small one. She and Esme had made plans that could change the outcome for all. "I should ask the same of you," she countered, crossing her arms. "I heard you two speaking behind my back. What is it you refuse to tell me?"

"Never mind!" Esme announced, turning with an angry huff. "I will return when your *Shadow* has flown! In the meantime, enjoy yourselves, because this day might be your last!"

Before Gwendolyn could stop her, or say aught more, Esme was gone.

"What was that about?"

Málik didn't blink. "What was what about?"

"I told you, I heard everything you said."

"If you did, you needn't ask." His lips curved slightly, perhaps even viciously.

"Why were you loitering outside *my* room whilst I slept? Really, Málik, did you stand here all night, guarding my room?"

"In fact, I did," he confessed.

"Why?"

"Because your *Shadow* is drunk on Hob cake and I did not believe it prudent to leave you alone." He cast his eyes in the direction Esme had gone. "Nor do I trust *her*." Gwendolyn's anger dimmed, if only a bit, replaced by a prick of guilt—for Bryn's sake as well as Málik's. She didn't like keeping secrets, nor did she like the fact that, because she had been so preoccupied with her own dealings, she'd left Bryn vulnerable. Neither was Málik her enemy. There was no mistaking the possessive gleam in his eyes.

"Did you not sleep?"

"Nay," he said. "But—"

"I know, I know." She waved a hand in dismissal.

"You do not sleep as we do, but you *do* sleep. And now that I am awake, perhaps you should go rest?"

"That is not what I need," he said, and for the first time since Gwendolyn presented herself this morning, his eyes dared to stray... to the long, flowing gown she'd worn to bed—another present from Esme, Gwendolyn presumed, when she'd discovered the garment on her bed. Gauzy and delicate, the fabric felt as though she were wearing a cloud. Gwendolyn followed his gaze and blinked.

Was he looking at...?

Even as she wondered, his eyes glinted *hungrily*.

Never in her life had she experienced such a look of hunger, and she felt suddenly... *nervous*? Like a vole facing a cat. She had never once found herself the subject of a man's lustful glances. But she recognized that look when she saw it, because she'd seen enough such glances directed at Ely.

Málik smiled, showing the barest hint of a long, white fang, and Gwendolyn couldn't help but remember his warning... *There are few occasions when the goddess' creatures are made without regard to need...*

Her heart beat a little faster.

As a matter of self-preservation, she hugged herself, covering the pebbled peaks of her breasts. He blinked, his long lashes lifting against silvery brows, and his *winterbourne* eyes blazed. "You won't tell me what you were discussing?" she said nervously, hoping to rediscover some inkling of her composure.

It wasn't a question; she knew he wouldn't answer, but for the moment, all she could think about was his lips... his kiss... his hands... the way it once felt to be held in his embrace. It had been too long, and she craved this as desperately as she did the Hob cake...

perhaps more. Only duty held sway over the desire she felt for his love.

A silver light shimmered in the storm of his eyes. "Perhaps you already know what Esme wishes to speak to you about?"

Gwendolyn hugged herself tighter. "If I do, it is not your concern."

And yet, it was.

Guilt forced her to avert her eyes.

Fear stilled her tongue.

Hope for her mother strengthened her resolve.

More than anything, Gwendolyn longed to confess... but for the sake of too many, she couldn't betray Esme's trust.

Wouldn't.

Not if there was the smallest chance to help her mother and save Málik as well. Regardless that he had lied to her, she didn't believe he wished her harm. And despite Esme's demeanor over these past weeks, Gwendolyn cared for her as well. Nobody was without fault here, and just as Bryn once thought it prudent to advise her... nobody was without secrets, not even Gwendolyn.

Most especially not Gwendolyn.

Dearest betrothed, Esme had said.

Gwendolyn's feelings were confused...

She lifted her gaze to Málik's beautiful, iridescent face.

Gods knew she would give everything if only she could return to the way it was... so her greatest worry was the uncertainty of giving her heart to a fellow.

Even if that fellow was not human.

"I do not wish to quarrel with you, Málik. Esme and I have business, but it does not concern you." Speaking with as much authority as she dared, she spun on her heels to go back into her room. "If she re-turns, please let her pass."

Málik caught her by the arm... his long fingers gripping hard, holding her fast.

Gwendolyn meant to shrug away, but twisted her arm and caught him by the forearm instead, locking her fingers about his as well, her fingernails digging into his flesh. And there they stood.

But two could play at this game.

For the longest moment, neither spoke, and for Gwendolyn's part, words refused to form. His steely eyes bore into her own... testing her resolve. But the hunger in his eyes had not abated, and instead, seemed to fortify as his fingers kneaded her flesh.

Gwendolyn swallowed convulsively as she soft-ened her grip on his arm. "Really," she said, much of the steel leaving her voice. "You should... go... rest."

More than anything, he should just go.

Now, before she said something she would later come to regret.

His look, his touch, was affecting her strangely.

A lump formed in her throat. And then he tugged and Gwendolyn tugged back, and though she didn't know what the gesture proposed... somehow, she did.

She didn't want him to release her.

She wanted him to come inside... with her.

She wanted to kiss him again.

Wanted...

His fingers sank deeper into the soft flesh of her arm, and Gwendolyn returned the gesture in kind, both staring at one another with gazes changing from ire... to surprise... to... unmitigated desire?

Hot points of desire burst behind her closed lids when she didn't even remember closing her eyes.

He tugged once more, pulling her toward him, and Gwendolyn said, "Málik."

"Do not tempt me," he begged.

And then, before she perceived how best to respond, he drew her into his arms, covering her mouth with his own, slipping his hot tongue between her trembling lips. A soft gasp escaped Gwendolyn as he enfolded her in his embrace, holding her possessively as he tasted and explored the depths of her mouth.

Gods. Oh Gods.

This wasn't a sweet kiss.

She could taste his *desire.*

And hers.

Her heart pounding all the while like a forger's hammer, they kissed ardently, exploring each other's mouths with the fervor of two starved beasts—both of whom had gone without sustenance too long. The groan that escaped Málik's mouth set fire to Gwendolyn's body, and when he attempted to extricate himself, she lifted her arms, locking them about his neck, pulling him down for another kiss. "No," she whispered. "Don't... go."

"I—"

"No," she said again. "Do not deny me."

His hands lifted to her cheeks, cupping her face between his hands—how and when they alit there, Gwendolyn didn't know for sure, because in her mind they were both still standing, arms entwined.

"Please," she begged.

"You have always been my weakness," he whispered, and the meadowy scent of his breath left her hungry and helpless...

"Come inside," she begged.

He shook his head, refusing.

Gwendolyn begged with her eyes.

"Who can say where we go from here, or whether we live or die? If, in truth, your father will flay you, what more will he do to me? I will not regret my death for this cause, Málik, but I will regret..." She swallowed. "Not having known..."

Gently, he lifted a finger to her lips, hushing her.

"Come inside," she pleaded, and though she had never in her life used her feminine wiles, she did so now, shrugging her gown off one shoulder to bare the pale moon of her flesh for his hungry eyes.

A strange haze passed over his wintry gaze... a film of burning ice. And then he lowered his hot lips to her shoulder, searing her flesh with a kiss. And swiftly baring his teeth, he rested his upper fangs against her bared shoulder, and there remained, pressing the points of his very sharp teeth into the tender skin.

As though aroused by the taste of her, he closed his eyes, and sank only the tip of one glittering tooth into her shoulder, drawing a speck of blood.

Gwendolyn blinked, confused.

And no matter... her body flushed with a different kind of hunger.

Her skin tingled.

Every part of her convulsed.

Her cheeks burned.

The tips of her breasts ached.

And before she knew what to say, a sense of certainty arose. Come what may, she would give herself to Málik and Málik alone, and if he would not take what she so willingly offered, she would beg. Death was a possibility, and she could not allow it to come for her without taking this small moment of joy. To say just that, she meant to speak—to tell him all that was in her heart, but words failed her as his fang sank a little deeper. Gwendolyn watched haplessly as he lapped a speck of blood.

"Gods," she groaned.

It was the only word she could have possibly uttered as he suddenly lifted her by the waist, pulling her hard against his body as he walked her back into the room, his intentions unmistakable...

30

T*his* was what her wedding night should have
been.

Like standing atop a sunlit mountain clad in her
mother's Prydein gown, sword in hand, singing a victory song.

Like a sweet drop of dew in a baby bird's beak.

Like the cool crash of the tide over sun-warmed
flesh.

Like a never-ending slice of Hob cake.

Like riding her sweet mare, with her air blowing in
the wind, unbound, uncut.

Like standing atop the prow of a ship, sails un-
furled, arms wide, embracing the wind.

Like the first wink of night after a blistering day,
bathing nude beneath the moon's soft caress.

Beautiful moments to inspire bards—it was...
everything.

Gwendolyn's heart was full even if her stomach
was empty, and when her belly grumbled in complaint, she daren't stir—not yet. Sated and spent, she
reveled in the weight of Málik's leg, hooked lazily over
her own, possessing her even in slumber. They'd
spent the entire morning and afternoon with Málik

exploring every curve of her body as though her form were a riddle to be solved. He'd kissed her gently and not so gently, and even now, she blushed over the memory of all they had done. It was... the most magical... titillating... wonderful... passionate... enriching experience she had ever known. At long last, she understood what it meant to lie in the arms of a beloved, *to feel* beloved.

And yet, tempering the joy she felt in arms was the fact that she had not come here to live joyfully ever after. She had a task to perform—one she could not afford to ignore, no matter how heavenly it felt to lie in his arms.

Nor, despite his professions of love, could Gwendolyn forget all that Esme had revealed...

Even so, she dared to linger abed, greedy for more.

In the half-light, she studied Málik's face, exquisite in slumber. His hair spilled over his shoulders like molten silver, pooling behind him atop the bed. And his face, perpetually youthful, appeared flawless with eyes closed and his mouth at rest. His iridescent skin was... perfect. His lips—ruby red, even after hours of putting them to wicked use—were magnificently formed, making her long once more to press her mouth to his, only to tempt him.

Every inch of him was as splendid as his face... and, in all ways that mattered, he was like any other man, but there were a few things he could do—and did—that left her breathless and craving more.

The one thing tainting this time together was the fact that all too soon, she and Esme would leave this village, but until then, she would cherish every moment.

Emitting a half growl, Málik turned and stretched out his arms, yawning... the gesture so utterly normal, and yet, so wonderfully feral. He then turned to her and grinned, revealing all his teeth in all their fierce glory. "Good eve, flower."

His voice was husky with sleep, and Gwendolyn returned his smile, certain as she was that he spoke from his heart. Málik had always seen her as something more than she was. He saw the good and the bad. And even when he had disapproved of her, he'd regarded her as a thing of beauty—unlike Locrinus, who'd revealed his true thoughts on their one and only night together.

Unconsciously, she reached to catch a lock of her hair, and twirled it. It was growing quickly now, and sometimes she was glad of it. Other times, she missed the fierceness of having it shorn. Even Caradoc had viewed her differently.

Málik seized her hand, drawing it to him and laying it atop his smooth, warm chest, holding it fast, and Gwendolyn smiled, remembering how, in his moment of most heightened pleasure, his horns had appeared. "*You* are a beast," she teased.

"I warned you. You were too persistent upon waking the dragon."

Gwendolyn laughed. "I only wonder... what did you... do... when..."

His brows lifted. "I bit you?" His eyes twinkled with amusement.

She nodded.

"Hmm," he said, once more rolling onto his back, pulling her with him. "In this world, perhaps the easiest explanation would be to liken it to the bite of a serpent." Gwendolyn's brow furrowed as she caressed his soft flesh beneath her fingertips—not one thread of hair... except on his head... and a bit *there*.

"So, you injected me with... venom?" She grinned."
"Do I need a *theriac*?"

He chuckled darkly. "Not precisely. But yes, I did. Though it was not venom. It was—"

"A wondrous *drogue!*" Gwendolyn proclaimed, and indeed, it was.

Not unlike the Hul Gil—a poison, to be sure, though in minute doses, it left the body with a delicious languor. When first they'd introduced it into Gwendolyn's *theriac*, it had given her the headiest sensation. However, it always left her with the worst of headaches and a mouth that felt dry and fuzzy. Not this. The aftereffects of Málik's bite were enduring bliss.

His lips twisting into a boyish grin, he bared his fangs again, and Gwendolyn only then realized how persistently he'd hidden them, because they were exquisitely *long*. "No *drogue* like any you know," he said. "Liquid *aether*. The essence of life."

"*Aether*," Gwendolyn said, rolling onto her back to stare up at her leafy ceiling. "So... this must be what gives your eyes the odd silver gleam?"

"It is."

"And your hair?"

"Yes."

She rolled to face him, smiling mischievously, poking at his bare chest with the pad of a finger. "And the color of this...?"

"Yes," he whispered, as she inched her finger down... down... down...

She tugged gently at the covers. "I'd see it again," she told him.

"Look at my head."

"Nuh uh," she said, tugging harder.

"You are most... unpredictable."

Her grin widened. "Insatiable, do you mean?" she offered, unapologetically.

Again, Málik laughed, the sound throaty and full of joy.

Gods knew she had so many questions—some perhaps not so lighthearted.

For one, Gwendolyn wished to know if the *aether* he'd injected was the reason his father might perceive they were bonded. She suspected it to be true, but she regretted nothing of what they had done within the privacy of this room. In fact, she hoped no one disturbed them—not Esme, and especially not Bryn. She wasn't yet through with Málik.

And then a sobering thought occurred to her...

Gods. Bryn.

She didn't know how she would face him again, after all the things she had done with Málik... after discovering at long last what a man's body was made for. Blushing, she recalled the many times she'd so naively swum with Bryn, never understanding why her father and mother had so heartily disapproved.

And all the times she had so unabashedly exposed herself... and now she understood why Bryn so quickly looked away—thank the gods!

It was not that Gwendolyn was ashamed of her body, nor of the fact that a man should enjoy it. She had simply never given much consideration to how it should be used, nor of the fact that it might give her so much pleasure in return.

And now she abruptly remembered a conversation she'd had with Málik whilst they were climbing the water shaft... *if you offered me your throat... I could be tempted.* She sat, tilting him a questioning look. "Did you... take... from me?"

The smile faded from his face, and he looked at

her—or rather, his gaze lowered to the breasts she'd so easily bared to him, the silver points in his eyes flaring like the cooling rays of a dying sun. "No," he said. "I did not."

"But you *would*?" she asked, merely curious.

"I would," he confessed, with a half-smile. "Are you offering yourself to me, Gwendolyn?"

Gwendolyn's brows collided. "Why did you not?" she persisted.

"Because it wasn't appropriate."

"*When* would be appropriate?"

"If you offered," he told her.

"Is it sustenance for you?"

"Of a sort."

"And do you crave it?"

"I crave you," he replied, his lips curving ever so slightly, this time without a trace of mirth. His eyes narrowed to slits, and the points in his eyes grew thick and black. "It is the first step of our mating ritual."

"So, if you partake of me, and I of you, we are mated?"

His eyes flared. "There's more to it, but yes."

Gwendolyn couldn't stop herself. She pounced on him, drawing her hair back, pressing her naked breasts against his chest, offering him her throat. "Have me," she demanded.

"Nay."

"Why?"

"You do not understand," he said, and despite what he said, he groaned inwardly—the sound tormented—and didn't resist. Like an animal starved, he lifted his lips unerringly to the pulse in her throat, his tongue flicking out to caress the throbbing vein. The feel of it gave Gwendolyn the most wicked sensation

—a ribbon of pleasure that tugged at her body in the most unexpected of places.

Her voice was husky when she spoke again. "Then, help me understand."

She leaned into the points of his teeth, seeking the same liquid drogue he'd injected so stingily all throughout the day—a little here, a little there, only teasing her when she knew there was so much more. Even as she did so, she felt his body respond, and she sighed with anticipation.

"Make me yours," Gwendolyn demanded, and Málik complied by sinking the tips of his teeth into her tender flesh and sucking gently from her vein. But even as he drew from her, he once again returned the elixir of life, mixing *aether* with blood... blood with *aether*, and Gwendolyn cried out as liquid joy rushed through her veins.

"Ohhh," she sighed. "Málik!"

Without distraction, he did this another moment, and then lifted his head, lapping tenderly at the slight wound as he withdrew, then licked his lips. "You may come to regret this," he said, but Gwendolyn could hear the remnants of his gratification in the raspy tone of his voice.

"More," she murmured, sighing as she felt liquid fire trickling through her veins and she grew reckless with desire.

Once more, he lifted his head, and before he consumed her, she saw the blue in his irises brighten to the hottest shade of a flame. His pupils elongated, then thinned, like that of a viper's, and he whispered. "By Dagda's hammer, you have been my weakness for a hundred thousand years, Gwendolyn... alas, I may well be your death."

Gwendolyn didn't care. "More," she whispered,

and he said, "No." Then he forced her head down to rest against his bare chest and kissed the top of her head. "Do not tempt me, Gwendolyn. No more," he pleaded, and there was again that note of finality, only tinged with despair. Disappointed though she was, Gwendolyn didn't press, perhaps understanding without being told that whatever it was he had been trying to avoid... she already felt stirring in the marrow of her bones. There was no regret in her for the things they had done, but perhaps there was some reason he could not share, and if she ignored his warning, they would both regret it—especially since this changed nothing: she still must go.

AMIDST THE DRUNKEN haze of pleasure, Gwendolyn didn't immediately recognize the sound that awoke her.

"*Danger!*"

Then again, more urgently. "*Danger!*"

Piskies?

Once more.

Málik was the first to find his feet. He bounded up from the bed before Gwendolyn could bring herself to stir. Sweeping up his sword from the bedside where'd he'd so gingerly placed it, he held it ready to strike.

Gwendolyn rose, groping for her sleeping gown, then quickly realizing that something terrible was amiss, she rushed for her *mithril* and leathers.

"*Danger!*"

The piskies warning grew impassioned.

"*Danger!*"

Behind her, Málik dressed, pulling on his leathers, his sword never leaving his hand. As soon as Gwendolyn was clothed as well, she rushed for her own sword, stopping short at the sight of its brightening runes—glowing blue. Not the same golden flare it had displayed when Esme first revealed it to her, but blue, like Málik's eyes in the heat of passion.

"Málik," she said, her gaze fixing upon the blade.

His gaze followed hers, then returned to her face. "This will be your first test," he said. "There can be no mistakes."

Gwendolyn nodded, swallowing, and swept up Kingslayer, even as the village stirred, and the first sounds of battle reached her ears.

Screams.

Men.

Oh, Gods, Bryn!

Blood and bones! What was happening?

The *piskies* flew away and the shadows deepened, as it happened in the last moments before the gloaming. Gwendolyn hurried for her boots, donning them hastily. And then, seizing Borlewen's blade as well, she tucked it into one boot, and turned at last, prepared to fight.

Move the sword with your body!

Keep your eyes on the sword.

Pull back as you thrust.

Don't forget to step.

Put your hip into the cut.

Don't spin.

Gods. Right now, she regretted not having practiced along the journey north. She had intended to do so here in the Druid village, but the opportunity had not yet presented itself.

Málik gave her the darkest of looks, and she knew he wanted to ask her to stay, but not even the gods could have made her comply. Knowing this, he didn't ask. Instead, he rushed into the courtyard, and Gwendolyn followed... only to stop short at the horror she discovered.

A creature unlike anything she had ever beheld—taller by far than Málik—came lumbering toward her. It had no flesh on its body, but its construction was not of bone. It was... more like... trees... with thorns... gnarled and twisting, with claws like spikes that protruded from each shoulder. A formation like antlers arose from its contorted head, and within the hollow of its eyes burned a ruby light.

"What is *that*?"

"A *spriggan*," Málik said.

"You said they did not exist!"

"Not in your world."

"You lied?"

"Not precisely," he said, readying his sword as the creature spotted them and lengthened its stride, moving toward them. "You were frightened," he said. "I did not wish you to be. There was no chance you would encounter any in the *fogous*."

A spriggan?

Gwendolyn swallowed, knowing intuitively the beast was coming after her. Automatically, she lengthened the distance between her and Málik, not so much hoping it would follow her, but not wanting it to go after Málik.

And then, it wasn't a matter of dealing with one.

Esme appeared, with Bryn behind her, both hurrying to defend Gwendolyn, but behind them came an army of *spriggans*.

A sleepy Druid made the mistake of emerging from his hut at that moment, and a *spriggan* swept its clawed hand across his middle, disemboweling him where he stood. Gwendolyn watched with horror, and then they were battling for their lives.

31

The squeals of the dying and injured accosted Gwendolyn's ears, and the sound rent the heart from her breast.

These creatures did not come for the Druids; they came for her.

As it was when Briallen wore Gwendolyn's torc, she could see their fiendish gazes alight upon her and her alone. Anyone who stood in the way would find themselves ripped to shreds, and Gwendolyn could not bear to see it happen again.

They know we're coming, she remembered Esme saying, and now Gwendolyn knew who they were.

Moving away from the melee—away from Málik, away from Bryn and Esme—she simply meant to draw the creatures to her. She didn't think, only acted— afraid not for herself, but for her friends. Gwendolyn ran, and the *spriggans* were quick to pursue. Unfortunately, she didn't go far, stopping short as she reached the adjacent cross point. *More spriggans!*

One after another, they were swarming onto the ramps, appearing from the mist and trees, teeming into the village...

Pressed between them, Gwendolyn searched,

trying to form another plan. Her gaze alit upon a fat, swooping branch, and with Kingslayer in hand, she ran, then jumped, as the *piskie* on her nose had done —with every bit of her might.

The tree might be difficult to climb with the sword in hand, but if she made it to the branch, she could jump again to the distant crossroad where no battle had yet engaged. One foot caught the limb she was aiming for. The other missed its perch, slipping. She dropped the sword. It fell with a clatter onto the ramp below.

Now what was she supposed to do?

She could drop, but despite hearing the clatter of her sword, she couldn't see anything below and couldn't be sure she would find the same purchase.

One lumbering creature prepared to leap, so she forsook the sword, dragging herself up, crying out in pain as the bark tore into the flesh of her hands. Opting for the path she could see, she swung her legs, trying to find a perch, but there was nothing—no small limb to use as leverage, nothing solid beneath her feet. Finally, as the creature crouched to leap, she found a knot in the tree, and hauled herself up, then turned at once to leap again onto the cross point.

No time for doubt. Once on the cross point, she sounded the alarm, knowing there would be Druids still sleeping in their beds. "Fire!" she shouted, hoping for an immediate response. "Fire! Run! Run!"

Fire was the one thing she knew these Druids must fear. She couldn't be certain they would know what a *spriggan* was.

One sleepy Druid emerged from his hut, and Gwendolyn felt the worst kind of horror for bringing this travesty to his door. She saw his gaze fix upon the creature that pounced onto the cross point, and she screamed, "Run! Go! Hurry! Arm yourself. Fight! Warn others!"

From the location she'd fled, she could still hear the sounds of battle engaged, but Gwendolyn expected most of the creatures to follow her.

Another *spriggan* leapt onto the cross point from the direction she'd come, and Gwendolyn turned to stand her ground, giving the Druid time to warn others.

These creatures carried no weapons—no need! They wore blades on their person—hooked protrusions like immense thorns stretching backwards from each forearm. With claws for hands, it swung at an overhanging branch, snapping it in twain as though it were nothing more than a small twig, then came lumbering after her, emitting a trilling sound like crickets, but louder.

At the moment, Gwendolyn had no better weapon than Borlewen's blade. She drew it from her boot and grew dizzy with relief as Málik dropped onto the platform beside her, wielding his sword to hack off the *spriggan*'s head. Thereafter, he tossed Gwendolyn the sword in his hand before removing his own from the scabbard at his back. Gwendolyn caught the sword, grateful to feel its weight in her hands. She daren't ask to whom it belonged. She hoped it wasn't Esme's or Bryn's.

Now she fought with two blades, one in each hand.

"Stabbing will do little," Málik advised. "Sunder the head."

Swinging the sword because it was the best she could do, Gwendolyn lopped off a forearm. "Will an arm do?"

With an angry burst of temper, the creature

swiped its uninjured arm at her, dragging its claws across her *mithril,* the sound like nails across steel, and leaving a scar across the otherwise unmarred *chainse.* It didn't penetrate, but the impact pressed the air from Gwendolyn's lungs and she fell backward onto her rump. Once more, the beast pounced, and this time, one of its claws penetrated her weakened armor, puncturing flesh and drawing blood.

Gwendolyn cried out in pain.

Furious over the blow, and her own stupidity, she rallied to her feet, slashing her blade across the smaller ligaments that made up the creature's mantis-looking legs. Unlike Málik, she hadn't the strength to sever them all at once, so she kept hacking until the creature stumbled backward, and then she kicked it off the ramp, and turned to face another. Success!

"I take it back," Málik said. "Cleave anything you can reach."

With glee, Gwendolyn thought, as she swung yet again, hewing through the wooden ligaments that connected one's arm, followed by another heavy chop across its thigh. The creature waddled forward and Gwendolyn sprang at it, swinging hard, slicing off another arm. Then she shoved this one, too, off the ramp.

Running toward the connecting bridge, mist blinding her, she swung and hacked at every gnarled limb that appeared in her periphery.

Behind her, Málik slashed through the middle of another creature, the sheer force of his blow severing the body from its legs. And then, when it lay squirming on the platform, he chopped at the creature's neck, separating the head.

"Go!" he demanded, hitching his chin toward the

adjacent bridge, urging Gwendolyn to run, even as a new mob leapt onto the cross point behind him.

"I won't leave you," she said, returning Borlewen's blade to her boot. It was difficult enough to maneuver the trees and ramps with one weapon, much less two.

"It's not me they want—go!"

"Not without you!"

"I will follow," Málik swore. "Stay and we both die."

Put like that, Gwendolyn could not argue.

She turned to run as Málik swung his blade at the ropes securing the bridge, hacking it so the ramp twisted under the weight of several *spriggans*. They slid into the gloom with angry squeals. Then, hacking at the other side, he untethered the bridge from its post, and the last of the *spriggans* tumbled into oblivion.

Gwendolyn stumbled into the mist, greedy for cover. But then, unable to see where she was going— the mist so thick—she kept running. When she heard footsteps behind her, she prayed it would be Málik.

"Follow!" Málik ran past, seizing Gwendolyn by the hand and dragging her deeper into the swirling mist. All about them, she could hear the clunking of wood as *spriggans* bounded from tree to tree. Her heart pounded fearfully because she couldn't see them.

"Why are they here?"

"To kill you, of course."

"Who sent them?"

"The one who commands them."

The Fae king.

Gwendolyn knew this without being told. Yegods. If he had such an army at his disposal, what else must she face? Even with the finest of skills, Gwendolyn couldn't have fought off these creatures alone.

Tripping over her own feet, she faltered behind Málik.

Apparently, someone else had the same idea of destroying bridges. She heard the chop and felt the bridge twist beneath her feet. Losing her footing, Gwendolyn slid across the bridge, only catching the edge, and nearly dropping this sword as well.

"Wait! Don't cut it! Not yet! Wait!"

Up ahead, the sound of hacking stopped, but behind her, a new *spriggan* emerged, and Gwendolyn could swear she saw the beast grin.

"Málik," she said. "Another!"

"I see it," he said, reaching for her, tugging at her arm. But unless Gwendolyn dropped the sword she held, there was nothing she could do to help until she could find a place to settle her foot. Beneath her, her legs swung frantically as the creature lumbered closer.

"Málik," she pleaded. "Go! Go! Go!"

If she must, she would release her grip on the bridge and drop into the gloom; come what may, anything would be better than this.

The creature raised its arm toward Málik, and Gwendolyn shrieked. He released her in time to turn and fend off the blow. But Gwendolyn watched haplessly as the creature swung its massive claw at Málik's throat. Once more, Málik ducked, then rose, but not before taking a wedge out of the creature's shin—was that a shin? Gwendolyn couldn't tell. Hanging as she was, she could only watch with horror as Málik battled for his life against a beast unlike anything Gwendolyn had ever witnessed in all her life. Formed like a man, it was no more than woody limbs and parts, with well-placed thorns the size of Borlewen's blade—one at the back of each calf, two on the back of each forearm. This one made the mistake of turning its attention to Gwendolyn, and Málik pivoted with his blade, severing the head from its shoulders, and then he turned to Gwendolyn, seizing her arm and hauling her up.

"Bloody Danu! About time!" she said, but it wasn't a complaint.

"Go!" he demanded. "Go, go, go!"

Once more, he led the way, somehow moving through the maze of cross points and ramps until they found themselves again at the village center. There, they dispatched another *spriggan*, and then dashed in the direction of Gwendolyn's bower, coming full circle to find Esme and Bryn fighting back-to-back. For a dread-filled moment, Gwendolyn had visions of Briallen and Jenefer that day in Chysauster when their village was raided, and both fell before her eyes. But here, now, Esme and Bryn were fighting in sync as though they had been fighting together for a lifetime. Wooden appendages littered the courtyard at their feet, some splattered by blood—human blood; these creatures would not bleed. It was only then that Gwendolyn's mind recognized the twisted shapes of human forms littering the ramparts.

Druids.

Fae.

Her belly turned, and she prayed Lir was wise enough to remain hidden along with his brother. She knew these creatures would not seek them. They were after Gwendolyn. But even as she thought this, one *spriggan* made a lie of her thought, and instead of turning its scrutiny to Gwendolyn, it pounced upon Bryn.

"No!" Gwendolyn didn't think, only acted. She flew toward the pair, leaping atop the creature's back, seeking to drag it away.

Bryn twisted and turned, trying in vain to dislodge the heavy creature from his back, and spying Gwendolyn, surprise widened his eyes—did he think she would leave him? "The legs," she charged. "Cleave the legs!"

Bryn wasted no time. He rolled forward, taking the *spriggan* and Gwendolyn along with him, and then twisting again, he sprang free, swinging his blade across the creature's legs, toppling it with Gwendolyn still on its back.

All about were screams and squeals, interspersed by the sound of snapping twigs and trills. The creature whose back Gwendolyn now rode turned and tangled its gnarled limbs in her hair. Yelping in surprise, she tried to free herself, even as the beast wrapped its woody limbs about her chest, reaching for her throat.

The sword in her hand would do nothing in close proximity, so Gwendolyn flung it away. Málik and Esme were too busy staving off fiends, and Bryn struggled ineffectively to free her, entangling himself in the creature's extremities. Vines shot out to enfold them both—as they had the day Málik saved her from Loc —squeezing tighter and tighter. Somehow, Gwendolyn kept an arm free, and reached for the blade in her boot, cutting vines as she lifted her arm, snapping them away until she could shove the knife lengthwise against the *spriggan's* throat, the razor-sharp edge pushing against the smaller ligaments of its neck.

Too hard! The blade accomplished nothing, and even whilst Bryn struggled against the creature's hold, all the while hacking at it wherever he could, its hands continued to twist about Gwendolyn's throat, squeezing tighter and tighter, sending out more and more vines that crept across her face, into her mouth, and poked at her eyes. Desperate for air, Gwendolyn began to saw her knife across the wooden ligaments of its throat, and kept sawing and sawing, even as the vines crept into every crevice and her eyes bulged. Her lungs threatened to explode.

Gods. She was going to die here!

With Bryn!

Imagining Ely's bitter tears, with the breath in her lungs burning for release, she remembered her promise to Ely and resisted a vine when it tried to catch her arm. With a singleness of purpose, she continued to saw.

No, no, no, no, no!

Not here. Not yet. Not now.

She had too much to do!

She would not die this day and allow these fiends to slaughter her friends.

With a sound like a pop, at long last, she severed the creature's head. It fell with a thunk against the wooden ramp, and then, gasping for breath, Gwendolyn rolled free of the tangle of wood, cutting and hacking at vines, then stood again to fight.

On the battle waged.

Together, they felled one *spriggan* after another—too many to count.

There was no clang of metal to ring against the night, no sword against sword—only the soft give of human flesh and the snapping of twiggy limbs.

At long last, when dawn broke, with the last of the *spriggans* dispensed, Gwendolyn sat, heaving for breath, tears burning her eyes as she met Bryn's gaze, then Esme's, and finally, Málik's.

All about lay twisted forms, some wounded, some dead—and despite that, they'd won, the spriggans had exacted a heavy toll. Exhausted, Gwendolyn fell back on the ramp, her head settling with a hard thump, only vaguely aware of the red permeating her black *mithril*—a thick pool of blood settled and congealed into the web of metallic fiber. The *mithril* had saved her from having the heart ripped from her breast, but she was wounded. She plucked at the vines that clung to her face, wincing as she removed one from the corner of one eye.

We won, she thought. *We won!*

That was her last coherent thought before she succumbed.

32

G radually, still disoriented, Gwendolyn regained consciousness, sensing after a time that she was in her bower, in her bed... alone.

"You underestimate her," someone whispered. "She's stronger than you know."

Female.

Esme?

Was there a note of pride in her voice?

Gwendolyn struggled to move her lips, only to wet them, but she couldn't. It felt as though she were still bound with twine. Even her tongue felt furry and constrained. Was she still covered in *spriggan* vines?

Gods. What was that terrible scent?

Pungent, woody, resinous...

Pine sap was oft used to disinfect wounds. Was this because someone was tending to her wounds? Gwendolyn's body hurt.

So did her head.

Where was Málik?

She tried again to lift her lids, but couldn't, so she settled for listening...

"She's a fierce one," said another voice, the conversation growing louder now—perhaps no longer concerned over waking her?

Male, this time.

"When she was a girl, scarcely able to lift a sword, she stole mine to drag it about the halls. Four she was when her father gave her a practice sword."

Bryn?

This said with a smile. "Who would not covet your sword?"

Flirtation?

No hint of sarcasm.

Only mirth.

Esme?

Gwendolyn decided she must be dreaming. There could be no other explanation for this strange discourse.

Giggles. Now laughter.

"Stop, lout! We'll wake her."

Disapprovingly. "I've cleaned her wound," said a third occupant of the room.

Lir?

"I found a bit of the claw still embedded in her flesh."

Concern. "Is it out?"

"Of course," said Lir. "I put it on the table if you wish to inspect it."

Now, again, Esme. "*Spriggan* poison is like yew poison," she explained. "That is what they used against your brother, I'm certain. Only at first, I did not recognize the symptoms. But that is no bruise he bears. His veins are gradually hardening." She must have lifted the claw in question. Gwendolyn heard it clatter softly against the wooden table as she laid it back down.

"Art certain?"

"Quite," affirmed Esme. "Fortunately for both, unlike yew, *spriggan* poison is slow to pass through the system. Neither is it fatal, so long as there is a ready antidote. I will administer it when I leave here. He will wake in a day or two."

There was no small measure of relief in Lir's tone. "Thank the gods!"

"No gods to thank for this one," said Esme, with a snide laugh. "If you wish to thank anyone, you may thank me."

"And her? Will you dose her as well?"

"No need," said Esme. "Málik has already done so."

Málik...

Desperately, Gwendolyn tried again to open her eyes, realizing Málik's was the one voice she'd yet to hear, eager to see his face. Her throat bobbed painfully, and she tried to speak, to no avail. Her words emerged as a hapless groan.

"Shhh... leave her to rest," suggested Esme, whispering again. "You, come with me," she demanded, and there was an answering chuckle.

Málik?

Gods.

No.

In her mind's eye, she saw him battling *spriggans*, wielding his sword like a creature possessed. But that battle was over now, wasn't it?

Gwendolyn was back in her room, safe.

Where was Málik?

Try as she might, she still couldn't open her eyes. Struggling against the weight of her closed lids, she lost. Awareness faded, dragging her back down into a dark, dreamless slumber.

. . .

GWENDOLYN BLINKED AWAKE.

"There you are."

To her greatest relief, it was Málik's face she first spied when she opened her eyes. "You're here," she said weakly, but unlike the torpor in her limbs, her heart leapt with joy. Only to be certain this was no dream, she reached out to touch his precious face, and then grimaced over the pain that assailed her.

"Where would I be?" Smiling, he seized her hand, laying it back down atop the bed, holding it fast, his long fingers curling about hers, squeezing gently.

Gwendolyn blinked away happy tears, not wishing to share the dream she'd had where he'd perished in the fight against the *spriggans*. Clearly, he'd fared better than she. Peering down at her aching chest, at the wound hidden by a mountain of furs, she found that Málik—or someone, perhaps Esme?—had removed her *mithril*, and dressed her in her sleeping gown. Unfortunately, despite the fresh clothes, the scent of her own blood persisted in her nostrils, and though it was difficult to see in the half light, she thought there might be bruises beneath her gown.

"They came to kill me," she said. "Didn't they?"

"Excellent conjecture," he said, his lips lifting at one corner. "Little did they realize my Dragon Queen is much too fierce to be brought down by a horde of wood-brained *spriggans*."

My Dragon Queen... the endearment squeezed at Gwendolyn's heart, the sound of it so full of pride. It didn't matter what Esme claimed; she believed their love was strong enough to overcome whatever influence his father might wield over him—his true name be damned. Gwendolyn tried to smile, but her face hurt. Instead, she lifted a hand to her breast, where it ached, and Málik seized it again, dragging it away.

"It's the *spriggan* poison," he told her. "It has a temporary effect, but do not let it concern you."

Gwendolyn gave him a nod, letting her hand rest beneath his, content enough for the moment to linger beneath its warmth. "How many attacked?"

"Thirty, perhaps, all intent upon you."

"Bryn?"

"Unharmed," he said. "Sadly, the same cannot be said for everyone. *Deartháir* Harri has sent men below to prepare a pyre."

Another pyre? Gods. The second in less than a sennight. But, of course, they could not light a fire in this tree-bound village.

Gwendolyn's heart hurt over the news, though it might be impossible to say whether it hurt more for the lost souls or the wounds she'd sustained in the attack. Her body truly ached, and it felt as though she had twenty stones resting atop her breast. The inexorable heaviness and pain extended well into her limbs. And this was all her fault. She was the one who had lured those creatures to this place. She alone was answerable for any injuries or death. Gods knew she could not lay abed and await another attack. She refused to endanger these people more than she had already. Gwendolyn tried to rise, intending to find Esme. "Argh!" The pain in her chest flared, radiating to every limb, every finger, every toe. Defeated by it, she laid back down, frustrated beyond measure. "How long have I slept?" she wondered aloud, worried that, once again, she had whiled away days, wasting time they did not have. Her plans could not change. More than ever, she was determined to cross the Veil and Esme's bargain afforded her the best opportunity.

"Not so long as you slept after the *pookies.*"

Gwendolyn wasn't in the mood for jests. "How long?"

"A few bells."

"How few?"

"Eighteen," he said.

Blood and bloody bones.

The night had gone and come again!

"*Spriggan* poison, did I hear you say? Did I dream it, or did I also hear tell it was the same that felled *Máistir* Emrys?"

"It was," Málik allowed. "Gwendolyn... I did not know they could cross the Veil. It never once occurred to me—nor to Esme—to examine h*is* bruise."

Or lie to her. She refrained from pointing out again. He'd assured her those creatures did not exist, and clearly they did.

It hurt to frown.

Gwendolyn stifled eyes, irritated though she didn't wish to be. She had come so close to losing Málik, and she could not dwell upon dark thoughts. She tilted a glance at the sleeve of her gown, where dark shadows were still visible beneath.

"The poison contains a spore that permeates the veins, congealing blood like sap. It works slowly, but if allowed to spread unchecked, it permeates the muscles and bones, hardening flesh as well."

"Is that what is happening to me?"

His smile was rueful. "No. Our... *bond*... saved you. The poison is not deadly to Fae. You will heal quickly," he promised.

"What about *Máistir* Emrys?"

"Esme dosed him yesterday. Luckily, he received very little of the poison—a pinprick. Someone perhaps intended it to put him out for a few days more than to kill him. I would guess that same person conceals the antidote, and perhaps intends to administer it once we are gone."

"Harri," Gwendolyn whispered.

She knew it. She would wager it was him, and if she could prove it, she would—what? Kill him? Already, too much blood had been shed, though she prayed he would weep actual tears for the men he would burn today.

"It could be," he said. "If so, Esme will deal with him."

Esme.

Gwendolyn needed to get up and go find her.

Esme was the only one who could help her now, and no matter what she and Málik had shared, she still, like Bryn, did not trust him to allow her to do what she must—not when he wouldn't even let her out of bed!

Wincing, she reached for the sleeve of her gown, attempting to lift it to see what the *spriggan* poison had done to her, and once again, Málik stopped her with a hand atop hers, pushing the sleeve back down.

"You may not wish to look," he suggested. "As I said, Emrys had only a prick. You received a bit more close to your heart. If we had not..." He gave her a meaningful look, his gaze alighting on Gwendolyn's shoulder, where his teeth had once pricked her. "You would be—"

A shiver passed down Gwendolyn's spine. "Dead?"

"Not precisely, though you might wish you were. The spores end life as you know it, but they do not end life. Those who fought here and succumbed to their wounds before the poison carried out its ill effects must be grateful. You may recall that feeling you had in the woods when Loc's men were in pursuit... still able to see, think, feel, but not move..."

Gwendolyn nodded and shuddered.

"Consider that permanent, irreversible. What I did to you that day was in some ways the same, but the effects of my glamour were fleeting."

Gwendolyn shuddered again, remembering that day in the woods, standing with Málik's arms entwined about her, like *spriggan*'s vines.

"What about the men who fell?"

He peered down at his chest, averting his gaze. "There was only one who did not die immediately of his wounds. Esme..."

"You need not tell me!" It was too awful to bear. "Why would your father send these creatures to kill me when I mean to face him? Does he not know?"

"Well... that would seem obvious, Gwendolyn. He does not intend for you to cross the Veil."

Gwendolyn's outrage deepened.

Neither did *Dearthair* Harri wish her to cross, and now she must wonder who else had been part of this scheme to keep her from the Fae realm.

Seizing the covers to toss them away, she flung one bare foot out of the bed, only for Málik to arrest her. "No," he said, and this time his tone brooked no argument. He shoved her leg back beneath the furs and drew up the covers. "Everything can wait. Rest, *Caer Ibormeith*."

How could he ask it of her?

Gwendolyn didn't wish to rest, but suddenly she hadn't any choice.

"Rest," he said again, and she sank down into the furs, powerless to resist, only to watch him as he turned to walk out the door. Her first thought was to get up and follow as soon as he was gone, but the weight of her covers felt like a load of tin, compelling her to close her eyes.

For two days, Gwendolyn drifted in and out of a dreamless sleep, each time waking stronger. But, unlike her first night in this chamber after the *pookie* stew, she experienced no prophetic dreams, only a healing rest that, oddly, made her feel... renewed. For all this time, no one intruded upon her respite. It was as though Málik had warned everyone against it, and despite Esme's previous urgency to be away, neither she nor Bryn once poked their heads in the door.

For two sleepy days, there was no sign of Málik either.

If Gwendolyn didn't know better—know how everyone supported her—she might even wonder if they had joined *Dearthair* Harri in his opposition, dosing her with a sedative to keep her resting.

When, by the third morning after the *spriggan* attack, Esme did not materialize, Gwendolyn decided she'd had enough rest.

Somewhere, her mother was waiting. She must retrieve her sword, and find her mother, and she intended to hold Esme to her bargain.

Dressing for war, intending not to return to this bower, she donned her black *mithril*, her sturdy boots, and leathers. Although the *mithril* was damaged, it seemed not to be damaged beyond repair. She put Borlewen's blade into her boot, then buckled the shoulder strap of her sword scabbard, prepared to leave. But then, seeing her mother's Prydein gown, she made her way over to it and laid a hand atop the buttery leather. Even if she wished to wear it now, she didn't believe it would fit, regardless that Demelza had tailored it for her. Along with her hair, Gwendolyn had lost most of her curves. And no matter that her hair was growing now, their respite in Trevena had not returned an ounce of flesh to her bones. Her mother had been tall for a woman, and Gwendolyn certainly inherited her height, but it had the opposite effect on Gwendolyn, giving her a sense of height, and not enough curves—at least of late. It wasn't so long ago that, save for her meager breasts, she'd had nothing but curves. However, much to her dismay, her breasts seemed to have diminished further along with the curve of her thighs, and she looked like a boy. Though reminded of the attention Málik had lavished upon them, she blushed hotly.

She didn't wish to leave him this way, but now, whilst he was else wise occupied, would the best opportunity to slip away. Nor could she leave him a note. Gwendolyn didn't know where Esme was, nor how long it might take to locate her, and she didn't want to take any chance that Málik might return before she had the chance to find her and be away.

As for the gown, she slid her hand from it, turning away, intending to leave it, along with her copper breast plate and golden tiara.

The crown, without her sword, would serve no purpose. These items had no place with her until they ventured north. They were simple adornments, intended to impress, but something told her that neither their beauty nor their import would influence the Fae king. Instead, she intended to face him, wearing only her humility. And if he did not comply and return her sword, she would take it perforce.

She would not be thwarted.

Family was everything and now that Gwendolyn had the chance to be reunited with her mother, nobody would keep her from this reunion—not even Málik.

Unbidden, her thoughts returned to Baugh, and Emrys' warning, remembering what Queen Innogen once told her—that Loc's brothers intended to ride north. She had announced this with such a slippery smile. At the time, Gwendolyn surmised they'd intended to attack the northern tribes, as they did once before. But what if instead they were going with the purpose of bargaining with her grandfather? Gwendolyn couldn't bear it if her own blood took Loc's side. But even if he didn't, Baugh still might not raise his sword to her cause. Having her mother by her side would help insure he might, and only Esme could provide Eseld's whereabouts.

34

Gwendolyn was running out of time.

Finding Esme nowhere within the village proper, she ventured to the *Máistir's* chamber, hoping to see for herself how he fared and, if Lir was about, perhaps ask him what he knew about Málik and Esme's whereabouts—the first to avoid, the second, so they could be away. To her relief and joy, she found the *Máistir* awake and well.

"At last!" he exclaimed when Gwendolyn walked in the door. He clapped his hands delightedly. "I see our beloved Prionsabail has finally allowed you to rise from your bed!"

Gwendolyn laughed at his exuberant greeting, but her laughter cut short when she neared the bedside to find that the small bruise he'd suffered had spread from the one small prick behind his neck, darkening his veins, so that it appeared he had a sprawling tattoo across one side of his neck and up the side of his face.

"Oh!" he said, waving a hand dismissively. "I am told it is harmless. It should fade, and if it does not, I will wear it proudly." He winked at her. "Not everyone can claim they survived a *spriggan* attack, now can they?" He laughed then, and Gwendolyn lifted her brow. She hardly shared the view. She could go a thousand lifetimes without seeing another or claiming such a thing. Unwittingly, she lifted a hand to the place on her breast where the *spriggan* had wounded her.

"I heard what you endured," the *Máistir* said, noting the hand at her breast. "I am relieved you survived. Alas, I am told *Dearthái*r Cathbad and *Dearthái*r Pikel did not. Poor, dear souls. We'll celebrate their lives as soon I can rise from this bed."

Gwendolyn had never heard him chatter so endlessly, and she wondered if he was attempting to make up for it now that he was awake and could. Remembering Málik's description of the disease's symptoms, she wondered how much the poor man overheard, and his next words made her wonder.

"My brother slept through the attack, 'tis no wonder! He spent every moment by my side begging me to wake. I don't know where he is now—no doubt sleeping again."

"He was quite beside himself," Gwendolyn agreed. "I've never seen him so dispirited. He, more than anyone in my party, has been the very spirit of good cheer." She tilted her head and offered a wink of her own. "If only he could learn to wield a sword."

"Alas, we are Druids," the *Máistir* reminded her. "We have no use for swords." He averted his eyes. "Until now."

Gwendolyn's belly turned, feeling the worst. But there was no recrimination in his expression when he peered up again to meet Gwendolyn's gaze. The best thing she could do would be to hasten her departure.

"I was wondering if you knew where Málik might be?"

The *Máistir* tilted Gwendolyn a look that gave her

every sense he knew but did not wish to say. "No," he said. "I do not."

He was lying.

No matter. Gwendolyn laid her fingers atop his black-veined hand. She'd not press him if he would not say. "Will they restore you to the *Máistir's* position?" She wasn't merely asking to make polite conversation. She wished to know where he stood on the matter of the portal.

Emrys shook his head sadly. "Neither do I wish to be." He sighed despondently. "My time in the mortal realm is done, *Banríon Dragan*. On this occasion, perhaps the cause of my illness was foul play, but eventually, death will be my fate." He shrugged. "I should like to linger a while."

Gwendolyn squeezed his hand fondly. "I would like you to linger, as well. Words cannot express how grateful I am that Cathbad and Pikel's fates were not yours." And then she furrowed her brow. "I do wonder though, did you perchance spy your attacker?" She was still suspicious of Harri.

The *Máistir* shook his head. "I did not. I descended to await my guest, and when he did not arrive, I grew tired of pacing, and meant to return. But then, I felt the smallest prick at the back of my neck—a bit lie a horsefly. I grew dizzy and sat to put my feet in the pool —sometimes the warm water calms me. But just then, as I removed my shoes, I remember nothing more. Esme tells me it was a splinter from a blowgun that struck me here." He moved his hand to the back of his neck, tapping the area where Gwendolyn had first examined his wound.

"We are both quite fortunate," Gwendolyn allowed, lifting her fingers to her mithril to trace the scar—barely discernible to look at, but easily distinguishable by touch. "They discovered you sleeping," she said. "That is how I found you, as well."

"Alas," he said. "Had I shuffled this mortal coil, I'd never even know."

"*I* would have known," Gwendolyn reassured.

He smiled warmly. "As I you, dear," he said, patting her hand, then suddenly lifting a finger, giving her a sharp glance. "But I should warn you... I've received word that Locrinus has journeyed north, in hopes of swaying the Parisi to his cause. That is who I was supposed to have met—an informant from this tribe."

"The Parisi?" Gwendolyn's brows collided. "Art certain?"

The *Máistir* nodded. "Quite. And yet, this news came to me first from the Brigantes. They wished to know my thoughts on this matter."

That didn't bode well. Like the Brigantes, the Parisi were never known to take sides, although perhaps Locrinus had discovered some argument to sway them.

The *Máistir* studied Gwendolyn, squeezing her hand. "I am heartily pleased you've awakened, but I must also tell you that no one here will support you in your quest to cross the Veil, *Banríon*—particular now, in light of this attack. In all our seven hundred years in this village, we have never once endured such a thing. We've been duly warned, and yes, I've been apprised of *Dearthái r* Harri's decision, and I would uphold this. But I can tell you, as an aside, your best hope is Esme."

"And Málik," Gwendolyn said, correcting him.

Regardless of her own plans with Esme, she knew Málik had not changed his mind or his heart. He supported her quest and had never wavered from the conviction that Gwendolyn must face his stepfather.

The *Máistir* shook his head. "Poor Prionsabail. I

have never seen him so stricken. It would not surprise me to learn he means to keep you from this quest."

Gwendolyn's brows collided. "He would not," she argued. "He, more than anyone, understands how important it is for me to retrieve my sword—now more than ever!"

Important enough that he'd had so many opportunities to fulfill his father's directive, and still he had not. Even during this *spriggan* attack, Málik had risked his life *to save her*.

"Does he?" asked the *Máistir*, his tone elevating, as though he himself did not believe it.

"Yes," Gwendolyn said with certainty.

And regardless, the *Máistir* had sewn a seed of doubt.

Once again, he patted her hand, as though to console her. "No worries, dear. Love is a force unlike any you will encounter. Your Prionsabail will move heaven and earth to keep you safe. I know this, as I know him. But please! Do not listen to me," he said. "What do I know? Except!" His eyes brightened, and he lifted a finger to wag at her. "I do know where else love has cast its capricious eye!" At once, he placed two fingers to his lips as though to turn a key in a lock, and then declared, "You did not hear this from me, but our Esme has... shall we say... kept your Shadow preoccupied... if you know what I mean?"

Gwendolyn drew back, surprised. "Bryn?"

The *Máistir* nodded, his eyes sparkling with something akin to titillation over the tidbit of gossip. "Oh, yes, I see you take my meaning," he said, and then he smirked. "I may be old, but I am not so old I do not recognize flirtation. I am told my brother went to locate your Shadow, and, well..." He shrugged then, pushing up a hand.

Gwendolyn blinked again.

Gods. She had never once suspected either, and if she had suspected Esme's feelings for anyone, it would have been Málik, or Lir.

Why then had Bryn suggested she might have feelings for Lir?

But did he say that? Remembering Bryn's words, all he ever claimed was that though Esme pretended to revile Lir, she did not. And, in fact, he believed she was trying to protect him. And now she wondered how he would have known this unless he knew her private thoughts?

So then, all those times Esme had slipped away, perhaps Bryn had slipped away as well? Somehow, this had escaped Gwendolyn.

"Sit," the *Máistir* said, grinning. "It appears you are not so well as you'd like to believe." He gestured at a stool beside his bed, and Gwendolyn sat.

35

E *sme and Bryn?*
Gwendolyn could not believe it!

Apparently, the conversation she'd overheard in her bedchamber, mistaken for a dream, wasn't a dream at all. And now she also remembered how often Bryn was so oft drawn to her side during the journey north. He'd claimed it was because he was protecting Lir—and perhaps he was at first—but those were the only occasions Esme had seemed more animated. And perhaps if Esme was vexed at Gwendolyn for something, it wasn't about her relationship with Málik; it was about Bryn.

Intending to confront Bryn and perhaps give him her blessings if this was true, she went straight for his bower, but the sounds she overheard coming from within stilled her hand before the knocker. They sounded as though they were battling a horde of *spriggans*!

Good for him.

Good for Esme as well.

And yet, thwarted once more, she left them to their clamorous affair, red-cheeked as she walked away, intending to investigate the village on her own. They would have to emerge at some point. Until then, Gwendolyn could prepare for the journey.

Counting on the chef's generosity, she found a small sack, intending to pack it with whatever sustenance she could find—preferably, not Hob cake.

She would need all her wits about her to deal with the Fae king.

STAYING clear of her own room, Gwendolyn made her way back to Bryn's.

If by now Málik had returned from wherever he had gone, that would be the first place he might look for her. But that he'd not yet come looking, led her to believe he must not have re—

"Where are you away to?"

Gwendolyn squealed with surprise, startled by the sound of his voice so near. She spun to face Málik, unable to hide the disappointment she felt over seeing him leaning against a tree, watching her.

"So pleased to see me?" he teased, but there was an obvious note of suspicion in the question. His gaze moved at once to the sack dangling from her hand.

"Oh!" Gwendolyn said, shaking her head, and then nodding. "I am... quite pleased," she lied.

"Indeed?"

She nodded jerkily. "Oh, yes. In fact, I was looking for you," she said again, lifting the pouch in her hand. This wasn't entirely a lie. She was looking to avoid him. "Victuals," she explained. "To share." Simply not with him.

His silver eyes pierced her as surely as would a sword. "Indeed," he said, again, but it wasn't a question.

Gwendolyn's cheeks burned. "Where have you been?"

"If I told you—"

"Yes, I know, you might have to slay me," she said, annoyed by the timeworn jest. It wasn't the least bit amusing the first time she heard it at six, when she'd first asked her father what was in his treasury. It wasn't amusing now, knowing that this was Málik's preeminent intention where she was concerned. She still couldn't believe it, and yet, somehow, she could. She had never felt assured by the circumstances of his arrival, nor by the way he had treated her before they became closer acquainted. She had to stop herself from blurting out everything Esme had told her.

"I was... you might say... making certain... of our options," he explained, his gaze inspecting her from head to foot, noting the sword on her back, the *mithril* and leathers, Borlewen's blade in her boot. He missed nothing before returning his gaze to her face. And Gwendolyn knew... he knew.

"Come," he said, launching himself off the tree with a foot, offering Gwendolyn a hand. But there was no affection in the glint of his eyes, and Gwendolyn hesitated.

He left his hand extended. "Art afraid of me?"

"Hardly," Gwendolyn replied, but not so quickly as it should be between lovers. In the end, she had no choice but to take the hand he offered.

36

There was a ramp hidden behind the bathhouse that wasn't easily detectable. One had to know it was there to venture at squeezing through the impossible space. And yet, whether one could or couldn't manage was less the point than whether one should. As Gwendolyn glimpsed the space beyond, she froze mid-stride, one leg already through the space between two trees, with no discernible place to lay down her foot. To one side lay a dark, unfathomable chasm that seemed hardly worth the risk of falling, particularly considering that, even once through, the path ahead seemed only precariously traversed. There wasn't even space enough for an entire foot on the visible ledge, and if one's balance went wrong...

Peering down at the sack of victuals in her hand, Gwendolyn reconsidered the sword on her back and cast Málik a wary glance.

"Art afraid of heights?"

For a moment, Gwendolyn considered the question. Normally she was not, but one glance down and her heart pounded traitorously. Only darkness peered back at her—an impenetrable gloom where light did not exist. This was the same inky void that inspired fear of *spriggans* and trolls, the unrevealed space beneath one's bed, the moonless corner about which one could never spy lurking danger, the darkest recesses of a grave, where life was neither welcomed, nor sustained. As much as Gwendolyn loathed to confess it, fear was the emotion it inspired—immediate and undeniable. And regardless, if it didn't stop Málik, she refused to allow a pair of trembling knees to hold her back, especially if he was about to reveal the portal.

Nor, in truth, did Gwendolyn wish to confess to fear, while Málik was grinning so impishly. The sight of it was like a gauntlet tossed at her feet.

He extended his hand again, and Gwendolyn groaned inwardly as she put her shoulder into the decision, wiggling through the space, like a cat would, then planting her foot wherever she could.

Once through, she had to tug hard to pull the sack through, and almost lost her balance. It was only thanks to Málik that she didn't fall.

With two hands at her waist, he steadied her. But the feel of his hands never failed to send a shiver down her spine. It was all Gwendolyn could do not to lean back into his welcome embrace.

Alas were it any other day, or any other place, she would have turned and wrapped her arms about his neck, then tugged him down for a kiss.

But this was not any other day. It was the day she meant to break faith with him, leaving him to wonder, as she now did, why he'd kept the truth from her.

"Steady?"

"Yes, thank you," she said, but she daren't look down.

Somehow, with help, she turned, slowly, carefully, and made her way across the impossibly narrow ledge to solid ground.

From there, another spiral passage led upward and Gwendolyn breathed a sigh of relief and tossed the sack over one shoulder as she followed Málik—up, up, up, up.

Only when it seemed they shouldn't be able to climb any higher, the path proceeded ever higher, and higher and higher.

Eventually, Gwendolyn wondered how such an ascent was even possible. The tallest tree she had ever known—the ancient yew outside their city, where she'd married Locrinus—wasn't nearly so tall.

Even more confusing, the mist thickened as they ascended, as though they were moving into and through the skies. But if this was the case, there was no sign of any living creature in this mysterious place —no birds, no buzzing bees, no insects at all. The air felt thin and growing thinner.

He was taking her to the portal. She knew it without question, but the realization that he was defying the Druids surprised her.

It was not like him.

She felt an immediate sense of disquiet.

Something was wrong.

Did he mean for them to abandon Esme and Bryn?

Curse the sun and the moon—all the while she and Esme had been planning one thing, he had been devising another plan.

"Where are we going?" Gwendolyn pressed. "And please do not say you would have to slay me—considering the circumstances, I don't find it amusing."

"What circumstances?"

"Never mind," Gwendolyn said fiercely.

It was bad enough that she had given herself to him so fully, even knowing what he'd intended. She was a bundle of confusion, and more than anything, she longed for him to confess what Esme had revealed to her, though she daren't give Esme away—just in case. For one, if he should ask her how she knew, or who told her, it would force her to tell him or lie. Until this task was through, Esme held her mother's fate in her hands, and Gwendolyn would not risk Eseld for pride. Though she felt the need ask, "Why do you despise Esme so much?"

"I do not despise Esme," he said. "Though regardless of how I feel about her, I've never trusted her. She is, without doubt, her father's daughter."

"Yet she is against him," Gwendolyn reasoned, clearing her way past an inordinately large spider web, one that appeared too large to be real.

Nor was there any sign of a spider—no prey on the web. What an odd, odd place!

"For now," he said. "But that is the problem with Esme, Gwendolyn. I could never construe her true motives. She stands to win the entire Fae kingdom as her father's only remaining heir, and I assure you, it is not me she has ever coveted to wed."

Knowing what Gwendolyn knew now, she could imagine that to be true. But she couldn't find it in her to tell him what she'd learned about Bryn and Esme. It might be better to let Málik continue without interruption.

"With me by her side, her father has promised her the moon. Our union would effectively quell the rebellion. There is little to be gained by Esme in championing the rebellion without some promise from me."

"What promise?"

"Without me—without my birthright—there is no one to oppose him."

"The Fae king?" Gwendolyn surmised.

"Yes," he said.

"I would see him deposed, but I'd not take the seat unless I know for certain my father cannot. My father is the rightful heir."

"The Dark One," Gwendolyn said, repeating what he'd told her on the ramparts in Trevena the night they took the city. The Banished Wyrm, the true-blood heir to the Tuatha'an throne.

"Yes."

"But if your father cannot be found, you are his heir?"

"Yes."

"So, Esme has championed a rebellion that will unseat her father and her as well?"

"Unless I wed her, which..." He peered back at Gwendolyn, his silver eyes glinting peculiarly. "For discernible reasons, I will not."

"None of this explains why you bear Esme such animosity," Gwendolyn pressed. "Mayhap she cares nothing for the throne. I certainly did not until Loc. Has she done something more?"

"She has," he said, without turning to meet her eyes. "Many ages ago, when she realized she would not get her way with me, she used my true name to sway me."

"What did she ask you to do?"

He ignored her question. "As yet," he said. "I cannot not determined her true purpose for you."

A quiver rushed down Gwendolyn's spine. "For me?"

"Make no mistake, Gwendolyn, she has one."

Gwendolyn's breath grew short now. The higher they climbed, the less visibility there seemed to be, and she clung tighter to Málik's hand.

"We're almost there," he advised, casting another glance over his shoulder. "Just a little further." The intensity of his gaze startled Gwendolyn, and the sudden appearance of his horns unsettled her. She blinked, pausing, if only to catch her breath. But really, she was growing confused.

Málik was rarely so forthcoming, and while his appearance discomfited her—more than what he looked like, she longed to know *why*—why did he look that way, why now, and why was he dragging her to this place without Esme and Bryn?

"A little further," he prompted, tugging her hand, and only because she trusted his love for her, Gwendolyn allowed herself to be led, until, at long last, they emerged into... She blinked, bewildered.

Some type of observation tower?

Nay, this was no tower. It was too expansive, and neither did there appear to be any boundaries. It was the most peculiarly beautiful place she had ever beheld. She was standing atop a dais, but like a cloud, and if she peered up, there were... trees upside-down? So far away that it would appear she was looking up at them from the heavens, but upside down. Turning her neck to see what she could see, she asked, "What is this place?"

"The portal," said Málik. "You wished to see it, and here we are."

Breathtaking.

Indescribably beautiful.

Terrifying.

Confusing.

As her jaw fell, Gwendolyn dropped the sack, holding the twine loosely in the crook of one finger, so it rested it at her feet as she peered out over the horizon. She was still inclining her head to alter the perspective so she could better comprehend the view. It was... fantastical. Over the immediate horizon, she could spy a canvas of green—trees? But at the far, far reaches of her vision... there was an endless expanse of blue. The sea? Even further, expansive new lands... and further yet, an icy tundra. But these perspectives were strange. It was as though she were looking upon her father's war table upside down, and if only she reached out far enough, she might move the pieces around. One tree there, another here...

Gwendolyn had no words.

"Come," Málik said, tugging at her hand, pulling her along.

Gwendolyn went. Neck craned, she gaped as the landscape changed, walking along like a twisted old crone as she examined the horizon, trusting Málik to keep her safe. One step brought them across the Tin Isles, another two, and they had crossed a cerulean sea. One last step and they were standing beneath a mountain of fire. "What is that?" she gasped, still looking up.

"A bolcán. A fire mound. There are many across the mortal realm and many points of entry into the Fae realm from this portal, but this one is nearest to my home."

"Your home?" Gwendolyn said, looking about, confused. There was no door here, no entrance she could see.

"I have told you many times, Gwendolyn. Nothing is ever what it appears."

"Gwendolyn," he said again, whispering her name as he pulled her upright to look straight into his face. His expression sober, he took her by the shoulders and held her steady to face him. "Do you remember what I told you that night on the ramparts—everything? About whom your grandsire is... your mother?"

Gwendolyn nodded, growing even more confused. "Fomorian," she said, only to appease him. She remembered, but there was a strange new light in his eyes.

"You remember everything?" he pressed.

Gwendolyn nodded once more, but said, "You are frightening me, Málik. Why are we here? Where are Esme and Bryn?"

He peered down between them, gripping Gwendolyn's shoulders tighter as he spoke. "Everything you know is *incorrect*," he declared. "But I can tell you no more, and Esme..." He peered up, meeting Gwendolyn's gaze, his pale blue irises burning like the hottest shade of a flame.

"Esme what?" Gwendolyn lifted a hand to her shoulder, trying to push off his grip, losing her patience. "Esme what!"

"Listen," he demanded, resisting her and shaking her gently. "I know what she has planned. I will not allow it!"

Gwendolyn's belly turned, seeing the fury in his eyes. "Málik, I can explain," she said, and truly, she meant to. But something about the look in his eyes made her afraid. She longed to find her mother and didn't wish to jeopardize her chances, but the way Málik was looking at her now—as though he could read her mind, as though he could kill her—it gave her a panic.

His fingers gripped her shoulders tighter, his pale eyes darkening with... sorrow? "Trust to no one," he demanded.

"You are scaring me!"

"Look with your heart," he persisted, giving her another shake.

"Málik! I dislike how you are looking at me." With her free hand, Gwendolyn tried to pry his fingers loose, but could not. "I can explain everything!"

"Remember, Gwendolyn. Remember!"

"Remember what?" Suddenly, Málik pulled her close for a kiss, wrapping his arms about her, kissing her so deeply, hungrily, thoroughly, it left her dizzy with confusion as he withdrew. "Málik?" she cried as he slid his hands back to her shoulder. *Blood and bones.* She hadn't the presence of mind to kiss him back, and now, she had the oddest feeling to swipe at her mouth. This... this felt like a kiss of betrayal, and his next words gave truth to the fear unfolding in her heart.

"Forgive me," he said. And then he shoved her.

Gwendolyn was unprepared for it, tumbling backward, snatching fearfully at Málik's tunic. Her fingers grasped at thin air as she flailed her arms, trying in vain to regain her footing, her eyes clinging to Málik as though he were a lifeline.

But he was not. He stood without moving. Without helping. Merely staring. And even as Gwendolyn stumbled backward, he continued to watch, a coldness settling in his bleak, wintry eyes.

37

"I t is done, then?"

Esme approached, and without looking at her, Málik echoed her words, fury darkening his tone. "It is done."

"It is for the best," she dared to console as he placed his arms akimbo, peering down at his feet.

"For whom?"

"You know, all I have said is true, Diarmuid. Any other way, and she will fail."

He spoke through clenched teeth. "You offered hope, then stole it away, and when all is done, her blame will fall to me, because I am the one who betrayed her, not you."

"We share the blame. And if she lives, I will give everything I promised, and more."

He could hear the note of sorrow in her voice, but it wasn't enough. She was the consummate siren, and he could not afford to believe her, or to lower his guard. He answered with silence, considering the journey Gwendolyn faced—a treacherous path to a potentially treacherous end.

"Where did you send her?"

"That is none of your concern."

She spoke now with that silky tone he recalled—the one she'd used to enchant him. "I could take a gander."

He spun to face her, his fist clenching and unclenching by his side. "Do it, but know this, Gráinne: If aught should befall Gwendolyn, I will split your belly and drag your entrails from your middle, then feed them to the trolls!" He lifted a finger to wag in warning. "And this is the last time you speak my true name. Do it once more, and before you utter a sound, I will rip out your tongue."

It would be pointless to tell her how desperately he regretted their intimacy, because he could not change the past, nor even the future.

Fate was no longer in his hands.

Without another word, he turned away from the creature, who had too long been the bane of his existence and walked away.

38

Gwendolyn tumbled backward into the void, the bright blue of Málik's eyes shrinking to pinpricks of light, which, even as she watched, grew smaller, smaller. And then, winking one last time, extinguishing, plunging her into infinite gloom.

No light.

No sound

Only peace.

Was this a portal?

To where?

Nowhere.

Cocooned within darkness, she convinced herself she was dreaming, but she was falling.

But nay, that was it; she'd never gotten out of bed this morn, never donned her weapons for war, neither her leathers. She'd never spoken to Emrys, never discovered Esme with Bryn... shouldn't that alone have given her pause?

Esme and Bryn—only in her dreams!

But she'd heard once that if, in a dream, one fell, and reach the bottom without waking, the end would come as surely as if one fell from the highest clifftop?

Or mayhap everything that transpired after succumbing to the *spriggan* poison was merely an illusion, and Gwendolyn was still up there, somewhere, lying abed, little by little, breath by breath, moment by moment, losing her will to live...

What if even now Bryn, Esme and Málik were sitting by her bedside, squeezing her hand... whispering sweet words and weeping?

"Don't cry," she whispered, but her words formed no sound, and somehow, despite her disembodied experience, she found a sting of tears pricking her eyes.

Betrayal wove itself through her heart like thorny vines. Only once before had she felt so betrayed... As it was the spriggan vines, pain clawed through her veins.

Why did he push her?

The answer spun away from her, even as she continued twisting and falling into... nothing. Falling, falling... until, finally...

Gwendolyn landed, disoriented.

The end of her journey was like that moment when she was six, twirling in a field of daisies, spinning, spinning, spinning and then tumbling down, everything wildly adrift—no solid ground, until abruptly there was, and the feel of it made her belly roil and her eyes close against a violent surge of nausea.

Groaning, she felt about for stability, grasping at what appeared to be rocks and soil... many little pebbles. Whatever the case, she was most definitely alive, judging by the pang between her shoulders where the hilt of her sword pushed against her *mithril*. She opened her eyes and blinked, to find herself dizzy and seeing stars... but nay, not stars... *piskies*... all buzzing about her face, winking furiously.

Gwendolyn sat up and, by the light of the swarm,

found herself stranded in a cavern that reminded her of her uncle's *fogous*.

Was this only a memory then, and at any moment, Málik would light the flame in his hand? She remembered falling down from her uncle's bedroom, into the fogous, the smell of dirt heavy in her nostrils...

"*Fáilte*," said a voice, and Gwendolyn blinked against the shadows to clear away the confusion. "Fancy meeting you here?" said the white and black creature that now reclined atop a small mound. And despite knowing the language was not her own, Gwendolyn somehow understood.

The Púca rolled onto its side, lifting a leg to lap at the inside of its thigh as a cat might do, its pink tongue stretching unnaturally. As she stared, it continued to clean itself until satisfied, and then sat upright and began to sing the same song Gwendolyn recalled from the Druid's hall, only this time she understood every word...

> A babe was bequeathed by two Fae,
> Two gifts, and a lie they all say.
> One younger, one elder,
> One wiser, one skelder,
> Then, sniggering, they stole awa'.

"Danger!" squealed the *piskies*, and with a thousand shrieks, the swarm scattered, taking Gwendolyn's light along with them, leaving her immersed in darkness and silence, but within that darkness, another flame kindled—this one in Gwendolyn's heart.

White. Hot. Fury.

Betrayed.

Even as she peered up, half expecting Málik to appear beside her, as he had in the fogous, she knew he would not. The sack she was still clutching between her fingers was a painful assurance that this was no dream, nor even a memory.

The Púca had stopped singing for a reason. Bewildered, Gwendolyn unsheathed Kingslayer, resting it atop her lap.

Málik hadn't simply shown her the portal. He'd shoved her through and then deserted her. And even as she grew certain of this truth, the runic inscriptions on the flat of her blade began to flicker, and glow... blue.

There's one final episode in this epic tale.
Don't miss Arise the Queen.

A HEARTFELT THANK YOU!

Thank you from the bottom of my heart for reading The Forgotten Prince. If you enjoyed this book, please consider posting a review. Reviews don't just help the author, they help other readers discover our books and, no matter how long or short, I sincerely appreciate every review.

Would you like to know when my next book is available? Sign up for my newsletter:

💜 Thank you! 💜

TANYACROSBY.COM/SUBSCRIBE

Also, please follow me on BookBub to be notified of deals and new releases.

Let's hang out! I have a Facebook group:

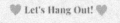

Thank you again for reading and for your support.

Tanya Anne Crosby

ALSO BY TANYA ANNE CROSBY

THE GOLDENCHILD PROPHECY

The Cornish Princess

The Queen's Huntsman

The Forgotten Prince

Arise the Queen

ONE KNIGHT FOREVER SERIES

One Knight's Stand

DAUGHTERS OF AVALON

The King's Favorite

The Holly & the Ivy

A Winter's Rose

Fire Song

Lord of Shadows

THE PRINCE & THE IMPOSTOR

Seduced by a Prince

A Crown for a Lady

The Art of Kissing Beneath the Mistletoe

THE HIGHLAND BRIDES

The MacKinnon's Bride

Lyon's Gift

On Bended Knee

Lion Heart

Highland Song

MacKinnon's Hope

GUARDIANS OF THE STONE

Once Upon a Highland Legend

Highland Fire

Highland Steel

Highland Storm

Maiden of the Mist

THE MEDIEVAL HEROES

Once Upon a Kiss

Angel of Fire

Viking's Prize

REDEEMABLE ROGUES

Happily Ever After

Perfect In My Sight

McKenzie's Bride

Kissed by a Rogue

Thirty Ways to Leave a Duke

A Perfectly Scandalous Proposal

ANTHOLOGIES & NOVELLAS

Lady's Man

Married at Midnight

The Winter Stone

ROMANTIC SUSPENSE

Leave No Trace

Speak No Evil

Tell No Lies

ABOUT THE AUTHOR

Tanya Anne Crosby is the New York Times and USA Today bestselling author of thirty novels. She has been featured in magazines, such as People, Romantic Times and Publisher's Weekly, and her books have been translated into eight languages. Her first novel was published in 1992 by Avon Books, where Tanya was hailed as "one of Avon's fastest rising stars." Her fourth book was chosen to launch the company's Avon Romantic Treasure imprint.

Known for stories charged with emotion and humor and filled with flawed characters Tanya is an award-winning author, journalist, and editor, and her novels have garnered reader praise and glowing critical reviews. She and her writer husband split their time between Charleston, SC, where she was raised, and northern Michigan, where the couple make their home.

For more information
Website
Email
Newsletter